Ramage and the Rebels

Lord Nicholas Ramage, eldest son of the Tenth
Earl of Blazey, Admiral of the White, was born in
1775 at Blazey Hall, St Kew, Cornwall. He entered
the Royal Navy as a midshipman in 1788, at the
age of thirteen. He has served with distinction in
the Mediterranean, the Caribbean, and home
waters during the war against France, participating
in several major sea battles and numerous minor
engagements. Despite political difficulties, his rise
through the ranks has been rapid.

Dudley Pope, who comes from an old Cornish
family and whose great-great-grandfather was a
Plymouth shipowner in Nelson's time, is well
known both as the creator of Lord Ramage and
as a distinguished and entertaining naval historian,
the author of ten scholarly works. Actively
encouraged by the late C.S. Forester, he has written
nineteen novels in the Ramage series about life at
sea in Nelson's day. They are based on his own
wartime experiences in the navy, and peacetime
exploits as a yachtsman, as well as immense
research into the naval history of the eighteenth
century.

BY THE SAME AUTHOR

DUDLEY POPE

Ramage and the Rebels

This edition published by Grafton Books, 1999

Grafton Books is an Imprint of
HarperCollins*Publishers*
77–85 Fulham Palace Road,
Hammersmith, London W6 8JB

This paperback edition first published by HarperCollins*Publishers in* 1996
9 8 7 6 5 4 3 2 1

Previously published in paperback by Fontana 1979
Reprinted four times

First Published in Great Britain by
The Alison Press/Martin Secker and Warburg Ltd 1978

Copyright © Dudley Pope 1978

The Author asserts the moral right to
be identified as the author of this work

ISBN 0-26-167356-4

Set in Times

Printed in Great Britain by
Caledonian International Book Manufacturing Ltd, Glasgow

For Joy, Douglas
and Katie
who also love the
Islands

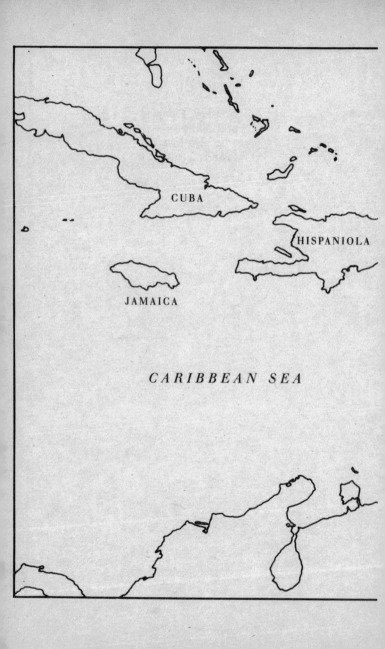

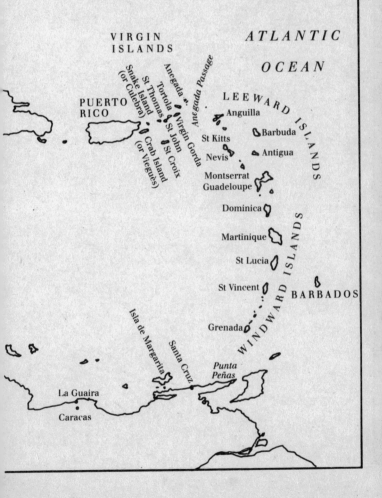

THE WEST INDIES

VIRGIN ISLANDS

ATLANTIC OCEAN

PUERTO RICO

Anegada
Tortola
St Thomas
Snake Island (or Culebra)
Virgin Gorda
St John
St Croix
Crab Island (or Vieques)

Anegada Passage

LEEWARD ISLANDS

Anguilla

Barbuda

St Kitts

Antigua

Nevis

Montserrat

Guadeloupe

Dominica

Martinique

St Lucia

St Vincent

BARBADOS

Grenada

WINDWARD ISLANDS

Isla de Margarita

Santa Cruz

Punta Peñas

La Guaira

Caracas

CHAPTER ONE

'It's not exactly making war, sir,' Ramage said, putting as much disapproval in his voice as he dared. 'It seems to me to be half-way between poaching and gamekeeping. I've never understood why we allow it ourselves.'

'It dam' well isn't war,' the Admiral said angrily, 'it's cold-blooded murder, and these orders – ' he tapped the sealed packet on the highly-polished table in front of him – 'tell you to put a stop to it all. These privateers are no better than pirates. Oh yes, they may have parchment commissions covered with big seals and signed by the king of this or the queen of that, but the fact is they're privateering just for plunder.'

He tapped the packet again. 'I say in here and I repeat it now, Ramage: any privateer you find, French, Spanish or Dutch, whose captain can't produce a regular commission, then we'll take him before the Admiralty Court and charge him with piracy, and he'll hang from a gibbet along the Palisades. So search well and warn each captain before you take him off his ship – I don't want any of 'em claiming afterwards they had no time to collect their papers. Commission, certificate of registry, charter party, muster list, log – everything. And witnesses – I want witnesses. The privateer's mate and at least two of your officers. Seal up in a packet all the papers you're given and make the privateer captain sign his name beside the seal.'

'Yes, sir,' said Ramage patiently.

'Yes sir, yes sir,' the Admiral repeated angrily, 'but just make sure you understand, Ramage: if one of these damned pirates escapes judgement in court because of some technicality that can be attributed to an omission by you, then I'll bring you to trial too, for negligence.'

'Yes, sir,' Ramage said deliberately, and he saw a copy of the latest *London Gazette* tucked under a pile of papers on one side of the table. The new 'Commander-in-Chief of His Majesty's Ships and Vessels upon the Jamaica Station' was not going to give his newest and most junior captain the satisfaction of knowing that he had just read half a page about him in the *Gazette*, detailing his latest exploits on the Leeward Islands Station, nearly a thousand miles to the eastward, at the windward end of the Caribbean. Yet William Foxe-Foote, Vice-Admiral of the Blue, one of the Members of Parliament for Bristol (it was said that bribing the voters to get the seat had cost him more than seventy-five thousand pounds), was by reputation one of the most sly flag officers in the Navy List. It was also said (and looking at the pink and perspiring face with its tiny eyes and bulbous nose, Ramage had no trouble believing it) that he had badgered the First Lord of the Admiralty into giving him the Jamaica Station – the richest in the service for prize money – so that he could recoup his purse after the Bristol election. Seventy-five thousand pounds a Foote – perhaps the Admiralty realized a fathom of him in London could prove too expensive and agreed to send him out to Jamaica.

'What do you find so funny?' the Admiral demanded.

'I was thinking of the shock these privateersmen are going to get, sir,' Ramage said, finding it easy to lie gracefully to a man who was so clearly a politician first and an admiral second, two roles which he combined to further his main ambition, which was to get rich. Ramage recalled some lampoon to the effect that the nation's taxpayers were lucky that there was only one Foote in Old Palace Yard, a neat reference to the space in front of the Houses of Parliament.

'So you are confident you can ferret them out?'

Ramage was thankful for the chance of repeating the one doubt he had, and which Foxe-Foote was trying to ignore. 'The coast of the Main, sir, from Maracaibo all the way round to Cartagena, Portobelo and then north to the Moskito Coast. It's all very shallow, with dozens of bays sheltered by reefs of coral.'

'Frightens you, eh? Don't be nervous, boy,' the Admiral said, not troubling to hide the sneer in his voice. 'You've got a good master on board – leave the navigation to him, and always stand out to seaward at nightfall.'

Ramage flushed at the man's insulting crudeness and stupidity. 'I'm talking of bays lined with mangroves, littered with cays and almost closed off by coral reefs, sir, where there won't be a couple of fathoms of water. My ship draws sixteen feet. That means any privateer can escape me by getting into one of these bays. Few privateers draw more than ten feet.'

'Send the boats in to chase 'em; a dozen Marines to capture the ship and a dozen seamen and a midshipman to sail her out to join you – nothing to it. Wish I was younger; just the sort of *fighting* orders I always enjoyed getting.'

'Of course, sir,' Ramage said admiringly, remembering the hundred men that most privateers carried – and a biographical sketch in a recent issue of the *Naval Chronicle*, the most interesting fact in it being that Vice-Admiral Foxe-Foote had, by design or the fortunes of war, reached flag rank without ever being in action. No man was braver than one who had never been shot at . . .

Ramage reached out for his packet of orders but then recalled one of the Admiral's remarks which he might later claim was an order. 'Standing out to seaward at night, sir . . .'

The Admiral raised his eyebrows questioningly.

'Out here it is more usual to stand *in* for the land at nightfall, sir,' Ramage said cautiously. 'If the privateers suspect one of the King's ships is in the offing they take the opportunity of creeping along the coast in the dark using the offshore breeze – '

'You have your orders,' the Admiral said abruptly, 'so carry 'em out. And don't go burning privateers when you catch 'em: send 'em back here to be condemned. Prize money for everyone, eh, Ramage? No need to burn money or strand it on a reef, or scuttle it, you know; good market for that type of vessel here in Jamaica; prices are high, so the prize agents tell me. Think you'll have any luck along the Main? At least a prize a week, I should reckon, eh?'

'No, sir,' Ramage said quietly. 'I'll probably sight one a day, but that'll be all. If I was commanding a privateer,' he added, 'I'd guarantee no frigate would catch me, nor would her boats get within a musket shot.'

Admiral Foxe-Foote's face dropped. Now he reminded Ramage more of an unsuccessful haberdasher than a flag officer, with the skin of his long, thin and bony face tightening and slackening like a flag in a breeze to signal his reaction to everything going on round him. 'Not catch any privateers?' he almost whispered, as though unable to believe his ears. 'But . . . but I've just given you written orders!'

Yet Foxe-Foote was far from sure of himself: when brought up all standing by a chance remark, he was usually quick enough to realize he had made a mistake or forgotten something. Now he saw this young captain was standing up and tucking his orders into his pocket, and in a moment would be taking his leave and calling for his sword and hat.

'I hardly expected to hear this sort of talk from you, Ramage,' he said in a voice drenched with sorrow and disappointment. 'From some of these other captains I've inherited on this station, men who've had it too easy for too long and who've grown fat and slothful, yes, I can understand a lack of enthusiasm; a lack of fighting spirit. Understand but not condone, you understand. Their dilatory methods of patrolling in the past are the reason why the Caribbean is now swarming with enemy privateers. I was hoping you'd be an example to them. But now . . .' he shook his head sadly, the picture of a bishop who had just discovered that his wife lusted after a choirboy.

'I don't know about the other captains, sir,' Ramage said quietly, 'because I've only just arrived on this station. But for myself I can't take a ship drawing sixteen feet into ten feet of water without running aground, and you've already refused me a tender or some sort of shallow-draught vessel.'

Foxe-Foote was enough of a politician to know when it was time to change sides. 'If you had such a vessel with you – a schooner, say – do you guarantee to root out those privateers along the Main?'

'Only a braggart could guarantee something like that,' Ramage said easily, 'but I would not regard it as good news if I was a privateersman, sir.'

'The schooner that came with you from the Leeward Islands, the *Créole*, is she suitable?'

'Yes, sir, absolutely ideal.'

'Why are you so sure? Have you sailed in her?'

'I captured her, sir,' Ramage said. 'My former fourth lieutenant commands her.'

'Oh, yes,' Foxe-Foote said lamely, 'that action of yours off Diamond Rock. Very creditable, too.'

'May I take it she will be placed under my orders, sir?'

'Yes, I suppose so. But you young fellows seem to think that frigates and schooners and cutters grow on trees. Very well, I'll send orders to her commander, and you can have him on board to give him your instructions. I want both of you under way by tomorrow morning!'

Foxe-Foote watched Ramage give a slight bow and leave the room. There was nothing in Ramage's behaviour about which a flag officer could complain; in fact his manners were perfect. But Foxe-Foote had the uncomfortable feeling that this young frigate captain was contemptuous of him. Officers of aristocratic birth were frequently offhand with the less well born, and there was little doubt that few came from more aristocratic families than this fellow Ramage – his father's earldom was one of the oldest in the country – but it was more than that. Admirals should not feel at a disadvantage when dealing with junior captains . . .

The Admiral reached out for the *Gazette*, opened it and began reading the small print. It gave two dispatches to the Admiralty and written by Ramage, describing his last two operations. They were remarkable by anyone's standards, even though written in what was obviously a flat style. Either action could have won him a knighthood, although he hardly needed it because he bore one of his father's titles.

The prize money from those two actions alone . . . and the admiral's share had gone to the commander-in-chief at the Leeward Islands, that blockhead Henry Davis. If only Ramage had been sailing from Jamaica . . . It must amount to thousands of pounds for both Ramage and Davis. Just think of prize money on that scale – and the young fellow never used his title either. He was Lord Ramage, and when his father died he'd be the Earl of Blazey. Yet few people knew it. Foxe-Foote picked up a pencil and scribbled on a piece of paper. 'Sir William Foxe-Foote,' he wrote, then added 'Kt'. He crossed that out and substituted 'Bt'. He would probably get a knighthood fairly soon – it was almost automatic when one became the commander-in-chief of a station like Jamaica. But a baronetcy tended to come to a naval officer only after a successful battle. That young upstart Horatio Nelson had received one after the Battle of Cape St Vincent. Wasn't this boy Ramage in that battle? Didn't he lose a ship, a cutter or something, while trying to prevent some Spanish three-deckers from escaping?

Foxe-Foote cursed the tropical heat, which made his uniform stick to him like dough on a baker's fingers, but smiled to himself and wrote, 'Lord Foote'. He'd have to watch the territorial part of the title, since he had had the misfortune to be born in a village with an odd name – one could hardly be 'Baron Foote of Piddleditch in the County of Essex'. But he'd get a barony if it took his last penny, and that was the advantage of entering politics. In the sea service you'd be lucky to get a baronetcy after a lifetime's work. A barony came only after a great victory, and then to the commander-in-chief. In either case it meant risking having a roundshot take your head off. That was the comforting thing about relying on a political title – the only risk was the party losing power, but a few votes for the party, a dozen entries into the 'Aye' lobby in Parliament, could earn you a baronetcy quicker than a dozen cutting-out expeditions, and without the slightest risk to wind or limb.

Yet . . . yet . . . it wasn't a title or the prize money or the handsome face that gave young Ramage that – well, what was it? Not an air of superiority, because obviously he didn't know he had it. Assurance? Confidence? It was hard to define. Certainly it was built on a foundation of confidence, because the *Gazette* showed he had a natural courage, quite apart from his reputation in the Navy. Confidence could and did take him into action and brought him out alive and well. Yet he had sat there on the other side of the table, Foxe-Foote suddenly realized, quietly and modestly, and he had manœuvred his admiral into giving him just what he wanted.

Earlier that morning, before Ramage arrived, Foxe-Foote had been determined not to be impressed by this youngster who some men reckoned would either have been killed in a glorious battle or be the youngest admiral in the flag list by the time he was forty. He had quite deliberately given him orders more suited to some callow young frigate captain who owed his promotion to influence rather than experience. Chasing privateers was work that had to be done, but it brought no glory and, for all his remarks, Foxe-Foote knew it could bring little or no prize money for anyone. A captured privateer was worth the price of its hull: it carried no cargo, which was where the profit was. The favoured few, the frigate captains who looked to him for patronage, were already patrolling where the real prizes were to be found – heavily laden Spanish merchantmen off Cartagena and Havana, San Juan in Puerto Rico and Santo Domingo, or Frenchmen making for Guadeloupe . . . Well, he had not asked for Ramage; the Admiralty had sent him to help sort out the mess left by the previous commander-in-chief.

The only job left, one without honour, money or glory, was chasing these damned privateers who, under a variety of flags, were seizing any British merchant ships they sighted, and taking them into – where? Mostly Curaçao, it seemed; the little Dutch island off the Main with its splendid harbour appeared to have recently turned itself into a privateers' haven. A row of three islands, rather, the beginning of the alphabet – Aruba, Bonaire at each end and Curaçao in the middle. Britain had no ally in the West Indies now: if an island or ship was not British, it was enemy. Spain, France, Netherlands – the only exception was Denmark, which had two or three tiny islands east of Puerto Rico.

The way this boy stared at you – it wasn't exactly insolence, but Foxe-Foote admitted it made him feel uncomfortable. The eyes were deep-set over those high cheekbones, and he tended to move his whole head rather than swivel his eyes so that when he turned to look at you it seemed he was turning his whole body, like training a gun, and this gave every look far more significance.

He certainly resembled his father, the old admiral. The same rather narrow face, beak-like nose and thick eyebrows. Two scars over his right eyebrow, one newer than the other, pinker, and possibly sword cuts. Or from falling out of trollops' beds, or tripping over while in drink. No, he was not a drinker; Foxe-Foote was sure of that, and thankful. There was none of the slight tremble in the hand, the slight but continuous perspiration, the shifty eyes, the excuse for a drink: indeed, Ramage had refused a rum punch, despite the heat of the day.

Foxe-Foote threw the *Gazette* on the top of the pile of papers. No, it had not been a satisfactory day so far. He'd been determined to send Ramage off in the *Calypso* frigate to clear out those privateers, and had vowed he'd neither listen to nor grant any requests; he was just going to tap the orders and say everything was written there and . . . And what had happened? The whippersnapper had calmly told him how to operate frigates in the Caribbean, virtually refused to catch a single privateer unless he was given a schooner as well, and – well, that had been all. And quite enough too. Just let him make one mistake, Foxe-Foote vowed to himself; no good ever came of giving young captains so many *Gazettes*; their heads became swollen, they expected all the pretty young girls to swoon over them, and they put their prize money in the Funds or bought themselves large houses in the country and – well, it was all damnably unfair; not every flag officer could make a reputation in battle, and thank goodness the First Lord of the Admiralty realized it. Just you send in the privateer prizes, Foxe-Foote muttered, or you might just as well send in your papers. He dismissed the tiny inner voice that murmured about jealousy; after all, Ramage was one of the most junior post captains in the Navy List while he, William Foxe-Foote, was one of the most senior of the vice-admirals of the blue. With luck and a few deaths among the flag officers above him, he'd be a vice-admiral of the white by next year and a vice-admiral of the red a couple of years later. By then he should have enough influence in the Commons to get the title that would assure him a seat in the Lords. They'd be listening to his speeches with respect long before that boy became the Earl of Blazey and took his seat.

Ramage acknowledged the salutes as he boarded the frigate and, glad to be under the shade of the awning once again, strode across the quarterdeck to go down the companionway to his cabin. He saw the master hesitating nearby, obviously with something to say but trying to guess the captain's mood after seeing the commander-in-chief. Ramage realized that his face probably looked angry, but the fault was more the sun than William Foxe-Foote, Vice-Admiral of the Blue: it wanted only a few minutes to noon, and with the sun vertically overhead the glare was fantastic, flashing up into his eyes from every ripple on the water. The humidity was so high that his uniform was sticking to him, while his hat seemed to weigh fifteen pounds and have shrunk. His head itched with the heat, his hair was soaked in perspiration, his feet seemed swollen and jammed into long boots far too small.

No, he was not angry; in fact apart from the heat he was in a fairly good mood. Foxey (as the commander-in-chief was generally known in the Navy by everyone from the cook's mate to fellow admirals) had lived up to his reputation, but Ramage was thankful he had seen that copy of the *Gazette* half hidden among the papers – that had been the clue to Foxey's manner: he wasn't going to be impressed by some young junior captain who had two dispatches printed in the

same *Gazette* . . . For all that, Foxey had given him the
schooner, and at this very moment was, no doubt, doing what
he should have done earlier – examining the charts of the Main
and discussing the problems with his second-in-command, who
had been out here a year or more, before drawing up orders.

'You want to see me, Southwick?' he asked the master.

'Not me, sir,' the old man said, 'it's the purser. He's been
cast into debt, I think, and wants to talk to you about it.'

Ramage grimaced. 'Very well, send him down in five minutes' time. And make the signal to the *Créole* for Lacey to
come on board.'

Southwick waited, hoping for some hint of what the *Calypso*
was to do, but his curiosity remained unsatisfied because of
his own efficiency: all the frigate's water casks were full, all
but one boat were hoisted on board and stowed on the booms,
all sail repairs had been completed and the old foretopsail,
worn and chafed beyond repair, had been sent down and
replaced with a new one. The ship could be under way in the
time it took to hoist in the last boat and weigh the anchors.

Ramage clattered down the steps of the companionway,
acknowledged the Marine sentry's salute, and ducked his head
under the deck beams as he went into his cabin. He tossed his
hat on to the settee, took off his sword and sat at his desk
as he took Foxe-Foote's written orders from his pocket.

He broke the seal and smoothed the paper, his hands sticky
with perspiration. There were the usual clichés, and then came
the orders: the Jamaica committee of merchants were complaining that ships plying between Jamaica and the Windward
and Leeward Islands (which meant from Antigua down to
Barbados) were being attacked by increasing numbers of
privateers holding Spanish, French and Dutch commissions.
These privateers were apparently using the Dutch islands as
the market place for the cargoes in the prizes they captured.

However, the Royal Navy frigates patrolling off Cuba, Hispaniola and Puerto Rico, and in the Mona Passage, reported
sighting fewer privateers than usual. From this it was apparent
that the privateers had retreated southwards right across the
Caribbean to the coast of the Spanish Main, and Ramage was
to patrol that coast for two months, paying particular attention to the island of Curaçao, 'and remove the threat'.

Ramage sighed, folded the paper and dropped it into the

top right-hand drawer of his desk and, after finding his key ring, locked it. They were not the sort of orders one would ever need to refer to again. The more cynical of his brother captains referred to such orders as an 'admiral's awning' because they were so worded that they sheltered him from any criticism by Their Lordships at the Admiralty should anything go wrong.

He wanted to look over the charts, such as they were, before Lacey came over from *La Créole*, but first there was the purser. Rowlands was an old woman, as quick as a lawyer to spot anything that might be to his disadvantage as the ship's businessman and prevent him balancing his books. This would 'cast him into debt', as all pursers described making a loss, forgetting that anyone in business was likely to make a loss at some time or another.

Ramage smiled to himself as he remembered Southwick's face at the head of the companionway. The old man's flowing white hair stuck out from under his hat like a new mop, and the order to make the signal for Lacey had obviously left him wondering what orders the *Calypso* had received. Ramage had decided to tantalize him for the time being, knowing that as soon as Lacey came on board Southwick would, with the ship's other officers, hear all about it.

The sentry announced the purser and Ramage called the man in. He was not carrying a handful of papers – that was a good sign. His plump face with bags under the eyes looked mournful (like a village grocer saying farewell to his best customers as he was marched off to the debtors' jail) but Rowlands always looked like that, the result of the Welsh-man's firmly held view that most people had a far too frivolous attitude towards money. To him it was not a means of enjoying life, Ramage realized; acquiring it was the whole object of life, as though dying a rich man was the ultimate satisfaction.

The man was nervous – that was only too obvious as he ducked his head like a pecking pigeon as he entered the cabin although he was only an inch or so taller than the five feet four inches of headroom. He was nervous and he had taken particular care in dressing himself to see the captain. Past experience had shown Ramage that this was a bad sign, the preliminary to announcing trouble. But trouble without a handful of papers, long lists and inventories, surveys and account books? Could it be personal? A confession of fraud? Or bigamy?

Ramage gestured to Rowlands to sit on the settee, and twisted his own chair round to face the man. 'Southwick said . . .' he began encouragingly.

''S the water,' Rowlands said hurriedly. 'I dunno what to do with it.'

Immediately Ramage pictured more than thirty tuns of water carefully stowed below in casks (and intended to last the *Calypso*'s men more than three months) suddenly going bad, or proving to be brackish. Now, within a few hours of sailing, the bungs would have to be started and the water run into the bilges and pumped out over the side. Then would come the tedious and laborious task of ferrying the empty casks over to Passage Fort with the boats and filling them and then swaying them back on board again and stowing them below . . . And all the time there would be the sneers (if nothing worse) of Admiral Foxe-Foote, who would see it as a ruse to delay sailing because to him all orders involving going into battle could only be unwelcome. Having never smelled powder, Foxe-Foote attached too much importance to the experience.

'It's only a few casks, sir,' Rowlands said eagerly. 'Two dozen butts, in fact.'

'Is that from here in Port Royal or did we take it on in Antigua?'

''Twas on board when we captured the ship, sir. I suppose the French loaded it in France. Must have, come to think of it; they couldn't get it anywhere else.'

What on earth was the man talking about? 'Is France the only place that supplies water, Rowlands? Or is this spa water, so good for the liver?'

'No, sir,' Rowlands said dolefully, ''tisn't spa water. Wish it was. Nor is it plain water. No, it's brandy, sir, twelve tuns of it, which is three thousand and twenty-four gallons, wine measure.'

Ramage was so relieved that he asked with mock seriousness: 'I trust it is *good* brandy, Rowlands? The French haven't fobbed some new, raw spirit on us, I hope? The sort of spirit more useful as liniment for rubbing into bruises than drinking?'

'I can't be for saying,' Rowlands said miserably, although

not so upset that his favourite expression was forgotten. 'No, sir, I can't be for saying, seeing as how I'm not a drinking man.'

Rowlands had a knack of being able to phrase an apparently innocent remark so that it put the other person in the wrong. No casual listener would guess that Ramage rarely drank even three pints of wine in a year, and detested spirits. But the purser had the ability to irritate Ramage more than any other man in the ship. He was smug, money-grubbing, self-righteous and self-seeking, and Ramage had done nothing about having him replaced because he was also reasonably (if tediously) efficient and, Ramage never co-operating in any of his hinted schemes, just as honest as he had to be.

Ramage heard a hail on deck that showed Lacey was approaching, and in the meantime he had more important things to think about than Rowlands's discovery of two dozen butts of brandy stowed down below, posing as water.

'Copy all the marks painted on the butts and give them to Southwick so we can enter it all in the log,' Ramage said.

'But, sir,' protested Rowlands, 'they're stowed bung up and bilge free, and some of the marks are on the under sides.'

'I should hope butts of brandy are stowed bung up and bilge free,' Ramage growled. 'I can just imagine the owners' joy on finding bungs popped out and butts sprung because they had been thumping against the ship's side in a heavy sea, and the bilges flowing with brandy, instead of milk and honey.'

'Milk and honey, sir?' the purser repeated, obviously puzzling over how two items never issued to the King's ships could have slipped into the bilge.

'Rowlands,' Ramage said heavily, 'get those figures for Southwick. Now, have you checked all the rest of the water casks? The ship's company might think that brandy is a good substitute for water, but I doubt if the surgeon would agree. And tell the Marine officer that we need a sentry guarding those butts until we get them stowed in the spirit room.'

Rowlands scurried from the cabin, reassured now that he had something to do and the responsibility for the butts had been lifted from his shoulders. He had informed the captain and, as far as he was concerned, the butts rested on Captain Ramage's shoulders, like the world did on that man in the print he once saw, Atlas or some such name; a Greek fellow probably; perhaps the first man to publish maps.

As Ramage reached up to the rack over his head to find some charts he reflected that the paperwork concerning the brandy could cause more trouble than capturing the frigate from the French in the first place. In fact, before he started his examination of the coast of the Spanish Main, he had better finish dealing with the matter which had started in France.

Southwick arrived in response to the sentry's hail with an alacrity which told Ramage that the master had not strayed far from the top of the companionway.

'Rowlands's problem is sorted out, sir?' he asked with what, for him, passed as a subtle enquiry.

'It's not Rowlands's problem.' Ramage made no attempt to hide his exasperation. 'It's mine and yours and Rear-Admiral Davis's and all those fools at Antigua who took an inventory of this ship when we brought her in as a prize.'

'What did they miss?' Southwick asked shrewdly.

'Two dozen butts of brandy . . .'

'Two dozen? Why, sir, that's three thousand gallons! Where is it?'

'Nestling down there with the water,' Ramage said sourly. 'And now you have the job of shifting it to the spirit room. It's a wonder it hasn't blown the ship up.'

'Those damned Frogs – just a lot o' smugglers! Why, they must have been smuggling it into Martinique. I'll bet they never intended to declare it to the Customs! Just sell a few gallons at a time to the planters, who're probably sick and tired of rum. Makes you wonder what the Revolution's all about, doesn't it, sir? The officers might be full of liberty and equality and fraternity, or whatever it is they shout, but they're not above a bit o' smuggling, given the chance.'

'Nor are we, as far as the Customs in Antigua and Port Royal are concerned,' Ramage pointed out.

Southwick's face fell. 'Oh dear . . . Officially I suppose we smuggled it out of English Harbour and into Port Royal. But whose is it? Who pays the duty? And who gets it?' he added as an afterthought.

'That can be decided later,' Ramage said. 'In the meantime we'll have to carry on smuggling, but Rowlands is going to give you the numbers on the casks. Make a full entry in the log for today stating how it was found, if the butts are full, and so on . . . And note that it was removed to the spirit room. In the meantime I've passed the word for Rennick to put a sentry on it – we're lucky none of the seamen discovered it first: I can just imagine us finding half the ship's company one morning lying drunk among the casks.'

'Those fools from the dockyard at English Harbour,' Southwick growled. 'They spent days on that inventory. They must have just made a quick count of water casks and assumed they held water. But anyone getting within a dozen feet should smell the brandy. Why, seepage alone!'

'Don't talk about it,' Ramage said. 'If anyone had walked round in the dark down there, using a lanthorn to count up water casks, the flame of the candle would have made the fumes explode, and the whole ship would have gone up.'

'By the time we've finished with all the extra paperwork this is going to create we might wish that it had,' Southwick said bitterly. 'Why, it affects the original inventory of the prize and the valuation; and that in turn affects the final valuation and the prize money paid. Which means our shares – everyone's, from Admiral Davis's down to the cook's mate's. Why, they could hold up payment for years – you know what prize agents are like. Any excuse to hold on to the money and draw interest.'

'Let's wait and see,' Ramage said. 'We can't be expected to bother Admiral Foxe-Foote with it now because he wants us to sail as soon as possible. We shan't be back for three months, and who knows what might have happened by then.'

'Three months, sir?' Southwick said eagerly. 'Where's it to be – let me guess. The Gulf of Mexico? Cuba? Moskito Coast? Surely not back to Antigua, sir?'

'Wait for Lacey. Is that him coming on board now? Very well, pass the word for the rest of the officers – Rennick, too. He might as well know what we're supposed to be doing, to see if his Marines can help.'

When Lacey came into the cabin he was embarrassed because the last time he came through that door he had been the *Calypso*'s fourth lieutenant and therefore the most junior commission officer on board. The frigate had just been brought into the King's service after having been captured by Mr Ramage's previous command, the frigate *Juno*. And,

Lacey remembered almost with a start, he had been fourth lieutenant in her, too.

Now, he thought to himself, he was twenty-five years old and the strides from his home in Somerset in the shadow of the Quantocks were beginning to show: he had not seen Nether Stowey for four years, not since he passed for lieutenant. And in those four years, thanks almost entirely to Mr Ramage, he had progressed from the most junior officer in the *Juno*'s gunroom to the most junior officer in the *Calypso*'s gunroom and then, after that last wild voyage, command of *La Créole* schooner.

His own command. Magic words and they could be as heady as a strong rum punch. He was still a lieutenant, of course; orders came to him addressed to Lieutenant William Lacey. But on board *La Créole* he was 'the captain', with two commissioned officers under him, second master instead of a master, and a sergeant of Marines.

La Créole was a witch of a ship. The French could build fast vessels, and it was fitting that he should be commanding one that he had helped to capture. And he was thankful that Admiral Davis had finally left her with her original French name, instead of calling her 'Diamond' after the Diamond Rock, off Martinique, where she had been captured. That had been the original intention.

'Creole' came off the tongue nicely. Most of the Creole women he had met so far had been extraordinarily beautiful; slim and sleek like the schooner, with jutting breasts under bright dresses. 'Your ship?' 'Oh, I command the *Créole*, that black schooner over there.' 'Weren't you at the capture of Diamond Rock, and then the cutting out of the *Jocasta*?' And he would admit – with becoming modesty, of course – that he was. At that moment he glanced up and saw Mr Ramage was watching him, and he flushed because the captain's deep-set eyes seemed to bore right into him, revealing his thoughts and fears – and perhaps his hopes, too.

When Ramage asked him if all was going well with *La Créole* he was thankful he could answer honestly that there were no problems.

'How many men are you mustering?'

'Fifty-one, sir, and ten Marines and a sergeant.'

'And you have ten 6-pounders?'

'And the two 12-pounder carronades they fitted at Antigua.'

'She handles well?'

'Like a witch, sir. Clean bottom, coppered – just the vessel for privateering!'

'Which she was doing up to the time we captured her.'

'Was she, sir?' Lacey was surprised. 'I thought she was a French national ship.'

'No, she was a privateer out of Fort Royal, but the French Navy took her over, and a sister ship, the day before they attacked us.'

Lacey would never forget the night those two schooners attacked the frigate in the darkness, trying to board. But – well, although it happened only a few weeks ago, it seemed part of another life: the nervous young lieutenant who had been hard put to keep his head amid all the cracking of muskets and pistols, the yelling and screaming and the clash of cutlasses – yes, and the screams of wounded men: that had surprised him. Now that frightened young lieutenant commanded his own ship, one of the two schooners that made the attack, and he wasn't frightened: at least, not in sailing her. It may be different when I take her into battle, he admitted to himself; but I haven't run away when going into action with Mr Ramage these several times, and maybe I've learned something from him. But keeping a clear head in the middle of a battle and never being frightened – that's what made Mr Ramage unique.

Suddenly Lacey felt cheerful because he thought he could see why he had been called on board the *Calypso*: the Admiral was sending the frigate on some operation or other and *La Créole* was to go with her . . . Perhaps Mr Ramage had even asked for him . . .

'You are up to establishment, then?'

'Yes, sir; Admiral Davis was very good at English Harbour: he gave me a full complement of men and Marines, and there's no one on the sick list.'

'And your officers?'

'Both lieutenants are excellent, sir. Young but good. The second master is steady enough – could be Southwick's younger brother. And the Marine sergeant is one of the best. I wouldn't change a man, sir.'

'You're lucky,' Ramage said soberly, looking back at some of the ships he had commanded. 'A captain's only as good as his ship's company. When you're considering whether or not to weed out a particular man it's worth remembering that. One rotten apple, you know. "When in doubt, weed him out!" '

Lacey sensed Ramage was waiting for something, and after a few minutes of small talk he heard several people coming down the companionway and the sentry's hoarse call: 'The orficers, sir.'

And suddenly they were all in the cabin – Aitken the first lieutenant, Wagstaffe the second, Baker the third, and young Peter Kenton, the small and red-haired youngster who had taken his place as fourth lieutenant, and Southwick, white hair flowing and looking even younger, his skin taut, as though years of salt spray had never given wrinkles a chance to get a grip. And Rennick, still looking as though he had been levered into his uniform with a shoe-horn, still red-faced and still with the cheery exuberance of a fairground barker.

This is what he missed when he sat in the captain's cabin of *La Créole*. It was hardly bigger than his old cabin in the *Juno* (from which he could talk to the other officers without bothering to open the door), but it was solitary. The lieutenants and warrant officers ate in their gunroom; he had his meals in his own cabin. On deck the officers walked the lee side and left him the weather side, the captain's privilege. But there was no one to whom he could chat; no one spoke to him unless first spoken to because he was the captain.

And even now he sensed it: there was a friendly smile from Aitken, who was way above him in seniority on the lieutenants' list, but the Scotsman's smile had that slight remoteness about it; the remoteness he sensed always existed with his lieutenants in *La Créole*, as though command had slipped a pane of glass between them. And the same from Wagstaffe and Baker, while young Kenton glanced at him with something approaching awe. He sensed it and now he understood it: these men were lieutenants in the *Calypso*, and in the case of Aitken likely to get command of his own frigate before long. But at this particular moment they did not command their own ships while he did: he alone among them was referred to in his own ship as 'the captain'. Of course, he did not have the rank of post captain, like Mr Ramage, allowing him to command a fifth-rate ship or bigger; he was still only a lieutenant, but officers in other ships would describe him as 'the captain' of *La Créole*, referring to the job he carried out, not the actual rank he held in the Navy List.

'The captain'. Those were the two words making that difference; they put that pane of glass between a man and those who had been his friends. Yet it had to be; this was what discipline entailed, a remoteness. A captain who tried to remain intimate with his officers or friendly with his seamen was, quite invariably, a bad officer, even though he might be a pleasant enough man. Mr Ramage never courted popularity; he was by turns surly, witty, bitter, silent, chatty – but he set the pace; he laid out the terms, as it were. The quarterdeck could be a chilly place on the hottest day if Mr Ramage was in a surly mood or angry over some incident. They weren't frequent, but he could remember them well enough. And, for that matter, he suddenly realized there were days when he too was surly; days when *La Créole*'s quarterdeck must seem chilly, and now he thought about it he realized they were more frequent than they should be, but he was still finding his way, sometimes irritated by mistakes he made and sometimes irritated by the mistakes of others; particularly when he had deliberately left them on their own to do something, determined not to nag and interfere – and then he had found he should have interfered; that few officers and petty officers had enough confidence to work on their own. And of course his own standards were rising, the more he learned about command.

In response to Ramage's wave, the men sat or stood where they wanted. Southwick subsided at his usual place, the single armchair; Rennick stood by the door, head bent because of the low beams, as if his uniform was too tight for sitting. Kenton, attending his first such meeting, stood looking lost until Ramage pointed to a chair.

Kenton was five feet four inches tall, exactly the height under the deck beams. Whereas Aitken's face was pale but slightly tanned, Kenton's was pink and peeling, and heavily freckled. Kenton loved the Tropics but the sun scorched him, making him pay a high price for his red hair. The son of a half-pay captain, Kenton was twenty-one years old and had passed for lieutenant within three months of reaching his twentieth birthday, the earliest that he could be promoted.

Southwick, who had served with Ramage for several years and was old enough to be the father of anyone in the cabin, guessed cheerfully: 'The Gulf of Mexico – patrol off Veracruz to look for the Spanish treasure fleet . . .'

'Of course,' Ramage said. 'You can have six men and the jolly boat, and start at dusk.'

The other officers grinned: Southwick's bloodthirsty attitude was well known. His round and cheerful face and white hair gave him the appearance of a gentle bishop or a benign village butcher: a man in his early sixties who could inspire confidence in old ladies and who would sit back in an armchair with a favourite grandchild on each knee. As the austere Aitken later admitted, this had been his first impression of Southwick, and one which lasted until the first time they had gone into action, when he saw the old man transformed into a formidable fighter wielding a sword of incredible size, a two-handed sword that might have come straight from a Viking legend. It was then that Aitken had christened him 'the benevolent butcher'.

'The Admiral could have sent us to Veracruz,' Ramage said, 'but no doubt he thought that because we have all done very well with prize money in the past few months, he'd better send us somewhere else.'

The officers all smiled, realizing that Ramage was tantalizing them.

'He's given us an interesting operation for the *Calypso* — just a comfortable cruise. Lacey and the *Créole* will be doing all the work – and getting all the glory.'

Everyone turned to look at Lacey, most of them more than a little envious, like members of a family at the reading of a rich uncle's will and wondering why their youngest cousin had been given all the sugarplums.

Southwick gave one of his famous sniffs, a great intake of air which signalled disapproval without actually putting it into words. Ramage had heard such sniffs scores of times in the past, when the old master had disapproved of something Ramage was planning. There were in fact various grades. A loud but brief sniff meant that Southwick would not have done it that way, although it might not be entirely wrong. If he thought something was wrong, the sniff was loud and long. If it was followed by a drawn-out 'Weeelll, sir', by the rules of the game Ramage would raise his eyebrows questioningly, which Southwick then interpreted as permission to disagree, and he would speak his thoughts.

It had taken Aitken some time to realize it was in fact a

code which had evolved between the master and Mr Ramage over a long period; they had served together from the very day that Mr Ramage received his first command as a young lieutenant. Since then the pair of them had gone into battle a dozen times or more, been dismasted in a hurricane, lost their ship on a reef, been marooned on an island, found buried treasure . . . It took a stranger a long while to understand the significance of the sniffs, and from the look of it only Aitken had suddenly realized that Southwick had in effect made a statement.

Aitken reckoned that Mr Ramage was ignoring it because Southwick's sniff was based on too little information. The fact that *La Créole* was going to do the work and get any glory meant that the task was one which could not be carried out by the *Calypso*. That much was obvious to Aitken, who was content to wait patiently.

'While we were in Antigua you heard about the increasing privateer activity, and how they are snapping up merchant ships sailing to or from Jamaica,' Ramage said. 'Well, it's worse than we thought and, more important, the frigates patrolling the coasts of Puerto Rico, Hispaniola and Cuba are all reporting *fewer* French, Spanish and Dutch privateers at the big ports.'

Southwick ran his hand through his hair and growled: 'They need to keep a sharper lookout.'

'Or look elsewhere for them,' Ramage said quietly, and everyone glanced up, realizing that those five words were not a chance remark but a clue.

'The Main,' Southwick speculated. 'Shallow water, dozens of likely bays lined with mangrove swamps – and swarming with mosquitoes, of course. Maracaibo, the Gulf of Venezuela, Riohacha, Santa Marta, Baranquilla, all the way round to Portobelo . . . Most of 'em too shallow for us, but not for the privateers, or for the *Créole* . . .'

Ramage nodded and turned towards Rennick. 'There's going to be plenty of boatwork for us, backing up the *Créole*. I shall want those Marines of yours getting in and out of boats as though they were born under the thwarts. And your men, Lacey. When a privateer escapes into water too shallow for *La Créole*, then you send boats in, and ours will follow when possible. I want you to exercise your men in hoisting out boats, rowing with muffled oars, using a compass in the dark, handling a boat gun, carrying pistols without them going off accidentally . . . And don't anyone expect we shall be doing this only in calm weather. You know the Trades blow half a gale out of a clear blue sky, with lumpy sea . . .'

'Which end of the Main do we start, sir?' Aitken asked.

It was a good question because the coast ran east and west, and the Trade winds blew regularly from east to west. Beginning at the eastern end meant that the *Calypso* and *La Créole* started up to windward, in effect starting at the top of the hill, and with luck would be able to chase the privateers to leeward, like wolves pursuing sheep downhill across a meadow, providing they did not make a bolt sideways for the shelter of the bays.

'We start well to windward of Maracaibo,' Ramage said. 'With the Dutch islands, in fact, because the Admiral has been told that the privateers are using Curaçao as a main base.'

'Could be, could be,' Southwick muttered, half to himself. 'The capital, Amsterdam, is a secure anchorage with a narrow entrance easy to defend, plenty of warehouses to store the loot, and well placed to intercept our merchant ships. Good market for prize ships and prize goods – those damned Hollanders are good businessmen, and wealthy, too. And a good rendezvous for all enemy privateers – the French from Guadeloupe, Martinique and Hispaniola, the Spanish from the Main only a few miles away, and from Puerto Rico and Hispaniola to the north. And of course the Dutch.'

Wagstaffe said diffidently: 'There's an advantage there for us, too: Jamaica is to leeward, so our prize crews will have a soldier's wind sailing back to Port Royal.'

Southwick sniffed yet again, and Ramage guessed what was coming: 'And every boarding party we send away with a prize we'll never see again: none of the King's ships in Port Royal will be coming to Curaçao; they'll just press our men. We'll end up with only fifty men left, having supplied the ships in Port Royal with two hundred well-trained men . . .'

It was a problem Ramage had already considered but put off any decision because that would only arise when they actually captured prizes, and remembering the sandbanks and cays and coral reefs littering the coast, he felt it unlikely to make him lose sleep.

He unrolled the chart on the top of his desk and weighted

it down to stop it curling up again. 'Gather round,' he said, 'I want you all to refresh your memories of this coast. How we carry out my instructions – which are simply to get rid of the privateers, and yours, Lacey, will put you under my orders – will depend on what we find among the islands.'

He jabbed a finger down at the lower half of the chart. 'There you have the island of Curaçao, the middle of the three lying just off the Main. There's Bonaire to one side and Aruba the other, but Curaçao is the only one that matters. Notice how Curaçao is like the centre of a clock – the islands of St Lucia and Martinique at three o'clock, Guadeloupe, Antigua, St Barts and St Kitts at one o'clock, Puerto Rico and Hispaniola at noon, and Jamaica here way over to the north-west at ten o'clock. And the Main to the south. All British merchant ships sailing between Jamaica to the west and the Windward and Leeward Islands to the east, have to cross these lines radiating from Curaçao . . .'

He took a pair of dividers from the rack and opened them up until they measured seven degrees, equal to 420 miles, against the latitude scale. Then he put one point on Curaçao and slowly swept the second leg across the chart until the other point finally rested on Grenada, the island at the southern end of the chain. 'You see, only 420 miles to Grenada and the rest of them, Martinique, Antigua, Nevis, St Kitts, no more than 500 miles because of the way they curve round. Puerto Rico, most of Hispaniola – all inside the 420 miles.'

He shut the dividers with a snap. 'Our merchant ships, whether sailing alone or in convoy, are passing east or west no more than four hundred miles north of Curaçao. Four hundred miles – that's probably no more than three days' sailing for the dullest sailor. Sail on Sunday morning, find a prize on Wednesday, and be back in Curaçao unloading the prize by Saturday night. A prize a week at least, and no reason why one privateer should not take three prizes in a day. A hundred men on board to provide boarding parties and prize crews . . . All on a shares-of-the-spoils basis.'

'Aye,' Southwick rumbled, 'making bigger profits than commanders-in-chief.'

'Taking more risks, too,' Wagstaffe said, and then glanced nervously at Ramage, who began taking the weights off the chart.

'Lacey – you have a copy of this chart? In fact you'd better go through our chart outfit with Southwick, so you can make copies of anything you don't have. And the French signal book – you have a copy? The one we captured at Martinique, I mean.'

'No, I don't have a copy, sir.'

Ramage turned to Kenton. 'You can help Lacey by making a copy. And Lacey, you treat it like our own signal book: always locked up when not being used, and always in the weighted bag ready to be thrown over the side . . .' He took out his watch. 'Sunset in five hours. Very well, we weigh in three hours – get busy with pencils and paper, gentlemen.'

CHAPTER TWO

The kneeling seaman carefully removed his plaited straw hat and took a soggy, stringy piece of tobacco from the lining, but before he put it in his mouth and began chewing he commented: 'My jaws are getting tired of overhauling this piece: it's the second day, and there ain't much taste left. You 'aven't got the lend of a piece, 'ave you, Jacko?'

'Since when have I ever chewed bacca?'

'I know, but you might've 'ad a bit tucked away.'

'Oh yes, as a charm against rheumatism and snake bites.'

'Oh, you're a Yankee misery. Now, 'old the cloth still. Cor, the sun's bright. You ready with those scissors, Rossi? Wait, let me flatten out that crease. Now, snip away!'

The three men were crouching down on deck, cutting out the pattern of a pair of trousers drawn on a piece of white duck. Alberto Rossi, the Italian seaman from Genoa, snipped carefully, the tip of his tongue poking out between his lips revealing his concentration.

The man in the straw hat, Stafford, was a young Cockney for whom the trousers were intended, and who scorned 'slops', the clothing sold by the purser, all of it made to standard patterns. One of the more crushing judgements that a self-respecting seaman could make of another man was: 'He's the sort o' feller who'd wear pusser's trousers.'

Rossi paused a moment with the scissors and inspected the cloth. 'Staff, I think you draw the line too tight here –' he gestured with the scissors – 'and you might damage yourself. Shall I leave extra cloth?'

Stafford looked at it doubtfully, certain that his pencilled line had been accurate, but Jackson nudged him. 'You pencilled round the outline of the trousers you're wearing but you forgot to allow for the seams.'

The Cockney's face fell. 'So I did; I was concentrating on holding the cloth still – in this wind. All right then; give us an extra 'alf an inch all round, Rosey.'

All three men stopped and looked round as another group of men kneeling nearby started a violent argument and one of them suddenly stood up, waving a ragged piece of cloth.

'You bluddy idjit!' he screamed. 'Look wotcher dun! Yer've cut froo two ficknesses, not one, an' took off the other leg! I sedjer coodn't be trusted wiv them bluddy scissors. Ten bob's worth o' cloft, that's whatcher've ruined. Why'ncher go'n sit on the jibboom tossing guineas over the side, heh?'

'As long as they're your guineas it's all the same to me,' the other man answered calmly. 'But you marked it and you held it, and I just cut where you said.'

With another scream of rage the first man flung the piece of cloth down on the deck and jumped up and down on it, shaking his fist. 'You rusty cuttle-bung; oooh you milk-livered jakes-scourer, why –'

' 'Ere, 'old 'ard,' the man with the scissors interrupted mildly, 'if you go on like that, I shan't 'elp you no more.'

Stafford prodded Rossi. 'Come on, snip away; don't pay no attention to them or you'll be doing the same. Don't forget, arf an inch outside the line.'

Stafford watched carefully and then muttered: ' 'Ere, Jacko, ain't there someone around what'll lend me a chaw of bacca?'

'Pay attention to your trousers, otherwise you'll end up with four legs and no seat, like a broken chair.'

Finally the trousers were cut out and the front section was held up against Stafford, who looked down at it critically. 'Seems all right,' he said doubtfully. 'Wotcher fink, Rosey?'

'Is all right,' the Italian said. '*Sta attenti* with the stitches. Not those great big ones you put in a sail.'

' 'Taint often the bosun catches me for sail mending,' Stafford boasted. 'I volunteered when the foretopsail split yesterday, but that was so's I could get my fingers on a sail needle.'

'I hope you picked a sharp one. Most of 'em are rusty,' Jackson said. 'They're the ones left on board by the French – poor quality they are. No guts in the metal; they won't hold a point.'

'I did get a nice sharp one, but I can't find it now,' Stafford admitted. ''Aven't got one I could borrow, 'ave you, Jacko?'

'Bacca, needle – I suppose you've got a reel of thread?'

'Well, not reely; I know Rosey's got some good fred, and I was 'oping . . .'

The Italian glared at him. 'This cloth we just make the cut, Staff; you buy him from the purser? I wonder. The purser not sell any slops since we leave Antigua, and I don't remember . . .'

'Well, I didn't steal it from any of me shipmates,' Stafford declared hotly, 'you know me well enough for that. Why, I'm – '

'Accidente!' Rossi said sharply. 'I was only going to ask why you didn't take the thread from the purser at the same time, and you need two buttons.'

'I got the buttons all right,' Stafford admitted, 'but old Nipcheese didn't get the fred out.'

'Old Nipcheese saw you coming,' Jackson commented. 'Not all pursers are daft!'

Ramage paused at the forward end of the quarterdeck and looked across the ship. It was a scene being repeated on board every one of the King's ships at sea: Sunday afternoon and 'make and mend', with the men off watch doing just what they wanted. Some dozed in the sun, others mended clothes, while yet more were cutting cloth and stitching, making new trousers and shirts and repairing old ones.

It was curious how fussy the average seaman was about his clothes, Ramage reflected. Expect him to wear slop clothes and he would be outraged; unless he was lazy or particularly unskilled with needle and thread he did not want to wear a purser's shirt of the same cut and cloth as his shipmate; he wanted a wider or narrower collar, or he sewed the whole shirt with French seams so he could also wear it inside out. His hat would be different; some preferred the natural straw colour of the sennett while others tarred it. Some liked a large hat almost resting on their ears with a wide brim which shaded their eyes and the back of their head; others wanted a narrow brim with a small hat worn high on the head and tilted rakishly forward.

Some captains tried to force the men to wear the same kind of clothes of the same colour and cut, a sort of ship's uniform, as though they were Marines or soldiers, but Ramage disagreed with them. His only rule was that his boat's crew should wear white shirts and trousers and black hats when they rowed him away from the ship on official business, but they were all volunteers and if they did not want to make themselves white trousers they could step down. In fact Aitken reported more than a hundred men clamouring for the dozen places . . . Eccentric captains (and he admitted there were a few of them) dressed their boats' crews in absurd rigs – Wilson had made a fool of himself when commanding the *Harlequin* and the story went that his admiral, taking one look at the men in the boat, asked him if he was commanding a ship or a circus. Wilson was such a fool that most people would have been unsure.

Ramage glanced at the dogvanes – corks strung on a line with feathers stuck in them – on top of the bulwark nettings, then up at the scattering of white clouds drifting westward in neat lines. The weather was holding and the wind had backed to the east. Sailing in the north-east Trade winds meant that one could be sure that they rarely if ever blew from the north-east. Today the wind had been mostly between east and south-east, so that he could short-tack along the Hispaniola coast and have something of a lee from the short, sharp seas rippling across the top of these larger swell waves which the *Calypso* did not like: they were just the wrong length, and each time she dug her bow into the bigger ones she came almost to a stop, the wind not strong enough to thrust her through.

Another few miles, though, and he would be able to turn south, direct for Curaçao. Almost direct, anyway; a course which counteracted a knot of westgoing current. With this wind a knot seemed about right. A week or two of strong easterlies always increased the current, but crossing the Caribbean from the Greater Antilles to the Spanish Main reduced navigation (the setting of an exact course, anyway) to inspired guesswork. You hoped for luck and nodded your head knowingly if you made a good landfall.

The approach to Curaçao from the north was clear of outlying reefs and rocks, and with luck and careful navigation the first the privateers knew that a British frigate and a schooner was after them would be when the island's lookouts sighted them coming over the horizon. Even then, there might be a few hours of uncertainty because both the *Calypso* and *La Créole* were French built and still used French-cut sails which were distinctive with their deep roaches, and with the ships too far off for their ensigns to be distinguished the worthy burgomasters of Curaçao might be forgiven for thinking their French allies were sending reinforcements or calling in for water and provisions, for which no doubt they would have to pay cash in advance.

Southwick, who had just been supervising the casting of the log, came up to report the ship was making a little less than six knots. There was land along the north horizon which ended to the eastward as Hispaniola gave way to the Mona Passage, one of the Caribbean's main gateways into the Atlantic. Just off the south-eastern tip of Hispaniola was the island of Saona, and Ramage pointed to it. 'As soon as the eastern end of Saona is in line with the Punta Espada we'll bear away for Curaçao.'

'Aye aye, sir. With this light wind it's going to be a long 330 miles.'

Ramage pointed at *La Créole* astern, her great fore and aft sails hardened in, spray flying up from her stem, the ship rising and falling on the swell waves with the easy grace of the flying fish which every now and then flashed up to skim the surface. 'Once she gets the wind on the beam you'll be hard put to hold her: she reaches like a bird, and these conditions suit her.'

'I know,' Southwick said ruefully, 'that's why I had the men overhauling the stunsails yesterday. We'll look silly if she has to reduce sail for us to catch up.'

'If I was young Lacey I'd be making my plans,' Ramage said. 'I'd have my best quartermaster chosen, staysails overhauled, largest flying jib bent on ready – and then I'd wait for the *Calypso*'s signal to alter course south, and I'd pass her before Captain Ramage had time to get another signal hoisted!'

Southwick was chuckling and rubbing his hands together.

'Reminds me of the time we were in the *Kathleen* cutter, sir. Pity we never had a schooner; then we'd know some o' the tricks.'

'If you haven't learned enough tricks in – what is it, forty years? – to beat young Lacey, who has been at sea perhaps eight years, and in command of the *Créole* for less than eight weeks, it's time you went back to England and cultivated cabbages. Forty rows of eight cabbages each.'

'She's French built, sir,' Southwick pointed out.

'So is this ship,' Ramage teased.

'Let's have a trial of sailing to windward in a blow, or running with the wind free. That'd show the whippersnapper. But reaching – that's what schooners are built for.'

'The trouble is the course is south, so the "whippersnapper" will probably show us,' Ramage said. 'And most of the privateers we chase will be schooners, too.' He looked towards the land again. Saona and Punta Espada were almost in line as the *Calypso* sailed along to the north-east, close-hauled on the starboard tack, as though struggling to stay up to windward and sail through the Mona Passage and into the Atlantic beyond.

'We'll cheat a bit,' Ramage said. 'Seniority must have its privileges. We'll go about now. That's an hour earlier than Lacey expects.'

Southwick gave an off-key sniff; one which neither acknowledged that he would have an advantage nor admitted that he needed it.

Ramage called to Wagstaffe, who was officer of the deck, and gave him his orders. A few moments later Orsini, the young midshipman, was busy with a seaman, bending signal flags to a halyard.

Southwick led the way to the binnacle and stared down at the compass card. 'We're heading nor-nor' east on this tack.' He looked up at the luff of the main course and then at the dogvane. 'The wind's due east, so steering south we'll have the wind on the beam. If it'd pipe up a bit . . .'

By now Wagstaffe, speaking trumpet in his hand, was giving the first of the orders which would turn the frigate and bring the wind from the starboard side to the larboard. The men stitching and cutting or just lazing, enjoying their 'make and mend', moved themselves out of the way of the men on watch who, in a few moments, would be hauling on tacks and sheets and braces as the great yards swung over.

The men at the wheel, one each side, watched the quarter-master who was standing to windward of them, alternately eyeing Wagstaffe and the luffs of the sails.

Ramage savoured the moment. Tacking a well-designed frigate was a joy if properly done, the ship swinging (in this case) through fourteen points of the compass without losing way and then sailing in almost the opposite direction at the same speed. A joy to watch the men you've trained moving in apparent confusion, but every man following his own special track, as if the deck was marked out with separate but invisible paths. The sails slamming and flapping, ropes squealing as they rendered through blocks – and then suddenly came peace and quiet as the last order was given with the sails trimmed on the new tack, and the quartermaster calling out the new course being steered. And the ship settled down to the ridge-and-furrow movement like the flight of a wood-pecker. Some hours of peace before the next bout of war . . . the fascination of sea life, he realized, was its strange variety.

Wagstaffe glanced across at Ramage who, seeing all was ready, nodded and wondered wryly as he looked astern at *La Créole* whether post captains had played similar tricks on him when he was a nervous young lieutenant commanding the *Kathleen* cutter. Small and at the time inexplicable episodes now took on meaning; sudden alterations of course, sudden and odd orders hoisted by signal flags when the wind direction meant the flags streamed out end-on and indistinguishable – yes, other post captains had done it. Now, years later, he could admit they were quite right, too: it had kept him on his toes. Even today, when he could rely on his men and had no need personally to watch a horizon for a strange sail or keep an eye on a flagship in anticipation of a hoist of signal flags suddenly appearing, it was rare for anyone on deck to spot them before him. Lookouts up at the masthead would sight a distant ship first because their height of eye gave them a longer range, but . . .

His thoughts were interrupted as Wagstaffe snapped orders at the quartermaster, and the men began to spin the wheel. Tacking or wearing off a coastline always gave this curious effect that the ship was still heading in the same direction and it was the land that was sliding one way or the other. Now the whole coastline of Hispaniola seemed to be sliding to the

west, as though someone was pulling a rumpled green baize
cloth across a table.

He still found it hard to leave an evolution entirely to the
officer of the deck. He had enough self-control to keep his
mouth shut, and thus give the impression of not interfering;
of treating the whole evolution with lofty disdain, as though
merely tacking the ship was beneath the interest of the captain,
apart from giving the initial order. Yes, he managed to keep
his mouth shut, but sometimes it was difficult – like now, when
the wind is out of the after sails and Wagstaffe is going to
be several seconds late in ordering: 'Raise tacks and sheets!'

Then he saw that as Wagstaffe put the speaking trumpet to
his mouth and bellowed the order the lieutenant's eyes were
in fact on Southwick, who was glaring at him. Southwick
knew it was late and now Wagstaffe knew, so why, Ramage
asked himself, don't I just admire the view?

The canvas of the sails was flogging with a noise like great
wet slaps. Wagstaffe was bellowing: 'Mainsail haul!' – and
what the devil were Jackson and his crowd doing? They had
suddenly begun pointing upwards after making sure he could
see them.

Up aloft the lookouts at the foremast and mainmast were
gesticulating wildly, their hails lost in the slamming of yards
and flapping of sails. Quickly Ramage ran to the larboard side
as the *Calypso*'s bow swung. Is that a fleck on the horizon?
Perhaps two? Specks that are the sun making light and
shadow of the sails of one or more distant ships? He could
not be sure.

Finally Wagstaffe gave the last order: 'Haul off all!' and
with the quartermaster watching the compass and the luff of
the mainsail and cursing the men at the wheel, Ramage heard
the excited hails from aloft: 'Deck there!'

For a moment he nearly cupped his hands to reply, but
Wagstaffe had the speaking trumpet and shouted aloft.

'Mainmast-head,' came the faint shout. 'One sail, probably
two, fine on the larboard bow, sir!'

Wagstaffe glanced round and saw Orsini, who was waiting
for the order to hoist *La Créole*'s signal. 'Quick, boy, take the
bring-'em-near and get aloft. What ships and what courses are
they steering!'

The young midshipman snatched the proffered telescope and
raced to the main shrouds. Wagstaffe looked at Ramage,

obviously worried about the signal, still bent on the halyard, a heap of coloured cloth, but a glance told Ramage that Lacey was already tacking *La Créole* without orders: he had probably seen the flags being bent on and saw Orsini suddenly scrambling aloft, and there was now only one order that mattered.

'Beat to quarters, Mr Wagstaffe.'

Already the deck was clearing of men: they had heard the lookouts' hail and were snatching up their pieces of cloth and rousing their sleeping mates and making their way to their quarters for action. The gunner was running up from below to ask for the key to the magazine and Bowen, the surgeon, who had apparently been dozing on the fo'c'sle, was hurrying below to set out his instruments.

Ramage looked out over the larboard bow, balancing himself on the breech of the aftermost 12-pounder gun. It took a few moments to spot the fleck again. Flecks, rather, because there were definitely two ships, though they'd seemed closer together when first he saw them.

And whatever they were, it was important to keep up to windward.

'Mr Wagstaffe, steer hard on the wind; man the lee braces and tend the weather ones . . . get those fore-tacks close down . . . Let's have those yards braced sharp up!'

Ramage stopped himself: there were plenty more instructions for getting the *Calypso* steering as fast and as close to the wind as possible, to cut off the distant ships' escape if they were enemy, but Wagstaffe knew them all, and any moment Aitken would be on deck.

Ah, there was the Marine drummer striding up and down, whirling his drumsticks with a flourish that sent men to quarters, and already several had anticipated the order and were rigging head pumps and running up on deck with buckets of sand while others were casting loose the guns.

'Mr Wagstaffe, make to the *Créole* "Sail in sight" and give the bearing.'

Southwick gestured astern, and Ramage saw *La Créole* was already hauling her wind to get into the *Calypso*'s wake, and at that moment three hoists of signal flags broke out.

'Should never trust young lieutenants with the signal book,' Southwick muttered, 'and Lacey must have seen Orsini going aloft!'

Wagstaffe had his telescope to his eye and began reading off the signals. '350 – *I have discovered a strange fleet* . . . 366 – *The strange ships lye-by*, and 315 – *The ship is ready for action.*'

'Acknowledge,' Ramage said, and winked at Southwick. 'He trumped our ace, don't you think?'

Southwick grinned ruefully. 'It's the way you've trained him, sir. He's picked up some of your habits. A rod for your own back!'

By now the lookout at the mainmast-head was hailing again, passing on Orsini's reports. 'Deck there . . . two ships, sir, both lying-to. One – the nearest, Mr Orsini says – is a merchant ship. The other is smaller . . . fore and aft rigged . . . much less freeboard, big sweep to her sheer . . .'

Wagstaffe acknowledged, but a few moments later the lookout was hailing again. 'Deck there . . . the smaller ship's a schooner and she's getting under way. The merchant ship's backing and filling as though there's no one at the helm, so Mr Orsini says, sir.'

From the moment the lookout had shouted down, '. . . both lying-to . . .' Ramage had known what was going to follow, and he turned to Aitken, who had just hurried up, buckling on his sword, and told him: 'Fine on the larboard bow, a privateer schooner has caught a merchant ship. She sighted us just as we saw her, and now she's getting under way.'

The masthead lookout hailed again: 'Deck there! Schooner's steering a couple of points to starboard of our course, sir, but the merchant ship's swung so everything's aback.'

Ramage saw Baker and Kenton hurry up to the quarterdeck and report to Aitken, who came up and said formally: 'The ship's company at quarters, sir: do you want the guns loaded and run out?'

'Not for the time being.'

And here was Jackson with his sword and a pistol. Ramage turned while Jackson clipped on the slings of the scabbard, and then took the pistol and clipped it into his waistbelt.

Now Southwick was reporting the wind freshening, and yet another glance showed *La Créole* was in the same position in the frigate's wake, heeling more now. There was no chance, Ramage realized bitterly, of her overhauling that privateer schooner out ahead of them. It would be dark in six hours, and the old saying that 'a stern chase is a long chase' was very true. And he was not going to risk splitting his tiny force at this stage.

Yet such was the contradictory nature of men, if he had told them that they would soon be going into action, with the inevitable corollary that some of them would be killed and others would be badly wounded and maimed for life, so that Bowen would have to saw off limbs with the patients biting a piece of wood and befuddled with rum to help them bear the pain, they would have cheered him. Instead he would soon be telling them that unless something entirely unforeseen happened, there would be no action today, and they would groan with genuine disappointment.

'Deck there! The schooner has tacked up to the nor' east, sir.'

And in half an hour, Ramage thought bitterly, she'll tack again, gradually working herself well up to windward, knowing no square-rigged ship like a frigate could get near her and sure that no schooner so far to leeward would ever catch her up. By nightfall she'll be out of sight, and the *Calypso*'s log will note that she was 'last seen in the south-east quadrant'.

By now, as the *Calypso* worked her way to windward, occasional spray flying over the fo'c'sle like a heavy shower of rain, the merchant ship's hull was beginning to lift over the curvature of the earth, the line of her deck just now visible in the telescope but the rest of her hull still below the horizon. Ramage saw that she was heading eastward, all her sails aback, and even as he watched she began to pay off and swing round, the wind pressing on backed jibs.

Had the schooner taken everyone on board prisoner? Was the ship abandoned? Curious that no one was attempting to trim her sails or furl them. Now she was making a stern board, one which risked wrenching off her rudder if the men at the wheel did not stop it spinning. There was, of course, another explanation, and he tried to avoid thinking about it; he would soon know.

'Mr Aitken, we'll need one boat, possibly two, so have them ready for hoisting out. Six Marines for each boat and a dozen extra seamen. And tell Mr Bowen to be ready with a bag of instruments, because he'll be going over.'

The first lieutenant stared at him, and then realized the significance of the reference to Bowen, because it was unlikely the merchant ship had been in action against the privateer. As he gave the orders he watched the distant merchant ship slowly turning, like a swan's feather on a pond, turning and drifting in the breeze.

Now Rennick was giving orders to his Marines while men ran to prepare the boats for hoisting out, and Jackson said to Ramage: 'Shall I get your boat cloak, sir?'

He had a light cloak, intended only for use in the Tropics, to keep the spray off his uniform, and there was enough of a sea to ensure a wet row to the merchant ship. He shook his head. 'I shan't be going over.'

The American coxswain's face fell. A visit to a merchant ship just out from England usually meant the gift of newspapers and often some tasty snacks like cheeses. Ramage said: 'You had better take Mr Baker.'

Aitken, overhearing the conversation, turned expectantly, but Ramage said: 'Send Kenton with one boat and Baker with the other and Rennick had better divide his Marines. And make sure the surgeon's mate goes with Bowen.'

'You think it will be as bad as that, sir?'

Ramage watched the merchant ship's sails fill for a few moments as she turned slowly in the wind. 'Yes, it'll be as bad as that.'

It was, in fact, far worse. As the *Calypso* approached Ramage saw that the merchant ship was low in the water and obviously settling, and Ramage wasted no time in bringing the frigate up to windward, backing the foretopsail and hoisting out the two boats, giving Baker orders that he was to board first and give any necessary orders to Kenton in the second boat.

Ramage had watched through the telescope as Baker boarded with Jackson, swarming up a rope ladder hanging over the merchant ship's quarter. He had paused on the poop, then walked forward, finally going below. He had emerged briefly to signal Kenton to come on board, and Bowen had gone up the ladder as well as Rennick and his sergeant. Then, as far as Ramage could see, they had systematically searched the ship's accommodation, although it was clear that the hatches were still battened down, the covers, battens and wedges still in place, showing that no one had been down into the cargo holds.

Half an hour later, with the ship settling so deeply that

she was becoming unstable, liable to capsize unexpectedly, Ramage had fired a gun to signal the boats to return, and when they were back on board Baker, Kenton, Rennick and Bowen had come to the quarterdeck to report, all of them white-faced and obviously distressed at what they had seen.

'You saw the name on the stern, sir, the *Tranquil* of London, but there are no ship's papers on board. The captain's cabin has been looted, his desk smashed up, every drawer emptied out,' Baker said.

He held up a bundle of papers. 'We shall be able to identify most of the bodies of the passengers from these letters, sir, and some of the crew too, I expect. There were some packages addressed to people in Jamaica. They're in the boat and I'll have them brought up.'

Ramage knew he was trying to avoid asking the question just as Baker was avoiding referring to it, but finally he said: 'How many?'

'Fifteen in the ship's company, sir, and nine passengers, five of them women.'

'All dead?'

'Three were still alive when I found them. One died before Bowen could get on board, and the others – both women – died before he could do anything. The women were raped and then shot or butchered. But the strange thing is none of them seem to have tried to run away.'

'Could they have been standing there, expecting to be taken over to the schooner as prisoners, but suddenly murdered by their guards?' Ramage asked.

Baker nodded miserably. 'I think that's what must have happened. When the privateer sighted us, sir?'

'Yes. The boarding party were probably about to secure the prisoners – or perhaps choosing those likely to be worth ransoming – and preparing to put a prize crew on board and get under way just as we came in sight.'

If I'd waited another hour before tacking, Ramage told himself, the privateer would never have seen us. Working beyond the rim of the horizon, she would have sent her prize off, and those people would still be alive, even though prisoners. As it was, there had been a senseless massacre. The ship was sinking anyway, scuttled with her boats still secured, so why kill everyone? Why not let them take their chance in the boats? It would have cost the privateer nothing. 'The quality of mercy . . .'

'Why was she sinking?'

'She carried two 6-pounders,' Baker said. 'Little more than boat guns, but the privateersman trained one down the companionway and fired a shot through the bottom.'

'And there's no indication of the name of the privateer?'

'No, sir, but she was French,' Baker said, motioning to Kenton, who opened the drawstring of a canvas bag and pulled out a handful of blue, white and red cloth. 'They had this flag ready to bend on her, but they left it behind in the rush.'

For a moment Ramage pictured the scene: women screaming as pistols and muskets fired, men begging for mercy as cutlasses slashed at them, and somewhere there, watching, the man who had ordered it all: the privateer captain who was not content with leaving all these people to take their chance in a sinking ship. No, he wanted the satisfaction of murdering them, twenty-four murders which did not put another penny in his pocket nor make his life any safer, because none of the victims could possibly have known his name.

Kenton held the hoist of the flag so the cloth unrolled like a sheet. He looked up at Ramage. 'It was a terrible sight, sir. Not like battle, where you expect to see bodies and men badly wounded. It was like a slaughterhouse.'

Ramage took the bundle of papers from Baker, and knew that for the next few hours he would have to read through many private letters, so that he could identify as many victims as possible. It was nothing compared with what the young lieutenants had just gone through. As Kenton had said, it wasn't like battle. Yet war wasn't made up only of battles, which was why he had sent these youngsters over to the merchant ship. Southwick, Aitken, Wagstaffe . . . they might not have seen this sort of thing before although they expected it, but for Baker and Kenton and probably Rennick, it was a side of war of which they had not yet even dreamed. And Ramage knew that in future they would understand if the captain of the ship in which they were serving refused to show any mercy towards a privateer or privateersmen.

'Look,' Southwick suddenly called, 'there she goes.'

Air trapped in the merchant ship's hull was bursting the hatches, hurling up the planks in showers of spray as canvas covers, battens and wedges tore free. Sacks and crates floated away as the ship began to heel, yards slewing and dropping as the lifts broke. She heeled towards the *Calypso* and for a minute they were all looking down on her, a gull's eye view, and then she capsized, fat-bilged and ungainly. The bottom was greenish-brown from the copper sheathing, but here and there small, rectangular black patches showed where sheets of the copper had ripped off. There was a swirling in the water, as though a great whale was submerging, and then she was gone, a few air bubbles making the floating wreckage, planks and sacks, bob and twist.

Ramage looked towards the eastern horizon. The privateer was now a mere speck several miles to windward, an anonymous killer sneaking into the haze. Astern *La Créole* was lying hove-to and like the *Calypso* her gun ports were open. Chasing the privateer was a waste of time; she would vanish in the night long before the *Calypso* or *La Créole* could ever get close.

Aitken looked questioningly at Ramage, who nodded, and a few moments later the men were bracing round the foretopsail yard while others unscrewed the locks from the guns and coiled up the trigger lines. Cartridges were returned to the magazine, cutlasses and pistols put back in chests. The sand had been washed from the decks and the hot sun had dried the wood in two or three minutes. Ten minutes later the *Calypso*'s off-watch men were back doing whatever they had been doing when the privateer and her victim had been sighted.

Ramage took one last look round the horizon and went down to his cabin with the handful of papers. It was cool and dark, and he was thankful to be out of the glare of the sun. Watching the funeral of a ship and twenty-four innocent people left him feeling shaky. Should he have read a funeral service as the *Tranquil* sank? He had not thought of it, because he preferred to mourn in his own way, in a quiet and dark place. He hated the pomp and ritual of church funerals, but he knew the ship's company were great sticklers for ritual. Not for ritual, perhaps, but for 'doing the right thing'. They had a healthy attitude towards the death of one of their shipmates, and their wish to give him what they called a 'proper funeral' was perhaps more because they wanted to please him; to give him the kind of funeral they thought he would like –

which in turn, Ramage supposed, meant the kind of funeral each man wanted for himself: a time when everyone, from the youngest boy on board to the captain, paid their respects.

The people represented by the handful of papers now on his desk had not been given a farewell wave. Yet he was sure that no one else had thought of it: Southwick would have been the first to whisper a hint; Jackson had heard Baker's report, and he had said nothing, and the American was not one for keeping his thoughts to himself if the captain's reputation was at stake. No, those who knew what that sinking ship contained had been too shocked to think of anything, and the *Tranquil* had gone down on her own with a quiet dignity and taken her people with her.

CHAPTER THREE

Ramage took up his pen and inspected the point. The quill was blunt but he could not be bothered to sharpen it. It was a miserable feather, taken from a moulting goose no doubt. At least it was from the left wing, for a right-handed writer. After unscrewing the cap of the inkwell he took his journal from a drawer and made a brief entry recording the encounter with the *Tranquil*. Then he took out a blank sheet of paper and began the draft of a report to the Admiral. Be brief, he told himself; old Foxey-Foote will examine every word, looking for trouble (an admiral's privilege, of course), and the fewer the sentences the fewer the loopholes. The obvious criticism from such an inexperienced admiral was going to be that he did not pursue the privateer, and the equally obvious answer was that in twelve hours of darkness the privateer could be anywhere, and Ramage knew he would be wise to point out that he was acting under the Admiral's orders to proceed to Curaçao. He read the draft through again. Less than a full page – that would please the clerk when he came to make the fair copy and also copy it into the letter book.

He took a piece of cloth from the top drawer and carefully wiped the pen dry of ink, then screwed the cap back on the inkwell and put it away. Then he knew he was deliberately putting off looking at those letters.

The first was from the *Tranquil*'s master to his owners, intended to be posted in Jamaica, because the Post Office packet would arrive in England weeks before the convoy with his ship. He was reporting that the weather had been fair for the whole voyage so that instead of anchoring at Barbados with the rest of the convoy he had sailed on alone. He had stopped at Nevis only to buy fresh vegetables for the passengers and then left for Jamaica. He explained that with so many ships calling at Barbados, the price of fruit and vegetables there was often three or four times that in Nevis. A piece of economy, Ramage realized, which had taken the ship out of the convoy and put her some fifty miles farther north than she would have been if she had remained in the convoy when it sailed from Barbados. The reason the ship had gone to Nevis and then come in sight of the privateer had been the high price of fruit and vegetables in Barbados; the reason the *Calypso* had tacked an hour early – and thus panicked the privateer – had been Captain Ramage's trick on *La Créole* . . .

The wife of a major in the 79th Foot was visiting her parents, who obviously owned a plantation in Jamaica. She had written a letter to her husband in the form of a diary, the last entry being the day before. Ramage pencilled in the two names on another sheet of paper, beneath the name of the master and the name and address of the owners of the ship.

A man living in Jamaica and returning there after a visit to England was writing an angry letter to his agent in London. He was probably a planter, so they would know him in Port Royal. For some reason the agent had not made sure that the furniture, cases of wine and boxes of crockery bought in London had reached the *Tranquil* before she sailed, and the letter told him in no uncertain terms what a stupid fellow he was. By now the goods would either be in another ship or still in a warehouse in London, but had the agent been sharper they would have sunk in the *Tranquil* – not that it mattered now, with the owner dead. Ramage copied his name and the name and address of the agent on to his list.

Another letter written by a woman. She was rejoining her husband in Jamaica after a visit to England, and she was writing to her mother in Lincolnshire – was it Louth? Her writing was not easy to read. She too described the voyage from London out to Nevis, and told her mother how she was

excited at the prospect of seeing her husband and children
again, and she wondered if she had been wise to be away so
long – eighteen months. But she was glad to be back in the
warm weather again – she apologized to her mother but, she
admitted, Lincolnshire was cold and damp. Then Ramage
realized the woman had written the last few lines only an
hour or so ago: a ship had just come in sight, she had
written, and was heading towards them. The captain was
afraid it was a privateer . . . The captain was sure it was; he
could see the Spanish flag . . . The Spaniard had fired some
shots across their bow and they were stopping and she was,
she told her mother, praying for their deliverance. The name
of the Spanish ship, the captain said, was the *Nuestra Señora
de Antigua* . . . a gentle name, she wrote, and in an hour or
two she would complete the letter and tell her mother what
had happened. And there the letter ended. But the woman
had perhaps not died in vain: the *Nuestra Señora de Antigua*,
and, Ramage vowed, God help her if she was ever sighted by
a ship of the Royal Navy.

Ramage found that the letters written by the men were
impersonal; they were names and addresses to be added to
the list. But the women – they were describing new sights and
ventures to distant loved ones, and although Ramage was hard
put to avoid feeling he was prying, as he read the written
words he felt he was getting to know the writers. And then,
as he held the letters, each so vital, each describing minutes
in the writer's life and looking forward to future events, like
seeing children, arriving in Jamaica, noting how much newly-
planted flowering trees and shrubs had grown, once again
came the shock of knowing that each writer had ceased to
exist; that now each was only someone's memory.

He thought for a moment, chill striking his whole body,
that Gianna could well have been in that ship; a passenger
for Jamaica. She could have decided on an impulse to sail
from England to join him, knowing that she would arrive
almost as soon as a letter warning that she was on her way.
His father and mother would try to dissuade her; but for too
many years the Marchesa di Volterra had ruled her own little
country among the Tuscan hills, had too many servants running around after her, too many ministers deferring to her, to
hesitate when she wanted to do something.

Her little kingdom had been overrun by Napoleon and she

had fled to England, and there she lived in Cornwall with his parents, old friends of her family, and they were treating her like a daughter. A somewhat wild and impetuous daughter, fiery tempered and yet gifted with a generous nature and, most important, a sense of humour. That the young Marchesa and their son had fallen in love they regarded as the most natural thing in the world, a fitting and suitable arrangement.

Ramage knew that his father had spent too many years at sea to see anything particularly romantic in the fact that Ramage had rescued the Marchesa from the Tuscan beaches as French cavalry had hunted her: Admiral the Earl of Blazey knew his son had his duty to do, and naturally expected him to do it. That the Marchesa had turned out to be a tiny, black-haired beauty then barely twenty years old and not an ancient and gnarled tyrant was – well, the old Earl had shrugged his shoulders and made no comment, recalling Gianna's mother, whom he had been expecting, not knowing that she had recently died.

Ramage tried to stop his imagination plunging on. Gianna could have been one of these bodies in the *Tranquil*, and because neither Baker nor Kenton had ever seen her, the first he would have known would be reading a letter if she had written one, and if Baker or Kenton had been able to find it.

Paolo would have been one of the boarding party had Ramage not forgotten him. Gianna's nephew, whom she had bullied Ramage into taking to sea with him . . . Paolo Orsini, the heir to the kingdom of Volterra, until Gianna married and had children of her own. Young Paolo would have found his aunt – how ridiculous referring to her as the boy's aunt; she was only five or six years older – among the pile of corpses.

Steady, Ramage told himself, bundling up the letters, and realizing that Jackson would have recognized her, this way lies madness: this was how young captains, isolated by the routine and tradition of command, became eccentric, even mad: they sat alone and in their cabins, brooded, thinking this and fearing that, playing the eternal game of 'if'. 'If this had happened, that would have been avoided . . . if I had done this . . .' The worst of the 'if' game was, of course, that it was very easy for a captain to lose confidence in himself: as he read his orders he could, without much difficulty, consider them far more difficult to carry out than they were, and then he would find himself wondering what would happen 'if' he failed.

The next stage after that was wondering 'if' he would succeed, and once he stepped into that quicksand he was lost; he would fail no matter what happened. That was the one lesson that Ramage had learned about command, dating back to the time when Commodore Nelson – as he then was – first gave him command of the little *Kathleen* cutter and put Southwick in as master.

Those first orders from the Commodore had been desperate enough, but looking back on them Ramage realized that, young and inexperienced as he was, he had not really thought of failure. There hadn't been time enough to consider it. The important thing was to avoid brooding. Keep your mind occupied – it could be a thick head from drinking too much wine at a reception the night before, or perhaps you were too preoccupied because the ship's company was badly trained – it could be any one of a hundred things, but you were too busy to think of failure, and often because of that you succeeded. Or perhaps you failed, but failed because success was impossible, not because you had gone into battle defeated by your own dark thoughts and lack of confidence.

At that moment Ramage acknowledged yet again how much he owed to Southwick. The old man had served with him for years, always the same, always cheerful, yet always grumbling. Cheerfully grumbling about the ship's company, whichever the ship and however well trained the men, but treating them all like unruly but much loved sons. And, of course, it was not just Southwick: there were those scoundrels Jackson, Stafford and Rossi.

Defeat, failure, even difficulties were hard to consider for long with those men around. Jackson, for example, an American who had an American Protection in his pocket and need only get word to an American consul to secure his discharge from the Royal Navy – but instead he was the captain's coxswain, a man who had saved Gianna's life once and Ramage's many times. Rossi, the plump and cheerful man from Genoa whose English was good and whose past in Genoa was a matter of conjecture. Rossi was a volunteer, and with Genoa under Napoleon's occupation Rossi was happy enough in the Royal Navy, where he was paid for killing the Frenchmen he hated. And Stafford, the third of the men always mentioned by Gianna in her letters. Stafford had, like Jackson and Rossi, helped rescue Gianna. He made no secret that before the press gang swept him into the Navy, when he had lived in Bridewell Lane in the city of London, and after having been apprenticed to a locksmith, he rarely went to work on the lock of a door with the owner's knowledge.

The three men argued interminably, although they never quarrelled; they had – Ramage thought for a moment – yes, they had been in the frigate that sank in battle as they went to fetch Gianna, and had helped row the boat used to rescue her. They had been in the *Kathleen* when she was smashed to driftwood by the Spanish three-decker at the Battle of Cape St Vincent. They had been with him in the *Triton* brig when he had taken command to find most of the original crew had mutinied, and they had been in her through the hurricane which tore out her masts and tossed her up on a reef near Puerto Rico. They had been with him in the Post Office packet brig when they were trying to discover why the mails were vanishing. They had been . . . and so it went on, and probably would go on.

Now, to their delight, they had on board the Marchesa's nephew (or, as Stafford had proudly announced to the rest of the ship's company when he first heard about it, 'the Marcheezer's nevvy') and it had been tacitly accepted that they kept an eye on him. Jackson had already saved the boy's life once when they boarded an enemy ship a few weeks ago with Paolo wielding a cutlass in one hand and a midshipman's dirk in the other.

Supposing the boy was killed – how would he ever tell Gianna? Then he checked himself: these thoughts were merely a variation on the game of 'if' – 'If Paolo was killed . . .' Paolo was lively, energetic, eager to learn, scared of nothing, and appalling at mathematics. As Gianna had said, in the argument which had finally persuaded Ramage, if the boy survived a few years as a midshipman and later a lieutenant in the Royal Navy, he would have learned lessons which would stand him in good stead if he should ever have to rule Volterra when the French had been driven out: he would understand men, and how to govern them, and that was all (whether midshipman in a frigate or ruler of Volterra) he needed to know to survive.

Ramage called to the Marine sentry to pass the word for his clerk, and as soon as the report and the list of names and addresses were handed over to the man for fair copies to be made, Ramage sent for Aitken. The first lieutenant was second in command of the ship; it was very easy to forget (or, more honestly, it was a thought that few captains cared to dwell upon) that Aitken would be in command if anything happened to the captain, and captains were as likely to perish from yellow fever or roundshot as any man on board . . .

The captain was brooding, there was no doubt about that. Aitken sensed it the moment he stepped into the cabin and sat on the settee in response to the captain's gesture. The deep-set eyes seemed positively sunken, yet one didn't need the second sight to guess why the captain was in this mood. There were plenty of men in the Highlands who still brooded over the rapine and pillaging of their villages half a century earlier, when they were still bairns, so it was hardly surprising to find a man like Mr Ramage brooding over that bloody murder in the *Tranquil* only an hour or so ago.

Now Mr Ramage was staring at him, as though he was a stranger.

'Do the ship's company know what happened in the *Tranquil*?'

It was a puzzling question; there was no way it could have been kept secret, even if it was necessary. 'Yes, sir, they all know.'

'And what are their feelings?'

'Violent, sir, particularly because of the women. We might . . .'

'Might what, Aitken?'

'We might have difficulty controlling them if we find a privateer, sir. If we board one, I mean.'

But instead of getting angry and saying the officers should be able to control their men, Mr Ramage was just nodding; not in agreement but in the way old men nodded their heads when told interesting news.

Aitken was thankful for this opportunity to discuss it. 'I was going to mention it to you, sir: perhaps you'd care to talk to the ship's company; to warn them against running amok when we start finding these privateers.'

The young Scot sensed the captain's interest was flagging, and was then not sure whether to be shocked or relieved when Ramage said: 'I propose giving no particular orders if we board a privateer called the *Nuestra Señora de Antigua*, Mr Aitken. We board other privateers in the normal way and I shall expect that strict attention will be paid to discipline.'

'Aye aye, sir. But no mercy for the *Nuestra Señora de Antigua*. Is she the one that . . .'

'Yes, she's named in a letter. The last line or two was written as she came close.'

Aitken reached for his hat and was about to leave the cabin, but the captain waved him to remain seated, and said quietly: 'I think you too sense there's something unusual in all this.'

He did too: he had felt it first when Baker and Kenton came back on board. He and Southwick had already guessed what the two lieutenants were likely to find (not the murdered women, of course) so they were not surprised. But with the return of the lieutenants, Aitken had become aware of a curious atmosphere on board. In a way it centred round the captain, yet Jackson and Rossi seemed affected. Not Stafford, and not Southwick: neither was an imaginative man; one could not imagine them having the second sight.

But he had felt very strongly this sense of – well, what? That the quarterdeck had grown chillier, like walking into the crypt of a church. That he had seen the whole episode before, although it was no stronger than a distant memory or a half-remembered dream. Yet he had known before it happened that Baker would produce a bundle of letters; he knew how the captain would take them and walk over to the companionway and down the steps, hunched as though the letters brought him bad news, instead of having been written by people of whom they had never heard.

That seaman Jackson, the captain's coxswain, he was just walking round as though bewildered, stunned almost, refusing to help Stafford finish cutting up a new pair of trousers. Rossi, too, the third one of that curious trinity, was sitting on his own, his thoughts miles away. Yet of all the men in the ship those two must have seen the most violence and bloodshed. What had upset them could not have been these senseless murders in the *Tranquil*. It was something else, as though a hand had reached out of the past and touched them on the shoulder.

The first time he had ever had this sensation of a touch from the past was when he was perhaps eleven or twelve years

old and had walked from his home in Dunkeld down the
steep hill towards the village.

It was a late autumn day with the last of the sun turning
the leaves of the great beeches into burnished copper, and he
had gone through the gate to the ruined cathedral. It was a
stone skeleton; only the walls stood; the roof had long since
gone. Yet it was easy to picture the fine stone building in its
glory, men and women and children singing hymns, their
voices echoing under the vaulted roof. The service would end
and they would be blessed, and slowly they would go to their
homes, pausing perhaps at the main door to talk for a few
minutes, to exchange family news and to gossip perhaps, but
feeling spiritually refreshed by the service.

Round the cathedral, lining the paths, were graves and the
entrances to vaults; carved marble, stained by age, mottled by
lichen, recording a couple of hundred years and more of the
story of the people of Dunkeld, and the people walking to the
gate would be passing the last resting places of their parents,
grandparents, great-grandparents . . . As a young boy on that
autumn evening he had sensed all this and had in his imagination seen people dressed in clothes he did not recognize, and
which he later discovered were the fashions of past centuries.

Between those earlier centuries and the time he stood there
as a boy, the cathedral had been burned; the pews and the
beams had gone up in flames and the roof had collapsed. No
one had tried to repair it; moss and lichen grew in the stones,
the grass spread over the tombs. It was something about
which his mother would never speak. But as he stood there
and thought about it the atmosphere had grown chilly. Not
cold and not frightening, even though he had been only a boy.
Just enough for him to realize he was experiencing something
he would never be able to describe or explain. Indeed, he had
never spoken of it.

Now the *Calypso* had changed. It was probably his imagination, but as he sat here looking at the captain, he knew that
around Jackson and Rossi and the captain there was – well, an
aura almost, as though they had stepped from the past.

Yet it was all absurd: the *Calypso* was a frigate built only
five years ago in a French shipyard, captured only a few
weeks ago by Mr Ramage, and Jackson was an American seaman who had volunteered to serve in the Royal Navy and
Rossi was a Genoese – what did he call himself? a Genovesi?

-- and that was that. He, James Aitken, a lieutenant in the Royal Navy and the *Calypso*'s first lieutenant, was rambling amidst superstition like an ancient widowed crone outside her croft high in the Perthshire hills, weaving with gnarled hands and prattling through toothless gums and staring about her with fading eyes, living in a world of vague memories and dreams of what might have been.

Yet here was the captain referring to 'something unusual in all this' and looking as if he had just seen a ghost.

It was nothing to do with Aitken, but it had happened as the young Scot had entered the cabin: Ramage had had this over-powering sense that he knew what Aitken was going to say. Earlier he had found himself giving orders as though repeating the words from a play or something said in a dream. Southwick had been puzzled because he had not gone on board the *Tranquil*, and even Ramage had been surprised to hear himself telling Jackson he was not going.

While Baker and Kenton had been on board her, somehow he had known what they were seeing; he had known that women had been murdered. But he had dismissed all that as something he did not understand; he had given his orders, come down to his cabin and gone through the letters, and had thought of Gianna, and all the time he had pushed aside this -- this what?

And then as Aitken had come through the doorway he had remembered a story his father had told him. He must have been very young at the time, and Father was telling him something of the Ramage family; how one day, when he was grown up, he would become the Earl of Blazey in place of his father.

At first he had not understood; then he had realized his father was saying that when an earl died his eldest son became the next earl; that his father was the tenth earl, and he had succeeded *his* father, Ramage's grandfather, who was the ninth earl and who in turn had succeeded the eighth earl, who was Ramage's great-grandfather.

It was great-grandfather, Charles Uglow Ramage, the eighth earl of Blazey, about whom his father had told him the story. He could not remember many of the details -- he had been so young that the story had little more significance than so many of the tales that his mother or father told him before he went to sleep at night.

But great-grandfather Charles, the second son, had been in Barbados during the Civil War, a Royalist, and for reasons which Ramage could no longer remember he had later fled the island and headed for Jamaica in the ship the family owned and which was used for supplying the plantation there. And something had happened which caused great-grandpa to become a buccaneer; he had hated the Spanish so bitterly that for years he harried the Main and the Spanish privateers – just as his great-grandson was doing now, only as a King's officer.

Ramage could remember faintly that there was some story of a privateer, perhaps more than one – indeed there must have been many of them at one time or another – but the details had gone, lost in childish memories of stories about pixies and gnomes and fairies with magic wands.

Had great-grandfather found a similar massacre? In his voyaging in the Caribbean – they called it the North Sea then, and the Pacific was the South Sea, and men were still alive who remembered Drake fighting the Spanish Armada as it came up the Channel – had he experienced something which made him so hate the Spanish that for the rest of his life he fought them?

Then he remembered the set of silver candlesticks used at dinner at home, three-branched candelabra, five of them but usually only two used unless there were many guests. Those candelabra had been part of the ransom paid after a raid on some town or other along the Main. There were several things – the candelabra, the smaller set of silver plate which was not used now because cleaning and polishing was wearing away the intricate design, said to be Moorish, those long-barrelled matchlock pistols and arquebuses which lined one of the halls, some of the armour, richly-chased corselets and helmets – all had been acquired by the eighth earl during his buccaneering days.

Of course the word buccaneer was used now to mean some-one akin to pirate, although in great-grandfather's day it was generally someone who, before there was a proper Navy, held a commission from the King or a governor allowing him (encouraging him, in fact, because the expense was entirely his) to wage war against the enemy. Drake, Ralegh, Hawkins – buccaneers all.

Aitken was looking at him, apparently puzzled. What had

he just said? The first lieutenant had been about to leave the cabin and he had gestured to him to wait, and he had said something, as an explanation. But now he could not remember what it was, so it could not have been important.

'Boarders,' he said for the sake of saying something. 'Exercise the boarders as much as you can. Get the grindstone up on deck and make sure the cutlasses are honed and the boarding pikes sharp. And boats, we must exercise hoisting out boats . . .'

'You had mentioned that, sir,' Aitken said patiently.

'Oh yes,' Ramage said, 'so I did. Very well, I think that's all for now.'

Aitken stood up slowly, hoping the captain would resume what he had started to say, but he had a faraway look in his eyes, and Aitken knew this was not the time to fetch him back from wherever his memories had taken him.

CHAPTER FOUR

The darkness immediately before dawn was depressing, chilly and damp, and Ramage pulled his boat cloak round him, hating the way the wool smelled because the salt soaked into it had absorbed the humid night air. In three or four hours the scorching sun would make him envy the seamen wearing only light shirts and thin trousers. But now, as they all waited for dawn, it seemed as cold as the English Channel. It wasn't, of course; he was now so accustomed to the Tropics that any time the temperature dropped below what would be a scorching day in England he felt frozen.

Baker was the officer of the deck; every ten minutes he called to the six lookouts posted round the ship, one at each bow, one amidships and one on each quarter. He called to them individually and received the same answer, that nothing was in sight, but this constant hailing was not because Baker was nervous or there was any particular danger: it was one way of ensuring the lookouts stayed awake. Staring into the darkness was peculiarly tiring; it was fatally easy to drop off to sleep, even though standing up. And sleeping on duty was a serious crime; not the mere fact of dozing but because in those minutes (even moments) of sleep an enemy could close in or a rocky shoal come into sight. One dozing man could lose the ship and kill every one of his shipmates.

Ramage accepted that lookouts might doze; his own days as a midshipman were not far behind him, and he could remember the tricks he had been reduced to as he tried to stay awake. Wetting your eyelids and facing the wind – that revived you for a few minutes, but never for long enough. Rocking back and forth on heels and toes, shaking the head like a wet dog, flexing the knees, knuckling the eyes and brow ... But best of all was the officer of the deck checking every man every ten minutes, and that was in his night orders. Perhaps other captains ordered it, although he had never been lucky enough to serve with one. But never in the years he commanded a ship had he needed to flog a man for sleeping on duty.

He imagined the earth slowly turning towards the sun, bringing dawn to start the day here, bringing twilight to end the day there, somewhere at the far end of the Mediterranean. In Cornwall, dawn had arrived four hours ago; by now it would be broad daylight with St Kew bustling: breakfast would be over and what would Gianna and his parents be doing? The old admiral would probably be astride a horse, cantering out to inspect a field of growing wheat or call on a sick tenant; his mother would be deciding the day's menus. Gianna – perhaps Gianna would be writing to him, another page in the long letters they wrote like diary entries.

The sun already shining over England (or hiding behind cloud) was lifting across the Atlantic and it would soon be here. The theory was interesting and there was no doubt – unless the world stood still – that it would occur in practice but, Ramage thought crossly, for the moment it was damned dark and damned cold here, just north of the Dutch island, with a ten-knot breeze and all plain sail set and, from the sound of it, the drummer buckling on his instrument to beat to quarters. Every ship of the Navy in wartime met the dawn with its men at general quarters; the ever-widening circle of daylight could reveal an empty horizon, but it could also reveal an enemy ship, even a fleet, within gunshot.

He listened to the ship noises, so much a part of life that normally one did not notice them: the creak of the great yards overhead and the occasional flap of a sail, like a deep sneeze;

the rumble of the barrel of the wheel as the men turned the spokes and the tiller ropes tightened or slackened, pulling the tiller below deck one way or the other, transmitting direction to the rudder to keep the ship on course and make that distant, ugly noise as gudgeons and pintles grated against each other, the metal lubricated only by the sea.

There was the creaking of the ship herself as she rolled and as the swell waves moved under her: creaks caused by slight movements of planking, of futtocks, of keel and keelson. Here, right aft, the intricate framing of the transom made more noise than in a British frigate, presumably because of some difference between British and French shipbuilding practice. The brief but deep noise of the trucks of the guns moving an inch, the distance the rope stretched when the ship rolled heavily. The lighter creak of rope shrouds stretching under strain, a curious noise which Ramage always thought rheumatism would make if it had a noise of its own. The animal squeak of the sheaves of blocks as rope rendered through them; blocks that the boatswain and his mates had missed greasing when they went round with the tallow bucket, although with all the hundreds of blocks in use it was a never-ending job.

The hiss of the sea, of the white horses riding crests, was more pronounced in the darkness; occasionally there was a thump and splash as the bow caught an odd wave and sliced off the top in a shower of spray; sometimes a sudden movement in the sky as a seabird wheeled in the darkness, probably startled as it slept on the surface of the water. Sometimes sudden slight flappings on the deck showed flying fish had landed on board and the officer of the deck usually gave permission to a lookout to grab them and put them in the fish bucket kept by the mainmast for the purpose.

Ramage gave a start as the drummer began rattling away, and below decks the boatswain's mates began their ritual, the calls shrilling with the noise that earned them their nickname, 'Spithead Nightingales', and followed by the bellows and threats to the seamen to get them out of their hammocks.

And once again the Calypso's ship's company went to their stations for battle: decks were sanded, guns run out (they had been left loaded, their muzzles protected from spray and rain by ornately carved wooden tompions), cutlasses, pistols, muskets and pikes were issued to the men, the Marines formed up under Rennick's sharp eye (Ramage had once heard a Marine grumbling that the lieutenant was a vampire who could see in the dark).

The sea was slowly turning a dark grey: because of a trick of the light the black, oily, fast-moving waves were slowing down and seemed higher, and one could see them approaching as the sky lightened almost imperceptibly towards the east.

Ramage saw that Southwick had come on deck and was standing at the forward side of the quarterdeck, his hands on the rail, looking forward. Of all the men on board, the master had most invested in what daylight would reveal today: he had predicted that they would see the land of Curaçao broad on the starboard bow, distant fifteen miles, while on the larboard bow would be the much smaller island of Bonaire.

Ramage would not be sorry to see Curaçao, though for a different reason from Southwick: with the *Créole* keeping station astern, it was necessary to keep a poop lantern burning because it had been a dark, overcast night, and Ramage did not want to risk the schooner losing sight of the *Calypso*. The lantern had been badly trimmed and was smoking slightly, and the sooty smell seemed to have penetrated all of Ramage's clothes as various random puffs of wind went round under the transom and came up over the taffrail.

Again Ramage shrugged his shoulders under his boat cloak, trying to make it fit more closely: the downdraught from the mizen topsail was like a miniature gale blowing down his neck and always particularly bad with the wind on the beam. Well, the draught was always there, he admitted to himself; it became a habit to say it was worse from whatever quarter the wind happened to be blowing at that moment. It meant, of course, that one hoped that the next alteration of course, bearing away a point or luffing up, would send the downdraught on to some other more deserving victim. It never did, of course.

The circle of grey was extending fast now, and Baker came up to him.

'Permission to send the lookouts aloft, sir?'

'Yes,' Ramage said, 'and send Orsini up with a bring-'em-near: Southwick will want to know the moment anyone sights land.'

Baker laughed, gesturing towards the master, who was still standing at the quarterdeck rail like a nervous punter waiting for his horse to come in sight.

The master's navigation had been accurate; twenty minutes later, as the ship's company hosed down the decks to get rid of the sand and secured the guns, replacing boarding pikes in the racks round the masts, Paolo's hail from aloft told them land was coming into sight through haze on the larboard bow, which was Bonaire, and from two to four points on the starboard beam (from south-south-west to south-west, Southwick noted on the slate kept in the binnacle drawer), which was Curaçao. There was no mistaking it: flat to the east, hills gradually rising until they ended in a cone-shaped mountain in the west, Sint Christoffelberg.

They were nicely to windward, Ramage saw; with the harbour half-way along Curaçao's south coast, the *Calypso* and *La Créole* could run in from the north-east with a commanding wind. Any alert sentries at the eastern end of the island should spot the frigate and schooner against the sunrise, but later, as they came closer, they would be up the sun's path and the glare would dazzle a watcher, making it more difficult for him to distinguish flags. All the more reason why such a watcher should assume that a frigate and a schooner so obviously French-built were in fact French.

Rossi swept up the last of the brickdust and looked at the brass rail on the top of the companionway. That polish would satisfy the first lieutenant – providing some *stupido* did not touch it before it was inspected. Fingermarks, fingermarks, he thought crossly. The fingers of half the men in this ship were used only to dab on newly-polished brasswork, or so it seemed.

Jackson and Stafford had half a dozen leather buckets lined up by the mainmast. The water had been emptied out and they were polishing the leather before they were refilled and hung back on their hooks, firebuckets which would be useless in case of fire but which, with the name 'Calypso' painted on them, looked smart. Looked smart from that side, but anyone with a little curiosity looking at the other side would see the faint scratches and scoring in the leather, done when the paint of the original French name had been removed with a sharp knife.

'Ever been to this Kurewerko, Jacko?'

'Sounds as though you're writing poetry. You pronounce

it Cue-rah-so. No, never been there; never had anything to do with the Dutch.'

'They're reckoned to be fighters, the Dutch.'

Jackson nodded. 'Hard people, so I hear. Hard in business, hard drinkers, hard fighters.'

'What've they gorn into business with the Dons and the French for, then?'

The American shrugged his shoulders. 'Politics or profit. Them and women are at the bottom of most things.'

'Women,' Stafford muttered nostalgically. 'Them Dutch women is usually very beamy, from what little I seen of 'em. An' what a clatter they make, them as wears those wooden shoes.'

He held up the bucket he was polishing so that its sides caught the sun. 'It's women what make me wish we was in the Mediterranington,' he said.

'Mediterranean,' Jackson said, correcting the Cockney out of habit. 'But I don't remember reckoning you as a lady's man when we *were* there.'

'Weren't much opportunity, were there? But Italy, and Spain . . .'

'I've seen some beamy ones there too. Built like three-deckers. Corsica, as well. Remember 'em in Bastia, selling fruit and vegetables? As round as their cabbages, some of them.'

'Oh yus, yus. And they had luvverly oranges, an' every now and again yer saw a real beauty. Woman, I mean.'

'You might have done,' Jackson growled, 'but I never did.'

'Yus, I prefer Italy. The Marcheezer,' Stafford reminded him.

'She don't count,' Jackson said firmly. 'There was only one of her in the whole of Italy.'

For the next fifteen minutes the two men reminisced about the rescue of the Marchesa from the Tuscan beaches and the subsequent voyage to Gibraltar, and then they were joined by Rossi who, finished with polishing brass, now had to help them with the buckets.

Rossi was, for once, not interested in discussing women, although it was a subject on which he claimed to be an expert. His verdict was always the same – that no women equalled those from Italy, and with it the implication that anyone who disagreed was probably a eunuch.

'These privateers, Jacko: you think we find them in Curaçao?'

'Preferably just outside,' Jackson said grimly. 'Then we can sink 'em or burn 'em while their friends watch from the shore.'

Rossi said with relish: 'Remember the *Tranquil* . . . let 'em burn.'

One of the bosun's mates, coming over to see how the work was progressing, looked up startled. 'What's burning?' The look in his eye showed that fire at sea was the fear of every seaman.

'Nothin's burning,' Stafford said soothingly. 'Not yet, anyway. We're just 'opin' to catch some privateers and make bonfires of 'em.'

'Use my flint and steel, then,' the bosun's mate said bitterly. 'You should 'ave seen those people. You did, Jacko. Slashed to pieces, particularly the women. Whoever killed those five was like a butcher's apprentice.' He looked at Jackson, who was regarded by most of the ship's company, quite erroneously, as being in the captain's confidence. 'Are we reckoning on finding privateers in Curaçao? Never heard tell of them using the place before. It's a Dutch island, ain't it?'

The American shrugged his shoulders and ran his hand through his thinning, sandy-coloured hair. 'Looks to me as though it's turned itself into a privateers' nest. I only know that's why we're going there, to look for 'em, though why they've all started using it as a base I don't know. Our frigates are probably making it too hot for them along the northern coasts, I suppose. Not many Spanish ships move around Cuba. Hispaniola's quiet, so's Puerto Rico.'

'That don't leave many other places except the Main,' commented Stafford.

'You don't understand the first thing about privateering,' Rossi said with a surprising fluency. 'The privateer, he capture a ship and he capture a cargo, and sometimes he capture passengers. Three things. He is not interested in anything else.' With a wave of his hand he disposed of the victim's crew over the side in a boat.

'He make his profit from these three things. He sell the cargo – for that he need a port and a market, a place where merchants have money. Then he sell the ship. He need the same thing. Port, merchants, men with money. For the passengers – well, collecting the ransom is hard work, and if he think he get enough profit from the ship and cargo *allora*, he let the passengers go in the boat – or – ' he gestured to the northwards – 'he kill them.'

'You seem to know about privateering,' commented the bosun's mate.

'In Genova I did not train to be a *prété*,' Rossi said simply. 'I do not have the face for a priest. But privateering – ' he held his hands out, palms upwards – 'it is like fishing, only no nets to mend.'

'Why is privateering all right there and not here?' Jackson asked shrewdly.

'Privateering is all right *anywhere*,' Rossi said emphatically, 'but in the Mediterranean only the *Saraceni* would kill passengers. Leave them only the boats, yes, but murder – no!'

Jackson could not remember having seen the Italian so coldly angry. In fact there was not a man on board the *Calypso* who had not been shocked by the death of those women, as though each could imagine a wife or mother or sister.

'*Era barbarico!*' Rossi declared, 'and if I find the man . . .' He made an unmistakable gesture showing how he would castrate them. 'That is to start with. And then – '

'Hold 'ard,' Stafford said, 'leave us to guess. My imagination's too strong and I can imagine it 'appening to me.'

'The Spaniards,' Rossi growled, 'they march about Italy for too many years.'

' 'Ere, Jacko,' Stafford said reminiscently, 'you remember that fortress near where we rescued the Marcheezer? Where you an' Mr Ramage went and fetched the doctor?'

'Santo Stefano, that was the place. The fortress was named after some Spanish king. The one that sent off the Armada. Philip the Second.'

'*La fortezza di Filipo Secundo*,' Rossi said. 'I know it, built high over the port. That Filipo – the worst of the Spaniards. He taxed everybody and used the money to build fortresses everywhere to guard them. Guard them against anyone ever rescuing them.'

'I thought it was the French you didn't like.' Stafford enjoyed teasing the Italian.

'I do not like the French, no, because they capture Genova

now and call it the Ligurian Republic. But in the past we not have the much trouble from the French. The Spanish, though. Always they rush to the Pope. They think all the Italian states belong to them. Always these cruel things for scores of years; centuries in fact. The rack for the heretic, the stiletto for the rival . . . and out here the cutlass for the women passengers.'

'These buckets,' said the bosun's mate, giving a shiver, 'they're polished enough now; let's get 'em filled and hung up again.'

All across the *Calypso*'s decks men were now finishing off various jobs. The tails of halyards and sheets, of dozens of other ropes which had been used in the last few hours, were neatly coiled; the bell in the belfry on the fo'c'sle gleamed as the sun caught it; occasionally there was the smell of wood smoke as a random eddy of wind brought it back from the chimney of the galley stove where the coppers were already boiling the meat for the men's midday meal.

In fifteen minutes the calls of the bosun's mates would have the men exercising at the guns, with the first lieutenant watching closely, a watch in his hand. In the meantime the *Calypso*, now pitching and rolling with the wind and sea on her larboard quarter, headed for the eastern edge of Curaçao, followed by *La Créole*.

The island was a bluish-grey blur on the horizon and with the sun still low the long shadows thrown by the few hills distorted the shape. But as the sun rose and the *Calypso* approached at almost eight knots, within an hour the grey gave way to faint browns and greens.

Ramage, newly shaven and beginning to feel fresher after an hour's nap and some breakfast, watched the island from the quarterdeck rail. He knew that by now the lookouts at the eastern end of the island would have sighted the ships – the *Calypso* anyway, with her higher masts – and no doubt a messenger on horseback would even now be galloping to the capital of Amsterdam with a report.

Southwick joined him, telescope under arm and judging by the contented look on his face, with a good breakfast inside him. He pointed at Curaçao, now on the *Calypso*'s starboard bow as she sailed down through the channel separating the larger island from Bonaire to the east.

'Must be the worst bargains in the Caribbean, these islands,' Southwick said. 'Just goats, cactus, aloes, salt pans, hardly any rain . . . must drive men mad to be stationed here . . .'

'Bonaire and Aruba, yes,' Ramage agreed, 'but not Curaçao: Amsterdam is reckoned to be one of the finest of the smaller harbours: a tiny Port Royal.'

Southwick glanced round at Ramage. 'Have you ever seen it, sir?'

Ramage shook his head. 'I've only looked at the chart. It seems to be a slot cut at right-angles to the coast.'

'Aye, calling it a slot is right. A ship sailing in could hit either side of the channel with a pistol. I don't know why we ever let the Dutch keep it. Impossible to cut out a ship – unless you first capture the fort on each side of the entrance.'

'Perhaps we couldn't get them out, and anyway we're usually at peace with them. I'd sooner have the green of Jamaica: plenty of fruit, beef, pork, fish . . . Here, from what I read, they live on goat, an occasional baked iguana – which doesn't appeal to me – with wild duck and snipe for the good shots. Pink flamingoes on Bonaire, I'm told. Hundreds of them.'

'Aye, they're quite a sight,' Southwick agreed. 'But Amsterdam itself is just a big warehouse. Tobacco brought in from the Main, liquor smuggled out, slaves from Guinea sold in the market by the dozen, salt shipped out by the ton. They're busy enough, the "*mynheers*". Wherever there's a chance of trade you'll find a Dutchman.'

'You can't blame them for that,' Ramage said. 'The merchants in Jamaica do their best, you know.'

'That's true,' Southwick admitted grudgingly. 'But *mynheer*'s a great smuggler, you know. To the Main.'

'But the Spanish are their allies,' Ramage pointed out.

'Aye, but the duty on Dutch spirits imported into Spanish ports is very high. On all Dutch goods, in fact. Leastways, that's what I've heard. So *mynheer* sails over on a dark night and lands his cargo of gin and slaves quietly up a river. Saves bothering the Spanish customs with too much paperwork . . .'

'They've been doing that for 150 years or more,' Ramage pointed out. 'Remember their old cry, "No peace beyond the Line", when Spain claimed that no foreigners could sail to the New World.'

'Ah, the buccaneers of the sixteen-fifties,' Southwick said wistfully. 'No commander-in-chief, no signal books, no orders, no forms for the Navy Board . . . you just captured any ship that was Spanish – and raided any Spanish town that took your fancy. Choose from hundreds of miles along the Main and the Isthmus, not to mention the Moskito Coast, New Spain, Cuba and Hispaniola . . .'

'And Puerto Rico,' Ramage said. 'But don't forget what happened if the Dons captured you.'

The master looked puzzled.

'The Inquisition,' Ramage reminded him. 'The Jesuits. All foreign prisoners were treated as heretics. The priests believed the only way to save heretics from Hellfire and damnation was to put 'em on the rack.' He glanced at Southwick's protruding stomach and plump cheeks. 'They'd halve your beam in half an hour. And by the time you'd spent the rest of your life digging in the salt mines, raking the salt pans or hammering rock into square rocks to build fortresses, you'd be as slim as a handspike.'

Southwick patted his stomach ruefully. 'That's a comfortable belly . . .'

'Well, a hundred years ago you'd have to be a Papist to keep it – or not get captured.'

'Just think of it, sir: suddenly sailing in over the horizon and holding a whole town to ransom . . .' Southwick was almost poetic. 'Putting a good price on the mayor's head – and the bishop, too,' he added, obviously recalling the rack. 'Searching the merchants' houses for chests of pieces of eight . . . killing and skinning beeves to put down fresh salt meat – aye, and finding a few demijohns of Spanish wine too . . . It'd have been worth it,' Southwick said with all the wistfulness of a worldly ecclesiastic condemning sin. 'I'd have spent the money as fast as I won it, just like the buccaneers; but the fact is, sir, forty years in the King's service hasn't left me a rich man, either.'

With that he began examining the coastline of Curaçao with his telescope. 'It's even more desolate than I remember it twenty years ago,' he said.

Ramage raised his telescope. He could just see along the south coast of the island as the *Calypso* rounded the eastern tip and then bore away to keep about two miles offshore. Thirty-eight miles long, and varying between two and a half and seven miles wide, the land was grey and arid in the glass, the sun – now almost overhead – harsh and mottling the landscape with shadows from bushes and cacti, as though each stood on a black base. Here and there the sparse divi-divi trees, each little more than a thin trunk with a wedge of thin boughs and leaves, were pointing to the west, away from the wind, like gaunt hands. Aloes – the people credited the leaves and bitter sap with magic properties, taking the pain or irritation from insect stings, burns, cuts . . . Ah, there were some of those huge cacti that grew like organ pipes. 'Datu', a book had called them. And there, beside that apology for a hill, a clump of kadushi, another cactus that looked like the same organ pipes but with joints in them. And round the cacti and moving over the ground, looking in the distance like swarms of insects, the flocks of goats, nibbling, ripping, finding food where most animals would starve. There a tamarind tree making arches; nearby the dark green bulk of a manchineel, and he could picture the little apples on the ground below it; apples which burned a man's mouth if he bit one, and killed him if he swallowed it. A strange tree, the manchineel; slaves always made a fuss when ordered to cut one down; they claimed the sap burned their skin, like drops of acid.

And what of the privateers? No sign of a sail, apart from some wisps of white cloth close in to the shore, little fishing boats tending pots . . .

CHAPTER FIVE

The study of the Governor of Curaçao at his residence in Amsterdam was hot. The ceiling of the white-painted room was high, the tall open windows facing west were shaded by jalousies, and the only one on the north wall was open, yet Governor van Someren's clothes were sticking to him, a thick and uncomfortable extra skin. He leaned forward in his chair to let the faint breeze in the room cool his back, but his feet felt swollen in his boots – and they probably were, although the damned doctor said there was nothing wrong – and his breeches were suddenly tight. Was he putting on weight? More weight, rather; the tailor had only just let out the waist and knee bands of all his breeches, and had several coats to work on.

He was not fat; rather a stocky man of medium height who, now past fifty, was getting plump. He had the high cheekbones and widely spaced blue eyes that would have betrayed him as a Dutchman anywhere, and his eyebrows were white and so thin that his face had an Oriental look about it.

He put down his long-stemmed clay pipe. It was too hot to smoke or, rather, the room was too airless. And the tobacco, a sample of the first of the Main's new crop from some plantation near Riohacha, tasted earthy. Some merchant was going to lose money, judging from the sample sent along to the Governor's palace.

There was a discreet knock on the door and a young Army officer, the cut of his uniform and aiguillettes showing that he was the Governor's chief of staff, came into the room carrying a letter. 'The British frigate and the other ship, sir. She has sailed through the channel and is coming westward along the coast, about two miles out. A messenger has just ridden in. The troop of cavalry keeping abreast the ship will send off a man every fifteen minutes to keep us informed.'

Governor van Someren nodded wearily. His pale blue eyes were bloodshot; the strain was emphasized by his lack of eyebrows, which made the eyes seem unduly swollen. 'Trouble from the west, Lausser,' he said gloomily, 'and now trouble from the east.'

Major Lausser, who not only liked the Governor but respected him, said: 'This British frigate, sir: she's probably just patrolling.'

'You said two ships.'

'The second is small – a schooner, I think the first message called it. We have little to fear from a single frigate, Your Excellency.'

'It's not a single British frigate that concerns me, Lausser, although one should never underestimate a frigate. A frigate is like a cavalry patrol: it can warn you that an army, or a fleet, is approaching.'

Lausser's eyes dropped to the Governor's desk because van Someren was tapping a sheet of paper. 'Our recent history on land – I ignore the sea for now – since we have been the "allies" of the French Directory has hardly been glorious. I was noting down some of it.'

He picked up the paper and began reading. 'In the East Indies – we surrendered Malacca to the British in August 1795 and Amboyna and Banda in the spring of '96. In Ceylon we lost Trincomalee in August '95 and Colombo the following spring. The Cape of Good Hope went in September '95 – although the garrison surrendered on the advice of the Stadtholder. And out here . . . what a sorry business: Demerara and Essequibo surrendered in April 1796, Berbice in May, and Surinam in August '99. Not a very inspiring history for the first few years of the Batavian Republic . . . The French have our home country; the British most of our colonies.'

He saw Lausser looking nervously at the door and added bitterly: 'You can open the door wide and let everyone listen: with five hundred revolutionaries and French privateersmen looting the western half of this island in the name of friendship, it is not I who lacks loyalty.'

'But help is coming, Your Excellency. Our frigate is due any day.'

'Any day, any day! That's all I hear. The French could have delayed her. She could have been captured by these damned British; she could still be at anchor in the Scheldt, blockaded. She could be sunk. Who knows, eh? And even when she arrives – then, Lausser? What good are a couple of hundred seamen? They'll only reinforce the brothels. I need a thousand well-trained Dutch soldiers; men who are used to this damned heat and whose loyalty I can rely on.'

There was a tapping at the door, and a smiling young woman came in. 'It's the ship, Papa!' she said cheerfully, but a moment later she stopped as both men looked away. 'Is something wrong? Papa! What's the matter?'

'Nothing – apart from these French revolutionaries, my dear. But she is not the *Delft*; she's a British frigate.'

The girl sat down, carefully arranging the skirt of her blue dress, and keeping her head turned from the two men. She had long, fine golden hair, braided and held up by large tortoiseshell combs which had obviously been fashioned by a Spanish craftsman. After a minute or two she looked up at her father, dry-eyed and obviously in control of herself.

'Why are the British paying us a visit? Who invited them?'

The Governor shrugged his shoulders. 'Not a visit; just a patrolling ship looking into the harbour. She'll pass by, like they always do.'

'And she'll see the only ships in it are French privateers!' the girl said bitterly. 'Oh, I am sick of the French; they treat us as the Spanish did. And we lose all our ships to the British – nine over there at Saldanha Bay; another nine ships of the line and two frigates surrendered under Admiral de Winter – '

'But six escaped,' her father interrupted, 'and four frigates!'

'Oh, I know that well enough: you forget Jules was serving in one of them.'

She was now on the verge of crying and her father said soothingly: 'Now, now, Maria, don't upset yourself: Jules will be here any day!'

With that the girl burst into tears and ran from the room. Her father was puzzled. 'What did I say wrong that time, Lausser?'

The ADC was equally puzzled. 'I don't know, Your Excellency. She seemed upset over the French, but it was when you mentioned that her fiancé was due that she – er, left the room.'

'Yes, yes, that was it: the mention of Jules. It has been a long engagement – although she is the one who keeps putting off the wedding day.'

'Quite, sir,' Lausser said dryly, and deliberately changed the subject. 'The British frigate will be off Sint Anna Baai in about two hours' time. Shall I tell the commanders of the forts to stand-to in an hour?'

Van Someren nodded. 'I shall watch from here. If the frigate opens fire I imagine she will aim at the forts or the ships, not the Governor's residence.'

Lausser, pleased to see a twinkle in the Governor's eyes, laughed dutifully. 'But where she aims at may not be where she hits, sir.'

'I'll risk that. But they'll stay well out: they've learned that our gunners are well trained. Four years ago – before you arrived, Lausser – one came in close and was becalmed, and we shot away a mast. She escaped because the current carried her clear and they could do repairs, but the British Navy learned a lesson.'

He picked up his pipe and put it down impatiently, irritated at being given a present of so much earthy tobacco. He examined a cheroot from a silver box on his desk and returned it with a grunt. 'I've been smoking far too much. I think I would like a drink. Ring for the steward, will you?'

Gottlieb van Someren was tired: tired not only because he had had very little sleep in the past two weeks, thanks to the revolutionaries rioting at the western end of the island, but also because he had spent too many years on the island of

Curaçao: he had been the Governor for three years when, in February 1793, the Dutch had found themselves attacked by France and two years later the Stadtholder and the Prince of Orange had to escape to England while their country was named by the French the Batavian Republic. And Gottlieb van Someren, with his wife and daughter, was left in Curaçao as the Governor, the republican king, as it were, of the three islands of Aruba, Bonaire and Curaçao. France had control of the Dutch fleet and gave orders to the Dutch officers, many of whom were privately torn between their loyalty to the Stadtholder and the Dutch admirals commanding the fleet.

Like so many Dutch officers serving in distant places, van Someren had to decide whether or not to serve the new regime: did it constitute disloyalty to the Stadtholder? And like so many others he had decided the wisest thing was to carry on: to resign or flee would, in the case of the islands, risk the French sending out a French governor, or a Dutchman who was a true republican.

His wife hated Curaçao; she swore the heat dried up her skin and accepting the French shrivelled her soul, and she was equally convinced that gin, good Dutch sweet gin, was the only medicine that could save her. So for the past four years she had drunk gin when others drank boiled water or wine. She had refused all attempts to send her back to the Netherlands because she hated the French even more than the Tropics. And because her family had in the distant past suffered dreadfully under the Duke of Alva's soldiers, she walked out of the room if a Spaniard entered.

It did not make a governor's life any easier, yet he had to admit it had some advantages. He had an excuse for having little to do socially with the Spanish – he never had to blame his wife; her dislike was well known. And, he reflected as Lausser ordered drinks to be brought, he must be one of the few governors of any nationality who cared little whether or not he would be dismissed from his post. He had saved some money; he would get his reward if the Stadtholder ever returned from exile in England. For the moment, though, the French seemed – well, omnipotent.

He took out his watch. 'Lausser, don't forget the orders to the forts.'

'I took the liberty of giving them earlier, Your Excellency.'

Van Someren nodded. Lausser was trustworthy and reliable,

and he wished Maria was to marry him, instead of that sharp-eyed young naval officer, Jules, whose sole topics of conversation were republicanism, the latest French victories, and the villainy of William V, the Stadtholder of Holland, and his son, the Prince of Orange, for having fled to England.

For several years, van Someren reflected, deliberately forgetting his prospective son-in-law, he had not only kept his job as Governor, but kept his head on his shoulders (no mean feat for anyone having any dealings with the French government) because he had drifted with the current. No republican could accuse him of disloyalty to the Batavian Republic; yet when the Stadtholder eventually returned to the throne, Governor van Someren had made sure he had clean hands to show. Clean, that is, until now.

There was a faint popping in the distance. Lausser looked up significantly. Those bands of ruffians were close; the musket shots must be from loyal Dutch troops – he had all too few of them – or local people trying to stop the rogues looting their homes.

He picked up the gilt paperknife on his desk and balanced the blade on the index finger of his right hand. For several years he had been able to sit on the fence without finding it too hard to balance. Now, however, he was dangerously poised, as though paying for all those past years. He was the Dutch republican Governor yet at this moment he was likely to lose his governorship (and perhaps his life) to a republican rabble scrabbling their way across the arid island, walking and staggering, riding stubborn donkeys, drinking raw rum or gin, raping or robbing as the fancy took them. They sang (when they were not too drunk) all the old French revolutionary songs of nearly a decade ago; they behaved as though Curaçao was some newly captured British spice or sugar island, not part of the Batavian Republic. They were stirring up the Negroes, telling them to murder their masters in their beds, burn the crops, scatter the salt, break down the walls of the salt pans . . .

He took a new clay pipe from the rack on his desk and began to fill it with tobacco. What the devil could he do? The worst of these rogues were French. Admittedly privateersmen, but was it just the desire for loot that had set them off? There had been young Dutch revolutionaries only too eager to listen to them.

'How many of these ruffians do our latest patrols report, Lausser?'

'More than five hundred, Your Excellency. About two-thirds of them are from the French privateers – the ten here in Amsterdam.'

Five hundred. It sounded highly likely because most of the privateers carried extra men to act as prize crews. But why? Revolutionary zeal? Hardly – most privateersmen could barely read or write; they were concerned with loot, not loyalties. The rest must be local revolutionaries, disaffected Dutchmen. The usual rabble.

'What the devil do you think it is all about, Lausser?'

'Robbery, sir. The privateers had little luck against the British – far too many privateers hunting too few prizes. The British frigates are patrolling to the north – many more than usual. I heard that the shopkeepers here stopped credit for most of the privateers some two weeks ago, just before all this started, so they were out of provisions and spirits . . .'

'Oh? I heard nothing of that. A very short-sighted policy, stopping credit. About as sensible in these circumstances as handing over your purse to a highwayman and asking for change. I'm sure that's what started off this – this insurrection.'

'But they had not paid their bills, sir.'

'Quite so,' van Someren said impatiently, irritated by Lausser's lack of imagination, 'but they aren't going to make money lying here at anchor, unable to go to sea without provisions. The shopkeepers have always done well out of them up to now: the privateersmen spend freely enough when they do capture something. The prize cargoes are sold here for whatever the merchants will pay. The merchants should welcome them, not cut off credit.'

'But they were not paying their bills, sir,' Lausser repeated, as though shocked at the Governor's more practical attitude.

'You can only threaten privateers when you have a frigate in the harbour, Lausser.'

'Well, sir, one is due.'

'I mean Dutch, not British,' van Someren said, smiling at his little joke. 'In the meantime, we have to prepare our defences against our friends the privateers, thanks to the island's shopkeepers, who may find that their shops will be looted . . .'

The very location of Amsterdam, which made it easy to

defend from the sea, made it almost indefensible from attacks overland. The channel to the Schottegat, like a wide but short river leading from the sea to the inland lake, divided Amsterdam in half: on the east side was Punda, the Point, with the Governor's residence overlooking the harbour entrance and waterfront, and defended by the Waterfort.

Otrabanda, 'the other side', was on the west and also had Riffort covering the entrance. But there were no defences covering either Punda or Otrabanda on the landward sides: the forts were no more than long gun platforms formed by wide stone sea walls, buttressed to seaward but open behind.

I can defend Amsterdam against my enemies, van Someren reflected, but I can't defend it against my allies. With two hundred Dutch soldiers and a couple of Negro companies (who had just refused to fight against the French ruffians) he was at the mercy of the rabble. And, into the midst of it all, came a British frigate. Perhaps he should be thankful the Batavian Republic had no other enemies – for the time being, anyway.

'Your Excellency,' Lausser said, a formal note in his voice indicating that he considered what he was about to say was important, 'ought the womenfolk to be sent to the forts for safety?'

The Governor held his clay pipe by the stem and tapped the desk with the bowl. 'Safe from whom? That's what I have to decide. If we are protecting them against an attack by the two British ships, then we should have them all here in the residence. But if we are protecting them against these drunken republican scoundrels, then perhaps they'd be better off in the forts. In fact, I'd be inclined to evacuate Otrabanda – after spiking the guns, of course – and bring everyone across to concentrate at Punda. And sink the ferries, of course.'

'Can we seize the privateers that are anchored in the channel, sir?'

'I can't risk it. Allowing ten soldiers to take possession of each privateer (and that means they have to row out in their own boats) needs a hundred men, which is all I have for both forts: the other hundred out trying to slow down the republicans will not be back in time. If the privateersmen remaining in the ships put up a fight . . .'

A knock at the door brought Lausser to his feet and he took a letter from a servant. He glanced at the superscription and proffered it to the Governor, who shook his head and gestured to Lausser to open it. 'It can't be good news.'

Lausser unfolded the paper – it was not sealed – and glanced over it. 'From Captain Hartog, sir. The republicans – that's what they are calling themselves, he says – are grouping on the main road half-way between Soto and Sint Willebrordus, about eleven miles from Amsterdam. He thinks that one man, or a committee, has just taken charge, so he expects them to advance much more quickly now. He is falling back on us but so far his casualties are light. He is deliberately conserving his men, he says.'

'Sensible fellow,' van Someren growled. 'Dead men lying among the salt pans won't help us. He understands that he's just fighting a delaying action, doesn't he?'

'Yes, sir: he seems to be quite successful.'

'Quite so, quite so. Now, about the women.'

Lausser knew this was the Governor's way of asking his opinion, and he said: 'Waterfort, sir. The republicans are the greatest danger, especially once they start looting shops and getting at the spirits. Keep the women in the residence until the last moment, then send them down to the fort.'

Van Someren nodded. There were perhaps fifty women involved: the rest had fled to friends owning plantation houses at the east end of the island many days ago, at the first sign of trouble, and he was thankful they had taken his advice. The fifty that remained were married to stubborn merchants who refused to have their household arrangements upset (even though in the end it might put the wives in great danger).

Finally the Governor made up his mind: 'Very well, we'll use Waterfort as the last resort. Tell the commander of Riffort – I always forget his name – to be prepared to spike the guns and join the garrison on Punda. They should bring their muskets and as much powder as they can carry, and pitch the rest of the powder into the sea.'

He tapped the desk with his pipe. 'Yes, and get more water taken to Waterfort. With all those extra women – and their children, and probably their husbands – we might get short. Get as many casks as you can find filled and rolled out to the Point. Food, too.'

By now he was tapping to emphasize each word, and at 'too' the pipe snapped. He looked at the stem which he was still holding. 'You know, Lausser, we can trust our enemies, the British. Our damned French allies are the danger.'

'You can just see the entrance to Amsterdam, now, sir,' Southwick said. 'From this angle the walls of the forts on each side look like a single big one. But the main part of the town – the Governor's residence, Parliament, the market – is this side, which they call the Point. The channel cuts the town in half and leads to an inland lake called the Schottegat. And the bay at the entrance, such as it is, they call Saint Anna's.'

'What guns do they have in the forts?' Ramage asked.

'Thirty in Waterfort on the Point, when I was last here, but it has three sides. Eighteen guns on the wall parallel with the coast, six on the first angled section facing south-south-west, and six more on the second, actually covering the entrance. The same guns in Riffort on Otrabanda, the fort on the west side. They're probably 24-pounders, but I'm not sure.'

'Sixty guns,' Ramage mused. 'But not all of them can be trained on us at the same time?'

'No, sir. As we approach, the dozen guns on the two angled parts of Punda won't bear. But all of those on Otrabanda will. About forty-eight altogether, I should reckon.'

'The same as the effective broadsides of two seventy-fours.'

'Yes, sir.'

'And how wide is the channel inside the forts?'

'About two hundred yards.'

'So a ship entering has Waterfort on Punda one hundred yards to starboard and Riffort on Otrabanda a hundred yards to larboard.'

'Exactly, sir.'

Ramage imagined the captain of one of the Dutch guns standing beyond the recoil, trigger line in his hand, and sighting along the top of the barrel. The *Calypso*, sailing into Schottegat, would seem enormous, and with the steep-roofed buildings and the fort taking some of the wind she would be making perhaps four knots. The gun captain would give a couple of orders to train left or right – and, unless he was poorly trained or over-excited, he should be able to put a roundshot or a round of grapeshot through whichever of the *Calypso*'s gun ports he chose. Or poke a roundshot through the hull along the waterline like a seamstress stitching the edge of a blanket.

Southwick was looking at him quizzically, his face covered

with perspiration from the heat of the sun. 'Not even on a dark night in pouring rain, sir,' he said, shaking his head.

Ramage grinned. 'It's a pity there's never fog in these latitudes.'

The master kept a straight face but he was relieved. Amsterdam was one of the most impossible ports to attack that he had ever seen, and, almost more important, the Dutch were tough fighters. You could panic a Spaniard and bluff a Frenchman, but a Dutchman – no, he was too like the British to do anything but fight man to man. Which wasn't to say Mr Ramage wouldn't attack the place if he felt like it, but the Dutch knew a British frigate and schooner were approaching because Mr Ramage had made no attempt to fly French colours, even though both ships were French-built and it would be easy to fool French privateers, let alone these *mynheers*. So the garrisons of the two forts would be ready; indeed, at this very moment, with the *Calypso* and *La Créole* now in sight of both, they would have their guns loaded and run out ready to fire; magazines would be unlocked and more cartridges and roundshot would be ready . . . The guns could lay down an invisible barrier some two thousand yards offshore and anyone stepping over it would be smashed to pieces by 24-pounder roundshot by the time the range was down to a thousand yards.

Ramage once again raised his telescope and murmured to Southwick: 'It isn't often you see that flag – look over the two forts and that large building on the Point, the Governor's residence, I suppose. The flag of the Batavian Republic.'

The French seemed to like renaming places. Genoa was now the Ligurian Republic, Holland the Batavian Republic; the Swiss were now inhabitants of the Helvetic Republic, while a group of Italian states round Bologna, Modena and Ferrara were now the Cisalpine Republic. From all accounts giving a new name was not the same as giving them their freedom . . .

Ramage turned to Aitken, who was the officer of the watch. 'Pass at least two miles off Amsterdam,' he said. 'We're being nosy, not provocative.'

Half an hour later they could see right into Amsterdam, neatly cut in half by the channel. Not quite in half, Ramage realized; the main part was on the Punda side – the Governor's residence, Parliament and most of the houses. On the other side, so quaintly called the same in Dutch, Otrabanda, it looked as though the merchants flourished. At the far end, where the small inland lake began, the privateers were lying at anchor. Aitken had counted nine, Southwick eight, the masthead lookouts ten, and Jackson and Orsini, sent up the mainmast at the rush with telescopes, confirmed that there were ten.

Southwick had been as puzzled as Ramage when Jackson had come down again and reported that most of the privateers looked as though they were laid up, or undergoing refits. There was no sign of sails; no squaresail yards were in sight. Nor, equally odd, was there any sign of activity on any of the privateers: except for two or three men standing at the rail of one of them, Jackson said, they seemed to be deserted.

Ramage had not known what to expect and for that reason had no plans. He turned to Aitken and said: 'Continue running along the coast. The chart shows two or three bays where privateers could hide. Keep a sharp lookout – we might be able to surprise some of them at anchor.'

With that he went below to his cabin, glad of the shade. He sat down at his desk, reached up for the chart from the rack overhead, and spread it out in front of him. Ten privateers: that meant the Admiral's information was correct: Amsterdam was being used as a privateers' base. Ten privateers. But they were the only vessels in the harbour. Certainly they could have a dozen prizes anchored in that lake, out of sight, but those privateers looked as though they were laid up. Why should the sails have been taken off? It was easy enough to do, but surprising. There might be a good sailmaker there in Amsterdam who was doing some major repairs on a single privateer's sails – even making new ones, because the Trade winds were hard on sail cloth and the sun and showers rotted the stitching. Would all ten have their sails on shore in the sailmaker's loft at the same time? No, there'd be no point: the sailmaker (at best a couple of men and three apprentices) could not work on ten suits of sails at once, and no privateer would risk having his sails on shore a day longer than necessary. He'd bring the sails over, wait for them to be repaired and take them back. If they were not on shore, then the sails certainly could be stowed below, out of the glare and heat of the sun and rain -- not that it rained much on these islands: they existed only because there were wells providing fresh water.

Was it likely, he asked himself, that only two or three

privateersmen would come on deck to watch a British frigate and schooner sail across the harbour entrance – something that happened perhaps once in three or four months? Two or three out of – well, more than five hundred men? Where were the rest of them? Some could be on shore, filling water casks or collecting provisions from the chandlers. A few dozen might be out at the salt pans, filling carts or bags with salt to preserve meat. Some might be in the brothels – though men and women preferred a siesta at this time of day. But two or three men . . . The privateers were not laid up for lack of targets, surely? He thought of the twenty-four dead in the *Tranquil*, murdered by the crew of the *Nuestra Señora de Antigua.*

The Marine sentry at the door called out that Mr Southwick wished to see him.

The master looked worried and without any preamble said: 'We're losing a lot of ground to leeward, sir. With these light winds, and the westgoing current, it'll take us a long time to beat back to Amsterdam . . . Leastways, I'm reckoning you want to stay close to Saint Anna's Bay . . .'

It was Southwick's duty to mention such things; as master of the *Calypso*, the navigation of the ship was his responsibility. But Ramage was angry with himself for reasons beyond his comprehension: certainly he had not been sure what he expected to find here in Amsterdam; he knew now only that those ten privateers, possibly all laid up, made nonsense of his orders. None of these privateers was going to put to sea with two British warships in the offing. And no British warship would get within a thousand yards of the harbour entrance by day or night without being smashed to kindling by the guns of those forts. No bluff or subterfuge could stop them firing.

However, Ramage thought ruefully, it is not a situation that William Foxe-Foote, Vice-Admiral of the Blue and one of the Members of Parliament for Bristol, as well as being 'Commander-in-Chief of His Majesty's Ships and Vessels upon the Jamaica Station', could visualize, understand or accept. Particularly understand, and especially accept . . .

Ramage gestured to Southwick to sit down in the armchair that was secured against the ship rolling by a light chain from the underside of the seat to an eyebolt in the deck planking. The master put his hat down beside him and ran his fingers through his hair, which was now matted with perspiration, and the mark of the hatband across the top of his forehead gave him a curiously puzzled appearance.

'Have you any idea what these privateers are doing?' Ramage asked.

Southwick shrugged his shoulders and gave one of his prodigious sniffs. 'With respect to Admiral Foxe-Foote, sir, all those privateers look just as if the owners have gone bankrupt. They look just like those old fishing smacks you see abandoned on the saltings along the bank of the Medway. Paint peeling, slack rigging, and one windy night the masts will go over the side. Not that I could see the rigging, of course; just the impression I had.'

Ramage nodded. 'I don't think many of them have been to sea for a month or more.'

'No, sir, at least that. And no one on board any of 'em. I saw maybe two or three men. Shipkeepers? Three men for ten privateers is not many. No, there's something damned odd about it all. Could there be more privateers at Bonaire, or perhaps Aruba?'

'Why?' Ramage asked. 'Why would privateers be at islands where there is no decent harbour? At Bonaire they have to anchor on a sloping shelf. Why be there when Amsterdam is such a perfect harbour? Sheltered from the weather, defended by the forts, provisions and water available . . .'

'That's why I'm so puzzled,' Southwick admitted. 'I expected to see half a dozen privateers, perhaps even a dozen, but all ready to go to sea. Perhaps one repairing damage and perhaps another replacing her standing and running rigging – but not ten like that. It's – well, almost ghostly, sir; as though yellow fever had killed every man on board as they were at anchor.'

For a moment Ramage thought of Amsterdam being in the grip of an epidemic of something like yellow fever, but plenty of people had been walking on the walls of the forts and in the few streets of Punda and Otrabanda when the *Calypso* passed. Southwick fluffed out his flowing white hair as it began to dry, making it look like a deck mop. 'Your orders from the Admiral, sir. There's not much you can do about them.'

'There are ten privateers in Amsterdam,' Ramage reminded him.

Southwick sat bolt upright. 'But you're not going to try to go in after them, are you, sir?'

Ramage grinned and waved to Southwick to relax in his chair. 'Nor am I going to send in the boats at night: they probably have a chain boom across the entrance that they haul up at sunset. But it's going to be difficult to convince the Admiral . . .'

'Those privateersmen can't afford to eat, lying there at anchor,' Southwick pointed out. 'They're all on a share-of-the-prize basis. With no pay, time in port is money lost. The shopkeepers will start wanting cash . . .'

'I've considered all that,' Ramage said mildly, 'but would *you* sail in one of those privateers with a British frigate and a schooner waiting outside?'

'I might try on a dark night, sir.'

'Come, come,' Ramage chided, 'it's never completely dark in the Tropics.'

'Hungry men get desperate!'

'The crew might, but don't forget that every privateer has an owner; and he's not going to lose his ship just because the men are hungry.'

'True, but I still don't understand it,' Southwick muttered. 'Why are these beggars laid up here when we know others – Spanish, anyway – are at sea? Think of all the prizes they're missing.'

'That's just what I have been thinking about,' Ramage said, 'and the only sensible explanation is that all the privateersmen are on shore doing something as profitable as being at sea, privateering. It obviously isn't selling fresh fruit in the market.'

Southwick slapped his knee, his face wrinkling into a broad grin. 'I hadn't thought of that, sir. I wonder what the devil they *are* doing?'

Ramage shrugged his shoulders. 'That's where I've come to a stop. You can be sure they aren't at a religious festival, nor are they sitting on the walls of the fort with fishing lines.'

'We can blockade the island for a week or two,' Southwick said. 'Catch a few prizes ourselves. Question prisoners . . .'

'That's what I've decided. We have to provoke them into doing something. By "them" I mean the Dutch rather than the French. Capturing a Dutch merchantman as she arrives off Amsterdam could do the job, and stopping all trade between Curaçao and the Main might force the Governor to make the privateers sail to drive us off. As a squadron they might stand a chance in the dark, if the Governor puts on board as many soldiers as he can spare.'

Southwick was brightening: Ramage saw that the prospect of action was cheering him up, having the same effect as an alcoholic sighting a bottle of spirits. Yet sitting there he still looked like a rural bishop, except for his eyes, which took on the glint of the owner of a knacker's yard. He reached for his hat. 'I'll be – ' he broke off as, high above them, a mast-head lookout hailed the deck, his voice too faint to penetrate the cabin. They heard Aitken answer, and both Ramage and Southwick made for the door. On deck Aitken, looking puzzled, walked quickly towards Ramage as he reached the top of the companionway.

'The lookout reports a lot of smoke several miles inland and we think we can hear occasional musket shots, sir. Very faint, and it might be duckhunters or something. But we can't see the smoke from down here – yet, anyway.'

'Is it new smoke, or something that's been burning for some time?'

Aitken looked crestfallen. 'I forgot to ask, sir.'

He stepped back a few paces and put the speaking trumpet to his mouth, bellowing: 'Aloft, there!'

'Mainmast lookout, sir.'

'That smoke – is it a new fire just started or have you only just seen it?'

' 'Snew, sir: increasing now, like houses catching fire. White and black smoke.'

Ramage looked across at the land. The arid flatness of the eastern end of the island was beginning to merge into rolling hills getting higher and higher as they approached the big peak of Sint Christoffelberg, ever-increasing waves suddenly turned to stone as they lapped the base of a pinnacle.

He saw a fleck of smoke a moment before Southwick and Aitken pointed and exclaimed. Smoke was common enough among the Caribbean islands: most of them spent more than half the year tinder-dry; the sun's rays concentrated by a broken bottle, a hunter's carelessness with a campfire, the sparks from a charcoal burner's crude furnace – all could, and frequently did, set a hillside ablaze in a fire that only died when the wind dropped at night, or mercifully backed or veered a few points to drive the flames back on themselves. But smoke *and* the sound of musket shots: that was a very different matter, and he was certain he could hear some distant popping, and Aitken now had the speaking trumpet to his ear, using it intently so that the young first lieutenant looked like a deaf seafarer straining to hear a mermaid singing a siren song from beneath a palm tree on the beach.

The brisk Trade wind was dispersing the smoke; instead of billowing clouds it was more of a haze by the time Ramage could see it from his low vantage point on the quarterdeck and Southwick lumbered over to crouch over the azimuth compass to take bearings. The entrance to Amsterdam, still in sight astern, the peak of Sint Christoffelberg, the next headland to the west, and the smoke. By plotting the first three he would be able to establish the ship's exact position; then drawing in the bearing of the smoke, he would be able to tell Ramage approximately where the fire was burning.

He hurried below with the slate on which he had noted the bearings and was back again within four or five minutes to tell Ramage: 'The smoke is coming from somewhere about half-way between the villages of Soto and a place called Sint Willebrordus. About eleven miles west of Amsterdam. Can it be cane fields burning?'

'There's no sugar cane on this island. And cane doesn't burn with a popping like muskets. It can only be houses.'

'Deck there! Foremasthead lookout!'

Startled, Ramage, Aitken and Southwick looked forward. The voice, almost disembodied, sounded excited, and Aitken answered: 'Deck here.'

'Sail on the larboard bow, sir, and I think I can see land beyond it. Might be a cloud but the bearing stays the same.'

'What type of ship?'

'Can't tell, sir; she's still hull down below the horizon, but I think she's steering towards us.'

Aitken looked round for Jackson, handed him the telescope and pointed aloft. Without a word the American made for the shrouds and began climbing the foremast.

Ramage said: 'It can't be land, but he may have seen a cloud hanging over Aruba.'

'What ship is it?' Southwick muttered to himself. 'Probably a cutter from Jamaica with fresh orders from the Admiral. Convoy work, more than likely . . .'

'Beat to quarters,' Ramage told Aitken.

Jackson hailed the deck the moment the drummer stopped

beating the ruffles.

'Her hull is only just lifting above the horizon but from the cut of her sails she's a merchant ship. Could be American, sir.'

'Make a signal to Lacey,' Ramage said. 'His lookouts are asleep.'

By the time the signal flags had been hoisted, acknowledged by *La Créole* and lowered again, Jackson was reporting from the foremasthead that the ship had just tacked, and was obviously bound for Curaçao. Aitken had just reported that the *Calypso* was at quarters when Jackson hailed once more to report that the strange sail was a merchant ship and almost certainly American.

American, and therefore wary of one of the King's ships, because a meeting at sea usually resulted in being boarded and having a Royal Navy officer checking through the ship's company for British subjects, who would be pressed immediately. Ramage pictured the American master groaning at the prospect of losing at least a couple of good seamen from a total of perhaps a dozen. On the other hand, masters of neutral ships were often good sources of information: they visited enemy ports, saw ships of war, and, because they were not taken as prizes, could talk about it afterwards. And the best way of making a master talk was to catch him in the moments of relief after he discovered that none of his men was going to be pressed . . .

The *Calypso* and the merchant ship were approaching each other fast; within minutes Ramage could see the American's hull above the horizon. 'Have the guns run out,' he said to Aitken, 'we want to look fierce. Then come below. I have more orders for you.'

Down in his cabin he explained his intentions. 'The master of that Jonathan is going to curse as soon as he sees the British flag – he'll have identified us as a French-built frigate, and to him there'd be nothing out of the ordinary in a French frigate heading west after apparently sailing from Amsterdam. Then suddenly he'll realize his mistake.

'So you'll board him and examine his papers. He could have sailed from a port on the Main, Aruba or direct from somewhere in North America. If he has just left an enemy port, I want to know what ships he saw there and what ships he's seen at sea, especially privateers. Dates, positions, courses being steered . . .'

Aitken looked worried. 'These Jonathans usually don't care to help us much, sir,' he said cautiously.

'No,' Ramage agreed, 'because they've usually just had some of their prize seamen claimed as British and sent down into the boat. But you will make it clear that, providing he co-operates, you will not even ask to see the muster book . . .'

'And he'll be so relieved . . .'

'Exactly,' Ramage said, 'but of course, if he is truculent, you know what to do.'

Aitken nodded. 'I hope I find a few Scotsmen; we're outnumbered in the *Calypso*, sir.'

'I want quality, not quantity, Mr Aitken,' Ramage said ambiguously, laughing dryly.

'Aye, sir. I've heard say that the Admiralty tell commanders-in-chief that when they ask for more frigates.'

'I'm sure they do,' Ramage said, 'that's why we make sure of having enough by going out and capturing our own.'

The young Scot gave one of his rare laughs. 'I've never thought of it like that, sir; I wonder how often a frigate and a schooner go out on patrol together manned by the people that captured them?'

'In a year or two we'll have our own fleet. We'll charter it to Their Lordships on a share-of-the-prizes basis!'

An hour later Ramage and Southwick waited at the quarter-deck rail. The *Calypso* was hove-to half a mile to windward of the American ship, which was lying with her sails furled, broadside on to the swell waves and rolling violently. Clearly her master did not trust her spars, rigging and sails enough to risk heaving-to. Shipowners often insisted that once in the Tropics their master used old sails as an economy. It was not an economy, of course, because tropical squalls were more sudden and vicious than people living in temperate climates realized; but most shipowners were men who cheerfully spent a guinea to save four pennies and congratulated themselves on the bargain.

The *Caroline* of Charleston, South Carolina. The moment he had seen the port of registry he had ordered Jackson to join the boarding party, warning Aitken to tell the American seaman what they were trying to discover, and explaining to the puzzled first lieutenant that Jackson had been born in Charleston.

The *Caroline* from South Carolina: it sounded like the beginning of some lullaby. If she was bound for Amsterdam (there could be little doubt about that) could he use her in some way, a Trojan horse that would get him among those damned privateers?

He could seize the ship and, putting his own men on board, send her into Amsterdam under her American flag. With his officers dressed in old clothes, they could pass themselves off as Americans and deal with all the paperwork with the Dutch authorities. They would, of course, anchor near the privateers. And soon after dark they would board them, set them all on fire, and then sail the *Caroline* of South Carolina out again, trusting that the Dutch would not fire on her, assuming she was getting clear of the flaming ships and never suspecting or guessing she was the cause.

Ramage shook his head. These were crazy thoughts: the diplomatic rumpus would be enormous; any British officer who used an American ship in this fashion would be court-martialled by the Admiralty and probably jailed; relations between Britain and North America were bad enough already; an incident like that could set off a war. Apart from all that, he thought ruefully, it was an excellent plan.

'Aitken and Jackson are getting ready to go down the ladder, sir,' Southwick reported. 'Ah, that fellow with the wide-brimmed straw hat, he'll be the master. He's shaking hands with Aitken. And with Jackson, too.'

Ten minutes later the boat was alongside the *Calypso*, and the *Caroline*, letting fall her sails, was getting under way again to continue her tedious series of tacks to get up to Amsterdam. It was unusual to see a square-rigged ship of her size sailing under the American flag: most of the trade in the West Indies was done with schooners. She was at least painted in the traditional dark green, the colour favoured by slave ships because it matched the mangroves which lined the banks of the rivers in the Gulf of Guinea where the slavers hid.

Aitken hurried over to Ramage, obviously excited, and Jackson, the next man up the side, was grinning broadly. Ramage saw the first lieutenant glancing astern, towards Aruba, and then he was reporting, making an effort to speak clearly.

'It worked just as you expected, sir: I suspect half his men are British. He says a French frigate anchored off Aruba was

due to leave for Curaçao a few hours after the *Caroline*
weighed. He half expected her to be in sight by now.'

'Has he seen any privateers?'

'No, sir: he commented on it. Normally he sees three or
four between the Windward Passage and the Main: they
always board him to check his papers. But he did say he has
seen more British warships: he wasn't surprised when he saw
us – or so he says. And Jackson was able to have a chat with
some of the seamen.'

Ramage looked at the American. 'Well, did you meet any
old friends?'

Jackson grinned. 'Not old friends, sir, but I knew one of the
men; he was sweet on my sister – when they were both about
five years old.'

'What else did you discover?'

'Quite a bit, sir, but it only confirms what Mr Aitken just
said. They – the men in the *Caroline* – met some of the seamen
from the French frigate on shore in Aruba. Said they were an
undisciplined crowd; they didn't pay much attention to their
officers. Called each other "citizen". And they wouldn't pay
the Dutch shopkeepers the prices they asked: they just took
what they wanted, paid half what was asked, and drew their
swords when a crowd gathered.'

Even as Jackson talked Ramage was thinking of the small
book in the drawer of his desk: the French signal book. He
looked at Aitken. 'You did very well with the *Caroline*.'
He turned to Jackson. 'You, too. Now make a signal to
La Créole: I want Mr Lacey to come on board at once.'

An hour later, long after the men had run in the guns and
secured them, put pikes, cutlasses, muskets and pistols back
in the arms chests, and swabbed down the decks, Ramage
looked round his cabin at the perspiring but eager faces of his
officers. He had finished explaining his plan and said to Lacey:
'Have you any questions?' The captain of *La Créole* had
none.

Aitken, however, was worried about darkness. 'Supposing
she comes up from Aruba during the night, sir?'

Ramage shook his head. 'With no moon and the risk of
cloud, would you choose to make a voyage of forty-eight
miles at night, the current foul, when you could time it to
make your landfall in daylight?'

'No, sir,' the first lieutenant said apologetically, 'it was a silly question. I'd hope to be about fifteen miles west of the island – west of Westpunt Baai – at dawn. Then if the wind was lighter than I expected I'd be that much later, and there'd be no risk of running ashore in the darkness.'

'And that's where we will be,' Ramage said. 'We'll be close to Westpunt Baai, and with the coast trending south-east towards Amsterdam, Lacey will be able to show how *La Créole* can pull with the bit between her teeth.'

He looked round to see if anyone had more questions, and Wagstaffe said: 'The privateers in Amsterdam, sir: are we leaving them alone?'

'For the time being, yes, although they won't realize it. Watchers along the coast will be reporting us going westward, but at twilight we'll turn back towards Amsterdam so that the Dutch lookouts report that we are doubling back and obviously intend to spend the night off the port – just the sort of trick one would expect. But of course once it's dark we'll turn back yet again . . .'

'And hope it is not so dark we run ashore,' Aitken said dryly.

'Sint Christoffelberg is twelve hundred feet high,' Ramage said. 'We should be able to see it from five miles off, and Lacey here has only to keep an eye on our poop lantern.'

He stood up and said slowly: 'Remember, gentlemen, that timing is vital. If we see the fish isn't taking the bait, we have to act immediately, otherwise dozens of our men will be killed or wounded unnecessarily.'

CHAPTER SIX

By dawn Southwick and a dozen men had about half of the smallest of the *Calypso*'s anchor cables, a ten-inch-circumference rope the thickness of a man's forearm, ranged on the foredeck after being led out through a hawsehole and back on board again, with a light messenger rope made up to the end. All her guns were loaded and run out, the decks had been wetted and sanded, and cutlasses, tomahawks, pistols and muskets had been issued. The *Calypso* was once again ready to greet the first light of day, the only difference being the cable lying on the fo'c'sle like a sleeping serpent.

Ramage, walking round the ship, could sense the men's excitement and he stopped here and there in the darkness to warn that they might have to wait two or three days for the Frenchman to appear. The men were delighted that the captain should stop and pass the time of day but were obviously ignoring his warning: they had made up their minds that the French frigate would show up today; that she would be reported in sight to leeward as soon as the lookouts went to the masthead at daybreak and had a good look round. One of the men had given it enough thought to realize that the Frenchman approaching from the west might see the *Calypso* against the lighter eastern sky and bolt, and he was relieved when Ramage assured him that in fact they would be hidden against the blackness of Sint Christoffelberg and the hills at the western end of Curaçao for that first critical fifteen minutes of the day.

The special lookout posted aft and staring into the *Calypso*'s wake continued to report every ten minutes or so that *La Créole* was still astern. Although it was a dark night there was plenty of phosphorescence, and every now and again a pale greenish swirl astern showed where the schooner was faithfully following and revealing herself occasionally as her bow sliced into a swell wave.

From his own experience in the past, Ramage knew that Lacey would have had little sleep, worried that his lookouts forward would lose sight of the *Calypso*'s poop lantern. The young lieutenant, knowing how important it was that he should be only a few hundred yards from the *Calypso* at first light, was unlikely to have left the quarterdeck: he had probably spent the night in a canvas chair, boat cloak over his shoulders, occasionally dozing and frequently nagging whoever had the watch and interfering as only anxious captains know how. Yes, Ramage thought to himself, I know just how you feel . . .

La Créole had to be close at daybreak, just in case: Ramage had been most emphatic about that. He personally did not think they would see the Frenchman at dawn whichever day she arrived, but there was always a chance that she sailed at the proper time and made a fast passage, which would bring her off Curaçao at first light. No gambler would ever bet on a Frenchman being punctual, but the whole success of the operation depended on *La Créole*: he had made sure that Lacey really understood.

Ramage looked through a gun port. He could just distinguish the toppling waves; they had a grey tinge, and the stars low on the eastern horizon were dimming slightly, Orion's Belt had crossed overhead and dipped, the Southern Cross and the Plough had revolved, Polaris had remained fixed, and the sun would soon be dazzling them all. Yes, Sint Christoffelberg was over there on the starboard beam so high that it was distinguishable as a black wedge pointing upwards and obscuring the stars low on the north-eastern horizon.

Somewhere in the darkness on deck three men waited, one at each mast, for the order sending the lookouts aloft – it would come from Wagstaffe this morning – and then each would race up the ratlines like a monkey, hoping to be the first to hail the deck that the French frigate was in sight. The competition, mast against mast, was traditional.

Ramage finished his walk forward along the starboard side and crossed over to make his way back to the quarterdeck along the larboard side. There was very little sea; the *Calypso* was hardly rolling, giving a gentle pitch from time to time, almost a curtsy, as a swell wave came along the side of the island, part of the movement westward that began off the western corner of Africa, crossed the Atlantic and Caribbean, and finally ended up, thousands of miles away, in the muddy shallows of the Gulf of Mexico.

Groups of men squatted round their guns. Usually they were half asleep, but this morning they were wide awake, occasional whispers and stifled laughter showing they were cheerful enough. Ramage never understood how men could laugh and joke when, within the hour, they could be dead, shattered by grapeshot or torn apart by roundshot. It was enough that they were cheerful.

Yet, he realized, they were cheerful because they were confident; they were confident that death would not touch them. And they were confident because – well, because so far, under his command, they had been lucky. All the actions of the last few months, including the original capture of the *Calypso* and *La Créole* from the French, had been fought with very few casualties.

Would there be a great change of heart among them if they fought a bloody action? Would they then be less martial?

He doubted it: most of them seemed like Southwick: as keen for battle as schoolboys for a game of marbles or poachers for fat pheasants. And as his heels thumped the deck and he balanced himself against the ship's roll, he knew he was slowly becoming a better captain. It had taken long enough, but now he had finally absorbed the apparent contradiction that the captain who worried too much about his men being killed in action was likely to kill them by the dozen because he would be too timid. The boldest plan was usually the safest. He realized he had never consciously taken a ship into action with that thought uppermost, but looking back on a series of actions, the fact was that he had often escaped with only a dozen killed and wounded when a prudent man with an apparently safer (more cautious) plan might have lost four dozen.

Was he being arrogant? Perhaps, and if arrogance on his part led to confidence among his men and success to an operation, then perhaps arrogance was no great fault. And of course it was the men's arrogance (that any one of them was worth three Frenchmen) that gave them the boldness which led them to succeed. The casualty lists usually bore them out, and certainly the Admiralty seemed to assume that one of the King's ships with a hundred men should be able to board and capture a French national ship with three hundred.

'Lookouts there – away aloft!'

Wagstaffe's shouted order broke into Ramage's thoughts and he realized he had not r. 'iced how much lighter it had become in the last few minutes, minutes when he had just stood at the gun port staring at the wavetops gliding past.

The men were getting up from the deck where they had been squatting or sitting, groaning as stretched muscles gave them a twinge, teasing each other, some shivering with the dawn chill and swinging their arms, others spitting tobacco juice over the side through the port.

Ramage climbed the quarterdeck ladder to find Wagstaffe waiting anxiously at the rail, speaking trumpet in one hand and night glass in the other, obviously awaiting the first hail from aloft, while Southwick stood at the binnacle talking to Aitken, who would take over from Wagstaffe if any enemy ships were in sight, leaving the second lieutenant free to go to his division of guns. The Marines were forming up with much stamping and thumping.

Not one of the *Calypso*'s officers approved of his plan. Ramage had sensed that when he had explained it to them. Only Lacey was full of enthusiasm, and that was because his role was exciting. But the rest of them, from Southwick (who had been in battle dozens of times) to Kenton (who was relatively untried) had misgivings. None had said a word; to most captains they would have seemed full of enthusiasm.

Looking round at them in his cabin the previous day, when he had asked if there were any questions, he could guess how each man's mind was working. Each was reacting differently because he had a different personality. Southwick regarded it as wasting time: to him there was little wrong in getting alongside the other ship as quickly as possible and resolving the battle with his broadsides and boarding pikes. The master's strength was in his right arm, wielding a meat cleaver of a sword. Aitken, the quiet Scot, was intelligent enough to see the purpose behind Ramage's plan but he did not believe it would work, and nor did he think it necessary. Wagstaffe did not think the French would fall into the trap – that much was clear from the questions he asked – but if they did he could see the trap would then work. Young Kenton had never heard of such a plan and, because he was young, he was conservative: why fence with a foil when you could slash with a cutlass? Kenton had been at sea long enough to see that wars could not be fought without men being killed, but not long enough to try to reduce the odds. To him – and, to be fair, to the other officers, including the Marine lieutenant – one British frigate and a schooner were a match for any French frigate, and given that historic truth, proved in hundreds of actions, why monkey about . . .

Aitken was a deep-thinking officer and Ramage could guess that the young Scot, wise beyond his years and almost certain to have his own command soon, was beginning to see things through the eyes of a captain, weighing risk against reward, risk against responsibility, risk against culpability. He knew that a senior officer, a commander-in-chief, Their Lordships at the Admiralty, were always reading the orders and looking at the results, rarely giving praise for success but quick to select and accuse a scapegoat if they saw failure (even though, often enough, the original orders were too absurd to allow success).

Yet there were times when a captain trying to make the

weights balance on those scales, putting the risk on one pan, the responsibility and culpability on the other, saw the responsibility and culpability pan drop with a decisive clang. So he did not take the risk because it would hazard his future. Rejecting the risky plan, he drew up a safe one. The risky plan might have saved many lives if it was successful; the safe plan was, all too often, safe only because the certainty of its success was bought with many men's lives.

As Ramage watched the lighter eastern sky push the darkness westward he felt his anger growing with the whole of the present system of command in the Royal Navy. It meant that no captain depending on his regular pay to support a wife and family dare take a risk where failure could blast his career. There were a few exceptions – very few indeed, and Rear-Admiral Sir Horatio Nelson was the only one who came to mind at the moment.

The officers who could and did take risks with their careers in order to save lives tended to be men who had private incomes. Alexander Cochrane, for instance, who was heir to the Earl of Dundonald, and although there wasn't much money in the family, it was just enough to make sure that Cocky would not starve if the Admiralty court-martialled him over one of his wilder exploits. Not that so far they had any reason to bring him to trial; he took quite fantastic chances – but he succeeded and his men worshipped him.

There were of course stupid officers, rich and poor, who took risks simply because they lacked brains; the kind of men who gambled every penny they had on the turn of a dice without realizing that, even if they won, the low winnings compared with the high stake they could lose made the risk absurd. No, he was thinking of intelligent men; men like Aitken, who had travelled a long way from a widowed mother and that grey stone cottage in Perthshire; who had managed by sheer ability and bravery to get well up to windward in his career, but who in a very few years would be unable to risk losing it.

Which, Ramage thought bitterly, boiled down to the fact that all too often the commander-in-chief and the Admiralty judged success by the size of the butcher's bill. An action in which a French frigate was captured by a British one which lost fifty men killed and a hundred wounded was regarded as a great victory, without anyone questioning whether the casualties were necessary. After all, the French frigate was captured . . . capture the enemy and no one questions the casualties. But capture the same frigate with only half a dozen casualties and the captain was given little credit, authority shrugged its collective shoulders and commented that the French were poltroons.

Perhaps it was the right attitude: Their Lordships could not be expected to weep because a hundred men died in a battle. If they did, the Admiralty would cease to function; no one would dare give orders. No admiral could order a ship into action if he stayed awake at night thinking of all the women who would be widowed, all the children made fatherless, as a result of his order. Admirals had to have hard hearts, and in his experience most of them did anyway, as well as an appreciation of captains responsible for payments into their prize accounts.

The trouble arose when a captain knew his ship's company too well; when he knew each man's quirks and habits, recognized his accent out of a dozen others, knew of his hopes and fears, perhaps had been asked for advice concerning some wayward wife or errant son. Then the question of taking a risk and hazarding his future did not apply. The captain was *involved*: he was the father of a large family.

Take Jackson, for instance. The muster book merely listed him as Jackson, Thomas, American, born in Charleston, Carolina, volunteer. Then there was Stafford, William, born in London, prest, and Rossi, Alberto, born in Genoa, volunteer . . . There were up to fifty other men now in the *Calypso* who had served with him for two or three years and sometimes more; who had been with him, for example, when the *Kathleen* cutter was rammed by the Spanish three-decker and reduced to kindling; had been in the *Triton* brig in various actions and saw her end up dismasted and wrecked on a coral reef . . . Yet men like Jackson, Thomas, had been with him when he rescued Gianna from the beach in Tuscany, with Bonaparte's cavalry galloping at them and Jackson making weird noises in the darkness which scared off the horses.

There was so much to remember; so many shared experiences with these people, men like Southwick, for instance, and more recently Aitken, Wagstaffe, Baker and young Lacey astern there in *La Créole*.

If any one of these men was killed in battle he would

mourn them like – like what, a brother, a nephew, an uncle? No, like one of his men; a curious relationship that encompassed all the others. With Southwick, for example, there was the combination of an eccentric uncle and an erratic nephew. Jackson, tall and sinewy, his sandy hair thinning, was like the most valued of family retainers. Officially he was the captain's coxswain, but over the years he had become the equivalent of bodyguard and head gamekeeper. Jackson had saved his life several times; he had saved Jackson's. There were no debits or credits, only mutual respect.

And Stafford. Not to put too fine a point on it, Will Stafford was a bright-eyed young Cockney picklock at the time the pressgang took him up, but even if his boyhood had been spent burgling, the result as a young man was a fine seaman, fearless and loyal in a way that reminded Ramage of old stories of knightly chivalry. Stafford could just about write his name with much effort and tongue protruding, but he would give his life for his friends, men like Jackson and Rossi. He had an engaging way of mispronouncing words, and Jackson patiently corrected him.

Rossi was the third man about whom Gianna always enquired in her letters. Plump, black-haired, olive-skinned and jolly, he was a Genovesi; had left Genoa in a hurry, hated the French with a deep bitterness, was proud – and completely loyal to his adopted country. He was a volunteer and, as far as Ramage could make out, had joined the Navy because it gave him the best opportunity of killing Frenchmen. He had left Genoa before the conquering French arrived there to set up a new republic, and no doubt the city records would show that the authorities did not believe the story that Ramage had heard – that Rossi had killed the other man in self-defence – but Ramage took the attitude of most captains: that a man's life before his name went on the ship's muster list was his own affair.

Rossi was inordinately proud of Gianna: proud that the woman his captain loved (that was no secret in the ship) was Italian. He might have a slight and secret reservation because she was not a Genovesa, but Volterra was in Tuscany and near enough to be acceptable. He would not have accepted a Neapolitan, a Sicilian or a Roman, and might have been doubtful about a Venetian, but a Tuscan was a neighbour, almost a *paisana*. Almost, but not quite; Tuscany was a different state; simply close to the Republic of Genoa.

Both Stafford (to whom she was invariably 'the Marcheezer', with Rossi trying to correct him, although the Cockney's tongue was incapable of uttering 'Mar-kay-zer') and the Genovesi regarded her as the most beautiful woman they had ever seen, and Ramage wondered if they speculated whether she would marry the captain. Ramage sensed that Jackson had no doubt, but Jackson's relationship with Gianna was slightly different: he had been with Ramage when they had searched an Italian town for a doctor to save the life of (as they thought) a dying Gianna.

A bellowing beside him made Ramage go rigid with surprise, but it was Wagstaffe answering a hail from the mainmasthead, whose lookout then reported: 'Horizon clear to the south and west, sir; only thing in sight is land to starboard.'

It was almost as if the ship shrugged and sighed with disappointment. Southwick sniffed, Wagstaffe rapped his knee cap with the speaking trumpet, a frustrated Aitken muttered some Scottish oath, and in the half-light it seemed that the men slumped at the guns.

No French frigate. She was still at Aruba. He looked astern – La Créole was so close it seemed her bowsprit and jibboom would soon ride up over the Calypso's taffrail. Lacey's lookout – Ramage could just make him out, a fly clinging to the mainmast – would also be reporting an empty horizon, and the schooner's men would be equally disappointed.

Ramage said nothing for several minutes, then commented to Wagstaffe: 'I can see a grey goose at a mile.'

That was the standard distance always used for visibility: from that moment each morning the life of the ship could go on. Small arms would be stowed in the chests, and guns run in, canvas aprons, or covers, lashed over the flintlock on each gun to shield the flint and mechanism from spray, and the cook would soon have the galley fire alight (it was always doused when the ship went to quarters). And then the cooking would start. Cooking . . . everyone could have their meat however they wanted it, as long as it was boiled; and the same went for vegetables. The Navy had a sense of humour when they called the man a cook: he had only to light the galley fire and boil the water in the coppers.

Today, Ramage remembered, was sauerkraut day. The pickled cabbage was good for the men's health, but he could well understand their lack of enthusiasm for it because when a cask was first opened it smelled like a privy. Worse, in fact. The stench lasted only fifteen minutes, but it quickly filled the ship. And, the dutiful captain, he always made a point of sampling it even though the thought, let alone the taste, made him want to retch.

In the meantime the damned French frigate was not in sight and the south and west coasts of Curaçao had little to offer by way of scenery. He would spend the day off the entrance to Amsterdam: it would help keep the Dutch quiet, and there was always a chance of capturing a fishing boat, so they could discover what was happening on the island.

He beckoned to Wagstaffe and took the speaking trumpet, hailing the lookout at the mainmasthead. 'Can you see any smoke over the land?'

'No, sir; nor smell it.'

The lookout was wide awake: they were dead to leeward of the island now, and a lookout high aloft would be much more likely to smell smoke than someone on deck, where the odour of bilgewater, tarred rope, the breath of the men chewing tobacco and the damp smell of clothing provided strong competition. There was, of course, the usual smell of hot and dry land. Not the rich herbs-and-spices of Spain or Italy, but a dried-hay-and-manure smell of an arid tropical island just before the sun gets high enough to scorch off the night dew.

The fires causing yesterday's smoke near the village with the impossible name had not been spread to the western end of the island by the night breeze, nor had he seen any glow. The lighter eastern sky now put this western side of Sint Christoffelberg into dark shadow and the hills rolling down towards the flat eastern end of the island looked more than ever like giant waves tumbling flat to their death on a beach. There was no sound of gunfire, cannon or musket. The island's troubles were obviously over. Ramage pictured cattle sheds accidentally burning, and men shooting fear-crazed animals. He shrugged his shoulders: fire in these parched islands was as dangerous as in a ship.

It was time to beat back to Sint Anna Baai and look once again at those privateers: a beat of twenty-five or thirty miles against a westgoing current of one or two knots, perhaps more, probably increasing as the wind came up. He looked round for Southwick and, relaxing, suddenly felt hungry. In ten minutes or so his steward Silkin would come on deck to report that his breakfast was ready. The sky was clear – an hour or so after sunrise the little white puffballs of cloud would begin to form up to the eastward and start their daily trek to the west; the sky would become a bright blue, the sea its dark reflection, hinting at great depths, the unmarked graveyard of the centuries and of secrets. And the sun would climb steadily to sear and scorch, withering plants and men, directly overhead at noon at this time of year and making everyone thankful for the cool of night.

For forty years or more the buccaneers had tacked along this coast. That was a century and a half ago, when it was always called the Spanish Main. Had his great-grandfather passed this way, heading for one of the towns on the Main? He had a sudden longing to know; to be able to sail up to a Spanish port and know that great-grandfather Charles and his men had once captured it from the Spanish. Even to take bearings of the peak of Sint Christoffelberg and Westpunt, and draw them in on a chart to fix the ship's position, and to know that Charles Ramage had done just that, using a crude chart for the lack of anything better and an even cruder compass. Old Charles had won a fortune from the Spanish along the Main; enough to rebuild and furnish a home shattered by Cromwell's troops, men who thought beauty was a sin and were offended by one of the loveliest houses in the west country.

'Old Charles': why *old*? He may well have been in his twenties at the time, the same age as his great-grandson was now. Curious how one rarely thought of a forebear as having once been young. Why, he wondered, these recent thoughts about Charles, who had succeeded a brother as the eighth Earl of Blazey?

Ramage had served in the Caribbean for several years without giving Charles more than an occasional moment's thought; now it was almost as though he was sailing with him. He then realized it dated from finding the *Tranquil* with her passengers and crew just massacred by the privateer with a Spanish name. That had jolted his memory, thrusting him into the past.

He suddenly noticed that Southwick was waiting patiently; the old master was used to finding the captain daydreaming, and he knew when to interrupt and when to wait, without appearing to be waiting. 'Disappointing, sir – not seeing the Frenchman, I mean.'

'I've never met a punctual Frenchman.'

'True, sir, true,' Southwick said soothingly, 'you did warn us we might have to wait a day or two. Still, we may pick up a Spanish prize by this evening – they must trade between Amsterdam and the Main. I seem to remember all the fruit and vegetables for the islands come from the Main in small schooners; they have a market in Amsterdam, selling direct from the schooners.'

Ramage nodded, already regretting his sourness. 'They have so little rain that they must get fresh food from somewhere. But a prize schooner laden with bananas and cabbages . . .'

'The men would be glad of fresh cabbage instead of that sauerkraut, sir. We have to open a cask today.'

Neither Ramage nor Southwick mentioned the prize regulations: there were times when a sensible captain ignored them. The regulations said that any ship taken in prize had to have its hatches sealed and be sent into a British port, where it would be inventoried, valued and sold at auction. There was no provision in the regulations for capturing a small Spanish schooner or sloop laden with perishable fruit and vegetables. A prize would have to be sent to Jamaica, some 700 miles to the north-west. The chances of such a vessel staying afloat for a long voyage (local schooners and sloops were roughly and cheaply built) were slight, and a fruit and vegetable cargo would be rotting within hours and almost explosive in a couple of days. A schooner full of exploding bananas . . .

A wise captain, ever on the watch for scurvy and the fresh fruit and vegetables that could prevent it, would in such a case take off the cargo, sink the prize, land the two or three men on board, or let them off in their boat, and make a note in the ship's log implying the capture was only the size of a rowing boat, and therefore scuttled. It would be different if a schooner was laden with tobacco, grown on the Main and shipped to Curaçao – that would be worth a lot of money.

'We'll return to Amsterdam, patrolling about five miles off,' Ramage said, 'and Lacey can take La Créole in closer every four or five hours to look at the privateers and generally rattle the bars.'

'Can we stay close in with the coast, sir? I'd like to have

another look at where we saw those fires.'

So Southwick was intrigued as well. 'As close as you want: there's deep water right up to the shore, isn't there?'

'My chart says "No bottom at 100 fathoms" to within a hundred yards or so, sir, and the water's crystal clear. I reckon once the sun's up you'll see the bottom at ten fathoms or more. Coral reefs just off the beaches and sometimes up to five hundred yards off.'

Ramage looked astern, and *La Créole* was still as close as if she were on a short tow. 'Mr Wagstaffe, we'll wear ship in a few minutes and make our way back to Amsterdam. Make a signal to *La Créole* – I don't want his bowsprit poking through our stern lights while I'm eating my breakfast.'

The foremast lookout gave an excited hail: 'Deck there!' Southwick, Wagstaffe and Ramage all stared at each other, then looked upwards. Wagstaffe ran to the binnacle drawer for the speaking trumpet, but Southwick cupped his hands and roared: 'Foremast lookout – deck here! What do you see?'

'Sail on the larboard bow, an' I think she's steering towards us. Reckon she's a ship o' war; could be a frigate, sir!'

'Wear ship at once and make a signal to *La Créole*,' Ramage snapped. 'Send Jackson aloft with a telescope. Muster a party on the fo'c'sle and make sure they have heaving lines handy.'

He waited until Wagstaffe and Southwick had given those orders and watched as the *Calypso* swung round, away from the distant ship and heading towards Amsterdam. Men hauled on sheets and braces, trimming the yards and sails so that the frigate was now sailing eastwards, parallel with the coast, the sun giving a hint that it was about to rise on the larboard bow.

'What the devil's happened to Jackson?' he snapped. He did not expect an answer and turned to watch *La Créole*. She was still in the *Calypso*'s wake and Lacey was handling the schooner well, but the next ten minutes would finally show whether he was a natural leader or just another lucky young man commanding by virtue of a piece of parchment signed by a commander-in-chief.

And then Jackson was hailing from the masthead: 'She's three-masted, sir; everything set to the royals. Hull below the horizon, but she's a frigate and from the cut of her sails looks French to me.'

Southwick caught Ramage's eye and winked cheerfully. 'That's her, sir; Jackson's never mistaken.'

Ramage nodded. 'Make the special signal to *La Créole*,' he told Wagstaffe, 'and as soon as she hauls clear of our wake, back the foretopsail and heave-to on the larboard tack.'

'Beat to quarters, sir?' Southwick asked.

'No, not yet; we've plenty of time and a lot to do.'

He glanced round and saw Gianna's nephew scurrying up the quarterdeck ladder. He was off watch, but obviously had heard the hailing.

'Orsini!' Ramage barked, holding out a small key. 'Top right-hand drawer of my desk – fetch me the French signal book. And lock the drawer again.' Then, just as the boy turned away, Ramage remembered, 'It's in the weighted canvas bag, along with the other papers. Make sure you secure the neck of the bag again before you lock the drawer.'

That small canvas bag, containing the secret daily challenge and reply for the next three months, along with the extra copy of the British signal book and his orders, and weighted with a six-pound bar of lead, was the most valuable object in the *Calypso*: if she was about to be captured by the enemy, that bag had to be thrown in the sea. If it fell into enemy hands and Ramage survived, he would be court-martialled as soon as the Admiralty could get their hands on him, and ruined. No excuses were ever accepted for that, and every captain knew it.

CHAPTER SEVEN

Captains, Paolo thought to himself as he scurried down the companionway; they always treat everyone else as a fool. All Uncle Nicholas need have said was: 'Get the French signal book from the top drawer.' If it was not on top, he'd have guessed it was in the canvas bag, and he'd have unlaced it, taken the book out, and laced the bag again. All without having to be told.

Nod to the Marine sentry and a quick explanation: 'On the captain's business.' The sudden darkness of the cabin, the key in the lock, and there's the bag. The canvas coarse, the brass eyelets for the roping going green with corrosion caused by the salty sea air. And that's it, the signal book – funny how he thought in English now, and saw the French language on the cover quite differently than when he lived in Italy and French was always the second language.

A wonderfully precise language, English: you could be so exact. But, he thought ruefully, remembering Mr Southwick's stern questioning during navigation and mathematics lessons, that was one of the language's drawbacks: Italian and French allowed you to give a more evasive, even imaginative, answer; there was more scope for disguising the fact you didn't know something; for dissembling. But Mr Southwick taught mathematics and navigation in English; good down-to-earth and unambiguous English.

Lock the drawer again, don't lose the key. What is Uncle Nicholas planning? All that amount of anchor cable ranged on the foredeck. 'Ranged' – a good word, that. Surely he's not intending to anchor close inshore? It is the lightest of all the cables, and there's no anchor bent on. Nor, for that matter, would the cable be ranged on the fo'c'sle if he was going to anchor.

If only he'd been on deck sooner he would probably have been sent to the masthead with Jackson. Paolo loved it aloft, the ship small and narrow-beamed below him, the men tiny, like lizards scurrying on a marble floor. Ah well, he was too late to go with Jacko, so belay the grumbling.

An odd man, Jackson. The men said that he and Uncle Nicholas had saved Aunt Gianna's life; had literally snatched her from under the hooves of the French cavalry. And, only a few weeks ago, Jackson had saved his own life. Aunt and nephew. But the American had said nothing about it at the time, nor had Uncle Nicholas: Rossi had finally told him, and then only to say that Uncle Nicholas had been angry with him for joining the boarding party when they cut the *Jocasta* out of Santa Cruz.

Such a glare on deck, and with a French frigate coming over the horizon they won't be stretching the awning, so the sun will be scorching, and where is Uncle Nicholas?

Paolo saw him standing at the taffrail watching *La Créole* working her way round to windward of the *Calypso*, which seemed curiously dead in the water. Dead in the water! *Accidente*, the foretopsail is backed and she's hove-to! What are they doing?

'The French signal book, sir.'

'Thank you, Orsini. Stand by me in case there are more errands.'

This was how Aunt Gianna said it would be. An hour at sea with Uncle Nicholas comprised forty minutes of waiting, nineteen minutes of wondering, and one minute of sheer excitement. Well, now he was fourteen years old he could make allowances for the way a woman saw things, but he could understand what she meant. Uncle Nicholas (the captain, he corrected himself, because he wasn't really an uncle, yet anyway, and good discipline meant that the relationship was never referred to) was rather like a cat. He sat patiently for hours outside the mouse hole, but once the mouse came out it was all over in a moment. The trouble was, of course, that the prey was rarely a mouse; usually it was something like a leopard, not that he'd ever seen a leopard, except in those paintings on the walls of Etruscan tombs. All spotted. And, *accidente*, what breasts those Etruscan women had, too, and lately he seemed to be thinking more and more about women's breasts. Men did, he knew.

Anyway, Aunt Gianna had said the captain would show him no favour; that this was the English system, and he'd probably be harder on Paolo than on anyone else, but it was all part of the training. Well, if that was the case then Midshipman Orsini would be the best trained in the Navy and would pass for lieutenant the first time he took the examination, and the examiners at the Navy Board would be amazed . . . except, if Mr Southwick was to be believed, for his mathematics and navigation. This spherical trigonometry— *Mama mia!* Galileo, Archimedes, Pythagoras, Copernicus, Leonardo—they were all Italians (or were some of them Greek? Leonardo was Italian, anyway, because he had visited the village of Vinci, where he had been born), and if they could do it, well, Paolo Orsini should be able to. But could Leonardo?

'Orsini!'

'Sir!'

'That signal from *La Créole!*'

'Yes, sir, I . . . er . . .' Where the devil was the ordinary signal book? And the telescope? *Accidente*, that *stronzo* Leonardo, and Vinci was not in Tuscany anyway; it was though, just north of Empoli, but it wasn't in the Kingdom of Volterra, so he didn't really count.

'It's all right, Orsini; it's a special signal. But you'd gone to sleep.'

'No, sir, I –'

He saw Aunt Gianna's face and heard her words: 'And, Paolo, you'll be blamed for things you didn't do and it'll seem unjust, but *never* make excuses.'

She really did understand the Navy – of course, she had made two or three passages in the King's ships. Or, he suddenly realized, perhaps she understood Uncle Nicholas – the captain, rather. She knew his moods, because he could be very moody, and his sense of humour, which was dry. Very dry, at times; like this island. Did she know how thoughtful he was, though? How he was always concerned for his men, doing something for them, and no one – except perhaps Mr Southwick or Mr Aitken, or perhaps Jackson – ever knew? Several times in places like English Harbour and Port Royal, bumboats had come alongside and put many sacks of fresh fruit and vegetables on board for the men, and most people thought it was Navy Board issue, but Jackson had told him the captain paid for it out of his own pocket, and it was to prevent the men getting scurvy.

What is going on? The *Calypso* hove-to and now a dozen or more seamen on the foredeck under Mr Aitken and Mr Southwick. Two men passing a line outside of everything to the jibboom end. And a seaman balancing out there – is that a heaving line he's holding, half the coil in each hand? Yes, and one end of the heaving line is being made fast to the line leading back to the foredeck. If only he could ask the captain, but Uncle Nicholas looked *preoccupato*: he was rubbing the upper of those two scars over his right eyebrow, and Paolo remembered one of the first lessons he had ever learned from Jacko, or perhaps it was Rossi: when you see the captain rubbing that scar, keep clear!

Accidente! Just look at *La Créole* now! They've eased the sheets and are just – what is the word, just 'jilling' – across our bow! They'll collide, rip out our jibboom, spring the bowsprit, tear away the forestay and bring the foremast down – why doesn't someone do – but the captain is just standing there watching. Rubbing the scar, but not bellowing orders. In fact, Paolo realized, no one was speaking a word: whatever was happening was planned.

With *La Créole* sailing slowly at an angle across the

Calypso's bow, the man holding the heaving line on the jib-boom end was balancing himself as the whole bow gently rose and fell on the swell waves. Now he's twirling the coil in his right hand and the men who had passed the heavier line from the foredeck to the jibboom end are holding it out clear, as though to prevent it snagging on anything. But why should it snag?

That schooner! There's Mr Lacey standing beside the men at the wheel. He's just standing there like a statue. One of the men heaves down a spoke or two. The hiss of the schooner's bow wave – he could see every plank in the hull, every seam where the heat of the sun had shrunk the wood. He wanted to shut his eyes as the schooner hit the jibboom but was even too frightened for that.

Suddenly the man on the jibboom jerks as though shot – now the thin snake of the heaving line is darting towards the schooner's mainchains. Men seize it as the schooner crosses ahead and the men along the *Calypso*'s jibboom jump back after letting go of the line, as though it was suddenly hot. The line is racing over the bow – it's secured to the cable and now that too is going over the side after the line, and they're hauling in like madmen in *La Créole*!

Now the first words in the *Calypso* came from Mr Wagstaffe, clear across the open water – to brace up the foretopsail-yard, so that it draws. Now he leans over for a quick word to the quartermaster and the men at the wheel heave at the spokes. And Uncle Nicholas is just standing there, quite still except his eyes move – from *La Créole* to the *Calypso*'s jib-boom, to the foretopsail, to the windvane on top of the bulwark nettings, to the foredeck and that heavy cable which is smoking where it chafes on the bulwark as it goes over the side. He hasn't said a word nor made a movement.

It had all happened, Paolo realized, exactly as the captain had intended. It had taken – well, perhaps three minutes. Three, Aunt Gianna, not one. But to what purpose? The cable was paying out slower than he expected – *La Créole* was deliberately spilling wind from her sails to move slowly; the *Calypso*, with her foretopsail now drawing, was gathering way and Mr Wagstaffe was getting her into *La Créole*'s wake. Now he could see the heaving line and the heavier line had been taken on board *La Créole* and men were hauling vigorously to get the end of the *Calypso*'s heavy cable on board.

Now Mr Wagstaffe was bellowing orders to furl the top-sails. And courses. *Furl*, not clew up. But the topmen are making a poor job of passing the gaskets: the sails look like so much old laundry. And Uncle Nicholas is just watching and nodding to Mr Wagstaffe, obviously approving. And the courses – bundling up the canvas, that's what the men are doing, not furling. The jibs are being dropped and just left at the bottom of the stays, as though milady was stepping out of her clothes.

What are those men doing with the ensign? No, it isn't the ensign, there's too much white. A broad expanse of white cloth. And of blue. And red, too, wide strips of plain colours with no design. Ah, now they have the blue ensign of old Foxey-Foote, and they are bending it on below this other flag. Mr Wagstaffe is pointing upwards, and they're heaving down on the halyard, and hoisting the flags.

Accidente! The fools! They've hoisted a big French Tri-colour above the British ensign! And Uncle Nicholas is look-ing at them as they go up, the cloth blowing out straight in the wind, and he is making some joke to Mr Wagstaffe.

A shout from Mr Aitken on the fo'c'sle and Mr Wagstaffe yells at the men at the wheel. They spin the spokes – ah, yes, the strain is about to come on the cable; all of it is off the fo'c'sle now; it leads direct from the *Calypso*'s bow to *La Créole*'s stern. And *La Créole* has hoisted a large French Tricolour. There's no British flag on it, though.

To anyone sailing past now, Paolo suddenly saw with almost bewildering clarity, it looked as if the French schooner *La Créole* was towing in a British prize . . .

Ramage flicked over the pages of the French signal book. Poor quality paper, bad printing, and very few signals, per-haps a third of the number contained in the British book, so pity French admirals trying to make their wishes known to their captains. Still, there were enough for his purposes and the sailmaker and his mates had made up enough flags, even if some of the cloth was stiff because it had been coloured with thinned paint.

It would never work. The captain of the French frigate would never fall into the trap. Instead of saving his men's lives, Ramage knew now he'd end up with half of them killed and the other half taken prisoner. He looked at the French frigate, a mile away and beating up to them fast. It was not too late to call it all off; to cut the cable, warn Lacey, let fall the *Calypso*'s topsails and fight.

A few words to Aitken, who was now officer of the deck, would be enough: 'Belay all this nonsense, Mr Aitken; cut the cable, let fall the topsails and we'll fight 'em ship to ship!' That was all it needed, and the only thing that prevented him from saying it was his pride, which was working like a gag.

Yet a few days ago – yesterday, in fact – he had been sure it would work. He'd thought of the idea, spent a couple of hours trying to find faults in his plan, and had spent many hours since looking for loopholes. So why did he now think it would not work? The explanation was quite simple, of course: he was a coward, and before any action he always had these moments of quiet desperation, quiet panic, quiet fear. The quiet coward. Some men were secret gamblers, others secret drinkers. Some were wife-beaters, and others had nameless secret vices. And you, Your Lordship? Oh, I'm a secret coward . . .

Now it was too late to change his mind; the French frigate was slicing her way up to them, spray flying from her bow, port lids triced up, guns run out, Tricolour streaming out in the freshening breeze. Her sails were patched and the wetness of her hull could not hide the lack of paint. She was being sailed well but her captain was letting her sag off, so she'd have to tack to stay up to windward . . . Now she was furling her courses. Very sensible and the standard move before going into action. She should clew up her topgallants, too – ah, yes, she was doing that now, and the men were going out on the yards to furl them.

The *Calypso* must be a puzzle to that French captain: sails bundled untidily on the yards, ports closed, a dozen or so men lounging on top of the hammock nettings, idly watching the approaching frigate just as they might look incuriously at passing bumboats in port. The large French Tricolour hoisted over the British ensign showed she had been captured. She was obviously French-built, so presumably had been a British prize. But there could be no doubt about the little schooner bravely towing her towards Amsterdam: French-built, Tricolour flying, her decks lined with men.

More important, Ramage had reckoned, the French captain of *La Créole* would have shifted to his new capture, the

Calypso. Apart from having considerably more comfortable quarters, it would be the obvious place for him. Now it all depended on the captain of the approaching French frigate. Was he a flashing-eyed revolutionary or a rough sea-lawyer the Revolution had dragged up from the lowerdeck and put in command? Or a former royalist who had hurriedly turned his coat in exchange for keeping his neck intact and getting promotion? By now France was getting over the shortage of trained captains caused by the Revolution's habit, in the first few months, of executing anyone that looked like an aristocrat, a bout of republican enthusiasm which had killed off France's best captains and admirals and often put in their place men who made up in political glibness what they lacked in seamanship or leadership.

Whatever the type of man in command of that frigate, Ramage knew the whole success or failure of his operation depended on him seizing (and keeping) the initiative. The enemy ship was now close enough that telescopes could distinguish flags.

'Hoist the French challenge,' he told Aitken, and warned Orsini: 'Watch for the reply.'

Two seamen hurriedly hauled at the halyard on which the three flags of the French code making up the day's challenge were already bent. Ramage was thankful that the French system of challenge and reply was less complex than the British – and the page on which it was printed in tabular form and which had been slipped into the signal book was for a whole year.

He aimed his telescope at the French ship. Over there the French captain would be puzzled all right. The Frenchman would be assuming that the schooner's captain would be only a lieutenant and therefore his junior. He had every reason to think that he would now take command of the whole situation; that he would escort *La Créole* and her prize into Amsterdam (and no doubt find a way of claiming a hefty share of the prize money).

Three flags were jerking their way aloft and almost immediately, before they were properly hoisted, Orsini reported, his voice squeaking with excitement: 'She's made the correct reply, sir. And there go her pendant numbers. I'll have her name in a moment, sir.'

The boy glanced down at the book. 'Pendant number one

three seven, sir.' He turned to the back of the book where ships of the French Navy were listed by their numbers. 'One three seven is *La Perle*, sir.'

Moments were counting now: *La Perle*, approaching from the *Calypso*'s quarter, would have read her name on the transom and wasted time looking her up in the list: she was not there because her name had been changed when she became part of the Royal Navy. So *La Perle*'s captain, already no doubt puzzled by the fact the challenge had been made by the *Calypso* and not the obvious victor, *La Créole*, would have no way of being sure of the seniority of the officer in the *Calypso* who had made the challenge.

'Quickly now,' Ramage snapped. 'Hoist one three seven and the signal for the captain to come on board – forty-six.'

So far so good: forty-six ordered 'the captain of the ship designated' to come on board the ship making the signal, and anyone seeing it hoisted would assume (Ramage hoped) that the officer making it knew he was the senior. The captain of *La Perle* would guess that whoever was on board the *Calypso* knew his seniority, but he knew nothing of the *Calypso*. More important, he knew no lieutenant commanding *La Créole* would have the impertinence to order him on board. *La Perle*'s captain should be very puzzled but, if Ramage's guess was correct, he would obey. Any officer in that Frenchman's position would (if he had any sense) obey because if he came on board and found that a junior officer had given the order, he could spend the next day or two making the fellow's life a misery.

The violent flapping of cloth, sounding like a squall hitting a line laden with wet laundry, made him glance up. The flags were being run up smartly, with Paolo almost dancing with impatience as he spurred on the two seamen hauling at the halyards.

Ramage resumed his watch on *La Perle*. As she danced about in the circle made by the telescope he could see just how scruffy she was; her guns were run out, of course: seventeen a side, so she was pierced for thirty-four. But as she heeled in the gusts there was a dirty mark all the way along her waterline, the mark of a ship that spent much time in harbour without her captain making sure a boatload of men with scrubbing brushes kept her clean. And the yards – rust streaks marked the wood and the canvas, showing no one bothered to have the irons of the stunsail booms chipped and scraped and painted. Rust marks weakened canvas, quite apart from looking untidy. The headsails sagged even though the wind was little more than a stiff breeze, showing that the forestays were slack and no one had bothered to take up the slack in the halyards as the ropes stretched. The sight of *La Perle* would give any British admiral –

'She's acknowledged, sir,' Orsini called.

Aitken did not even look round; Southwick was still taking a bearing of her. The only person to catch Ramage's eyes as he glanced across the deck was Jackson. Was the American the only one who realized that everything had depended on that signal? Not everything, Ramage corrected himself, but at least the success of the first part of his plan.

How odd to see the *Calypso*'s decks so bare! A French frigate within three cables (he could distinguish men on board her now, so she was less than 700 yards away) and getting ready to heave-to to send over a boat – and the only sign of life on the British ship's decks was the men lounging on the hammock nettings, two or three watching from the fo'c'sle, and a few men on the quarterdeck.

He was wearing a seaman's white duck trousers and an open-necked blue shirt with a cutlass belt over his shoulder; Aitken and Southwick had also borrowed clothes from some of the men and also wore cutlass belts, without cutlasses. No breeches in sight – hurrah for France; this was the age of the *sans-culottes*. Breeches meant oppression; trousers stood for democracy. The *Calypso*'s decks were a picture of egalitarian slackness – viewed from *La Perle* anyway. The Frenchmen could not see the men waiting below, more than one hundred and fifty of them, ready to race up, trice up the port lids and run out the guns, which were already loaded, with handspikes, rammers and sponges lying beside them, and trigger lines neatly coiled, not in their usual place on the breech of each gun where they might be spotted by a sharp-eyed Frenchman aloft with a telescope, but on the deck.

The captain of *La Perle* was going to have to scramble on board as best he could: the *Calypso* was making only a couple of knots or, rather, *La Créole* was, and could not be expected to stop for him. Scrambling (and the prospect of it as his boat approached) would help keep the French captain's mind occupied, Ramage thought; he must be wondering why the *Calypso* had no canvas set to help *La Créole*. The frigate could of course be under tow for several reasons, not the least was damage to her steering, but some canvas set would make the schooner's task much easier.

Now *La Perle* was heaving-to; her foretopsail was being hauled aback and a boat was being hoisted out with the stay tackle.

Orsini and his seamen had hauled down the flags and were bundling them up again. The boy was bright enough, the way he had learned the French signal code in a few hours. It was a pity he had such difficulty with mathematics, but Ramage always felt hypocritical at punishing the lad when an exasperated Southwick insisted. Ramage's own mathematics were poor; they had been sufficient to let him pass the examination for lieutenant and be thankful that no one would ever test him again for the rest of his naval career; once past lieutenant promotion did not depend on the mysteries of mathematical figures.

The boat was being held alongside *La Perle*; now the men were settled in it. And the last man going on board must be the captain. A squat, powerful-looking man with a fighting sword slung over his shoulder: no dress sword for him. They let the sternfast go, then the painter, and then the men at the oars were pulling briskly and clumsily for the *Calypso*.

'Look at them, sir,' Jackson muttered disgustedly. As the captain's coxswain he always commanded the boat carrying Ramage, and he was offended by the way the French boat was being rowed. 'I'll bet they'll lose an oar before they get alongside.'

Ramage laughed – louder than he intended, but it was a relief to have *La Perle*'s captain on his way, even if his boat's crew rowed like drunken smugglers dodging a Revenue cutter.

'Mr Aitken, I want four men ready to take that boat's sternfast and painter, but warn them not to speak a word while they're doing it; I don't want those Frenchmen to get any warning.'

Five minutes later Ramage was waiting a few feet back from the entry port. Jackson, Stafford and Rossi were standing nearby, looking like undisciplined seamen, but each had a pistol tucked into the top of his trousers and wore a cutlass. To *La Perle*'s captain they were obviously some of the guards who were having a breath of fresh air, relaxing from the task of guarding the English prisoners held below.

Aitken stood beside Ramage, a telescope under his arm and clearly the second in command. As Ramage waited, finding himself rubbing the scar over his eyebrow and cursing the sun's glare – he could not wear his hat – he knew the deception need last only two or three minutes, perhaps less; just the time it took to get the captain on board and the French boat astern, where it would tow with its crew still on board, a perfectly normal procedure.

Suddenly a plump, wine-mottled face topped by a narrow-brimmed straw hat appeared at the entry port, rising as its owner climbed up the last of the battens. The man was the same height as Ramage with broader shoulders and a stomach long ago run to fat. His arms were long and he walked two or three paces without swinging them. Creased, unbleached canvas trousers, a dark-red shirt, blue eyes, a face unshaven for a couple of days, greasy skin that had not been washed for the same length of time . . . But, Ramage realized, *La Perle*'s captain had the look of a reliable man and was probably a good seaman. A boatswain promoted by the Revolution?

'*Citoyen* Duroc,' the man said, holding out his hand to Ramage, a huge hand whose fingers seemed as large as bananas. 'Pierre Duroc.' His eyes flickered over the *Calypso*'s decks and seemed satisfied with what they saw.

Ramage did not move and Duroc, his hand still proffered, looked surprised, and then Ramage said: 'Do you speak English, Captain Duroc?'

The Frenchman stepped back a pace and instinctively looked towards *La Créole* and then over at *La Perle*, obviously intending to run back to the entry port.

Three metallic clicks stopped him in his tracks: he recognized the noise and looked round slowly, careful now not to make any sudden movement. Jackson, Rossi and Stafford had cocked pistols aimed at him, and Ramage and Aitken had each taken a pace sideways, out of the line of fire.

Duroc was still puzzled and obviously not frightened. 'I have no English,' he said in French, his heavy accent showing he came from the Bordeaux area. He pointed up at the Tricolour. 'What is happening? Were you prisoners? Have you escaped?'

Ramage shook his head and said in French, gesturing at the

Tricolour and blue ensign, 'A *ruse de guerre*, Captain Duroc, to secure your capture!'

Duroc's face, already purple from years of heavy drinking, looked swollen: his eyes narrowed, his hands clenched: he was about to step towards Ramage, remembered the three pistols, and contented himself with sneering: 'You fight under false colours, eh?'

'Fight?' Ramage enquired innocently. 'There's been no fighting, and you know the rules as well as I: one hoists one's proper colours before opening fire.'

'That schooner, then!' Duroc burst out. 'She's French. I recognize her. From Fort de France.'

'She was French and you probably did see her in Fort Royal –' Ramage deliberately used the old name – 'but we captured her, along with this ship.'

Duroc shook his head, like a trapped bull. 'What are you going to do now?' he demanded.

'Take possession of *La Perle*.'

The Frenchman shrugged his shoulders and waved at the *Calypso*'s decks. 'I have three hundred men on board – you have a couple of dozen.'

Ramage bowed. 'Thank you; I was expecting you to have fewer.'

Duroc, unaware what he had revealed, held out both hands, palm upwards. 'You'll never take her. Let me go back on board my boat and let us continue our respective voyages.'

Ramage watched the man's eyes. It was a curious offer, curious and not in keeping with the man's character. Duroc was a fighter; it would have been more in character if he had sworn at Ramage and told him to do his damnedest to capture *La Perle*. Duroc had a reason for avoiding a fight, and the reason, Ramage guessed, was because he had a particular purpose in wanting to get to Amsterdam. An important passenger? Special supplies? Reinforcements? No, not reinforcements because he had boasted of his three hundred men, which was the number of men the French like to have in a frigate of that size. Whatever it was, Duroc had a reason for wanting to get to Amsterdam. And while the ship was lying hove-to over there, Ramage knew Duroc would never reveal it. Afterwards, he might.

Ramage looked again at the eyes – they were bloodshot now, from rage – and the hands, which were clenched, looked like shoulders of mutton. He turned to Aitken. 'Pass the word for Mr Rennick – we'll keep this fellow in irons for the time being.'

La Perle was soon a mile astern and still hove-to as *La Créole* continued to tow the *Calypso* eastward. Orsini, whose French was fluent, had been sent aft to order the French boat crew to climb on board up a rope ladder slung from the taffrail. The nine men had climbed over the taffrail to find themselves staring into the muzzles of pistols and were only too glad to be led below as prisoners.

Ramage wished the Royal Navy would abandon breeches for its officers – in the Tropics, anyway: cotton duck trousers were loose and so much cooler and more comfortable than breeches and stockings. And there was much to be said for a loose-fitting shirt. The French *égalité* had sartorial advantages.

Very well, he told himself, the first part of the plan has worked: *La Perle* now has no captain, but whether or not she is also a snake with her head chopped off depends on the French first lieutenant. If he's like Aitken, there is hard and bloody fighting ahead. If he's a fool – well . . .

'Mr Orsini – let me have the French signal book, please.'

He knew the wording of the signals almost by heart, but he dare not risk a mistake in the numbers. It was such a thin volume, it contained so few signals, especially – especially, he made himself say under his breath, when you are going to try to use it to capture a ship. The only ally he had at the moment was the fact that the officers in *La Perle* would assume that any orders signalled to her from the *Calypso* would have the approval of Duroc, and would promptly obey them.

La Créole and the *Calypso* were now a couple of miles from the coast of Curaçao and steering diagonally away from it to the south-east. That was no good; he was going to have to crowd *La Perle*; crowd her just at the time her first lieutenant was getting into a panic.

'Mr Aitken, make a signal to *La Créole* to tack. But don't hoist it: I want the flags hung over the bow where *La Perle* can't see them and have Lacey's attention drawn to them by a musket shot. If the Frenchmen see flags being hoisted that they don't recognize . . .'

'Aye aye, sir,' the first lieutenant said briskly.

'And I hope he has plenty of way on that schooner when he puts the helm over.'

'I warned him about that,' Aitken said dryly. 'I didn't want our dead weight pulling his stern back again and putting him in irons.'

Ramage nodded and looked over towards the island. Once they were on the other tack they would be steering almost directly for the shore. It would take them half an hour to reach the beach, and although half an hour sounded a long time it would seem a matter of moments if anything went wrong. Particularly, Ramage thought grimly, if the person involved was a French lieutenant upon whose shoulders the fate of two frigates and a schooner was suddenly and un-expectedly thrust.

CHAPTER EIGHT

Aitken stood by the binnacle watching the schooner. Lacey had acknowledged the signal to tack and had then turned away a good point to starboard and eased sheets to increase La Créole's speed. The cable running from the schooner's stern to the Calypso's bow now had less of a curve in it, straightened by the extra pull, and when the strain suddenly brought several feet of rope jerking up out of the sea, water spurted from between the strands, like a burly washerwoman wringing out sheets.

Then, with the Calypso now moving faster, the schooner began to turn slowly and deliberately to larboard. Aitken snapped out the order to the quartermaster, who relayed it to the two men at the wheel, and they hauled at the spokes. Almost at once the Calypso began to turn inshore and Ramage watched. The frigate should be round and on her new course by the time La Créole had completed her tack, and during that time the cable would have slackened just enough, dipping deeper under its own weight so that it would act as a spring to dampen the jerk as the frigate's weight came back on it.

'Mr Orsini,' Ramage said quietly, 'you have La Perle's numbers ready to hoist?'

'Aye aye, sir.'

'And number fifty-six?'

'Yes, sir – *"Ship indicated shall take disabled vessel in tow, the course to be steered to be made known in the next signal"*.'

'The signal for the course is bent on ready?'

'Yes, sir.'

'And what course is that?'

'North-east, sir.'

'Very good. Don't get them mixed up.'

Paolo Orsini was angry. His olive skin was flushed; his brown eyes glared. For a start he was wearing a seaman's shirt and white duck trousers, instead of his uniform, and he had no hat, except this straw thing woven out of palm fronds and painted. He was more proud of his uniform than anything except perhaps his name, although fortunately no one had so far strained his loyalties to find out, and he resented his present garb, even though all the officers were similarly dressed.

Not only had Uncle Nicholas – the captain, he corrected himself sarcastically – made him wear these wretched clothes, so that he looked like some damnable *sans-culotte*, but he kept asking silly questions about the signals. They were the right ones, they were bent on different halyards, they had been checked half a dozen times. Five times by himself, and once furtively by Jackson and Rossi who, with Stafford and the sailmaker, had sewn up the French flags in the first place and had written what each one was in small figures at the bottom of the hoist. Orsini had been angry when he first saw the figures and had rounded on Jackson, who had just listened and then winked.

Winked! Not offered any explanation to the officer whom the captain had made responsible for signals, which was himself, but winked. Admittedly no one else could see the wink, but a wink was no way to behave towards a midshipman. Why, he could have taken Jackson to the captain and reported his insolence. Not that that would have done any good, he admitted, his anger melting as quickly as it had arisen, because the captain would have pointed out that Jackson was helping him. And so he was; it was the kind of thing that Jackson did, quietly and without anyone else seeing, and Paolo sheepishly admitted to himself that he was grateful. It was so hot down here in this latitude; too hot to think and certainly too hot to remain good-tempered.

Anyway, the signals made no sense. Was the captain going *pazzo*? What was the point in this French frigate *La Perle* taking the *Calypso* in tow instead of *La Créole*? Did he have some other task for the schooner? And why tow the *Calypso* anyway? Why didn't the *Calypso* cast off the tow and get alongside *La Perle*, then pour in a few broadsides and board her in the smoke? That's what *he* would do if he was the captain. Captain Orsini. *Dunque*, three broadsides and *allora*, it would be all over.

And this tacking. Just look now: *La Créole* is towing them straight towards the shore! *Mama mia*, if she gets into stays on the next tack offshore we'll all end up on the beach. And you can be sure the *Calypso* will bilge herself on the only rocks along a mile of sand and spring some planks, so all we'll hear for the next couple of days will be the clanking of the chain pump and the creak of our own muscles. Every man will have to take his turn – in this heat too, when it is too hot to think, let alone pump. And the Dutch cavalry will come galloping along and start sniping at us. Then they'll bring up artillery and the *Calypso* will not be able to fire back because she'll be heeled to seaward and all her guns on the landward side will be pointing up in the air. *Accidente*, what a mess, and all because Uncle Nicholas didn't – then, to his surprise, he saw they were still a mile from the beach, the *Créole* towing steadily, and the French frigate still hove-to. The way his imagination ran away with him . . . if Uncle Nicholas had the slightest idea, he'd send him back to Aunt Gianna!

Ramage looked at his watch. Five minutes to go. There were nearly two hundred men waiting on the *Calypso*'s lower-deck, which must be like an oven.

'Carry on, Mr Aitken!' he said, 'I'm just going below for a few minutes.'

He clattered down the companionway, noting yet again the comfort of the trousers: going up or down steps in breeches always caused an uncomfortable tightness across the knees. He made his way forward to the messdecks, where the men waited. Not only was it appallingly hot but it was smelly. There was the sickly stench of bilgewater, the last gallons that no pumps could ever clear, and the smell of which was usually cleared away by the downdraught of the sails. At anchor the water settled, but now, with the ship rolling under tow and no sails set, the effect was like stirring up a stagnant pond on a hot, windless day.

The men were grouped round the ladders with their officers. Wagstaffe, the cheery Londoner, was obviously keeping his men amused; he had a good fund of stories and could mimic Stafford's Cockney accent. Baker, the burly young third lieutenant from Bungay, in Suffolk, was quiet; the chance of him telling a funny story to amuse his men was remote, but they all seemed to like him. And finally, of the sea officers, the fourth lieutenant, young Peter Kenton. His shortness and red hair made him conspicuous, and because his heavily freckled face was usually peeling from sunburn, he seemed younger than his twenty-one years. His men looked contented, while Rennick and his Marines were a compact mass of pipeclay.

All of them fell silent as soon as they saw Ramage, a silence not caused by awe but because they were obviously expecting him to say something. He had not intended to do more than show himself, but rows of expectant faces made him climb a couple of rungs of a ladder up to the main hatch so that he could be seen by all the men.

'While you fellows are resting down here,' he said, and they all gave murmurs of mock protest, 'we have been busy on deck. We have the captain of the French frigate on board as a guest – of the Marines, who I hope have him in irons in the gunroom – and the *Calypso* is being towed by *La Créole*, as you know, to save you all the effort of sail handling on a hot day.'

The laughter showed that the men liked this teasing, simple as it was, but time was passing and he was anxious to get back on deck. 'At the moment the French frigate is hove-to astern. Within an hour I hope we shall have captured her. You'll get your orders. Speed is what will matter. Speed will mean success. It'll also be your best protection. In the meantime *La Perle* – that's the name of the French frigate – is quite convinced we are *La Créole*'s prize. Well, we'll see. We know how much Their Lordships reckon French frigates are worth in prize money and we know the deductions for damage, so we'll be gentle with *La Perle*.'

With that the men cheered him and he swung up the ladder into the bright sunlight. In the past few months each of the men had earned a considerable amount of prize money – from ships including the *Calypso* and *La Créole* – and they obviously liked the idea. Each of them was now entitled to more prize money than he could earn in wages in twenty years at sea. Curiously enough it did not seem to affect their attitude to life – or death, rather. A man with several score guineas due to him, enough to go home and set up a little business which would keep him comfortably into a prosperous old age, might well be more anxious than usual to stay alive; he might show some reluctance when going into action. Wasn't it Frederick the Great who berated his tardy Prussian guards with: 'Dogs, would you live for ever?' A sensible man's answer, Ramage reflected, would be an uncompromising yes, but fortunately the Navy (and the Army too!) comprised men born without an excessively strong sense of self-preservation.

On deck once again the sun's glare was harsh and it took him a moment or two to adjust his eyes. Curaçao seemed startlingly near but automatically he checked: he could see the beach clearly so it was less than three miles; he could see a shrub the height of a man growing at the back of the beach but not quite distinguish the colours of the flowers growing on it – so it was between two miles (colours indistinguishable) and one (colours distinguishable). Call it a mile and a half. On this course, making an angle to the coast, *La Créole* had two miles to sail before she ran up on the beach, followed by the *Calypso* nearly one hundred fathoms, or two hundred yards, astern. *La Perle* was still hove-to and he could make out her main rigging, so she was a mile away: the *Calypso* and *La Créole* by tacking, were in effect sailing along the tangent of a circle of which *La Perle* was the centre.

As he walked to the quarterdeck Ramage began rubbing the scar over his eyebrow. He knew he had gone below to see the men because the tension of remaining on deck was getting too much: he hated the split-second timing on which the next part of his plan depended, the split-second timing which depended not on the hands of a watch but on his own judgement. And through making that speech – the mouthings of bravado – he had probably wrecked everything by starting the second part of the plan two or three minutes late. But stay calm, he told himself: if you try to rush people they just make silly mistakes.

'Orsini – hoist *La Perle*'s pendant number!'

His voice was so calm that he surprised himself, but he could afford it because earlier he had made the boy check the flags. Now the midshipman and his two seamen hoisted them smartly.

'Now number fifty-six of the French code.'

'Aye aye, sir.' As the boy and the seamen hoisted Paolo repeated: ' "*Ship indicated shall take disabled vessel in tow, the course to be steered to be made known in the next signal.*" '

'Very well,' Ramage said. 'Let me know when she acknowledges.'

But even before he finished speaking three telescopes were trained on *La Perle*: Aitken was standing with his back to the quarterdeck rail, balancing himself on the balls of his feet against the *Calypso*'s gentle roll, Southwick was watching with the complacency of a prosperous farmer inspecting a ripe field of corn, half of which had already fallen before the reapers' scythes and with the weather set fair, and Paolo had snatched up a telescope with the speed of a conjurer producing an out-of-season apple from the rector's hat.

Even Ramage could see without a telescope as *La Perle* answered. 'They had the flag already bent,' Southwick commented.

'Now, Orsini, hoist the signal for north-east, and make sure it is acknowledged.'

Aitken and Southwick walked over to join Ramage, who had remained by the binnacle, which for the moment was shaded by the furled mizentopsail.

'I'm glad I'm not that French first lieutenant,' Aitken said to no one in particular.

'Why not?' Ramage was surprised at the Scotsman's gloomy tone.

'Well, sir, he's been ordered to take us in tow, but how is he to get the cable from *La Créole*? By the time he gets up here the schooner will be nearly on this coral reef running parallel with the beach. There'll be hardly any room for him to manœuvre. If he stays too far off he could hit the reef; if he gets too close to the *Calypso* he runs the risk of hitting *La Créole*. But somehow he has to get that cable secured on board!'

'You've forgotten two other things.'

'What, sir?' Now Aitken was surprised.

'First, he thinks his own captain is watching every move from this quarterdeck, with another senior officer beside him. Second, he's sure his whole future depends on what he does.'

'Aye,' Southwick said with a prodigious sniff, 'and he knows how easily he could get all three ships caught up in such a mass of tangled yards that we all end up on that reef like three battered tankards in an alehouse brawl.'

'Two and a half pints,' Ramage said dryly. 'Yes, I'm glad I'm not that Frenchman. In fact I can't see how he can do it.'

Aitken and Southwick both swung round to stare at him. The skin of Aitken's face had suddenly gone taut, and Southwick ran a hand through his flowing white hair, and licked his lips uneasily. 'But you – you've just given him the order, sir,' Southwick said nervously.

'Yes, though I'd sooner give it than receive it.'

'I . . . well, sir, should I get an anchor cleared away for letting go, sir?'

'Won't help much, Mr Southwick. It's deep right up to the reef, so by the time the anchor's beginning to get a bite we'd be on the coral. Staghorn, isn't it? Dreadful stuff . . .'

'Could we hoist out the boats ready to tow if necessary, sir?' Aitken ventured, still watching Ramage closely.

'No,' Ramage said lugubriously, 'we shouldn't envy that poor French first lieutenant.' He turned to Jackson, who was holding up a cutlass: 'Ah yes, slide it in.' He settled the leather belt more comfortably across his shoulder. 'And the pistols, thank you.' He took the pair from the American and clipped them on to the waistbelt of his trousers.

Orsini called excitedly: 'La Perle's acknowledged the signal giving the course, sir. She took long enough.'

'Hoping we'd made a mistake, no doubt, and would annul it,' Aitken commented as he turned to look at the frigate. 'But she's slipping along now. But that fellow hasn't made up his mind whether to approach us on the windward or leeward side.' He looked at Ramage, who nodded as though the subject of La Perle no longer interested him.

'I wonder what the devil all that smoke and musketry was yesterday,' Ramage said. 'And the captain of La Perle was so anxious to get to Amsterdam.'

'Was he, sir?' Aitken said in surprise.

'Oh yes, no bridegroom was more anxious to get to the church on time than Captain Duroc.'

Ramage felt hot and he felt a fraud. Standing under this scorching sun, which was now directly overhead so that you had to lean forward slightly to see your own shadow, the deck was so hot that the wood could be a stove top curling the leather of the soles of your shoes. Nor was the wind doing very much to cool anything: the *Calypso* was making only two knots and the wind barely had the energy to lift itself over the rolls of hammocks piled in the bulwark nettings to blow across the deck. The glare from the sea, from the sails, and from the near-white sand of the beach, gave the impression of heat, even though its only real effect was to make you screw up your eyes so that you peered out on this tropical oven through slits, like a short-sighted Oriental.

And the fraud: that was a different thing altogether. Aitken and Southwick had suddenly looked at each other and then they had laughed: the captain, they thought, was playing a neat joke on them, pretending he did not know what would happen when *La Perle* arrived to carry out her orders. They were sure the captain had a trick hidden away; a trick which would solve everything and leave them with *La Perle* as a prize.

The fraud arose because he had no trick ready, and if Aitken and Southwick gave the matter any thought, they would know it was impossible to have one waiting. He had explained yesterday the only plan he had was the one which would get *La Perle*'s captain on board, leaving the ship – he hoped – in the hands of less experienced officers. Well, that plan had been executed; Captain Duroc, no doubt sadder and wiser, was now sitting below in irons, with Marines guarding him.

What happened next depended entirely on what *La Perle*'s first lieutenant did. Given that he tried to carry out the order to take over the tow of the *Calypso*, how would he approach? How would he get that heavy cable from *La Créole* and secure it on board and take up the tow? Would he come up to starboard, on the windward side, or on the larboard side, which had the advantage of being to leeward but the disadvantage of being the land side, reducing the available room to the stretch between the long reef and the *Calypso*?

Ironically the anonymous French lieutenant now had the advantage; that much Ramage admitted. The Frenchman knew what he was going to do, but Ramage knew nothing. It was a game of chess – that's what neither Southwick nor Aitken realized. At this stage of this particular game, your move depended on your opponent's move; it was a response. You *hoped* that your opponent moved a piece which allowed you to checkmate in one move, but there was always the danger that you would be the one who was checkmated.

La Perle was beating up fast in the *Calypso*'s wake and Ramage stared at her. The three masts were in line. She could pass one side or the other at the very last moment. Suddenly he realized why she looked a little strange: all her guns had just been run in and the gun ports closed. The French lieutenant had – wisely from his point of view and fortunately from Ramage's – done it presumably because he wanted his men ready to handle sails and secure that cable; as far as he was concerned there was no fighting to be done; simply a problem of salvage.

CHAPTER NINE

Lieutenant de vaisseau Jean-Pierre Bazin bitterly regretted the day he had ever gone to sea. As a boy growing up in Lyon, where the placid River Saône joined the turbulent Rhône after its race through the mountains, he had watched the Saône passing within a hundred yards of his home in one of the narrow streets in the shadow of the cathedral. He had also walked the other way, to the Fort de Lovasse. He had walked up to the Fort scores of times, hundreds in fact, to watch the soldiers drilling, the bands playing, men marching and counter-marching to the beat of a drum. But soldiering had never excited him; the pressed uniforms, the polished buttons, the pipeclayed belts (for this was before the Revolution) had seemed a lot of unnecessary work every day, especially to a boy who was for ever accounting to his mother for the latest holes in breeches and boots.

In contrast the rivers had captured his imagination. Along the Saône men sat on the banks or stood among the rushes, fishing from dawn to dusk, with a sleep in the middle of the day when the sun was high (as it was now, but never reaching such an altitude or heat, of course). Horses had plodded along the banks of the Saône, towing barges and disturbing the *pêcheurs*. The barges were usually painted in gay colours and carried cargoes from places which seemed as distant to a young boy as China: from Tournus and Chalon, and towns on the Saône's tributaries, like Dijon and Dole.

Then, as a change from the placid Saône, he would walk across the bridge and past the arsenal and watch the Rhône which, in spring, as the ice and snow melted up in the Swiss mountains, was a torrent. The water sluicing past, noisy over the rocks along the banks and cold, gave the impression of movement and travel; starting from way beyond Lac Léman it passed Genève and twisted and turned to Lyon; then, always rushing onwards, it began its great surge to the Mediterranean. The Mediterranean – the cradle of civilization, the route to ancient Greece and Tyre and Nineveh, or even to Corsica, where Columbus was born at Calvi, no matter what those blackguards in Genoa claimed. Born within the walls of the Citadel, he was, and a credit to the island – to the whole of France, indeed.

Anyway, the quiet Saône and the racing Rhône (except occasionally in summer when it almost dried up, usually after a winter of only very light snow in Switzerland, and barge traffic was stopped for weeks on end) had given him the idea that they represented the two extremes of the sea, the smooth and the rough. So at the age of fifteen he had packed a bag, said goodbye to his widowed mother, travelled by barge down the Rhône to Avignon, and then ridden by cart (for the price of helping the carter with his train of four horses) to Toulon, where he had joined the French Navy. It was slavery; even in port it meant fourteen hours' work a day while the officers spent their time on shore . . .

By the time the Revolution came he was an able seaman, a nimble topman and, thanks to his mother's patient teaching, one of the few seamen who could read and write. Read well enough, fortunately, to understand the revolutionary pamphlets and help persuade the other seamen of the necessity of disposing of several royalist officers for whom the men had an absurd loyalty. For all this work the Revolutionary Council had made him a lieutenant, and he had long since learned that the Rhône at its wildest had as much similarity to the sea as – well, the *grande rade* of Toulon to a puddle.

More recently, he remembered the excitement when *La Perle* had been at anchor in Martinique, at Fort de France, as Fort Royal was now called, and Captain Duroc had finally noticed the royalist sympathies of the frigate's first lieutenant, that braggart from Gascony. Denunciation, trial and execution had taken only a few days, and *Citoyen* Jean-Pierre Bazin, the second lieutenant, had suddenly found himself promoted: at thirty he wàs second in command of this great frigate.

The journey from the house in the shadow of the cathedral in Lyon to walking the quarterdeck of *La Perle*, frigate, as the man next only to the captain had taken but fifteen years. That showed the opportunity which the Revolution gave to men of character and leadership. Captain Duroc, for example, had been the boatswain of an old xebec trading from Sète to Marseille when the Revolution began.

Now, though, Captain Duroc was on board that damnable prize frigate being towed quite competently towards Amsterdam. And he, Jean-Pierre Bazin, had been left in command of *La Perle* for the first time. At the beginning, that had been far from daunting; with the foretopsail backed the ship had stayed hove-to, like a gull resting on the water. The captain's boat had been rowed briskly to the prize frigate, Duroc had gone on board, the boat had been hauled round to tow astern: all what one would expect, because whoever was on board the prize was obviously senior to Captain Duroc. One would have expected the captain to return in, say, fifteen minutes, half an hour at the most, and *La Perle* would then continue on her way to Amsterdam: the captain had made enough fuss about the rush to get there.

But had Captain Duroc come back on board? Oh no, he had stayed on board the prize, no doubt clinking glasses and reminiscing. And then suddenly the signalling had started. Without any warning or explanation he had been ordered to take that thrice-damned frigate in tow. Not only that; he had to take over the tow from that damned schooner. Somehow he had to transfer the actual cable from the schooner, not pass one. How? And the fools, the criminals in the schooner, had tacked. From heading offshore, leaving plenty of room for *La Perle* to manœuvre, the cretins had quite unnecessarily tacked, heading inshore, and by the time *La Perle* reached her there would be no room on their larboard side, which was the lee side, which meant (unless he risked running *La Perle* ashore) that he could only approach from the windward side.

Merde! Approach from to windward with a ship like *La Perle* that handled like a haystack and was manned with crippled imbeciles who jumped to obey orders with all the alacrity of royalist mules! And if he made a mistake (because he was not given proper orders) and *La Perle* found herself alongside the other frigate, yards and rigging locked, or her jibboom caught in the other frigate's shrouds, with masts toppling like sugar cane before a machete, who would get the blame, eh? Why, he would be hauled before a tribunal and put in jail (if not worse) for damaging the property of the State. Not Duroc, will you please note, but *Citoyen* Bazin, who had been abandoned by his captain.

Just his luck, too, that most of the ship's company were also Gascons, followers of that traitorous first lieutenant. Little wonder that '*gasconnade*' had become part of the language: just listen to them now, bragging, boasting, arguing. At least they had managed to get *La Perle* under way without having a committee meeting about it – that was where Duroc had an advantage: he was big enough to knock down any man that argued. *Lieutenant de vaisseau* Bazin, on the other hand, would have to draw his sword and threaten (and risk having a man laugh in his face, as had happened once already).

Now, anyway, *La Perle* was steering for the prize frigate. The fourth lieutenant had reported that she had the name 'Calypso' painted on her transom, but there was no such name in the list of the French Navy, so the English must have renamed her. What did it mean, anyway? The name of a town, or of a battle? Perhaps one of these barbaric Roman or Greek gods.

It is so hot. This sun, it scorches, dazzles, and soaks you in perspiration. This island, too; what a wretched place. It looks more like a collection of rocks and sand which has been used for a camp by a passing army. Just cactus and shrub and, if Aruba was anything to go by, pudding-faced Dutch women with breasts like sacks and red-faced Dutchmen with bellies like casks who prefer their gin to the best wine.

All this thinking is wasting time. What is he going to do? If only the schooner tacks again to head the *Calypso* out to sea, and then drops the cable with a buoy on it. That would be the easiest; then *La Perle* could heave-to, use a boat to retrieve the buoy and get a line on it, and haul it in, all without risking a collision or drifting on to the coral reef. That damned coral reef along the shore just went on and on, like the border round a flower garden, a deceptive band of brown and gold with light-blue water beyond, showing how shallow it was.

No, he simply would not take the responsibility. Duroc was the captain; he should be on board now. He would – ah! Suddenly, with a spasm of irritation that he had not thought of it before, Bazin saw what Duroc obviously expected him to do: pass within hail of the *Calypso*. Then Duroc would shout across instructions. After all, Duroc would not want to risk damage to his own ship.

In the meantime he didn't want those damned guns run out with all those port lids triced up so that even the slightest touch of ship against ship would tear off lids and wrench guns from their carriages. The *Calypso*, he noted, did not have her guns run out.

He shouted orders to the second lieutenant, who was leaning on the quarterdeck rail as though expecting the ladies of the town to parade across the deck in front of him. Soon he could hear the rumble of the guns being run in, then the crash as port lid after port lid was allowed to slam shut, leaving the side as smooth as the walls of a house with the windows shut. Ah, he felt better now; he knew that Duroc would not have let him down like that. He looked round for the speaking trumpet: he might need to reverse it and use it as an ear trumpet. Duroc did not speak very clearly, even when sober, and he had been on board the *Calypso* for a good half an hour by now, so . . .

Ramage looked astern at the approaching frigate. Masts still in line, her jibboom and bowsprit sticking up at an angle directly towards him like a hussar's lance. If you didn't know, you'd think she was going to ram the *Calypso*! Was she? The thought suddenly struck him that perhaps she had discovered that the *Calypso* was a British frigate and, not trusting to her guns, was trying to disable her. Had he made some silly mistake in the signals (in the challenge, perhaps) that had given him away?

Then Southwick ambled up and stood beside him, patting his ample stomach as though he'd just finished a good dinner. 'So he's unsure of himself, eh?' the master commented. 'That Frog is going to range alongside and ask for instructions on how to pick up the tow.'

Ramage nodded, hard put to stop himself slapping Southwick on the back from sheer relief. 'That must be it. He's just run his guns in and closed the ports – must be worried in case he comes too close and rips them off.'

Southwick glanced at him, uncertain whether the remark about ripping off gun ports was serious or not. 'We've enough way on to be able to give ourselves a bit of a sheer one way or the other to dodge him.'

'A bit of a sheer.' Ramage repeated Southwick's phrase to himself and looked across the narrow stretch of sea between the *Calypso* and the reef. Half a mile? Already the dark blue had gone from the water; now it was much lighter, lacking the near-purple which showed extreme depth. Then, quite abruptly, the water became light green and then brown as it reached the reef. Or, rather, the brown tops of the staghorn coral showed near the surface. And then, beyond the reef, a band of very light green showed the shallow water (a fathom or two) running up to the beach, with an occasional splash of white where a wave had enough strength to break.

Take a bit of sheer, a bit of panic, and a bit of a chance, too! He called Orsini and snatched the signal book from him. Feverishly he flicked through the pages. And there it was, a single flag. 'Hoist number eight!' Ramage snapped. It might be too late, but its very lateness might be a help.

'Number eight, sir – "*To turn to larboard*".'

Ramage caught Southwick's eye and smiled: he knew exactly what was passing through the master's mind: young Paolo seems to have memorized the whole French signal book, but he can never remember for more than a day the simplest mathematical formula.

An intermittent mouse-like squeaking high overhead showed a halyard was spinning the sheave of a block, and Ramage deliberately continued looking astern, defying himself to glance up at the flag. The squeaking stopped; the flag must be hoisted now. And *La Perle* was perhaps three lengths astern, a little over a hundred yards. If it worked it was going to be a close-run affair.

He said to Southwick: 'Give her a sheer to larboard of one point.'

The master turned and shouted to the quartermaster.

To Aitken, waiting by the binnacle, Ramage called: 'Warn the men below to stand by!'

He could see a Frenchman perched out on the end of *La*

Perle's jibboom gesticulating aft and pointing at the *Calypso*, as though drawing his quarterdeck's attention to the signal.

Now *La Perle* appeared to be sliding to Ramage's left as, below him, he could hear the rudder grinding a little as pintles rubbed against gudgeons. The *Calypso*'s 'bit of a sheer' to larboard was beginning, swinging the ship's bow to larboard a few degrees and moving her bodily towards the reef, narrowing the gap, like a drunken man walking along a road and curving slightly towards a wall.

Ramage turned forward towards Aitken. 'Are those men with axes standing by on the foredeck?'

'Yes, sir.'

It would take them at least two minutes to chop through the towing cable. Looking over the *Calypso*'s bow he could see the sheer had taken her well out on *La Créole*'s larboard quarter. Let's hope Lacey has the wit to bear away, otherwise the *Calypso*'s weight will haul his stern round (like someone hanging on to a dog's tail) and get the schooner in stays.

By the time Ramage looked aft again *La Perle*'s topsails were fluttering slightly – the *Calypso*'s sudden movement had, not surprisingly, caught the French first lieutenant unawares, and now he was trying to luff up to obey the order to turn to larboard.

Lieutenant Bazin had been watching the transom of the *Calypso* grow larger as they approached. Her sternlights seemed occasionally to wink as the rippling surface of the sea reflected the sun from the glass. With the telescope he could see that the old nameboard had been replaced with a new one: the paint and gilt making up the name *Calypso* was much fresher than the rest of the design on the scroll.

There were very few people on board the *Calypso* – two or three officers on the quarterdeck (Duroc presumably among them), and a dozen or so men along the gangways. Ah, and a few seamen waiting on the fo'c'sle. So he could reckon on some help from the *Calypso* with that damned cable.

By approaching in the *Calypso*'s wake, Bazin wanted to be absolutely sure that Captain Duroc realized what he was doing. He was sure it was what the captain would want – Duroc was always interfering, never considering anyone could do anything properly without detailed instructions and constant overseeing. So by steering straight for the *Calypso*'s stern and then bearing away to starboard at the last moment, ranging to windward close along her starboard side, he could listen to Duroc's shouts. Probably Duroc's drunken ravings in fact, because he couldn't imagine Duroc still sober and letting pass such an opportunity to show a senior officer how clever he was and how stupid everyone else. He had to admit he hated Duroc.

The *Calypso* is a handsome ship: one can tell by that graceful sheer that she is designed by a Frenchman because the British can never achieve that elegance. But what is wrong with her that she has to be towed? It can only be damage to the rudder because her masts, yards, bowsprit and jibboom are all right. She is not leaking – there are no spurts of water streaming over the side, showing her pumps at work. And, oddly enough, no battle damage. At least, none that can be seen from astern. No shotholes in the hull, no fished yards. Not even a pane missing from the sternlights. Can that schooner towing her have actually captured her? It seems unlikely; there is some other explanation. Most likely another ship captured her and ordered the schooner to tow her to port. Yes, that is what happened!

He swore at the two men at the wheel as *La Perle* yawed in a momentary wind shift. They were nicely lined up now; he could even see the smooth trail, a path across the sea, which was the *Calypso*'s wake. Another half a dozen ships' lengths or so, and he'd begin the turn to starboard which would let him pass alongside. Already the *Calypso* was being hidden by *La Perle*'s bow; he'd have to perch on the breech of a gun and peer over the bulwark, or rely on seeing her masts.

Actually it isn't as difficult as one might think, commanding a frigate. Duroc makes a great performance of it, cursing everyone, clutching his brow, stamping a foot, shaking his fist, spitting to show his contempt, but it is only necessary to keep calm. Keep calm and make sure orders are obeyed promptly. One needs a dozen eyes, of course, but Duroc makes hard work of it by all the drama.

What is that fluttering in line with the *Calypso*'s mizen? He lifted his telescope. *Merde!* Another signal, and at this stage! Number eight. Hurriedly he mentally skimmed the first page of the signal book.

'Deck there!'

Now a blasted lookout aloft is hailing.

'Deck here!'

'Foremast here – she's hoisted a signal!'

'I know. Keep a sharp lookout.' He looked round and spotted the second lieutenant. 'Where's the signal book, *crétin*?'

When the lieutenant handed it to him he snatched it and began flicking through the pages.

'It's number eight,' the second lieutenant said.

'I know that!' Bazin snarled.

'It means to turn to larboard.'

'Why the devil didn't you say so, then, instead of giving me the book?'

'You asked me for it. The book.'

Now there was shouting from the bow.

'What goes on there?' Bazin shouted back.

'The frigate's hoisted a signal!'

'I know. Just keep a sharp lookout.'

'We'll ram her in a minute,' the second lieutenant said lugubriously. 'Captain Duroc will have you court-martialled.'

'And I'll tell him how you fooled around with the signal book,' Bazin said hotly, and then looked ahead again.

The *Calypso* was no longer ahead: suddenly she was way over to larboard.

'*Crétins!*' Bazin screamed at the men at the wheel. 'What are you doing? Who told you to turn to starboard?'

'We didn't. The *Calypso* suddenly turned to larboard.'

And Bazin saw she had: the schooner was still some way to starboard, but the *Calypso* was so far over to larboard it was now doubtful if he could get *La Perle* to point high enough to pass her to larboard.

Snatching up the speaking trumpet that he had been expecting to use as an ear trumpet, he began bellowing orders to get the yards braced sharp-up, and a moment later gave more orders to the men at the wheel.

The *Calypso* seemed glued on *La Perle*'s larboard bow; then slowly, almost reluctantly, she began to move slightly to starboard. Or, Bazin corrected himself, she appears to, although of course it is *La Perle* turning to larboard at last. But now the wind is increasing – that helps her up to windward but it is also increasing her speed, and she is approaching the *Calypso*'s larboard quarter crabwise.

Then Bazin glanced up and saw the luffs of the sails fluttering, beginning to be starved of wind.

'Bear away, you fools!' he bawled at the men at the wheel, but even before they could haul down on the spokes he realized that bearing away, turning to starboard, would inevitably bring *La Perle*'s starboard bow crashing into the *Calypso*'s larboard quarter.

'No, no! Luff up, luff up!'

'*Merde!*' screamed one of the men, stepping back from the wheel, 'make up your mind – sir!'

Bazin saw that the name *Calypso* was painted in blue on a gilt background, and edged with red. The colours were bright. The studding-sail boom irons on the outer ends of the *Calypso*'s yards were newly painted in black, in contrast to *La Perle*'s, which were stained with rust.

This is a funny time for the *Calypso* to be hauling down the Tricolour. They have the Tricolour on one halyard and the British flag on another, so they can haul down one independently of the other. Perhaps the halyard has chafed through. Anyway, there is only a British flag now. And it is going to be a dreadful collision.

Southwick gave yet another of his prodigious sniffs, a sniff that contained a lifetime's contempt as well as a lungful of air. 'That Frog lieutenant couldn't be trusted with a bumboat full of whores,' he said crossly. 'Just look at those luffs fluttering. Ah – now he's having the yards braced up, but that isn't going to help him. And – the fool, he's paying off so much he's making more leeway than headway!'

La Perle was now coming crabwise down on to the *Calypso*'s quarter. Two ships' lengths, Ramage reckoned.

'General quarters,' he snapped at Aitken. 'Guns run out, boarding party to stand by.'

The flapping of flags overhead reminded him. 'Orsini! Get that Tricolour down! Leave our own colours flying.'

'She'll stave in our larboard quarter, spring a dozen planks and carry away the mizen,' Southwick said matter of factly, drawing the great sword he had been wearing slung round his waist. 'But if she damages us too much we can all shift on board her . . .'

Seamen were streaming up from below. Some were tricing up the gun ports while others ran out the guns. Men grabbed boarding pikes from the racks round the masts, others took up pistols from wherever they had stowed them. Marines scrambled on to the hammocks stowed in nettings round the quarterdeck, muskets loaded and waiting for orders from Lieutenant Rennick who suddenly appeared on the quarterdeck and posted himself near Ramage, ready for instructions.

Aitken, having passed all his orders, was now steadily and fluently cursing *La Perle*'s first lieutenant, his Scots accent becoming more pronounced as he pictured the damage that would soon have to be repaired along the *Calypso*'s quarter. None of them thought to look at Ramage; none except the quartermaster, who was Thomas Jackson. The American watched him from habit. He was not sure quite what the captain intended, but there must not be the slightest delay in passing a helm order. Jackson knew the men at the wheel were reliable, quite competent to watch the windvanes and the luffs of the topsails, and for the moment had to admit he could not see how the captain was going to get out of this situation. He heard the grumbles of the first lieutenant and the contemptuous snorts of Mr Southwick, and he noted that oddly enough the only person who was not worrying about any damage to the ship was the one man who would be held entirely responsible for it, the captain, and from long experience Jackson knew that if the captain was not worrying, then the odds were that there was nothing to worry about.

Personally, he had to admit that if he was the captain he would be – well, worried: that French frigate was not only sagging down on them but moving faster than the *Calypso*. Now she looked as if her bow would hit amidships: she'd shove her jibboom and bowsprit through the mainshrouds and the wrench would probably carry away the mainmast.

Ramage, rubbing the scar over his eyebrow and then snatching his hand away as he realized what he was doing, took one last look at *La Perle* and then briskly said to Aitken: 'Cut the cable!'

He walked over to an open gun port and looked over the side. The *Calypso* was still making more than a couple of knots; she had steerage way. The Frenchman was making a good four but slowing fast. And she would not hit the *Calypso*'s quarter for two reasons – first, that foolish French lieutenant was still trying to luff her up, but was losing speed and control instead, and second, the sheer which turned the *Calypso* towards her could, with the wheel turned back, swing her away; swing her just enough that instead of *La Perle*'s bow ramming the *Calypso* amidships she would crash her whole starboard side against the *Calypso*, as though she was intending to board. And the moment that happened . . . He gestured to Jackson and gave the order which began the *Calypso*'s sheer to starboard, swinging her stern away from *La Perle*, but agonizingly slowly.

He glanced back at *La Perle*: already her towering jibboom was abreast the *Calypso*'s quarterdeck but passing it. Now the bow, and he could see the black paint peeling, rust weeps from iron fittings, stains where garbage was thrown carelessly over the side. Now the foremast . . . French seamen just standing there or peering over hammock nettings, astonishment or fear showing on their faces, but none wielding a cutlass or aiming a musket.

Now *La Perle*'s sails flogging overhead, not drawing, and the sloshing of water as waves rebounded between the two hulls. But, Ramage realized, no orders being shouted across the French ship's deck.

La Perle's mainmast passing now. She is slowing down appreciably, her sails not drawing, and she is very close: you could lob a grapeshot on to her deck. The sheer to starboard is working well: the two ships are now on almost identical courses but just slightly converging, and both are slowing down: *La Perle* because a desperate first lieutenant has braced up the yards too much and starved the sails of wind, the *Calypso* because the cable has been cut and *La Créole* has let the rest go and is already wearing round, determined not to miss the next few minutes.

Then the crash. For a moment Ramage, nearly flung off his feet, thought they had hit a rock, but the rending of wood as *La Perle*'s hull scraped along the *Calypso*'s told the story.

Crisp shouts along the *Calypso*'s decks showed the junior lieutenants had their men in control. Grapnels flew through the air to hook into *La Perle*'s rigging and hold the two ships together, and then there was no more movement of the ships: *La Perle* was stopped alongside, her transom level with the *Calypso*'s quarterdeck rail so that Ramage could see her three officers, one of them no doubt the first lieutenant, standing rigid on the quarterdeck, looking more like statues. They were all watching the *Calypso*'s quarterdeck, as though expecting the devil to appear.

Ramage held the speaking trumpet to his mouth and shouted forward: 'Away boarders!'

'Sir!' Southwick said pleadingly, and Ramage nodded, and the master ran down the quarterdeck ladder to join the boarding parties streaming over the bulwarks.

In the meantime the two ships began swinging to starboard: *La Perle* had more way on when she hit and she was slowly turning the *Calypso* to starboard, away from the beach. And that, Ramage realized, was what he wanted: the *Calypso* would end up to leeward of the French ship and, by letting fall her sails and cutting the lines to the grapnels, could get clear.

The shouting on board *La Perle* was unbelievable but, Ramage noted thankfully, there had been no pistol shots so far. The metallic clang of cutlass against cutlass was dying out – he'd heard only a few, less than a dozen. And all along the larboard side of the *Calypso* the guns' crews waited in their respective positions trying to see what was going on, and no doubt frustrated at not being allowed to fire even one broadside before the boarders were ordered away.

Ramage now aimed the speaking trumpet at *La Perle*'s quarterdeck and shouted in French: 'Do you surrender?'

The French first lieutenant must be the tall, thin man, and he looked dazed. He had heard Ramage and turned to stare at him, jaw slack and puzzled. But he was giving no orders. In fact, Ramage suddenly realized, the poor fellow probably had not noticed the *Calypso*'s Tricolour coming down at the run several minutes earlier, and at the very moment the *Calypso*'s boarding party streamed over the bulwarks he had been expecting to hear a stream of abuse from Captain Duroc . . .

Jackson called to him, pointing almost overhead. Ramage looked up to see *La Perle*'s Tricolour coming down, and hauling at one end of the halyard was one of the officers. The man he thought was the first lieutenant was watching; not with interest but with the same fascinated stare of a rabbit facing a ferret.

'What,' Southwick grumbled, 'are we going to do with three hundred French prisoners?'

The two frigates, still alongside each other, were slowly drifting westward off the coast of Curaçao with *La Créole* circling them like an anxious mother hen worrying over her chicks that were now fully grown.

'First we attend to the ceremonial,' Ramage said, nodding to where Lieutenant Rennick, a sergeant and six Marines were climbing back on board the *Calypso* with three French officers in their midst. The officers were wearing their swords and once they were on the *Calypso*'s deck, with Rennick leading and shouting brisk orders and the Marines stamping their feet as they marched in time, they walked along nervously in the centre, trying to get into step.

Rennick and his Marines were enjoying themselves, and Ramage waited until the three French officers were standing to attention in front of him on the quarterdeck, covered by the Marines, and Rennick was reporting in a stentorian voice the presence of French officers who wished formally to surrender. At least, he added in an outburst of honesty, he did not speak French but he thought that was what they meant.

But for the fact that the Marines rarely had a chance to show off their drill, Ramage would have cut short the ceremony: *La Perle* had been taken without a shot being fired from a pistol or one of the great guns, and she had been handled like a bumboat coming alongside with vegetables to sell. The French officers deserved to be bundled below without so much as a nod.

'Please introduce yourselves,' Ramage said in French. 'I am Nicholas Ramage, *capitaine de vaisseau*, and commanding His Britannic Majesty's ship the *Calypso*.'

At the mention of his name two of the lieutenants glanced nervously at the third, the tall and thin man Ramage had seen earlier on *La Perle*'s quarterdeck and who still seemed to have a fixed stare.

'Jean-Pierre Bazin, *lieutenant de vaisseau*, formerly second in command of the French national ship *La Perle*.' He drew his sword, making his movements very deliberate, obviously worried in case the gesture might be misunderstood by the Marines. He held the sword hilt-first towards Ramage. 'I surrender my sword.'

'And the ship,' Ramage reminded him.

'Yes, and the ship, milord,' Bazin said hurriedly.

Ramage was puzzled by the 'milord' but turned to the next Frenchman as he handed Bazin's sword to Aitken. The second lieutenant gave his name, surrendered his sword and was followed by the third lieutenant. The fourth lieutenant, Bazin hastily explained, had died of yellow fever two weeks earlier.

'Do you speak English?' Ramage asked Bazin casually, and when the Frenchman shook his head signalled to Rennick to take them below.

As soon as they were marched off, Ramage turned to Aitken and realized he was still holding the three swords.

'Share them out,' he said. 'Have one yourself. How about you, Southwick?'

The master shook his head. 'I don't need a memento,' he said. 'But just think of it – a French frigate captured without a shot fired and not one man killed or wounded. On our side, I mean. You'll get a *Gazette* for that, sir. Only ten lines, perhaps, but what a dispatch! Three hundred men and a 34-gun frigate captured with a 100-fathom cable!'

'Aye, just look at her.' Aitken gestured at the great bulk of *La Perle* with his free hand. 'Not a sail to mend nor a bit o' rigging to knot or splice. Not a shothole for the carpenter to plug. Aye, and not a man to be buried either . . . Just one or two Frenchmen for Bowen to stitch up.'

He put the swords down on the deck beside him. He looked embarrassed as he turned back to Ramage; his usually pale face was slightly flushed and now he was not holding the swords he did not seem to know what to do with his hands.

'I think – we, I am sure, sir, the ship's company would want me to say on their behalf – and mine, too, sir – that . . .'

By now Aitken's accent had deepened and he came to an embarrassed halt. Ramage was puzzled and gave the first lieutenant a minute or two to recover, then said: 'Well, Mr Aitken, take a deep breath and finish what you were going to say!'

'That-they-appreciate-how-you-managed-to-save-lives, sir.' It came out as one long word, and Southwick nodded as Ramage heard Jackson, the men at the wheel and the crews of the nearest guns murmuring in agreement.

'You took the devil of a chance, if you don't mind me saying so, sir,' Southwick said in his usual blunt way. 'If we'd failed, no court would have believed what you were trying to do.'

Ramage nodded in acknowledgement to Aitken and said dryly to Southwick: 'If I'd failed we wouldn't have been alive to face a trial.'

'Don't you believe it, sir. Their Lordships have a deputy

judge advocate stationed permanently in Hell: he has a quire of paper, a gallon of ink, a bundle of quills, and a copy of the Articles of War.'

'And if I go to Heaven?'

Southwick shook his head. 'Doesn't matter, sir; they have another one sitting beside St Peter . . .'

'But!' Ramage said, grinning broadly.

'But what, sir?' The master screwed his eyes up in concentration, knowing Ramage was teasing him and trying not to fall into any trap.

'But we succeeded, so Their Lordships won't worry.'

Southwick gave one of his more-in-sorrow-than-in-anger sniffs, and Ramage said: 'I'm just going down to have a word with that French first lieutenant. Pass the word, please, Mr Aitken, I want him brought to my cabin. And don't be too hard on the French. I wonder if we could have resisted poking our noses in, if we'd seen a small schooner towing a frigate . . .'

CHAPTER TEN

Bazin could hardly believe his eyes when, a few moments before *La Perle*'s bow crashed into the *Calypso*'s quarter, the prize frigate suddenly began to move over to starboard, as if deliberately moving over so that *La Perle* could come alongside without a collision.

At the same moment a seaman by the mainmast began shouting at the quarterdeck something about the *Calypso*'s gun ports, and Bazin saw that they were opening, and her guns were being run out. It is all very strange, he thought; first they drop the Tricolour and now they run out the guns. And here is Roget, the second lieutenant, his face as white as a sheet and shaking him by the shoulder and screaming at him, his teeth bared like a mad dog. But the words are slurred – by fear, though there's no need to be scared now; there will be no collision. 'Control yourself, Roget; speak slowly.'

Roget swallowed hard, took a deep breath – and Bazin gave him credit for the way he controlled himself – and then said, very distinctly: 'It's a trap. She's English.'

'Don't be stupid! She made the correct challenge. And all the signals!'

'She's English, I tell you – she's dropped the Tricolour; there's just the English flag now. Look, you fool! It was a *ruse de guerre.*'

At that moment the two ships touched, hull against hull, like a fat couple walking down a narrow alley, and the second lieutenant turned and ran to the quarterdeck rail, shouting at the seamen to stand by to repel boarders, but even as Roget shouted Bazin saw grapnels flying through the air on the end of ropes, and as the crunching and banging ended with *La Perle* stopped alongside the *Calypso*, he also saw the bulwarks of both ships suddenly become alive with men: seamen from the *Calypso*, waving cutlasses and pistols, and wielding long boarding pikes, and shouting weird cries.

It is indeed a trap, Bazin realized, his brain in a fog, and someone is hailing in French from the *Calypso*'s quarterdeck. Surrender? Of course he surrendered; how could he fight? He turned to the cleat on which the halyard of the Tricolour was made up, but Roget was already undoing the figure of eights made by the rope and a moment later the flag came down. What will Captain Duroc say, he wondered. Where is he? Why didn't he shout a warning?

And then Bazin found himself staring at the point of an enormous sword held by a red-faced Englishman with a big paunch and flowing white hair. Not an officer, because he wore only a shirt and trousers. Then he remembered everyone on the *Calypso*'s quarterdeck was wearing shirts and trousers, which was another reason why he had fallen into the trap.

The Englishman was shouting something in English – *sur rendre?* That made no sense, but the man was sheathing his sword as if in disgust, and waving to men in blue uniforms. These must be the famous English Marines.

Bazin felt it was all a dream as he was taken across to the *Calypso* and lined up with his two officers on the quarterdeck. There was that fat man with white hair, looking very pleased with himself. And a pale-faced officer, who would never tan. And this other man, obviously the captain.

An aristo, too, that was certain; one had only to look at him, the slightly hooked nose, the high cheekbones, the tanned face, the dark hair bleached by the sun, the arrogant way he stood there, just looking at his prisoners. He too wore a shirt and trousers, but it was all part of the trap. Then Bazin looked carefully at the man's face and found himself staring at deep-set brown eyes that seemed to bore into him. He had to glance away because he knew those eyes would set him trembling. For the first time, Bazin realized, he was facing an aristo who could kill *him*. For years he had lived in an atmosphere where aristos – or men simply accused of being royalists – were hunted down like sheep and killed. Now a live one was looking at him – and, he realized, speaking in French and giving his name, Ramage. That word meant the song of the birds. The music of birds, rather. A pleasant word. Then he pronounced the name the English way, with a hard 'g', Ram-aidge, and he suddenly felt dizzy: this was the man, the famous English milord, Lord Ramage, although he had just given his first name, not the title. *The* Lord Ramage, the mad English aristo whose most recent escapade had been to capture two frigates off Diamond Rock only a few weeks ago, and sink two more, and seize the entire convoy on which Martinique was depending.

And Bazin suddenly knew why the *Calypso* had seemed familiar, a French ship. She was one of the frigates this milord Ramage had captured at Martinique. And that schooner towing her – Bazin remembered that two French schooners from Fort de France had been captured by this *assassin* a few days before the convoy arrived.

This milord was looking at him curiously. Oh yes, he had to surrender his sword. He was careful to hand it hilt-first, just in case one of those Marines thought he was threatening the captain.

'*Et le vaisseau,*' this milord was saying.

Had he the authority to surrender the ship? Yes, of course; there was no one else to do it, now Captain Duroc was not here.

'*Oui, et le vaisseau,* milord.'

Now Lord Ramage was turning to Roget, and Bazin realized that several times he had said 'milord', using the English word. It was the first time he had ever called any man 'lord', and here he was, only too anxious to say it to a foreigner. He knew he wanted to do anything to please this man, but he was not quite sure why, except that it was not only a desire to please. In France they guillotined the aristos, but here, under this blazing tropical sun, with English seamen

aloft in *La Perle*, furling the topsails, it was not France; here
the aristos could guillotine him – or order it with a snap of
finger and thumb.

They were marched down to the lowerdeck, and made to
stand by the mainmast, and all that fool Roget could say was:
'I told you so.'

'Told me what, cretin?'

'That it was a trap!'

'Ah yes, the moment before we crash alongside you scream
at me like a girl defending her virginity. It would have helped
if you had made that discovery five minutes earlier.'

'You were in command,' Roget retorted.

'I can't be watching everything!' Bazin snarled.

'You have to, if you're the captain.'

'You know who that man was?'

'The one with the eyes?'

'Yes, the captain,' Bazin said.

'Why should I know who he is?'

'You've heard of milord Ramage?'

Roget went pale. 'That's him? I didn't recognize the name
when he said it.'

'That's him! He pronounces it differently.'

'He'll have us shot . . .'

'Probably,' Bazin said. 'Duroc's already dead.'

'How do you know?'

'I just know. These aristos – as soon as they get their hands
on a true republican it is like that!' He made a chopping
motion with his hand.

Roget, the colour coming back to his face, shrugged his
shoulders. 'I suppose it's only fair.'

'What's fair?' Bazin asked suspiciously.

'The aristos killing republicans. After all, every aristo I've
ever seen was hauled off to the guillotine, or shot.'

'That's different.' Roget irritated him; Bazin was the first
to admit that. Only a fool like Roget could make that sort of
argument.

'Sometimes I think you are a royalist at heart, *Citoyen*
Roget.'

'Just because I point out that if we kill every aristo we find
we can't blame the aristos if they kill any republicans *they*
find?'

'Yes. Aristos are criminals. Like murderers. You have to

see justice done. We republicans have the duty of administering it.'

'Well, that milord doesn't look like a murderer to me. I'm glad my wife can't see him; she'd fall in love with him at once.'

'There you are,' Bazin said triumphantly, 'they run off with our women, and when they've had enough they cast them off. Like Moorish pashas. This one probably has a harem, too.'

'I envy him, then,' Roget said unexpectedly. 'If I was a milord I would have a *dozen* women. One of them would be Chinese. I saw a Chinese woman once. What eyes! No bosoms to speak of, I admit, but the eyes . . . A Chinese, an Italian, perhaps a Creole, and – now, let me see . . .'

Bazin listened, wide-eyed. Roget *was* a royalist; he had just given himself away with all that talk about a harem. But what did he mean about the Chinese woman? Did none of them have bosoms, or just the one that Roget saw? The Italian women (some of them, anyway, when they were young) were nearly as beautiful as French women. But black women, certainly not – though there are many in Martinique, tall and slim, their skins like ebony. Yet there are only a few white women out here that one can bear to look at – most have skins dried, voices shrill, always nagging at their husbands. Still, Roget was a royalist, although no one had previously suspected it.

And now that Marine lieutenant had come down the ladder and was looking at them. And he was pointing and beckoning. One of the sentries pulled him by the arm. Now Bazin knew they were going to shoot him. He turned to Roget. 'I forgive you,' he said, 'but for my sake stop this royalist talk.' He looked at the third lieutenant. '*Courage*,' he said, like a benediction. With that he braced his shoulders and began to climb the steps. After the second step his knees had an unfortunate tendency to fold, like shutting a pocket knife, but he managed to continue climbing. This was how the aristos felt when they climbed up to the platform of the guillotine . . .

On deck the sun was dazzling, and he followed the Marine lieutenant. He glanced astern, but no sentry followed, nor could he see the firing squad. Up the quarterdeck ladder *La Perle*'s topsails were now neatly furled and the two ships were still drifting alongside each other – and now down the companionway. This, Bazin knew, led to the captain's quarters.

At the foot of the companionway there was a Marine sentry who stood smartly to attention and saluted as the Marine officer passed, and he called some word into the cabin. Then Bazin was in the cabin, his head bent sideways to avoid hitting the beams overhead, and facing him, sitting at a desk, was this milord Ramage, who waved towards a settee and told him to sit down. The door shut and Bazin glanced up to see that the Marine lieutenant had left the cabin. He was alone with the milord. And his uniform was sticking to him and the perspiration was turning cold, and fresh beads of perspiration sprouting from his upper lip and forehead were cold, too, like rain on a glass window, and his breathing was shallow and he felt as though he was going to faint.

'Lieutenant Bazin, I must apologize for the ruse.'

His accent was perfect. He must have lived in France before the war – no foreigner could speak French like a Frenchman without living in France. The accent of Paris. In Lyon he would pass for a Parisian, Bazin was sure of that. But ruse?

'What ruse, milord?' There was the damned 'milord' again: it seemed so natural when talking to him, but he must guard his tongue against it.

'The flags, M. Bazin. But I am sure you know perfectly well that it is a legitimate *ruse de guerre* to fly another flag as long as it is lowered and one's own flag hoisted before opening fire.'

Bazin was puzzled. 'Yes, of course. We always do it when we sight an English merchant ship, or a privateer.'

'You do? So you have no ill-feelings about me doing it?'

Ill-feelings? What is he talking about? Bazin knew it was his own fault that he had not grasped the significance of the *Calypso*'s Tricolour coming down at the run. He shrugged his shoulders. And this milord was smiling, as though pleased. Bazin felt less chilly, but wondered if all this polite talk was not the prelude to another trap, another pat at the mouse by the cat's paw before the end came in a flurry of pain and blood.

'*La Perle* was a few hours late in leaving Aruba, M. Bazin?'

What a curious question. 'Several hours. In fact we nearly didn't leave at all.'

'Oh. Why was that?'

'The leak, of course. Touching that reef made it a lot worse.

The captain waited for some time before we left to make sure the pumps could hold it.'

'And they could, of course.'

'Only just, but there was no point in waiting in Aruba because we couldn't careen there to make repairs. Curaçao is the nearest safe place – and of course it would have to be to windward. That's why Captain Duroc was not going to stop for you – but he was curious when you made the signal.'

The milord was looking at him strangely now. He was leaning forward slightly in the chair that he had twisted round to face the settee. 'You had *all* your pumps going?'

'Oh yes – chain pump, deck wash pumps and men with buckets. Every available man took his turn.'

'And you were just holding the leak.'

'Yes, just. It was getting no worse, thank goodness. If only we could have reached Curaçao we'd have saved her.'

The milord stood up slowly and walked out through the door, and the Marine sentry came into the cabin to guard him. He heard the milord's shoes clattering up the companionway. He had gone to arrange for the firing squad. He will not bother to question Roget or the third lieutenant. He would bother to question only the man who had been commanding *La Perle* (admittedly very briefly).

Bazin was proud that, with the firing squad only minutes away, he had kept control of himself and told this milord nothing. Nothing except that they were going to Curaçao, and that was obvious enough to anyone who saw which way the ship was heading.

A few minutes later the milord came back again and the sentry left the cabin. The milord still had this pleasant smile on his face; the smile the cat has as it plays with the mouse. However, no aristo was going to fool Jean-Pierre Bazin with a smile.

'The privateers are waiting for you in Curaçao, M. Bazin.'

This is an obvious trap. 'Are they, milord?'

'I saw ten of them a few days ago. Perhaps more have arrived by now.'

'Very interesting, milord. There might be fifty, then.' That would worry him, Bazin knew. 'But they can get on quite well without *La Perle*, because we did not intend to call there. Not until we sprang this leak, rather.'

'Forgive my ignorance about all this, M. Bazin: I did not have time to talk to Captain Duroc.'

Look at those eyes: Bazin now knew what an *assassin* looked like. He had large brown eyes, the sort that would fool a woman like Roget's wife, and they were sunk deep below bushy brows, and he smiled such a friendly but false smile. No, milord had not bothered to talk to Duroc before murdering him, so he did not know that Duroc was making a desperate rush to get to Curaçao to careen the ship in the hope of finding the leak. No one was very optimistic, though; the whole garboard seam on the starboard side was leaking, and it seemed the entire transom was working loose because all the butt ends of the planks were weeping, although the caulking was still in the seams. The carpenter was puzzled and Duroc was frightened and he – ah, a chain pump had just started working somewhere this very moment because he could hear the distant clank-and-thump. And running water, like a distant stream. Now the clank of a head pump, and a second one has just started up. And a third and fourth, which was strange because *La Perle* had only two.

The milord was speaking again; something about *La Perle* working with the privateers. It was hard to concentrate, worrying about that leak, and he repeated the question.

'Does *La Perle* really not work with the privateers at Curaçao?'

Did this milord, this *rosbif crétin*, really think that *lieutenant de vaisseau* Bazin was going to give away secrets? 'No, she does not.' Nor did she, but there was no point in giving the enemy information.

'This patrol of *La Perle*'s, M. Bazin – might one ask if you were co-operating with the Spanish or the Dutch?'

'With neither.' That would puzzle him. This evil man could not imagine that *La Perle* was on an ordinary patrol, having arrived in Martinique from France with dispatches and being sent on a patrol of the eastern end of *la mer des Antilles* on her way back to France. But *La Perle* had first begun to leak a few days after leaving Brest; they had pumped her across the *Atlantique* to Fort de France; they had careened her there and the caulkers had hammered away at their cotton and the pitch had been heated and poured. And the leaks were stopped, but Duroc, always anxious to please and always impatient, had left for the patrol and for France without trials, and the leaks had started again the minute the frigate had sailed beyond the lee of the islands and reached the full strength of the Trades. Why Duroc called at Aruba no one knew, and the reef they hit was not shown on the chart – or, rather, it was shown with more water over it, but more coral must have grown. Anyway, the leak was now twice as bad, and the nearest careenage was Curaçao. However, you know nothing about all that, milord aristo.

Ramage found that after five minutes' conversation with Bazin he felt grubby. The man had a face which was startlingly like a weasel's; his manner, way of talking, and probably his way of thinking was the same. No doubt he was quick to pounce and bully or kill a weaker animal; but he was ingratiating when in the company of a stronger. And a fool, too; he had seen the Tricolour being hauled down, leaving only a British ensign flying, and he had thought nothing of it.

Out of curiosity it might be worth talking to the other two French lieutenants, just to find out their view of Citizen Bazin, but Ramage felt he could guess. And now Bazin was below again, under Marine guard, and no doubt quite certain that he had told the *rosbif* captain nothing . . .

Ramage went up on deck again and found both Aitken and Southwick waiting for him, shamefaced and looking like naughty schoolboys caught red-handed.

'I'm sorry, sir,' Aitken said. 'Southwick and the carpenter were just going on board her when you came up and told us about the leak, but –'

'But they should have finished their examination by then ...'

'Yes, sir.'

'And you've no explanation for this lapse.'

'No, sir,' Aitken said contritely. 'None at all.'

'I'll give you one,' Ramage said, 'and it's a lesson we've all just learned. Just because no shots have been fired, don't assume a prize isn't damaged and sinking.'

'Aye,' Southwick said, 'and it's worse than that, sir: they could have scuttled her – they should have done, in fact – and I just leaned on the quarterdeck rail and looked at her. I even noticed she rolled more than we did and had less freeboard, but I never thought the reason was that she had several feet of water in her.'

'Well, how's the pumping going?'

Southwick grinned cheerfully. 'With three hundred prisoners and our own pumps on board as well, it's no problem. No man has more than a quarter of an hour at a pump, but he has to work like a madman. It's the only way we'll get the level down.'

'She's making seven feet an hour,' Ramage said.

'Yes, but if we can empty her while she's alongside us, then the French can hold her with their own pumps without much trouble. We've got all the Frenchmen pumping – purser, bosun, sailmaker, captain's steward, everyone is taking a turn.'

Aitken was still rather chastened, and he said to Ramage: 'After we've pumped her dry and left the French prisoners to hold their seven feet an hour, what are we going to do with her, sir?'

Ramage shrugged his shoulders. 'After capturing her for the price of some cloth to make flags, it seems a pity to let her sink; but our orders are to deal with those privateers. I can't spare fifty men to take *La Perle* to Jamaica. More than fifty, because the prizemaster would need enough men to sail her and enough to guard three hundred Frenchmen and keep them busy pumping.'

'But losing a prize like this, sir!' Southwick protested.

'The chances of her reaching Jamaica with these leaks even if I put a hundred of our men on board are remote.'

'How so, sir?'

'The leaks are getting worse. I don't think she's just spewing her caulking; I'm sure she's rotten and the fastenings are going. The planks are loosening as the hull works in anything of a sea and popping 'em out. The next thing will be the butt ends of planks suddenly springing, and then she'll sink in ten minutes.'

Southwick scratched his head. 'Well, we can't take three hundred prisoners on board, that's certain. Still, we could put 'em on shore right here, in Curaçao. Land 'em on that beach there.'

'And give the privateers in Amsterdam another thirty men each?'

'I hadn't thought of that,' Southwick admitted. 'But if we don't bring 'em on board and don't put 'em on shore . . . ?'

Ramage began walking up and down the quarterdeck, hands clasped behind his back. If all revolutions replaced uncomfortable breeches and white stockings which showed every dirty mark with loose-fitting trousers, he thought wryly, then officers would be well advised to change their politics. With *La Perle* captured he had no excuse for not going down to his cabin and putting on his uniform. The same applied to the rest of the *Calypso*'s officers. Perhaps they were waiting for the captain to give a lead, afraid of offending him by appearing in uniform when he still wore trousers. Perhaps (and much more likely) they were as comfortable as he was and in no hurry to return to the uncomfortable and hot smartness of breeches.

All this thinking about trousers and breeches was wasting time; he had to make up his mind as soon as possible about *La Perle* and her three hundred men. Very well, state the problem. Well, three problems, sir. I can't spare a prize crew to sail (and pump) her to Jamaica, and anyway she'd probably sink in the first gale she met. But, problem two, I can't leave her drifting. She has to be sunk – or set on fire. That leaves me with problem three, the three hundred prisoners whom I daren't land in Aruba or Curaçao, because they'll immediately become privateersmen.

Given that *La Perle* was eventually bound back to France and would have sunk on the way, her meeting with the *Calypso* is hardly a stroke of good fortune for the British, least of all the *Calypso*, which loses prize money and head money, and whose captain will have to face the wrath of Admiral Foxe-Foote, who is not going to like losing his share of the prize money.

Very well, milord, as that wretched Bazin insisted on addressing you, with true republican regard to ingratiating himself, reduce the problems to their simplest terms. God it's hot; the deck throws up waves of heat. No sails set to cause a cooling downdraught, no awning stretched to make some shade. And here is Jackson with a straw hat for me to wear. A thoughtful act: he felt as though his brains were already frying, and his eyes seemed scorched from the glare.

The problem, he reminded himself, tipping the hat farther forward so that it shaded his eyes more completely, the problem is really quite simple: how to dispose of a French frigate without drowning her ship's company or handing them over to the French privateersmen in Curaçao.

Quite simple, milord: turn both ships and men over to the Dons.

He stopped in mid-stride. That *was* the answer! Where it

came from he was far from sure; probably lurking inside this straw hat. The French could land from *La Perle* on the Spanish Main, but they must not be able to repair the ship. His head buzzed with ideas, but none was any use until he looked at a chart.

He glanced over at *La Perle* and saw clear streams of water pouring out of her scuppers and from the hoses of head pumps rigged on the sides. *La Créole* was tacking back and forth to windward; the two frigates were drifting slowly to leeward, westward along the coast of Curaçao. The weather seemed set fair. The only really miserable men on board the *Calypso* should be Duroc, Bazin and the two junior lieutenants.

Down in his cabin he pitched the straw hat on to the settee and pulled a chart out of the rack, unrolling it on his desk and holding it down flat with weights. The nearest part of the Main was in fact a long semicircle stretching from the tip of the Peninsula de Paraguana, the hatchet-shaped piece of land forming one side of the Gulf of Venezuela and leading down to Maracaibo, round to (for practical purposes) San Juan de los Cayos, a hundred and fifty miles to the eastward. Notes on his chart showed that there was not a port along that stretch where *La Perle* could be careened and repaired, nothing on the Peninsula apart from a mountain range topped by Pan de Santa Ana, a peak nearly 3000 feet high and visible for sixty miles on a clear day – which meant that any ship sailing south-west from Curaçao would sight it within a few hours. Just where the hatchet-handle joined the mainland was La Vela de Coro, a large village on the bay. A soft mud bottom, frequent breakers, a sea whipped up by almost any breeze . . . Yes, hardly the place to careen a fishing smack, let alone a frigate.

Then came Cumarebo, which although the Spanish gave it the name 'Puerto' was simply an open roadstead in front of the town. After that was another small village, and then nothing for a dozen miles to Punta Zamuro, a coastline formed by sandy beaches, clay bluffs, shallow water . . . Punta Aguida had a red clay bluff and shallows of less than three fathoms more than a mile offshore . . . And, after a long stretch, the Bay of San Juan. The point sheltered it from the Trade winds coming from the east and north-east, but there was only twenty feet of water a mile offshore. As long as *La Perle* was not half full of water, she could get fairly close in, but she would not careen . . .

Now for the distances. He opened the dividers. Fifty miles would bring *La Perle* to anywhere on the Peninsula; a hundred miles would take her down to San Juan de los Cayos. The wind would be on the beam so she would make a fast passage, but give her the benefit of the doubt and say she averaged only three knots and went to San Juan de los Cayos. Thirty-three hours, a day and a half at the outside.

He called to the Marine sentry to pass the word for the first lieutenant, lieutenant of Marines, master and purser. The purser was the last to arrive, looking alarmed at suddenly being summoned to the captain's cabin.

Ramage decided to deal with him first, to put him out of his misery. 'Tell Mr Southwick the quantity of water needed for two days by three hundred men working extremely hard in this climate.'

'Water, sir? You don't mean beer?'

'No, nor cheese nor butter. Just water.'

Rowlands's lips moved as he did some mental arithmetic. Finally he gave a figure. Ramage thanked him and the man left the cabin.

'Remember that figure, Mr Southwick. Now, gentlemen, at midnight *La Perle* leaves us, escorted by *La Créole*, bound for the Main – anywhere between the entrance to the Gulf of Venezuela and San Juan de los Cayos. Come and look at this chart and refresh your memories.'

The three men inspected it, and Rennick said: 'All the Marines on board her as guards, sir?'

His face fell when Ramage shook his head and said: 'There'll be no guards. The Frenchmen will be alone on board: just *La Créole* to keep them company.'

Aitken was the first to grasp what Ramage had said. 'But, sir, what's to stop them making for Martinique?'

'Or attacking us?' added Southwick. 'No good putting them on parole; they'd never keep their word.'

'Sit down,' Ramage said. 'You all have jobs to do, so pay attention. *La Perle* sails at midnight under the command of Duroc, and he has the choice of the destinations I've just shown you, and –'

'But what's to stop him going somewhere else?' Southwick interrupted.

'Because all his charts will have been removed,' Ramage

said patiently. 'Removed by you. And your mates will comb
the officers' cabins for anything resembling a chart. And just
before he boards *La Perle* you will present him with an
accurate but not overly-detailed copy of this section of the
chart – ' Ramage tapped the chart on his desk. 'This section
only. That means he has little choice of destinations. He
could go to Aruba, but he left there because there was nowhere to careen *La Perle*. It is unlikely he knows the coast
of the Main – this section, anyway – so he won't know there's
nowhere there for him to careen, either.'

'He doesn't need a chart to get up to Martinique,' Southwick pointed out. 'He knows the latitude of Fort Royal . . .'

'That won't help him. He'll have only two days' water on
board because you, Southwick, will empty the rest of the
casks and that fresh water will be pumped over the side with
the salt. With three hundred men and water for only two days,
he needs to get somewhere in two days, which rules out
Martinique by several days. You will also dispose of all the
wine and spirits – over the side, of course.'

'Sir,' Rennick said anxiously, 'the guns . . .'

'Aitken will supply you with a working party and you will
flood the hanging magazine. I don't want an ounce of usable
powder in the ship. All the great guns are to be spiked and
you'll cut the breechings. All the locks for the guns are to
be brought on board the *Calypso*, along with all flints,
muskets, pistols, cutlasses, tomahawks and pikes.

'Leave the shot in the locker – we don't have time to get
them out, and anyway we are not concerned in reducing her
draught – but all those on deck can be hove over the side.'

Southwick combined a doubtful sniff with a vigorous
scratching of his head, and Ramage smiled as he looked at
the master. 'What's worrying you, Mr Southwick?'

'Well, sir, I still can't see why this fellow Duroc *has* to
make for the Main, and what good it does when he gets
there.'

'He has water for only two days,' Ramage repeated
patiently. 'Obviously that limits his range for two days' sailing. But, more important, his ship is making seven feet of
water an hour. That means with every man taking his turn
at the pumps and bailing with buckets he can just keep her
afloat. But for how long can he pump and bail? The men have

to get some rest, quite apart from sailing the ship – and in this heat they have to drink a lot of water.'

'But when he arrives off the Main – say at La Vela de Coro – and anchors, he can get fresh water from the Dons and careen the ship.'

Ramage shook his head. 'Even supposing Duroc can get water, he has only enough casks for two days – he'll never get more locally – he's still tied to a radius of two days' sailing from La Vela. Don't forget Martinique is almost dead to windward, six hundred miles or more, and that much punching to windward will double the leaks. So he's condemned to stay and pump wherever he first anchors, and my guess is he'll end up so exhausted he'll have to run the ship ashore – or land his men in the boats and let the ship sink. He has no other choice. But whatever happens, we're rid of her and the three hundred men.'

'And *La Créole*, sir?' Aitken prompted.

'She's our insurance. She keeps *La Perle* company until Duroc is anchored somewhere. Lacey has nothing to fear from the Spanish and the French frigate will not have even a pistol on board. Drilling out the spikes in the great guns will be beyond them – tell the carpenter to take off all suitable drill bits and small awls, Mr Aitken. Lacey could batter her to pieces in an hour or two, if Duroc tried any tricks.'

By an hour before midnight the two head pumps and hoses from the *Calypso* were being brought back on board from *La Perle* and Southwick reported that the French frigate's own pumps were holding the leaks. Ramage had gone through the ship in the last of the daylight, inspecting the nails which had been hammered into the touchholes of all the great guns to spike them, the heads cut off, the ends riveted to make it impossible to pull them out. Only drilling would make the guns usable again – many hours of patient work with the proper tools which only an armourer would have. *La Perle*'s armourer did have them, but his elaborately carved and brass-bound box of tools was now on board the *Calypso*, whose armourer was walking round with the unbelieving smile of a small boy given the Christmas present about which he dreamed but never thought to get.

Water casks had been smashed and the hoops thrown over

the side, the staves lying about in the holds like dozens of pieces of melon rind. A few casks had been left untouched: the two days' supply of water for the three hundred men. The hanging magazine, a lathe-and-plaster-lined cabin whose deck was three feet below the normal deck level so that it could be flooded with hoses, was now a small rectangular pond, the water slopping as the ship rolled, with scores of what seemed like dead cats floating in it – the cartridges for the guns. Casks of powder had their bungs removed; the grey powder they contained was sodden and some had washed out so that the water had the consistency of a thin grey soup.

Southwick and Aitken had made a thorough job of limiting *La Perle*'s range. Bags of bread had been ripped open and the hard tack they contained soaked with salt water, taking care that none of the resulting mash went into the bilge, where it would plug the strainers and block the pumps. Casks of cheese, jars of oil, barrels of sauerkraut (which accounted for the vile smell), sacks and casks of oatmeal – all had been smashed, cut open, or the contents spoiled with salt water.

All the books and papers from the cabins of the captain and the master – they included another signal book, and the order book giving every order Duroc had received since before leaving France – were now stacked in Ramage's cabin, while the charts were in Southwick's. At the purser's suggestion, only a couple of dozen candles had been left in the ship. It was a very good idea but Ramage had been amused at the reason behind it. In the Royal Navy the purser had to pay for and supply free all the candles used in a ship, and now the *Calypso* had a windfall of several hundred, admittedly thin and of poor quality. No doubt Rowlands was hoping – though he would not dare suggest it – that the captain would not mention the acquisition in the *Calypso*'s log. This would, Ramage noted wryly, make the purser the only man to make a financial profit from *La Perle*'s capture.

The French prisoners were quite cheerful, despite the pumping, and Ramage had stopped to chat with several of them. A few grumbled about blistered hands and aching backs from the hours they had spent at the pumps, but the only real complaint was the heat: it was the heat that was exhausting them. Curiously enough, no one had asked what was going to happen to them, yet with several of the men – the master, carpenter and bosun, for example – Ramage had chatted for some time, with none of them realizing that he was the *Calypso*'s captain.

An hour to midnight, and there was *La Créole*'s lantern: Lacey had been on board the *Calypso* to receive his orders and was obviously delighted with them. Ramage recognized the expression on Lacey's face when he realized he was going off on his own – or, rather, would be free of his senior officer for a few days. How in the past Ramage himself had prayed for such orders, and luckily Lacey had grasped the need to obey them implicitly. If there was any sign that *La Perle* was trying to make for anywhere but the agreed stretch of the Main, he was to warn her by firing a shot across her bow, and, if that was not sufficient, he was at once to rake her with broadsides until she obeyed or was a wreck.

On the other hand, if she was obviously going to sink before reaching the Main, Lacey could leave them two of his own boats because the frigate had more men than her own four boats could carry. Aitken had already made sure that two of *La Perle*'s boats had compasses. None had water, though; the breakers were left in them, but the French master had been warned that they were empty and, in any emergency, would first need filling.

Once again Ramage looked at his watch. The two frigates had drifted well to the west of Curaçao now, and there was half an hour to go before *La Perle* would be cast off. Now was the time to give Duroc his instructions, and to spring the final (and, he admitted, quite malicious) surprise on Citizen Bazin.

He went to his cabin after passing the word that Duroc was to be brought up, but without the other prisoners seeing him. At the moment the Frenchman knew absolutely nothing, other than what he could have guessed from the evidence of his own ears. Ramage had not been down to talk to him; the Marine sentries guarding him in Aitken's cabin had been warned to say nothing, in case Duroc could in fact speak English. Bazin and the other lieutenants did not know he was there; they knew nothing of him.

The man brought into Ramage's cabin by two Marines was a shrunken version of the burly braggart sent below under guard before *La Perle* was captured. The dim light of the lantern emphasized the deep lines of worry, marking his face like crevices in a cliff, and he was licking his lips nervously like someone caricaturing a nervous man. His shoulders were hunched, as if unconsciously hiding his neck from a guillotine blade.

Ramage kept him standing so that the man had to cock his head to one side.

'Ah, Captain Duroc, you know what has happened to your ship?'

'You captured her. I hear her alongside. And the pumps, I hear them working.'

Ramage nodded. 'Your men are still on board her. The five who were wounded have been treated and put back on board – their wounds were slight.'

'Five? How many dead?'

'None.'

'And now, sir?' Duroc's eyes revealed his fears of what would happen when the French Ministry of Marine in Paris heard those figures. The captain not on board, no one killed, the ship lost to the enemy – it could only mean treason to minds so accustomed to finding or manufacturing it.

Ramage handed him the chart which Southwick had drawn. 'Sit down there, on that settee. You can read the chart – there is enough light? Good. Now, you know your ship is sinking?'

Duroc nodded miserably.

'But you are confident your pumps can keep up with the leaks?'

Again Duroc nodded. 'Yes, but if they get worse . . .'

'Quite, you risk the leaks getting worse, and your men are becoming exhausted. That was why you were making for Curaçao, to careen her?'

Duroc nodded for the third time, studying the chart.

'Your destination is now changed. You will be put back on board your ship in a few minutes, and you will have that chart, and water for all your men for two days. There is no powder, the guns are spiked, and my schooner will escort you to Spanish waters.'

Duroc looked up at him, accepting the situation but obviously assuming some trap. 'We shall not be prisoners, then?'

'Only of yourselves and your ship. For two days the leaks and the pumps will be your guards.'

The Frenchman used his fingers to measure distances. 'One

day, perhaps two,' he said, almost to himself. 'Yes, that is good. But . . .'

'Have you any questions?'

'Yes, M'sieur. Why are you freeing us?'

'I don't want three hundred prisoners,' Ramage said frankly. 'I have orders from my admiral and I need all my men.'

Duroc made no secret of his relief: he believed the answer, perhaps because it was a logical one, and said: 'I do not know your name, M'sieur. You are being very fair to us. I would like to know to whom I am indebted.'

The Frenchman had spoken very formally and was obviously sincere. Ramage remembered Bazin and said casually, giving his name the English pronunciation: 'Nicholas Ramage, *capitaine de vaisseau.*'

Duroc nodded and repeated the name. Suddenly he looked up, wide-eyed. 'Lord Ramage?'

Ramage nodded.

'*Merde!* Then this is a trap!'

The change was so sudden Ramage was unsure whether to be flattered or insulted. 'What do you mean, a trap?'

Clearly Duroc was now a very frightened man; he was folding and refolding the chart like a nun with a rosary. 'Well, you – why, it is well known that . . .'

'That what?'

'I don't know,' Duroc admitted lamely. 'But capturing that convoy off Martinique, and the frigates . . .'

'I could of course smash *La Perle*'s chain pump, stave in all the boats, and cast you adrift. The ship would sink and you'd all drown in – half an hour?'

'Less. And I cannot swim.'

'But instead I have left you water and boats, given you a chart so that you can sail to safety, and provided an escort. This "trap" has a strange bait, Captain Duroc. I wonder if you would be as generous if our positions were reversed?'

'No, forgive me,' Duroc said. 'I spoke hastily. It was the shock of finding out who you are. You have a certain – well, a certain reputation.'

'Not for cruelty, I trust.'

'Oh no! Nothing to your discredit, milord.'

Ramage waved to one of the sentries. 'Fetch the French officer called Bazin.'

He sat down at his desk and turned the chair so that he

could see the door, telling the Marine sentry: 'Take this prisoner into the coach, and keep him there until I call you. You won't need a lantern; just keep your cutlass pressing against his shoulder blades.' He then explained to Duroc that he would have to wait in the next cabin.

Bazin, in contrast to Duroc, had regained some of his courage or, Ramage thought, more likely he had been goaded by the other two lieutenants into truculent belligerency.

'Sit down,' Ramage told him. 'The time has come for us to say farewell.'

'I expected nothing more,' Bazin sneered.

'Nothing more than what?'

'You haven't shot us; I presume you will now throw us over the side.'

'Yes,' Ramage could not resist saying, 'you are all going over the side in a few minutes.'

'Ha! I knew from the first you were an *assassin*!'

'Tell me, how did you discover that?'

'The way you murdered Captain Duroc.'

'Oh, *that*!' Ramage said in an offhand voice, suspecting that the Frenchman in the next cabin would be amused. 'What else did you expect? Surely such a man does not deserve to live?'

'That may be so,' Bazin exclaimed angrily, 'but who are you to kill him?'

Ramage shrugged his shoulders. 'He was not a true republican.'

'I know that well enough,' Bazin said as he half rose but sank back when he saw the Marine's cutlass. 'But that is no reason for you, an aristo, to murder us.'

'But why should I murder him but spare you?' Ramage enquired mildly.

'Because . . . well, because . . . what I mean is, you should not murder me because I am a true republican; I believe in the freedom and equality of man. But Duroc – he was an *opportuniste*. He was a bosun before the Revolution. He joined the Revolution only to get promotion!'

Ramage took out his watch and inspected it. 'Ten minutes before midnight, *citoyen*. For us,' and he could not resist putting a slight emphasis on 'us', 'the new day is about to begin.'

He called to the sentry in the other cabin, and a minute

later Duroc stamped through the door. Bazin leapt to his feet like a rocket, white-faced, crashed his head against the beam, and fell flat at Duroc's feet. The French captain looked across at Ramage, a grin on his face. 'He knows all about revolutions. By dawn he'll know all about working a chain pump, too. You have a droll sense of humour, milord, but it brings out the truth at times.'

CHAPTER ELEVEN

Amsterdam's houses were painted in gay colours which the glaring sun emphasized without making them garish. The owners on the Punda side obviously preferred pinks and light blues while Otrabanda favoured reds, greens and white, but most of the roofs, steeply pitched and gabled in the Dutch style, had red tiles, in contrast to the wooden shingles favoured in the British islands. It was curious about the colour preferences but, Ramage thought, the explanation was probably mundane: the paint shop on one side stocked some colours; its rival the others.

The channel separating the two halves of the town was stained brown as it joined Sint Anna Baai, probably due to the slight rise and fall of tide draining out some of the water as it ebbed from the Schottegat, the inland lake.

The fort on Punda, Waterfort, seemed quiet enough; nor was there any sign of movement at Riffort on Otrabanda, 'the other side'. The Dutch flags were flying from flagpoles on both forts; it was also flying from the building that Ramage assumed was Government House.

Amsterdam, Ramage decided, was an oddly attractive and typically Dutch town set down on an arid and desolate island whose sole function was to be the main Dutch trading post in the Caribbean. The Dutch had done their best to make the town look cheerful and they had succeeded. If you forgot the heat and the bright glare, Amsterdam could be any town built along a canal in the Netherlands. Certainly the general flatness of the island (if one did not look to the west as the hills began and rolled up to Sint Christoffelberg) made you think that the average Dutchman was only happy on flat land, although from seaward small hills gave the appearance of waves in a choppy sea.

The privateers were at anchor just at the entrance to Schottegat and still had the laid-up-out-of-commission look about them. He had only a fleeting glance of them through the telescope as the *Calypso* tacked in towards the shore, but it was enough to show him that nothing had changed since they had passed on their way to the west end of the island.

Aitken shut his telescope with a snap. 'That fresh lot of smoke near Willebrordus puzzles me, sir. I'm sure it's from burning buildings. Black smoke with the white. If it was just scrub and grass burning, it would be white.'

'And I'm sure I could hear gunfire,' Wagstaffe said. No one else had heard it, but they had been almost to leeward of the smoke at the time and Ramage was quite prepared to believe the second lieutenant. Rennick, in his usual impulsive way, had wanted to be landed in Bullen Bay with a platoon of Marines to investigate, but as Ramage pointed out, gunfire and smoke in Curaçao was the concern of the Dutch Governor, and the Dutch, like the French and Spanish, were the enemy . . . Fire could only mean the destruction of bush and cactus, a few scraggy divi-divi trees, aloes and agaves, and perhaps some plantation houses (not many because there were few plantations). The goats and iguana would bolt, the wild doves would take off for quieter corners of the island, and the fire would eventually burn out.

The *Calypso*, under topsails alone in a fifteen-knot breeze that occasionally whipped up small white caps in sudden gusts, was steering north-west towards Piscadera Baai as Ramage looked up the channel into the Schottegat. But so far the only reaction to the frigate's presence in this part of the Caribbean seemed to be fish leaping away from her stem, like dogs dodging a careering carriage, and swarms of flying fish coming up out of the water like small silver arrows without making a ripple, then skimming above the waves for scores of yards and suddenly vanishing without the tiniest splash. The frigate birds, broad-winged with thin bodies, black and white, graceful in flight (yet to Ramage always ugly and menacing), swooped down on the flying fish, showing a fantastic skill in flying but attacked by the tiny laughing gulls. The chubbier boobies flew low, and often rested on the water like old ladies sitting in a market selling their wares, beady eyes alert, or dived for a fish. Very occasionally half a dozen dolphins played under the *Calypso*'s bow, swimming at enormous speeds and crossing ahead of her so close it seemed they must be hit by the cutwater. The cry of 'Dolphins' usually sent the off-watch men running to the bowsprit and jibboom, from where they would 'ooooh!' and 'aaaah!' until the dolphins vanished as quickly as they arrived.

Ramage decided to make one more tack across Sint Anna Baai, passing two miles off Waterfort and Riffort to wake up the gunners and perhaps provoke them into firing. This rattling of the bars was useful because although the *Calypso* had nothing to fear from shore guns at that range it was usually too close for them to resist firing. Careful observation of the puffs of smoke could reveal how many guns a fort had, and if they had not been fired for a long time they could sometimes do their owners considerable harm: a wooden carriage with hidden rot could send a gun barrel weighing a couple of tons spinning away in a shower of smoke and flame like a carelessly-thrown stick. Roundshot painted too frequently or neglected and rusted invariably ended up larger than they should be, like swollen grapefruit, and they could stick in the bore, with the gunners left unsure whether or not to fire the gun to clear it in case the barrel blew apart. Tacking back and forth in front of the forts and just outside their effective range was as good a way of teasing the enemy as any and always pleased the ship's company.

Taking the ship in closer than intended was also a way of ensuring smart sail handling, Ramage mused. Lucky shooting which took away a mast or yard when fifty other shot had missed altogether seemed to happen more frequently at long range than close in. And many ships sailing in boldly with a nice fresh breeze to intimidate a shore battery had been lost when the wind suddenly vanished, leaving them becalmed, a stationary target and an artilleryman's dream.

He lifted his telescope for one more look at the town – from this angle he could see the third side of Riffort on Otrabanda. Beyond it, on Punda, there was a curious movement round the flagpole at Government House. In fact the big Dutch flag was being lowered. He looked at the flags on the two forts, but they were still flying. Yet – yes, there were several men round the bases of each flagpole.

Now a bundle was going up the flagpole at Government

House and breaking out to stream in the wind – a plain white flag. Another was being run up to replace the Dutch flag on the fort at Punda. And now a third was being hoisted at Riffort.

A white flag, the flag of truce? Well, there was no question about its meaning; everyone treated it as a truce flag, the signal for a parley. But here, in Amsterdam, with ten French privateers safely anchored inside the two forts guarding the entrance? What could –

Aitken suddenly exclaimed as he saw the flags; then the lookout at the foremast hailed the quarterdeck. In a few moments the whole ship was buzzing with comment and speculation. Southwick, quite inevitably, sniffed and announced that it was a trick; that the *Calypso*, with *La Perle* hardly out of sight, should not get caught on her own bait.

'They can see we've a good breeze out here and there's probably a dead patch close in under their guns that we don't know about and where we'd be becalmed,' he announced. 'It's no good trusting *mynheer*; he's a cunning fellow. Drives a hard bargain – and fights hard, too.'

Ramage walked over to the binnacle and looked at the compass card. The wind was due east; with the yards braced sharp the *Calypso* could lay north-north-east, almost direct for Amsterdam. A bow-on approach gave the Dutch gunners the smallest target and made it harder to estimate – or guess – the range, because calculating the speed of an approaching ship was difficult. More important, the wind allowing him a direct approach also gave him a choice of direction if he needed to escape: ease sheets and bear away to the west or tack and bear away if he preferred the east.

A quiet order to Baker, who was the officer of the deck, had the Marine drummer beating his ruffles, which sent the men to quarters. A second order had the coxswain watching the compass and the men at the wheel as they brought the ship round three points to starboard.

By the time the trucks began rumbling as the guns were run out, the *Calypso* was headed for the channel separating the two halves of the town. In the distant days of peace, Ramage reflected, the *Calypso* would be preparing to fire a salute to 'the place', as the Regulations and Instructions termed it.

He checked the compass and noted the *Calypso*'s bow was

now heading a fraction to the north of north-north-east, although the men at the wheel were on course.

'Watch for the current, Mr Baker; it seems to be westgoing and quite strong, perhaps a couple of knots.'

It did not really matter because the *Calypso* most certainly was not going up the channel, but young lieutenants are supposed to be quick to note currents. In many Caribbean ports a few degrees to one side or other of the course meant you would hit a rock waiting alone and unmarked for the careless mariner. Many rocks were named on charts after the ships that had hit and sunk beside them. It was the kind of enduring fame, Ramage thought, that he would gladly avoid.

Southwick had put down his quadrant and looked up after consulting a volume of tables. 'We're a mile and three-quarters off the forts, sir.'

'Very well, Mr Southwick.'

Ramage opened his telescope once again, careful to set it at the focusing mark he had filed on the brass tube, and looked at the forts. There were a few people standing on the walls. Although it was impossible to be sure at this distance, they seemed to be watching rather than preparing for action. From their point of view the *Calypso* was approaching fast (they had an excellent view of her bow-wave, which must look like a white moustache), and one would expect even the most controlled of battery commanders to open fire at a mile if he meant to be unfriendly. At the speed the *Calypso* was making, she'd be a mile off in about seven minutes.

Now Aitken was officer of the deck; Wagstaffe, Baker and Kenton were standing by their divisions of guns. Paolo Orsini (wearing a seaman's cutlass as well as that wretched little dirk, Ramage was glad to see) was waiting, telescope in one hand and the signal book in the other. Southwick, his usual burly self, was at the starboard side of the quarterdeck rail, using his quadrant, quite convinced that the Dutch were up to some trick but obviously unperturbed at the prospect.

The master turned and said casually: 'A mile off the fort on Otrabanda, sir.'

'Very well, Mr Southwick.'

A mile . . . why the devil was he going in so close? Ramage felt a sudden chill. Just because the Dutch had hoisted flags of truce, he had taken the *Calypso* almost into the port; yet the Dutch could just as easily lower the white flags, suddenly rehoist the Dutch colours in their place, and open fire – and quite fairly claim it was all a *ruse de guerre*. After all, he'd just done it himself to *La Perle* . . .

Yet his telescope still showed men standing on the walls of the fort at Otrabanda. And at Punda. But – what *was* going on there now, on the Punda side of the channel?

'Mr Orsini, hurry! Aloft with your telescope and tell me what that boat is doing in the channel.'

While Paolo bolted for the shrouds both Aitken and South-wick trained their telescopes forward, having to move across the quarterdeck to find a place where their view was not obscured by the bowsprit, jibboom or rigging.

'It looks like a boat the size of our gig, sir,' Aitken reported. 'Pulling perhaps six oars a side. And they are in a hurry!'

Ramage left Aitken to keep an eye on the boat: the *Calypso* was approaching the port so fast now that if there was going to be any treachery it would happen in the next few moments. The first warning would be those men vanishing from the walls of the forts: they would have their eardrums burst if they stayed there while the Dutch guns fired. If they vanished from the battlements, the *Calypso* would immediately tack out again: they would be his danger signal.

'The boat's hoisting a mast, or something, sir,' Aitken said, his voice showing uncertainty. 'It's bigger than an oar but seems too short for a mast. And I can't think why they'd step a mast now: it would have been easier to do it alongside the quay.'

The *Calypso* was almost gliding now as she came in with the land, which was flat enough not to interrupt the wind but formed a lee from the swell waves, so the sea was almost flat. Suddenly, just as Aitken reported he could not make out what was going on in the boat because he could not get a clear view, an excited Paolo hailed from high up in the mainmast. 'A boat is pulling out towards us, sir . . . Twelve oars . . . Only one or two people in the sternsheets . . . Now they're holding up a white cloth on an oar . . . they're waving it, sir . . .'

Ramage noted the men on the battlements had not moved and called to the first lieutenant: 'Back the foretopsail, Mr Aitken: we'll heave to and let the boat come out to us.'

'We're three-quarters of a mile off the forts, sir,' Southwick reported as Aitken shouted the orders which sent men running to haul on the braces, swinging the foretopsail yard round so that the wind was blowing on the forward side of the sail, pressing it against the mast.

The *Calypso* slowly came to a stop. With the wind thrusting on the forward side of the foretopsail and trying to push the bow off to leeward and the rest of the sails trying to push her round to windward, the frigate was in a state of equilibrium, with the waves passing beneath her as though she was a sitting gull having a rest.

Flags of truce at the flagpoles, an open boat rowing out from Punda and waving a flag of truce . . . It was unlikely to be a trap; Ramage felt reasonably sure of that much. The men were still on the battlements and the boat needed to cover only a few more hundred yards before the *Calypso* could blow her out of the water with a round of grape or canister. It could still be a trap: sacrificing a dozen men in a boat would be nothing compared with the capture of an enemy frigate, but he did not think the Dutch mind worked like that. Nor was the boat a necessary part of any deception: the *Calypso* was already heading in to investigate before the boat left the quay.

'It looks as if we are going to have visitors, sir,' Aitken commented, looking through his telescope as soon as he was satisfied that the foretopsail sheets, tacks and braces were properly settled. 'I can see that the men sitting in the sternsheets of yon boat are wearing a deal of gold braid.'

Ramage glanced down at his own coat. It was faded, but no more than one would expect; his breeches were clean and so were his stockings. His shoes had lost their polish in the salt air but the gold buckles gleamed. He was wearing his third best hat. All quite sufficient for entertaining enemy officers who chose to pay unexpected calls, and only the cutlass looked out of place. He preferred a seaman's cutlass to his own sword, even if it was a fine example of the sword cutler's art: Mr Prater of Charing Cross, who made it, would be upset if he knew that Lord Ramage usually went into action with a cutlass like any of his seamen, leaving his fine sword in its scabbard on the rack in his cabin.

Now, however, was a time when courtesy (custom, anyway) demanded that he go down to his cabin and put on the sword. When dealing with one's own people, clothes rarely counted (except when paying official calls on officers like Admiral Foxe-Foote, who was the sort of man who never paid his own

tailor but was very fussy what his officers wore); but foreign
dignitaries set great store by braid, buttons and buckles, and
the lack of a few inches of gold braid could easily give the
wrong impression of the rank or worth of the wearer.

As he acknowledged the Marine sentry's salute, the door
of his cabin opened and his steward stood there, a cheerful
expression on his face.

'I have fresh stock and stockings and your uniform ready,
sir.'

'What on earth for, Silkin?'

'Why, to meet the deputation, sir!'

'Deputation? It's probably the mayor's brother who owns
a bumboat business and wants to sell us limes, or some worn-
out goats. Or, from the look of the island, wanting to know
if we'll sell *them* some water.'

By now Ramage had reached his sleeping cabin and Silkin,
like an Arab carpet vendor displaying his wares, was holding
up clean breeches, and nodding towards stockings, shirt and
stock. They looked cool. The stock he was wearing was tied
a little too tightly and, damp with perspiration, chafing the
skin and rasping, particularly on a patch by his Adam's apple
which he had not shaved very well. He looked down at his
stockings. There were black marks on the inside of the left
ankle where he had accidentally caught it with his right shoe.

The boat had a long way to row, even though the wind and
sea were on its quarter, and Ramage knew that it needed no
effort to change, either, with the ship hove-to; the roll was
almost imperceptible and she was not pitching. In fact it was
an invitingly refreshing prospect: the cabin was cool because
a breeze had been sweeping through it while the ship was
under way. Changing his clothes also delayed him having to
go back to the heat and glare on deck . . .

He sat down on a chair and kicked off his shoes, getting
immediate relief because his feet were swollen. The size of
shoe that fitted in the early morning and evening was much
too small when the midday heat made feet swell and throb.
Feet and head: the glare of the sun made your eyes want to
pop, and the heat, even coming through a hat, seemed to fry
your brain.

He stripped off his clothes and pulled on the fresh garments.
For a brief couple of minutes the stockings were cool; then
he pulled on the breeches. The tailor had sworn it was a light-

weight cloth, but no tailor in London could visualize the oven-like tropical heat – that was the regular lament of naval and army officers posted abroad.

Shirt, stock, swordbelt, jacket . . . even the sword and scabbard seemed cool. Silkin had fresh shoes and Ramage slid his feet into them (if an admiral had been approaching, they would have been high boots). Now Silkin held out his hat after giving it a ritual brushing with his sleeve to make the nap lie in the same direction. Ramage nodded and left the cabin, irritated that Silkin had in fact manœuvred him into changing, yet feeling all the fresher for it.

On deck, blinking in the glare, he saw Aitken by the binnacle looking at him anxiously.

'There are three men in the sternsheets of the boat, sir. Two are wearing uniforms I don't recognize. Could be the Dutch army, I suppose. But the one not wearing uniform is much older than the others who, as far as I can make out at this distance, are both wearing aiguillettes, as though they're his aides.'

Ramage grunted, more because he was still irritated by Silkin than the fact that a trio of foreign officials were coming out to the ship. 'Perhaps Britain has signed a peace treaty with the Dutch,' Ramage said. 'They might have just received the news and realized we couldn't know . . .'

One of the most potentially dangerous situations facing the captain of one of the King's ships patrolling in waters distant from commanders-in-chief or the Admiralty was that war would break out – or a peace treaty be signed – with another country whose colonies heard about it first. Britain could have been at peace with the Netherlands when a ship left Jamaica for a routine patrol of three months which included a visit to Curaçao. But a Dutch frigate might arrive at the island to report that war now existed (and a British ship get to Jamaica with the same news). So that the only person completely in ignorance that his erstwhile friends were now his enemies would be the British captain on his long patrol. He might be lucky in accidentally meeting a merchant ship and hearing the news, but merchant ships were usually the last to know, and in consequence were often captured. He might also make the discovery after anchoring in Amsterdam and finding his ship seized. Equally a war existing when he sailed might now be over.

All this would explain that boat, which was now only three or four hundred yards away, and it was the only explanation that made any sense. The Dutch did not have scores of British prisoners for whom they would want to arrange an exchange. And – he was pleased with himself for the deduction – it would explain the ten privateers anchored and looking abandoned: if the Netherlands had just signed a peace treaty with Britain, she would now be neutral or an ally. In either case these French privateers would not be able to use Amsterdam as a base. They would have been seized or interned. It was so obvious that he was almost angry with himself for not having thought of it the first time the *Calypso* passed Amsterdam. Yet the first time – only yesterday, he realized – there had been no flags of truce. Nor was there a ship in the port now – not that he could see, anyway – that could have brought the news while the *Calypso* had been up at the western end of the island dealing with *La Perle*.

He turned to Aitken: 'Side ropes are rigged? Sideboys ready?'

'Yes, sir,' Aitken said patiently, making a note, like hundreds of first lieutenants before him, that when he became a captain he would not interfere in routine affairs. Of course the visitors, as they climbed the battens forming a ladder up the ship's side, would be able to grip a rope in each hand for support. Boys would be stationed at various points down the battens, holding the ropes out and away from the ship's side, making it easier for a climber to hold on.

Ramage watched the boat and considered the position. Supposing it was in fact peace with the Netherlands – the Batavian Republic, as it was now called. The *Calypso* would be the first ship to arrive after it, and no doubt Ramage and his officers would be entertained by the Governor to celebrate. In return, the *Calypso* – Ramage, rather – would have to give a dinner. Or, better still, a small ball. Dancing on the quarterdeck with awning rigged and lanterns in the rigging – women loved it. The true romance of the sea, one of them had once said at a ball he had attended in a flagship. Soft lights from lanthorns (which, if you inspected them closely, contained sooty and smelly candles), the atmosphere of a ship of war (comprising mostly an unpleasant odour from the bilges, but sometimes this could be drowned by a shrewd captain who, a few hours before the ball began, had the rigging near the quarterdeck liberally soaked with Stockholm tar, which was the smell most landlubbers associated with ships), and the sight of the shiny black guns and the roundshot in racks nearby (producing girlish shrieks, though none of the visitors ever stopped to think that the roundshot represented death and destruction) – all this provided an atmosphere of seduction far more potent than the most carefully prepared boudoir.

It was hard to understand but it was a fact. Any officer with designs on a woman's virtue was more likely to be successful if he could get her on board one of the King's ships for a couple of hours than he would be in a couple of hours of her company in an elegant drawing room. Stockholm tar was, apparently, more romantic than the perfume of roses; the faint smell of a ship o' war's bilge outbid any pomander filled with all the aromatic spices specially mixed by a knowing Cupid or procurer. The train of thought which took him from the sight of a boat bearing foreign army officers to thoughts of seduction on the quarterdeck showed him that he had been at sea too long . . .

Now Aitken was at the entry port, leaning out and giving orders. Seamen forward were taking a boat's painter; more men farther aft were throwing down a line to be used as a sternfast. As he walked slowly forward Ramage hoped that, whoever the visitors were, they spoke English or had brought a translator with them: he did not speak a word of Dutch. Or perhaps one of them spoke French (or even Spanish, a hangover from Spain's long occupation). The Netherlands, he admitted, was a country about which he knew very little; in fact, like most Royal Navy officers, his knowledge was limited to a healthy respect for the Dutch both as seamen and fighters.

A black shako with a red, white and blue cockade and a small peak (too small to keep the sun out of the wearer's eyes), a blue tailcoat which had each side of the tail turned back and buttoned to show a white lining, a high collar with white piping round the edge, white epaulets with two red stripes along them, aiguillettes, blue breeches, high brown boots – and no sword. Ramage watched as the young officer scrambled up the last few steps and stepped on to the gangway. There he stopped, obviously a stranger to ships. Then he saw Aitken and, recognizing him as an officer, was about to speak, but the first lieutenant gestured towards Ramage.

As the officer walked a few steps towards him Ramage saw

another head at the break in the bulwark. The fat man was sending his aides on ahead!

'You are the captain, sir?'

The English was good, slightly guttural.

As Ramage nodded the young Dutch officer came smartly to attention and saluted, giving his name, which Ramage did not catch as he returned the salute. By now the second officer had arrived and took the place of the first, who stepped two paces to his left and said something in Dutch which resulted in another smart salute. Ramage gave his own name but cursed himself for failing to catch the second officer's name, though it sounded something like Lausser.

The second officer, a little older than the first and obviously his senior, said carefully: 'Captain Ramage, we come under a flag of truce, and His Excellency Governor van Someren wishes to pay you a visit.'

'Where is Governor van Someren?' Ramage asked, wondering about the plump man still down in the boat.

'He is waiting,' the Dutch officer said warily. 'He wishes to be assured that you will observe the flag of truce.'

'You have my assurance,' Ramage said formally. 'The truce will of course end once your boat is safely back in Amsterdam.'

'That is agreeable, sir. If you will excuse me for a minute.'

He did not move until Ramage, for a moment expecting him to turn away at once, nodded his approval. With that the officer walked to the break in the bulwark and called down something in rapid Dutch, and then waited.

The two highest sideboys holding out the manropes were obviously taking a strain; then a stocky man with high cheekbones and widely-spaced blue eyes with thin white eyebrows was stepping on board. His face was shaded by a straw hat; he wore a mustard-coloured coat and matching breeches with highly-polished brown knee-boots. His skin was tanned; he was used to the Tropics. He was not nervous, but he was not entirely at ease either: he had obviously come to ask for something.

That was as much as Ramage could absorb before the officer had led him over to Ramage and said: 'Governor, may I introduce Captain Ramage of His Britannic Majesty's Navy. Captain Ramage, I have the honour to present His Excellency the Governor of Curaçao and the representative here of the

Batavian Republic, Citizen Gottlieb van Someren.'

Protocol demanded a salute and Ramage gave it. Governor van Someren removed his hat and gave a deep bow, but not before Ramage noted the flicker of annoyance which had shown round his eyes when his aide introduced him as 'Citizen'. No doubt when the House of Nassau ruled the Netherlands – until February of 1793, in other words – van Someren had been one of the Dutch nobility. Since then he had managed to keep his head on his shoulders while the occupying French renamed his country the Republic of the United Provinces and then, more recently, the Batavian Republic. Now, anyway, in public and in front of strangers, he had to be '*citoyen*'.

Now what? The Governor replaced his hat but the two aides were still rigidly at attention. Did the Governor speak English? Whatever it was, he was more likely to speak freely if he did not have witnesses of his own nation.

'Should we go below, Your Excellency? My cabin is cool.'

'Very well, very well,' van Someren said thankfully.

Ramage signalled to Aitken and said with an apparent casualness that he knew the Scot would immediately understand: 'Perhaps you would be kind enough to show these two gentlemen round the ship, and then provide them with refreshment.' Then, before either of them could demur, he said to the Governor: 'If Your Excellency would follow me . . .'

Down in the cabin, van Someren sank into the single armchair with a sigh of relief, though Ramage was not sure whether the relief came from getting the weight off swollen feet or boarding the *Calypso* without incident.

As Ramage sat down on the settee opposite, van Someren said conversationally: 'What happened to the French frigate?'

'You would like some refreshment, Your Excellency? A rum punch, perhaps?'

Van Someren shook his head impatiently. 'Thank you, nothing. The French frigate?'

Ramage inspected his nails. 'I understood from your aide – what was his name?'

'Lausser, Major Lausser.'

' – that you were visiting this ship under a flag of truce . . .'

'But I am, I am!'

'One might get the impression,' Ramage said almost dreamily, clearly absorbed with his nails, 'that you are in fact conducting an unarmed reconnaissance.'

'My dear Lord Ramage – you see, I know who you are –
I am merely asking a polite question. However, if you do not
care to answer . . .'

'According to my information, the Dutch – the Batavian
Republic, if you prefer the term – are at war with Britain and
they are allies of France, which is also at war with Britain.
You, sir, are my enemy, so perhaps you will forgive me for
not supplying you with news of your allies.'

'You captured her,' van Someren said, and Ramage was
startled to hear the satisfaction in his voice. 'You captured
her and you've sent her off to Jamaica with your other ship,
the little schooner, escorting her.'

Dutch lookouts along the coast could have seen everything,
of course; indeed, they obviously had reported to the
Governor, who was perhaps curious to know how it had been
done, because his informants would also have noted the lack
of gunfire and smoke.

'If I can be of some service to Your Excellency while you
are on board under a flag of truce,' Ramage said heavily,
'please feel free to mention it.'

Van Someren's eyes twinkled and he slapped his knee.
'Lord Ramage, we can do business. Or, rather, we can do
business if you have definitely disposed of that French frigate.
She was not expected here and she was sighted only about
the time you saw her. But I must be assured you captured her.
Without that assurance I can do or say nothing more.'

Van Someren was not deliberately talking in riddles; Ramage
was sure of that. But what would he propose once he knew
that *La Perle* was not coming to Amsterdam – could not
come, rather? On the other hand, the flag of truce could be
just a trick to get information. Perhaps *La Perle* was needed
urgently, and this flag of truce and talk of 'business' was just
an elaborate charade to find out.

Van Someren was deliberately staying silent, giving him
time to think. Very well, think. Assume the Governor is
speaking the truth when he says the French frigate was not
expected, and the first the Dutch knew of her presence was
sighting her off the west end of the island – from a lookout
position on the slopes of Sint Christoffelberg, no doubt. A
French frigate in the offing and ten French privateers anchored
in the harbour. Van Someren doesn't know that Duroc was

making for Amsterdam to careen and mend the leak, and that his visit had nothing to do with the privateers. Yet . . . was Duroc speaking the truth?

Supposing van Someren expected the frigate because she was in fact bringing Frenchmen to help man the privateers? Duroc had boasted of having three hundred men on board – not a large number for a French frigate, but a hundred more than an equivalent British frigate would have. Duroc could have left a hundred men behind for the privateers and still had a strong crew for the voyage back to France. A hundred men, ten privateers. Ten men for each ship. That was nonsense, unless the ships had only nucleus crews, because each needed at least fifty or more.

Start again. Van Someren, alarmed at finding a British frigate and schooner arrive off Amsterdam and (as far as the Dutchmen knew) about to blockade Curaçao for the next couple of months (and probably Bonaire and Aruba as well), was anxious to see the French frigate arrive to lift the blockade. That sounded much more likely – except for two things.

The first was that Duroc would not have been lying when he said he was going to Curaçao only to careen, for the simple reason that Aruba was west of Curaçao. Any frigate bringing reinforcements of any sort – men, powder, shot, provisions – from Martinique would go direct to Curaçao, not sail past it for thirty miles in a leaky condition and have to beat back. The second was that van Someren had seemed both relieved and pleased when he thought that Ramage had disposed of *La Perle*.

'You talk of "business". What have you to offer?' Ramage asked bluntly.

'Did you capture or sink that French frigate?'

'Before I discuss her, I want to know what you want.'

'Stalemate,' van Someren said gloomily. 'We have reached a stalemate.'

Ramage shrugged his shoulders. 'I am sorry, but remember that our countries are at war.'

'Have you seen any fires burning on the island?'

Ramage glanced up, trying to keep the surprise from his voice. 'Yes. Quite large fires. And we've heard gunfire, too.'

Van Someren's eyes were narrowing now; the twinkle that accompanied his remark about doing business had gone.

Indeed, looking at that so very Dutch face, Ramage found it hard to visualize it ever smiling.

'You are a man of honour,' van Someren said suddenly. 'And you are a brave man. All this I hear from many ship captains who know what happens at sea. This very ship, for instance . . .'

Ramage again shrugged his shoulders: it was gratifying that the Governor of Curaçao knew of him, but that same Governor had just used the word stalemate.

'Lord Ramage, I mentioned that we could do business together, providing you assured me you had captured or sunk that French frigate. You suspect a trap and I suppose I cannot blame you. You remind me we are enemies. However, stalemate helps neither of us.

'Therefore, young man – you will forgive me so addressing you; I am more than twice, nearly thrice, your age – I am going to tell you why I need to know if you have sunk that French frigate. But before I do, I must warn you that my life could be forfeit if you betray what I am going to tell you. I am going to show you my hand of cards without knowing if you will then show me yours. But I rely on your honour.'

Ramage said nothing. The Governor sounded sincere, but the fact was that he commanded an island thirty-eight miles long by seven miles wide, must have sufficient troops, had an excellent and impregnable port as a capital, and as such was the most powerful representative of the Batavian Republic in the Caribbean – in the New World, in fact. Why, then, was he out here under a flag of truce trying 'to do business' with the captain of a British frigate?

The man *was* sincere, Ramage suddenly felt sure of that, and as he waited he felt a tingling of excitement. Whatever it was would be a challenge. He raised his eyebrows, feigning only idle curiosity: 'Well, Your Excellency?'

'I want to surrender the island of Curaçao to you,' van Someren said quietly and added, 'to you as the representative of His Britannic Majesty.'

Ramage stared at him in surprise. 'Why?'

CHAPTER TWELVE

Amsterdam as a harbour was excellent for any ship wanting to unload cargo at one of the quays lining each side of the channel, or for other vessels, including privateers, needing to pass through and anchor at the far end or in the Schottegat. For a frigate wanting to anchor across the channel to block it, to be outside the arcs of fire of the guns of Riffort and Waterfort, and also to be able to swing herself round far enough to fire into the Punda side of the port in case of emergency, it presented difficulties, with only a couple of hundred yards in which to anchor.

Governor van Someren, Ramage realized, now regarded the island's surrender as an accepted fact, with only the actual document, the 'instrument of surrender', to be drawn up, signed and sealed. He did not realize that Ramage still had no guarantee of good faith, no hostages to make sure the Dutch kept their word, and had no explanation of the sudden surrender. Van Someren, on the other hand, had a British frigate in the harbour and would, within an hour or two, have her captain sitting down with him in Government House, a guest or a hostage.

As the *Calypso* sailed in towards Waterfort and Riffort, the Governor and his two aides had stood beside Ramage on the quarterdeck, commenting, explaining and exclaiming at the sight of Amsterdam from seaward on a sparkling, sunny day. Their boat was towing astern; their crew was in the waist, keeping out of the way of the British seamen as they hurried back and forth, trimming yards and sails. Southwick had a party preparing the anchor, Aitken had the topmen standing by to furl the topsails, and Ramage, acting the role of host, was thankful none of the Dutch trio enquired why lieutenants Wagstaffe, Baker and Kenton remained with groups of men who, while not ostentatiously standing by each gun, would be recognized by trained eyes as being the guns' crews. If the Dutchmen had asked why the guns were left run out, and why a few men swilled water over the deck from time to time and sprinkled more sand, Ramage was prepared to say with a straight face that this was the way in wartime that ships of the Royal Navy always entered port.

The thunder of 12-pounder guns firing at five-second intervals would echo up the channel and carry for miles across the flat countryside, advertising the *Calypso*'s presence, so Ramage had avoided the question whether or not to fire a salute by explaining, again with a straight face, that Admiralty regulations forbade him saluting anyone who was actually on board the ship. His Excellency thought this a splendid joke and, revealing a lively mind and a good memory of peacetime routines, commented that Ramage would not in fact fire a salute anyway without first sending an officer on shore to satisfy himself that a salute would be returned 'in due form'. (No one pointed out that a salute was also to a place, as well as an individual, a point covered by paragraph fifteen in the 'Of Salutes' section in the Regulations and Instructions.)

Ramage had laughed politely at the phrase but it was difficult to maintain polite conversation while judging distances, calculating how much way the ship would carry in the channel with a backed foretopsail, and where to drop the anchor because the *Calypso* would end up with her stern very close to the Otrabanda side. More important, he had to see the arcs of fire of Waterfort and Riffort. One thing was clear now that the *Calypso* was only a cable or so away – they were not so much forts as walled batteries facing seaward.

Under the guise of using his telescope to examine the house which Major Lausser described as his, Ramage was able to see that the guns of Riffort on Otrabanda could cover only the entrance to seaward; there was no way they could fire inland, down the channel. Once inside, a ship was safe. The same went for Punda's guns: Waterfort was a reversed replica of Riffort.

He saw exactly where he wanted to anchor the *Calypso* – half-way along the channel. A single anchor to the eastward would keep her head to wind and with springs to the cable he would be able to haul the *Calypso* round far enough to fire into each side of the town, should it become necessary.

The temptation to take command, to give all the orders direct through the speaking trumpet, was very strong, but he knew it was also the sign of a weak and an unfair captain. Weak because it showed he was uncertain of his ship's company (and probably of himself as well) and unfair to the first lieutenant, particularly one of Aitken's ability, because it deprived him of responsibility for handling the ship at just the time when it would do the most good: at a time when no mistakes could be made. Few captains, Ramage reckoned, were as cold-blooded as himself: if Aitken sailed the *Calypso* on to the rocks in front of either fort, or let the ship get into stays so that she drifted on to one of the sandbanks inside, the captain would get the blame anyway: courts-martial rarely departed from the tradition that captains might not have much work to do, but they carried *all* the responsibility at all times. So Aitken might just as well have the experience.

'Mr Aitken,' he said, 'you see the long house with the pink walls and red roof to starboard, and the grey warehouse to larboard?'

'Aye, sir.'

'We'll anchor between the two, about a third of the way to the eastward.'

'Aye aye, sir.'

'I was thinking of springs,' Ramage said casually, to make sure Aitken left enough room for the ship to swing, and warning the young Scot without the Dutch knowing that the *Calypso* might end up having to open fire on the town.

'Aye, sir.' Aitken let his accent become so pronounced that even Ramage could only just understand him when he said, ''Tis a bonny spot for clapping a spring on the cable.'

Ramage watched the walls of the batteries pass the *Calypso*, with the channel narrowing so that he felt a couple of good men could throw heaving lines to the shore on each side. Van Someren turned and said anxiously: 'You will not go too far in, I hope: it gets shallow towards Schottegat, where the privateers are anchored.'

Did it really get shallow or was His Excellency worrying about the privateers? It was hard to be sure. Ramage had no chart of the inside of Amsterdam, but it seemed likely the channel would get shallow that far in. Until those signatures were on the instrument of surrender, he thought to himself, it is wiser to be suspicious and wary.

Then suddenly he realized what Southwick had meant. A few minutes after he had come back on to the quarterdeck with the Governor, Southwick had been fussing round taking compass bearings of various points in Amsterdam, and as Ramage had passed him the old master had muttered, rather loudly: 'Numbers three, five and six.'

Ramage had not paid much attention. Obviously they weren't bearings, but the numbers had no significance, until now. Southwick knew nothing of what was going on with the Dutch; there had not been time or opportunity to tell him anything. But Southwick, in his own wise way, was trying to remind his captain.

The Articles of War were unambiguous on the question of dealing with the enemy. It was one thing for one of the King's officers to capture an enemy ship or island in battle; it was quite another to be involved – as he now was – in negotiations.

While Aitken gave the order to clew up the maintopsail, Ramage recalled the wording of Article number three: 'If any Officer, Mariner, Soldier or other Person of the Fleet, shall give, hold or entertain Intelligence to or with any Enemy or Rebel, without leave from the King's Majesty, or the Lord High Admiral or the Commissioners for executing the Office of Lord High Admiral, Commander-in-Chief, or his commanding officer, every such Person so offending, and being thereof convicted by the Sentence of a Court-martial, shall be punished with Death.' Death with a capital 'D'. Well, Captain Ramage did not have leave from anyone, least of all Admiral Foxe-Foote.

Neither Articles five nor six specified death with a capital 'D' (it meant in fact that if a court found you guilty it had to sentence you to death). No, they laid down death or whatever punishment 'the nature or degree of the offence shall deserve'.

Five dealt with 'all spies, and all persons whatsoever' who came as spies 'to bring or deliver any seducing letters or messages from any Enemy or Rebel', or try to corrupt any captain or anyone in the Fleet 'to betray his Trust'. That could cover His Excellency and his aides.

Number six would catch Ramage if he so much as offered His Excellency a drink. He had already done that, he reflected grimly, and was not guilty because His Excellency had not accepted it. If he had *accepted* a rum punch, though, then Captain Ramage would have been guilty – 'No person in the Fleet shall relieve an Enemy or Rebel with Money, Victuals, Shot, Arms, Ammunition, or any other supplies whatsoever, directly or indirectly . . .'

The phrase 'directly or indirectly' took on a new meaning: at this moment the *Calypso* is coming head to wind, foretopsail backed, and ready to drop an anchor. If she goes aground – indeed, if the whole thing is a trap – Captain Ramage will have provided the Governor of Curaçao with all the items, and a few score tons of 'any other supplies'.

Like most laws passed by Parliament in its infinite wisdom, the Articles of War were a fine-meshed fishnet which caught without discrimination everything from sprats and sharks to waterlogged tree-trunks. And splash went the bower anchor, just where he wanted it, and the smell of burning drifted aft as friction scorched the hemp rope as it raced out of the hawse. Now the *Calypso* had sternway, pushed by the backed foretopsail, putting a strain on the cable and digging the anchor in. Later when the Governor and his aides had gone on shore, the springs would be put on the cable, and the *Calypso*'s broadsides would be able to rake both sides of the town, if necessary.

The Dutchmen had been chattering to each other and Ramage cursed his lack of knowledge of the language. Van Someren turned to him: 'If I may borrow an English expression and "give credit where credit is due", I must congratulate you and your men: I have never seen anchoring so well done with a ship of this size, even by captains who have been in a hundred times. You have visited here before?'

Ramage grinned and shook his head. 'None of us has. But perhaps you would repeat your kind remarks to my first lieutenant: you saw he was handling the ship.'

Van Someren nodded and Ramage called Aitken. It would do no harm to make the point to these Dutchmen that, in the *Calypso* anyway, the captain was not the only man who could handle the ship in a confined space. Aitken showed sufficient surprise at the Governor's congratulations that Ramage sensed that His Excellency had in mind that the junior lieutenant would probably be handling the ship when she left . . .

The Governor said to Ramage: 'I would like to go on shore now to prepare for our formal meeting. Then this evening perhaps you and your officers would have supper at Government House?'

He saw Ramage hesitating and added: 'I am sure our negotiations will be completed by then. And my wife and daughter will be glad to have new partners for dancing.'

Ramage thought of the daughter and agreed at once. Young Kenton, the junior lieutenant, was going to have to stay on board, unless Southwick decided to miss an evening on shore in favour of a few hours' peace and quiet on board.

An hour later Ramage and Aitken, in full uniform, were seated in what was obviously a small council chamber, with the Governor and Major Lausser sitting opposite them. The dark reddish-brown of the big rectangular table contrasted with the cool white of the stone walls and the black marble floor. Paolo had come on shore with Ramage and, as soon as they had all been introduced to the Governor's wife and daughter, the boy had been swept off by the women for a tour of the city.

The daughter was beautiful; as unexpectedly beautiful in such a dull island, Ramage thought, as a frangipani blossom. She had corn-coloured hair that glinted gold; blue eyes that betrayed a sense of humour; full lips that hinted at – well, they more than hinted. She was physically the opposite of Gianna: she was only a couple of inches shorter than Ramage, while Gianna was a fraction under five feet tall. She had full breasts while Gianna's were small and firm. If Gianna was the imperious little Latin, then Maria van Someren was the typical blonde Amazon, not large-limbed or heavy-featured but a young woman who could look a man straight in the eye without shyness or coyness. And, Ramage was sure, she had known immediately that the moment he had first met her in the drawing room, when she had been wearing a cool, long white dress in the French fashion, clinging and cut low in front, he had in his imagination seen her standing there naked, elegant and proud. She had given a slight curtsy as they were introduced, a curtsy when Ramage had imagined her breasts moving slightly, her nipples caressing the silk of her clothing.

'You agree, My Lord?'

Ramage, his lips kissing those nipples, suddenly found himself in the Council room and the three men waiting for him to answer. To answer what?

'I'm sorry,' he said heavily, 'I was thinking of something else.' Deep thoughts, his voice implied, weighing, for instance, the importance of Curaçao against Antigua, or comparing Amsterdam with English Harbour. They would be large nipples. 'Would you repeat that question?'

The Governor's smile showed that he understood how important matters required careful consideration. 'I was asking if we should begin.'

'We are ready,' Ramage said, glancing at Aitken, who was going to take notes if necessary.

The Governor said: 'You are curious why I wish to surrender the island to you – to Britain, rather.'

'I have been trying to find out from the moment you first mentioned it, Your Excellency,' Ramage said dryly. 'It seems to be the point upon which all negotiations must pivot.'

'It is, it is. But I regret the surrender is not entirely straightforward.'

There is always a catch, Ramage thought sourly. Now come his terms: you can have my island wrapped up in Bruges lace on condition that you . . .

'Nor,' van Someren continued, 'is it very complex. If I may explain some of the background, you will understand at once why you have been seeing smoke at the western end of the island, and hearing occasional gunfire.

'First, you know the circumstances by which the French claimed the United Netherlands as an ally and that our Prince Sovereign had to flee and is now a refugee living in England. Anyone who disagreed with France or the Revolution was – ' he made a chopping gesture with his hand to imitate the guillotine.

'Those of us in distant colonies at the time had to decide how best we could serve our country. We had three choices. We could become refugees and get to England or a British colony. We could withdraw from public life (and risk being arrested, accused of being traitors to the republican cause and then executed). Or we could appear to be prepared to serve the republican cause in the hope of safeguarding our own countrymen, because if we did not serve them the French would put in their own men.

'Rightly or wrongly I allowed myself to continue as Governor in this last category, and until recently I have been able to spare my people the worst excesses for which the Revolution in France has become famous – infamous, rather.'

He paused and poured water into a glass from a carafe in front of him. He drank and then continued. 'But recently – in the past few months – some of our wilder young men have come out violently in support of the French Revolution, or its revolutionary principles, rather. They gathered in the western end of the island, freed slaves, and began threatening to overthrow my government, which they claim is not truly revolutionary – although, ironically, it is approved by Paris.'

'Do they have a leader?'

'To begin with they had their own committee. The Committee of Liberation they called it. Now their new leader is one of the French privateer captains, who has taken all the men from the ships to reinforce these – these revolutionaries. It seems an odd word for the Governor of an island belonging to the Batavian Republic to use, but these rebels want to destroy all that most of us in the island consider justifies Curaçao's existence.'

'The smoke . . .?' Ramage prompted.

'Villages and plantation houses being burned down by these rebels.'

'Why?' Ramage was curious at what seemed a self-defeating activity.

'In some cases because the people would not join the rebels; in others my troops were using them as defences. But mainly because this privateer captain, their leader, is a murderer who enjoys killing and destroying – and robbing and raping. They say he is mad . . .'

'Where are your troops now?'

'I have withdrawn them here to defend the port.'

'Are they loyal?'

'To me, yes. There are only one hundred of them, plus the gunners from the forts and a score or so infantrymen.'

'And the ordinary people here in Amsterdam and the island – what are their sympathies?'

'Against these rebels: they are mostly tradesmen who want to be left in peace to carry on their business. They want no part of the present war – as you know, Curaçao was one of the great trading centres on this side of the Atlantic. This war has brought business to a standstill. Trade with Britain is cut off, France has no money to buy, and nor has Spain. We are reduced to a precarious trade with the Main. Our warehouses are full – with goods that have been there for years.'

'Your Excellency,' Ramage said deliberately, making it clear that he was about to speak as the official British representative, 'you realize that to my government you and your – is it a legislative council? – are rebels: men in arms against the House of Nassau, which my government regards as the rightful rulers of the United Netherlands? Now you are in turn attacked by men *you* call rebels. Your problem is, in effect, a revolution within a revolution.'

For several moments van Someren was silent. His eyes had narrowed, giving him a slightly Oriental appearance; his hands clasped on the table in front of him, showed the knuckles white. 'You speak like a diplomatist, My Lord,' he said without animosity, but choosing his words with precision, 'and like a diplomatist, you want to drive a hard bargain. For myself, though, I am concerned only with saving lives. There are many hundreds of innocent men, women and children living here in Amsterdam. We have reason to believe the rebels intend to loot the city and then burn it down.'

'Why do they want to do that?' Ramage asked bluntly.

Van Someren gestured to Major Lausser, who sorted through papers in front of him and handed the Governor a letter.

'You read French, My Lord?'

'I do, Your Excellency.'

Ramage took the proffered letter, hard put not to smile at the way each of them observed the courtesies with their titles and reflecting how inappropriate was a naval uniform at a negotiating table. The letter, comprising only a few lines, was from some group that called itself 'The Revolutionary Committee of the Batavian Republic in the Antilles', and was addressed to the Governor by name. It said, without any preliminaries, that unless he surrendered Amsterdam by noon on a given date – it used the new revolutionary method of dating which Ramage could never remember – it would be burned down, and the Committee took no responsibility for the safety of the women and children while the men would be treated as traitors.

Ramage folded the letter and went to give it back to the Governor; then he unfolded it again, read the signature, and said to Aitken: 'Make a note of the name "Adolphe Brune, chief of the privateers".' He spelled out the names and then returned the letter to van Someren.

'I trust that decides you,' the Governor said.

'You have about a hundred men, trained troops?'

'Yes, mostly artillerymen.'

'And there are a thousand republicans?' Ramage guessed the figure, curious to see van Someren's reaction.

'Not as many as that. We estimate about five hundred at the most. The privateers were all short of men – we guess at a total of three hundred and fifty. There were about one hundred republicans when all this began, but they may have been joined by others, the inevitable – how do you call them? – opportunists. About fifty, we think.'

'All short of weapons and powder, though?'

Van Someren shook his head. 'Unfortunately they have plenty, because each privateer has weapons – muskets, pistols, cutlasses – for at least fifty men, so they can arm five hundred. Before I brought my troops in, patrols were reporting capturing men holding positions with three loaded muskets in reserve beside each of them.'

'How many men are left in the privateers?'

Even as he asked the question Ramage realized that he had made a bad mistake: he had taken no steps to prevent someone from the privateers getting on shore to ride off into the hills and report to Brune that a British frigate had just come into the harbour and her captain was at Government House.

'One or two men in each vessel,' and then, perhaps reading Ramage's thoughts, van Someren added: 'I left sentries concealed who will seize anyone landing to carry the news of your arrival to the rebels.'

Ramage wished he had a pen or pencil to twiddle. Sitting here with his elbows on the table and one hand resting on the other was comfortable but it seemed to stifle coherent thought. Ideas must come through active hands. Clasped hands reminded him of contented parsons and portly priests mumbling things by rote or making embarrassingly obvious remarks in portentous voices. The true artists in this form of activity, he thought sourly, became bishops, and the lords spiritual never found themselves sitting in the residences of governors of enemy islands trying to think what to do next.

'You are satisfied?' van Someren demanded, his voice slowly becoming almost querulous from anxiety as he realized that this English officer seemed far from delighted at the prospect of having the richest Dutch island in the Caribbean surrendered to him.

The Dutchman watched carefully. This Lord Ramage sat

quite still, like a cat waiting for a mouse. He did not move his hands – nor crack the joints of his knuckles like Lausser. It was impossible to guess what he was thinking: his eyes gave nothing away, sunk beneath bushy eyebrows. He had tapped the table with his left hand when he wanted his lieutenant to make a written note of something but van Someren saw it was always a figure or a name, never a phrase. Obviously he was not a diplomatist because he was concerned only with facts, not phrases.

Whether or not this Lord Ramage eventually accepted the surrender – and it seemed far from sure at the moment – van Someren knew that it was fortunate for Curaçao that he was commanding the frigate that suddenly appeared off the port. Had that French frigate come in, she would have provided more than enough men for the rebels to swing the balance: she would have made sure the rebels were left in control of Amsterdam. Which would in turn mean his own arrest and execution. By a miracle, this Ramage had captured her. In fact, having the *Calypso* anchored in the port almost made up for the fact that the *Delft* was so long overdue. Thank goodness he was not bothered daily by demands from Maria for news about the *Delft*. The frigate was due almost exactly six weeks ago, and that was all he knew. Either she is delayed in the Netherlands or she is delayed by storms or calms. Or she has been captured or sunk.

Now Lord Ramage is watching me. Those brown eyes do not miss much. And he is rubbing one of two scars on his forehead, as though a mosquito bite has started itching. The lieutenant suddenly glances sideways at him, van Someren noticed, as though this rubbing of the scar is significant.

'Would you just repeat briefly, Your Excellency, exactly what you are proposing. Slowly, because I want Mr Aitken to write it down, so that we have a record for my admiral.'

Van Someren was almost thankful because for the captain's own sake he ought to have something in writing to show his senior officer – indeed, he would have been much wiser to have demanded a document from the Dutch. Yet, van Someren realized, if surrender terms are agreed and signed, Ramage will have no use for such a document. He thought how satisfying that his English was coming back to him. Talking English and French to Maria when she was a young girl had done wonders for her command of both languages, and he had to admit it had been good for him, too. Now, to choose the words, words for naval officers, not diplomatists . . .

'As Governor of Curaçao, I wish to surrender this island, with all its people, fortifications, troops, stores, vessels and armaments, to His Britannic Majesty –' he paused when Aitken raised a hand for him to go more slowly – 'in return for His Britannic Majesty's guarantee of protection of the island and its people.'

'A straight exchange,' Ramage said. 'We get the island, you get defended against these republicans. These rebels, rather.'

One has to smile at such bluntness. A diplomatist would have taken five minutes to say the same thing. 'Yes, reduced to its simplest terms, that is so.'

'And, Your Excellency, you give your word of honour that the situation in the island is as you have described it?'

'You ask a great deal! I cannot possibly give you my word of honour about that because I have had to rely on the reports of patrols, and they have now been called in. In all honesty I cannot say what the island's position is at this moment. I can give you my word – and I do – that what I have told you is truly the position as I understand it.'

One had to be honest with this young man. He was not guileless; far from it. But obviously he had no time for all the tact, vagaries and deceptions normally used by diplomatists: if he accepted the surrender of the island, clearly he wanted to know exactly what obligations it brought him.

'You want a guarantee that the island and its people will be defended by the British?'

'Yes.'

In face of such a simple question one could give only a simple answer and the question and the answer were critical: this Lord Ramage might lack (or spurn) the approach of the diplomatist, but he had a sharp enough mind to distil what really mattered.

And now he is shaking his head. His lieutenant has put down his pen and Lausser gives a muffled sigh which is quite unnecessary and tactless: there is no point in revealing disappointment to this young man. Disappointment! Hardly the word to use when a man shaking his head means your eventual execution, and God knows what treatment of your wife and daughter . . . But one must smile. One must remain cheerful. One must bluff, too.

'The prospect of reporting to your commander-in-chief that you have captured the island of Curaçao does not appeal to you, My Lord? I would have thought that it would be – how do you say, "a feather in your cap".'

'The *idea* appeals to me, Your Excellency, but you ask for a guarantee that the British defend the island. I am the person who – for the time being, and that is the only time that really matters – has to give that guarantee.'

'But I can see no difficulty . . .'

'Your Excellency – ' the voice was crisp now, van Someren noted – 'I have about two hundred seamen and forty Marines. How can I possibly *guarantee* to defend you with such a small force?'

'There are my own troops as well! Together they make a strong force.'

Again he shook his head. 'You assume that because I have two hundred and forty men I can land them all like a few companies of infantry. But only the Marines have any training as soldiers. The seamen have been barefooted for months, and if they put on boots or shoes I'm afraid their feet would be blistered within an hour. And I need to keep fifty men on board.'

'Very well, if you don't want to fight . . .'

Again those eyes. It was an insulting thing to say, and not really meant: the words were only a measure of the disappointment at realizing that the *Calypso* would be sailing out of Amsterdam within – well, a few hours.

'Your Excellency, you should not assume that because we captured a French frigate yesterday without firing a shot we did not want to fight.'

'Accept my apologies, please.' It was the only way, and one wanted this young man's respect. 'But is there no way you can help us? Have I not shown you that the French are now as much our enemies as yours?'

'I may be able to help you, Your Excellency, but not on your terms.'

What is he offering? Is he a sly fellow after all? Have I misjudged him? No, it is not possible. Anyway, words cost nothing except time. They can always be denied or twisted.

'But I have not insisted on any terms!'

'You offer to surrender, Your Excellency, on one condition. Perhaps I should have said "condition", not "terms".'

'Please explain more fully.' There might be some hope yet.

'I cannot *guarantee* to defend the island. I can accept the island's surrender and hope that my commander-in-chief will agree to send troops and ships for its defence. But four weeks or more would pass before they arrive, even if my admiral agrees, and that would be much too late. The next four days are the critical ones for you. If you can survive the next four days you will be safe for more than four weeks.'

'But we can't.'

'No, I don't think you can, Your Excellency.'

'And you refuse to help us?'

'As things stand, I can't. At the moment you are our enemy – you forget we are here under a flag of truce. If I helped you, I would be guilty of treason, of helping the enemy.'

And of course he is quite right; this Ramage has not let himself be dazzled by the idea of taking the surrender of an island. 'So, My Lord, we reach stalemate?'

He is shaking his head; quite a definite movement. But has he an alternative proposal after all? His lieutenant is looking round at him, obviously surprised. Lausser is sitting rigidly in his chair. 'What do you propose, then?' The words sound strangled, but Ramage seems not to notice.

'That you surrender without conditions, Your Excellency.'

'But, My Lord, you cannot expect me – why, you could sign the instrument and just sail away, leaving us to be slaughtered by these rebels.'

'I could.' And now he looks me straight in the eye. 'But then all I would have would be a worthless sheet of paper, not an island, so do you think I would?'

'No, I do not.' In all honesty one has to admit that. 'But why do you reject my condition?'

'Your Excellency, I have told you. I can't sign a document guaranteeing you something which cannot be guaranteed. Some men would sign a document guaranteeing to make the sun rise in the west. I am not one of them.'

'What do you suggest we do?' And here at last, in the sixty-third year of my life, I, Gottlieb van Someren, Governor of Curaçao, once honoured with several titles which had been held by many forebears but now officially addressed as 'Citizen', am asking a young British frigate captain what he suggests I do with the island I govern. The ironies of wars and revolution – and of Nature's delays too: where is the *Delft*?

'You have only one choice, Your Excellency. I think you know what it is.'

'I prefer to hear it from you.'

'Surrender the island without any condition, and put yourself under the protection of His Britannic Majesty. I repeat the last part – "put yourself under the protection of His Britannic Majesty". You get no guarantee about anything.'

'How will that help me or my people?'

Now he gives a boyish grin; not an artful or sly grin, but one of satisfaction.

'All it does is help me to help you. At this moment I can't help you in any way – indeed, it is doubtful if I should even be talking with you – because you are "the enemy". If you surrender and put yourself under British protection, you become my ally. And with a clear conscience I can do all I can to help you. But I could not sign any *guarantee* with a clear conscience. Shall we now compose a brief "instrument of surrender" and the four of us sign it?'

The English lieutenant's eyes light up. With his name on a document in which the British accept the surrender of Curaçao, he knows his name goes down in history. And so does mine, but for the opposite reason. 'Yes, let us begin with a rough draft . . .'

Aitken looked at the sheet of paper which Major Lausser had slid across the table towards him. It was a large sheet which had been folded in half to make four sides, and three of them were covered with the neat, copper-plate handwriting of the Governor's clerk, who had painstakingly copied the draft agreed by the captain and the Governor.

Aitken wiped the quill on a piece of cloth and dipped it in the ink. This was a fine thing, his name on a document (an 'instrument of surrender' was its proper name, apparently) by which the captain took the surrender of this whole island. Why, running before a fair wind it took the *Calypso* five or six hours to sail from one end to another. At least 400 square miles, perhaps more. The captain insisted he read it right through and say aloud, for them all to hear, that he understood it. Then, and only then, was he to sign it as one of the two representatives of His Britannic Majesty.

It would be printed in the *London Gazette*, that was certain. The *Gazette* would refer to the surrender, print the wording of the instrument, and give his name as well. A document of state, signed by him. But he wanted to read more slowly, even if the foreign gentlemen were showing signs of impatience, because he knew his hand was trembling, and he did not want to write a shaky signature.

It was a long way from Dunkeld to Amsterdam, from the Highlands of Scotland to this parched tropical island perched on the edge of the Spanish Main, and, despite the excitement and actions of the past few months, these latest twenty-four hours almost passed belief. At this very moment the frigate of which he was first lieutenant – of which he was second in command – was moored across the entrance channel of the port of the island of Curaçao, the Netherlands' most important base in the West Indies. Not a man or vessel could stir without Captain Ramage's agreement. And now the captain was becoming impatient, too, but his hand still felt shaky.

'Sign under Major Lausser's name. Your full name, and then "Lieutenant in the Royal Navy and second-in-command of His Majesty's frigate the *Calypso*" underneath. Don't blot it.'

The captain was speaking quietly, just as he had been doing for the past couple of hours. And what a couple of hours. There were times when Mr Ramage had refused some Dutch request and it had seemed unreasonable: he, James Aitken, would have agreed with the Dutch on that. Then a few minutes later it would become clear that the refusal was proof of how quickly the captain's mind had been working; he had looked far ahead and seen difficulties, and the Dutch Governor had finally agreed, often looking very crestfallen that he hadn't thought of it first.

Well, there was the result of it all: a folded sheet of paper in exchange for an island nearly forty miles long and with a harbour third only to Port Royal in Jamaica and Cartagena on the Main. And there were the signatures – Gottlieb van Someren, Governor; Lausser, Major; Ramage, Captain; and now James Aitken, Lieutenant.

And he had managed to write it without making a blot. The writing *was* a bit shaky, but Lausser had been nervous, too; he had wiped his hand before signing because it was obviously damp from perspiration. And perspiration meant nervousness because this room was delightfully cool, built so that the Trade wind blew along its entire length, and the sun was kept out by the jalousies.

Now a second copy was being passed across. This was the French version. The Governor had wanted the second copy to be in Dutch but Mr Ramage had refused because he did not speak the language. Finally they had agreed on French, which he suspected Mr Ramage spoke better than the Governor.

Now they all shook hands. The Governor paid him a nice compliment, too, about handling the *Calypso* and helping with the negotiations. And the Governor suddenly said, pointing at the signed documents: 'Before we were enemies; now we are friends.'

'But we have quite a task ahead of us,' Mr Ramage said, obviously warning the two Dutchmen that signing papers might end wars but it didn't win battles.

CHAPTER THIRTEEN

Back on board the *Calypso* Ramage returned Wagstaffe's salute and commented on the springs now on the anchor cable. With only three hours of daylight left, there was a lot to be done. The *Calypso*'s other three boats had been hoisted out and now floated astern of the frigate, the ducklings behind the mother.

The officers were all within sight of the gangway: obviously they had expected a surge of activity the moment the captain and the first lieutenant returned from Government House. Ramage decided it was too hot for them all to go down to his cabin and pointed towards the binnacle.

Briefly and quickly Ramage gave each of them his instructions. Rennick was to divide his Marines among the *Calypso*'s four boats. Wagstaffe was to command one, Baker another, Kenton the third, and Ramage himself the fourth. This had resulted in protests from both Southwick and Aitken, but Ramage had silenced both of them by asking if they spoke French. When they admitted what he knew well, that they did not, he had shrugged his shoulders, as if that was the reason why they had not been chosen.

In fact Ramage had decided to lead the little expedition simply because he was bored; there was no chance of any action, but the walk to and from Government House had been the first escape from the *Calypso*'s quarterdeck for weeks, and his cabin was beginning to feel like a cell. None of the other officers had been off the ship, but they had each other's company in the gunroom while the captain lived in almost monastic seclusion.

Ramage took out his watch. 'We start in fifteen minutes. Mr Kenton, will you pass the word for my coxswain?'

With that he went down to his cabin and, with Silkin's help, changed into an old uniform. Jackson arrived before he had finished and, told what was about to happen, began methodically to load the pair of pistols which were kept in the case in the bottom drawer of Ramage's desk. They were a matched pair, beautifully balanced, a present from Gianna and bought the day he had been made post. In fact the visit with Gianna to the gunsmith in Bond Street had been his first foray in his new uniform, when the single epaulet showing he was a post captain with less than three years' seniority seemed to weigh a ton and pull his shoulder down.

First Jackson snapped them to make sure each flint gave a strong spark; then he opened the chamois-leather bag of lead shot, looking like dull grey marbles, and selected two that had no dents or flaws. Then he opened the box of wads, small circles of felt the diameter of the bore of the guns, took out four, and reached for the two powder horns. From the larger he poured a measure down the barrel of one pistol – a lever on the spout of the horn measured the exact amount – and, with a rammer, pushed home a wad, then a shot, and then a second wad. He then took the smaller horn and poured some of the fine powder it contained into the pan and shut it. He then repeated the process with the second gun.

He looked at the two guns critically. They were beautifully made and no doubt very accurate but, he wondered, how would they stand up to the kind of harsh use that was usually the pistol's lot in a ship of war: fired and then often hurled at an enemy's head, dropped on the deck, used as a club? The regular Sea Service pistol had the grace of a hammer compared with these, but it could also stand up to being used as a hammer, a bung starter or a wedge driver. Accuracy as such was not really important; it was rare that a man with a pistol fired at a target more than twenty feet away; in fact, Jackson realized, he could not remember ever aiming at a target even that distant: fighting on board a ship was a close-range business, often little more than jamming the muzzle of a pistol in an enemy's ribs and squeezing the trigger.

As Ramage came into the cabin, having changed, Jackson held out the pistols, which Ramage took and slid the belt clips into the waistband of his breeches. Jackson saw that he now wore a cutlass belt over his shoulder: the usual sword, used for ceremonial occasions and which he had worn on shore for his visit to the Dutch Governor, must be back on its rack on the bulkhead. It was a good job that the Marchesa, who had also bought that, did not know . . .

'Do you think we'll have any trouble, sir?'

Ramage shrugged his shoulders. 'I doubt it.'

'The lads hope we will,' Jackson commented, and when Ramage raised his eyebrows questioningly he added: 'After what that Spanish privateer did to those people, the lads won't be giving quarter to privateersmen . . .'

'These are French, though,' Ramage said, more because he was interested to hear Jackson's reaction than by way of defending privateersmen.

'They're as bad. Any man that goes privateering is no better than a thief and a murderer, sir. Why, they say most of the privateersmen are on shore, attacking the Dutch and burning their villages. They'd loot this place as soon as look at it . . .'

Ramage knew only too well that Jackson, in his unique position as the captain's coxswain and respected by the ship's company, was well placed to relay information to the men, information that was in effect official but not announced by the captain on the quarterdeck.

'The chief of these privateers, a man called Brune, has already warned the Governor that they'll burn down this town and murder the people unless he surrenders it to them.'

'Brune, eh?' Jackson repeated. 'Means "brown", doesn't it, sir? Must be a nasty sort of man to want to burn down his ally's capital . . .'

Ramage led the way out of the cabin, knowing that the information would pass through the ship like a gust of wind, and was soon walking along the gangway to the entry port, where Aitken and Southwick were waiting.

'Your gig's ready, sir,' Aitken reported, 'and the rest of the boats are holding on astern, each with the number of seamen and Marines you specified.'

Aitken's voice was polite, as became a first lieutenant reporting to his captain, but the tone made it clear that the Scot was not overly keen on staying behind while Ramage went off, even though the expedition seemed little more than routine.

Southwick, telescope under one arm, said lugubriously: 'I've been watching those privateers for an hour or two. There's something odd about 'em, but I'm damned if I know what it is.'

'They might be like us, brandy in the water casks.'

Southwick grimaced: he had not been allowed to forget the purser's concern, nor had he yet devised a satisfactory way of disposing of it.

Ramage settled himself in the sternsheets, careful that the butts of the pistols did not jab his ribs, and the gig cast off. Jackson steered the boat at the head of a small armada: immediately astern was the launch with twenty-four boarders and commanded by Wagstaffe, then the pinnace with sixteen under Baker and finally the cutter with another sixteen under Kenton, who was enjoying his first command in what he hoped would be an action.

In Ramage's gig Rennick sat stiffly on a thwart with his Marines, and, although his head did not move, his eyes missed nothing: any sign of movement on board the privateers, a grease stain on a Marine's tunic, a button missing, a musket butt whose woodwork showed a scratch which had not been carefully stained and then waxed.

As the gig leapt forward, the rowers' faces soon glistening and then running with perspiration, Ramage watched the sides of the channel and the privateers with all the concentration of a hungry poacher uncertain whether the gamekeeper really was ill in bed. Small rowing boats from which two or three men had been fishing suddenly scurried for the shore as they saw the boarders leaving the *Calypso*; men who had been working on the quays or walking along the paths lining the banks farther down stopped to watch, the more prudent of them then disappearing. A woman snatched up a small child and ran back towards Punda; a soldier on the Otrabanda side stood still, obviously uncertain what to do. Shutters slammed shut across many windows of houses facing the channel and sent gulls squawking off in alarm.

Then, as the gig approached, Ramage watched the privateers. The ten were anchored in pairs, the Trade wind swinging them diagonally across the channel. Presumably each pair was secured together to make it easier for the maintenance parties: half a dozen men could just as easily look after two privateers rafted up alongside each other as one. The first pair soon obscured his view of the rest, but they were all big vessels. The nearest was the largest and smartest – a schooner perhaps a little smaller than *La Créole*. He counted the ports – she was pierced for ten guns, and a couple of bowchasers. Were they carronades, intended to sweep the victim's deck with grapeshot as she approached? Black hull, buff masts, white topmasts. Booms black, which was strange. All the paint was dull and neglected, yet the sun reflecting from some of the rigging showed that it had been recently tarred.

The second privateer, beyond, was ketch-rigged, her hull painted green, the dark-green of slave ships, the colour of mangrove leaves so that they could hide in the narrow inlets, their hulls blending with the bushes lining the banks. Her lower masts were buff and her topmasts white, so anyone looking for them would be unlikely to spot them against the white of clouds. Ramage once remembered explaining all that to an Army officer, who expected the topmasts to be blue, to match the sky, not realizing that in the Tropics, and particularly on the Guinea coast, there was nearly always broken cloud scudding along. Yes, with that sweeping sheer and low freeboard the ketch was probably a former slaver now finding that in wartime privateering was more profitable.

He felt sure that the nearest privateer, the schooner, belonged to Brune; the leader, or most senior of the privateers, would choose the best berth. In an emergency, the schooner would be the first out of the harbour because she was the nearest to the entrance. And when Brune was on board but felt like an evening in one of Amsterdam's brothels or cafés his boat had the shortest distance to row.

There! A definite movement behind that bowchaser, which was a carronade. And a blur of blue behind the first gun, the washed-out blue that French seamen always favoured. Ramage stood up, drawing his cutlass and waving it a couple of times to attract the attention of the boats astern before pointing to left and right. Even without looking astern he knew that Wagstaffe had started to turn the launch to larboard and Baker would swing the pinnace out to starboard, while Kenton moved over to larboard a few yards with the cutter to be between Ramage and Wagstaffe. The four boats, in line abreast, now made a series of individual targets and as they took up their positions the men rowed even harder at the oars.

Suddenly the schooner's carronade and first two guns were run out, their barrels jabbing from the ports like black, accusing fingers. Ramage, feeling that the gig was rowing right into the muzzle of the carronade, suddenly stood up again and, using the speaking trumpet that he had brought with him, shouted in French: 'If you fire, we will give no quarter!'

For more than a minute nothing happened and Ramage reckoned that the threat, the sight of four boats laden with boarders, and the harbour entrance blocked by a British frigate, was going to be enough to make the men in the privateers surrender. But the carronade gave an obscene red wink; suddenly yellow, oily smoke spurted out and with a noise like ripping calico the sea fifteen yards away to starboard erupted as if a hundred great fish had broken the surface in a gigantic leap to escape a marauding shark.

The crash of the gun firing was deafening but a moment later, as if from a great distance, Ramage heard Stafford's voice, a mixture of awe and scorn: 'The capting'd flog us if we aimed that bad!'

'And he'll flog you anyway unless you put your back into that oar,' Jackson snarled. 'They shouldn't miss with the next round.'

'The Frog wiv the grapeshot'll drop it on 'is foot and waste time cussing.'

Ramage saw that the second and third guns, 6-pounders, were trained more to larboard, at the launch and the cutter.

'Quick,' Ramage snapped at Rennick, 'have your men fire at the ports!'

He cursed himself for not doing it sooner. The chances of a musket ball hitting Frenchmen were slight – any Marine who could fire through a port from a fast-moving boat would be a king among sharpshooters – but the thud of musket balls into woodwork might spoil the enemy gunners' concentration. The gig's oarsmen's ears would soon be ringing as the muskets fired over their heads, but it was the only chance of saving the men in the other boats.

Rennick snapped an order that could be heard in all the boats and in a moment the Marines were standing, one knee on the thwarts. Ramage could hear a succession of clicks as the men cocked the locks and then, within a couple more seconds, all had fired and some were coughing as the smoke drifted back and caught their throats.

Forty yards to go: Ramage could see dried salt forming a grey band two or three feet broad above the privateer's water-line and the black paint had the mauvish tinge that came from too much sun, salt – and age. The seams of the hull planking were opening up with the heat of the sun constantly on one side.

'The bow!' he called to Jackson. 'Stand by, men; we'll board over her bow: up the bobstay, anchor cable, anchor stock – men with broad shoulders give the little chaps a leg-up!'

The Marines were frantically ramming home fresh shot as they reloaded their muskets, and now most of them were priming. 'One more volley through the ports, sir?' Rennick asked. 'They've all got pistols.'

And why not, Ramage thought: they were close enough now that at least a few shot should get through the ports, and discharged muskets could be left in the boat because, as Rennick had just pointed out, each Marine had a pistol, like the seamen.

'Very well, but aim with care!'

Again there was what seemed a ragged volley which in fact showed that each man was firing carefully, aiming for the narrow gap between gun and bulwark. There was more space at the top, but they were now so close that the barrel of the gun helped protect the French gunners.

Suddenly there was an enormous crash, a thump of invisible pressure, and smoke filled the boat, followed by a distant shriek and confused shouting. The sun darkened and then lightened, and Ramage felt his lungs burning as he breathed in gun smoke. But his men were still rowing; the oars were still squeaking in the rowlocks and they came out into the sunlight again.

He glanced round to larboard, guessing what he would see. The second gun had fired and the cutter was now just a swirl

in the water with splintered planking and oars floating away.
Heads were bobbing about in the wreckage – several heads.
Wagstaffe and the launch were still rowing fast but farther
away now because, Ramage was glad to note, the second
lieutenant was making for the schooner's stern, which also
took him out of the arc of fire of the first gun. With Ramage's
men boarding over the bow and Wagstaffe's over the transom,
with luck Baker would board amidships, providing Ramage's
men could silence that carronade.

Ramage twisted his cutlass belt round so that the blade hung
down his back and would not trip him; he pushed the pistols
more firmly into his waistband and jammed his hat firmly on
his head.

Twenty yards, ten, five – and then the gig was under the
privateer's bow, the oars were backing water to stop the boat,
and there was a wild scramble as men began climbing. Ramage
grabbed the thick, rusty lower fluke of the spare anchor and
kicked upwards. The top edge of the planking, doubled for
a couple of feet below the sheer line, made a narrow ledge
for his feet so that he was held horizontally. He paused for a
moment and saw that one swing up with his legs would enable
him to catch his feet in the bottom edge of the port for the
bowchase gun, the carronade that had missed the gig but
which by now must have been reloaded and ready to fire.

He tensed his muscles and heaved upwards, and a moment
later was standing spreadeagled across the port, off balance
and leaning inboard with his belly against the wide muzzle of
the gun. At the breech, four feet away, he saw a blur of movement: a man to one side cocked the flintlock; a second man,
behind and beyond the recoil of the gun, began to take the
strain on a lanyard – the trigger line which fired the gun.
Within a moment the carronade would fire and blow him in
half – the men were apparently aiming for Baker and the
pinnace at the very moment that Ramage appeared at the
port. He tugged for one of his pistols. It came clear of the
waistband and his thumb cocked it as one of the Frenchmen
screamed a warning to the others and lashed out at Ramage
with a handspike, a six-foot-long steel-tipped lever used to
move the other guns and which would have crushed Ramage's
head if the tip had not caught the side of the face of another
man in the French gun's crew.

Ramage, still seeing it all as a blur, aimed along the lanyard towards the man at the end and fired; then regaining his balance he wriggled sideways round the barrel and in through the port just as the man with the lanyard – the gun captain, in fact – collapsed within a foot of the man hit by the handspike.

As he tugged his second pistol free he sensed rather than saw men rushing past him: his own men from the gig who, coming over the bow, had not found so fast a route on board. The rest of the carronade's crew had vanished – fled aft, presumably, when they saw the Calypsos coming over the bow. But as Ramage looked back out of the port to see where the other boats were, he realized that the fighting had stopped: the privateer's crew were dead or had surrendered.

Then in the sea a few yards away he saw the expanding circle of splintered wood, the remains of the cutter with men clinging to the wreckage. Wagstaffe had obeyed his orders and not stopped with the launch, but now a boat could go back and pick up survivors. Jackson was standing in front of him, grinning cheerfully. 'All surrendered, three wounded, and this chap here – ' he pointed to the man hit by the handspike – 'and one dead, the one you shot, sir.'

'And our casualties?'

'None on board here, sir, but the cutter . . .'

'Yes, get back and pick up the survivors; I can see several men holding on to wreckage.'

Then Wagstaffe was reporting and then Baker, and after making sure the prisoners were being guarded, Ramage led them in a dash to the second privateer alongside, but there was no one on board. There were still eight more privateers to be secured, and after returning to the schooner and leaving instructions for securing the prisoners, he ordered the men back into the boats. As an afterthought he ordered one of the guards to lower the French flag, and the man paused a moment and said: ' 'Sfunny thing, sir: she's flying French colours, but she's got a Spanish name on her transom: I noticed it as I climbed on board.'

'What name?'

'Can't rightly pronounce it, sir, but summat like *Newstra lady of Antigua*. I know it was "Antigua" 'cos I thought of English Harbour.'

'Was it *Nuestra Señora de Antigua*?'

The tone of Ramage's voice and his correct pronunciation made the seaman stare at him. 'Cor, sir – then this is the privateer what murdered all them in the *Tranquil*!'

Ramage nodded. A French privateer with a Spanish name and probably commanded by Adolphe Brune, who had described himself as 'chief of the privateers' in the letter to van Someren demanding Amsterdam's surrender. If Brune survives this affair in Curaçao, Ramage vowed, he'll end up dangling on a noose from one of the gibbets on the Palisades at Port Royal.

By five o'clock that evening the gig, launch and pinnace were back alongside the *Calypso*, secured to the boat boom. More than sixty French prisoners from the ten privateers – more than ten times the number Ramage had expected – had been ferried on shore and locked up in the town jail. Because Amsterdam was a large port and accustomed to acting as the forcible host to crowds of drunken and rioting seamen, the jail was a large stone building, and the Governor assured Ramage that the jailers were quite capable of dealing with up to a hundred prisoners without the cells seeming crowded.

The capture of the rest of the privateers without a shot being fired had been luck: Ramage realized that none of the Frenchmen in the remaining eight had seen the shot smashing the cutter to pieces; the whole action had been hidden by the sheer bulk of Brune's schooner and the ketch. They had heard a carronade and a 6-pounder each fire once, apparently without effect on the British, and the nearest of them had heard a single pistol shot, and then the French flag had come down at the run on board the *Nuestra Señora*. That had been enough to make each of them surrender immediately one of the *Calypso*'s boats came alongside.

Now the ten privateers were still at anchor in Amsterdam, but on board each one were two Dutch soldiers who had simple orders: if any French came into sight on the quays and looked as though they might board, they were to light the slow matches leading to the magazines and escape in the rowing boats which had been commandeered from local fishermen. The fishermen had made no protest at losing their boats temporarily; they had lost their appetite for fishing.

Bowen was still busy patching up the wounded. Three of the cutter's crew had been badly cut and bruised by splinters but were in no danger; two were missing and obviously killed and one man, with no mark on him, was just cold and trembling, unable to walk or talk. Kenton was once again his lively self but swearing he would always wear shoes, not knee-length boots, on any further boat operations. If he had to swim again, he declared, he could kick off shoes, but his boots had acted like ballast. An otherwise sympathetic Aitken had agreed with the problem of boots but warned Kenton against kicking off the shoes, pointing out that: 'Ye never know but y' might have to walk a long way back to the ship.' His Scots accent made 'ship' sound like 'sheep', and Kenton had gone off muttering that he was a sailor, not a shepherd.

Southwick and Aitken had watched the action through their telescopes and seen Ramage momentarily draped over the muzzle of the carronade and knew it must be on the verge of firing. The master hid his feelings with the comment to Ramage that: 'Then I remembered you were wearing your oldest uniform and had left behind the new sword the Marchesa gave you, so only the pistols would be lost.' For a moment Aitken had been shocked, then he had seen Ramage's grin and had joined in with: 'Aye, I thought for a minute or two I'd be moving up a deck. I find my present cabin both small and hot in this weather . . .'

Then, with Southwick's assurance that he had no wish to spend the evening on shore and Bowen declaring he would not leave his patients, Ramage and his officers went below to prepare themselves for dinner with the Governor. Ramage was worn out, but he could think of no possible excuse to avoid at least an hour or two at Government House. After going below to chat with the wounded men – and finding them cheerful but chagrined, complaining bitterly that before they could 'get a swing' at the French they found themselves swimming – he went to his cabin, let Silkin pull off his boots (Kenton's vow about shoes made sense: apart from anything else the hot decks and walking had swollen his feet so much that pulling off his boots needed as much effort – or so it seemed – as pulling off his feet), and then sat back for ten minutes, trying to relax.

Relaxing, everyone told him, was a very fine thing. Relax for ten minutes, banish all worrisome thoughts from your head, and at the end of it you were as refreshed as a flower garden after a summer shower. It probably worked for some people but it depended on relaxing in the first place. If you could not relax, then you felt (and probably looked) like a flower garden after a long drought.

His feet throbbed as though someone was pounding them with clubs; his eyes were sore from the day's scorching sun; his hands were not visibly trembling but like his knees they gave that impression. If he tried to rest his mind for a moment – the first stage, as it were, to relaxing – he felt the muzzle of that carronade pressing against his belly, the iron barrel warm to his hands from the heat of the sun, and hunched there, unbalanced and frightened, he could smell the garlic, the Stockholm tar, the bilges and the sheer stink of unwashed French seamen. Then once again he heard, almost felt, that sharp metallic click of the gun's second captain cocking the lock, and he could see the gun captain's eyes staring at him, startled and momentarily paralysed by his sudden appearance at the port. The bloodshot eyes were close together, and seemed slightly out of focus, and afterwards he had noticed that the corpse reeked of wine. Drink had slowed the Frenchman's reactions by – well, perhaps only a couple of seconds, but just long enough for Ramage to cock and fire his pistol; one of the two pistols given him by Gianna and which she had thought plain, preferring a far more ornate pair.

Well, he had *not* been blown in half by an enemy carronade; young Kenton had *not* had his head knocked off by the 6-pounder shot that smashed up the cutter. There was, therefore, no more point in thinking about it. Think instead of – well, the privateers were captured, which would please old Foxey-Foote. The Admiral's orders did not actually say the privateers in Curaçao were to be captured; from memory the orders were in fact rather vague about what was to be done. Anyway, all ten of them were captured and could be sunk, burned or blown up if necessary in minutes.

The French prisoners had sworn that those ten were the only ones using the Dutch islands of Aruba, Curaçao and Bonaire as a temporary base, so any new arrivals would be ships that came in by chance. Ramage had been interested to discover that they had not been expecting *La Perle*, so her captain's story was probably true.

Suddenly he sat upright in the chair, then stood up and went over to his desk, unlocking a drawer and taking out his orders from Admiral Foxe-Foote. Yes, they *were* vague about exactly what he was to do about the privateers based on Curaçao, but they were quite clear on one point which had just occurred to

him with the suddenness of a sword thrust: as soon as he had
dealt with them he was to return to Port Royal. So, if Foxey-
Foote was liverish when the *Calypso* finally returned, he could
sermonize and wax wrathful because Ramage had paused to
take the surrender of an island. Islands, after all, yielded no
prize money; nothing from which a commander-in-chief could
take his eighths. Ten privateers, on the other hand, undamaged and requiring only the sails hoisting up from below
and bending on . . .

Maria van Someren. He put his orders back in the drawer
and turned the key, and then returned to the armchair. There
was nothing restful about Maria van Someren. She was no
blushing young girl overcome with the vapours if she saw a
naval officer casting an eye over her body; nor was she one
of those brazen young women who made up for dull and
vacant minds and vapid personalities by wearing daringly cut
dresses out of which a reasonable man could expect a bosom
to pop any moment and which, temporarily, took his mind
off the mental drabness of the owner.

No, like Gianna she preferred the company of men to being
caught up in a crowd of women chattering about the merits
of a newly-discovered dressmaker, hinting at the behaviour of
some absent wife (or her husband) or (with a brisk flapping
of fans) remarking how hot it was for the time of year. Or,
Ramage suddenly realized, he assumed she did: he had seen
her once for a few minutes, and already he thought he knew
her. Instead, of course, he was creating a person in the image
of the kind of woman he liked. He had seen her once, he
would see her again this evening, and then it was unlikely he
would ever see her again. The disappointment was physical
rather than mental; he felt it in his loins. He would see Gianna
naked, hold her body closely, share her bed – at least, he
could have reasonable hopes of all that – but he would always
wonder about Maria van Someren: was she one of those
women who clasped her hands across her breasts, shut her
eyes, breathed shallowly and went rigid, like a day-old corpse?
Or was she – well, his mind was in enough turmoil to stop
speculating further.

Many a man had metaphorically or literally lost his head
because of the curve of a bosom but, he asked himself, have
we anything to lose by dining at Government House tonight?
The *Calypso* was safe enough; Southwick was quite capable

of turning her on the springs and firing into the town – and likewise dealing with the unlikely prospect of a ship unexpectedly sailing in after dark. The privateers were safe enough under their Dutch guards – safe inasmuch as they could not fall into enemy hands. And since Ramage had to discuss the military situation with the Governor before doing anything about the rebels, the *Calypso's* officers might just as well be present and have a good dinner afterwards.

At the moment Ramage finally stood up from the armchair, Silkin knocked on the door and came into the cabin, freshly-ironed shirt, stock and stockings over his arm and polished shoes in his hand. Ramage, always irrationally irritated by Silkin's ability to keep out of sight until the moment he was wanted, began stripping off his clothes and walked through to his sleeping cabin where he knew the handbasin would be precisely two-thirds full of water, with soap, shaving brush, razor freshly stropped, and towel neatly laid out.

Relax indeed! Those captains who were court-martialled for 'not doing their utmost' against the enemy, admirals criticized after a battle for not pursuing a beaten enemy, junior officers not promoted because they lacked initiative – they were the men who could and did relax.

He soaped his body and then rinsed it. He twirled the shaving brush in the soap dish and lathered his face. He paused and rubbed the lather deeper into the skin with his fingers before resuming with the brush. Finally he picked up the razor. He had no need to test the blade; Silkin was not intelligent enough to do something wrong, like forget to put out the shaving brush, or not hone the razor, so that the captain could spend a couple of minutes being angry, and then brighten up for the rest of the day. Instead, with nothing to grumble at, he became angry with himself for being so ill-tempered, and this discontent sometimes lasted for hours. If the ship's company understood all this, Ramage thought to himself, they'd cut Silkin's throat and feed him in small pieces to the gulls.

A mirror hung on the bulkhead, although Silkin knew well enough that Ramage always shaved without a mirror, a habit picked up as a lieutenant when frequently there was not enough light in a tiny cabin. Ramage rinsed the razor, wiped the blade and then closed it. Shaving was a relaxing activity.

One glance at the mirror to make sure no flecks of lather remained in the ears or nostrils (he was always irritated when he saw it in other men) and he turned to the clothes, laid out neatly on the top of his cot, and began dressing.

Pulling on silk clothing after a leisurely wash and shave . . . he was thankful he had enough money to afford it, though officers who wore silk shirts in the Tropics instead of the linen on which he insisted for himself were silly fellows: a hot evening meant that the silk stuck to the body like a coating of glue.

Finally he tied his stock and Silkin was ready with his frock coat, shoes, sword and hat, and the news that he had passed the word to the first lieutenant that the captain would be ready in five minutes. One of the advantages of being the captain was that you were never kept waiting; by tradition the senior officer was the last in and first out of a boat.

Governor van Someren was in a cheerful mood, anxious to hear from Ramage the details of the capture of the privateers. He had sympathized with Aitken that the first lieutenant had to stay on board during the operation, listened carefully when Ramage had Wagstaffe explain how he and his men had boarded over the stern of the *Nuestra Scñora*, and been startled when Kenton gave a hilarious description of the cutter disintegrating.

Van Someren called over his wife and daughter and made Kenton repeat the story, and they laughed until Maria discovered men had been killed and wounded. Then she turned to Ramage and asked how they could laugh over such a tragic episode.

The question was completely unexpected and Ramage took a few moments to realize that she had misunderstood both Kenton and the attitude of all the Britons. 'We are not laughing at the tragedy. We are laughing because at one moment Mr Kenton is sitting on a thwart – on a seat – in the boat, and the next moment he is sitting in the sea.'

'Yes – but some of his men were smashed to pieces. Why do you laugh at that?'

'We were not laughing at that; we knew them all very well.'

'Then that is far worse,' Maria persisted, tears beginning in her eyes. 'You are so ruthless. Dead men cannot fight and cannot be of any more use to you, so you laugh, but they have mothers and wives and sweethearts who will weep for them.'

'We are not laughing at them, ma'am,' Kenton said, obviously very upset at her accusation. 'We – well, as the captain said, we were laughing at me!'

'But all round you in the sea was the blood of the dead and wounded . . .'

Ramage wanted to end the conversation: this kind of reasoning brought back memories which for years he had struggled to drive away: of friends, of men he liked, and even men he disliked, who had died round him in battle, lingeringly or instantly, bloodily or unmarked, silently or screaming in agony.

'Madam,' he said, making little effort to keep a chill out of his voice, 'we laugh to avoid weeping. Today some of our men were killed. We knew them and we grieve, but inwardly. We don't wail and tear our hair. Tomorrow fifty might be killed, and a hundred the day after. Are we to weep for every one of them? Are we to weep because fifty of us might be killed on the third day? I might be dead tomorrow, Kenton and Baker the day after, and then Aitken. If we thought too much about it we would never sleep, we'd never be able to look at each other without bursting into tears. But we have a war to fight so each of us hopes he is immortal, laughs when he can and mourns in his own way when he must.'

Maria was angry now, the hint of tears gone and the skin of her face tautening to give her a beauty which was absent when her features were in repose. 'It is all very well for you to speak thus,' she snapped, 'but you are the captain! These young men risk their lives while you just give them their orders, and stay safely in your own ship.'

Ramage smiled in agreement and gave a slight bow which, he hoped, would end the conversation, but Aitken's Scots voice said quietly: 'I haven't served with His Lordship long, ma'am, but he's been wounded twice to my knowledge – look at the scars over his right eye – and has done things that make men like me tremble even to think about. And,' he added, giving the words the broadness that only the Scottish accent allowed, 'today he was nearer death than any of us who lived.'

Maria stared at Aitken, obviously disbelieving him. 'You defend your captain – as indeed you should.'

'Aye, madam, because he won't be bothered to defend himself against what – if you'll forgive my presumption – is a very ill-informed attack. I'm a simple naval officer not used to Governors' palaces, so I'm wrong in speaking out like this, but I canna stand here and listen to you talking about the captain staying behind and giving orders.'

'But he does!' Maria snapped. 'Mr Wagstaffe has just told us how he boarded the French schooner over the stern.'

Rennick grunted in protest and Wagstaffe had none of Aitken's shyness. 'Madam,' he said sharply, 'the first person to board that schooner was the captain. He climbed through a gun port at the bow. You probably don't know what a gun port is but you know the fortresses here. It was as if he climbed the wall and went through one of the embrasures so that he was standing right in front of the muzzle of a gun which was just about to fire.'

'It didn't though,' she said bitterly. 'He's alive but the other men are dead.'

'The gun did not fire because Mr Ramage had time to kill the gunner the moment before it fired.'

'So four men died today, not three!' she exclaimed.

Before anyone had time to react, Kenton, his cheeks flaming with anger, took a step towards her and said angrily: 'Yes, and nearly *five* – Mr Ramage. Would that have satisfied you, ma'am? The French may be your allies but they're our enemies. *They* killed three of *our* men today, not Mr Ramage.'

He stopped and Ramage was just about to order his officers to change the subject when Wagstaffe said: 'Madam – that schooner has a Spanish name, the *Nuestra Señora de Antigua*. You are sorry that Mr Ramage shot one of her seamen, but I can tell you that every man on board the *Calypso* would volunteer – aye, would be proud – to hang every Frenchman that normally serves in her. Hang them, or cut their throats. Some of them – and that includes me – would like to kill them even more slowly. Especially her captain – I could take a week to kill *him*.'

Maria stared at Wagstaffe contemptuously. 'So you are a – a hired assassin; that's what you've just admitted!'

Wagstaffe turned to Ramage, a questioning look in his eye. 'Can I tell her what I saw, sir?'

Ramage hesitated and glanced at van Someren, who was deliberately staying out of the argument, but before he could

answer a white-faced and angry Wagstaffe turned back to the
girl and described how the *Calypso* had found the *Tranquil.*
He then told how they had found everyone on board had been
murdered, including the women passengers.

'What has that to do with the *Nuestra Señora de Antigua*
and Captain Brune?' she demanded, obviously horrified by
the story.

'She was the privateer, he was the captain,' Wagstaffe said
quietly. 'Captain Brune had all those people killed, unnecessarily and in cold blood. Now he threatens to burn down
Amsterdam, your town. He,' Wagstaffe added with biting
sarcasm and giving a slight bow, 'has been your country's ally
for nearly ten years.'

Maria half turned to Ramage and collapsed at his feet. In
the second before she fainted Ramage saw in her eyes such
agony of mind that he found it hard to forgive himself for
not having stopped the conversation many minutes earlier.
He was the first to kneel beside the girl and half-turn her so
she faced upwards. Her father did not move, and when
Ramage glanced up to see if he was going to give any
instructions he saw that the Governor's face was rigid and
that he had held up a hand to stop his wife going to the girl.

'She has fainted,' he said, 'which seems a fitting end to
insulting every one of my guests. I can only apologize and
say that I do not agree with a word she said and hope you'll
forgive her – she is a young girl who has led a sheltered life.'

His wife nodded in agreement. Apart from an occasional
glance down at her daughter – a glance combining irritation,
exasperation, disdain and concern in equal proportions, each
competing for a leading position but none winning – she
seemed to consider that the kneeling Ramage was all the attention the girl needed, and none of the other officers moved.

She recovered slowly and finally her eyes opened and
focused on Ramage and as she recognized him he found he
could not fathom her thoughts. Hate, contempt, distaste,
horror? One of them, surely, but the blue. eyes closed again
before he could be sure.

He felt a tap on the shoulder and looked up to find her
father standing beside him. 'We'll put her on the settee. It will
soon pass.'

By the time she was sitting down and obeying Ramage's
instructions to breathe deeply, the colour was coming back

to her face and her hands were exploring her hair, in case some strands had escaped. Aitken had walked the three lieutenants to a large painting on the wall which showed a group of people skating on a frozen lake, and now the four lieutenants, perspiring from both the tropical heat and the situation, examined the ice and the surrounding snow with great concentration.

Van Someren pointed to a door Ramage had not previously noticed. 'To the balcony,' he said. 'Perhaps you would be kind enough to take Maria outside, for some fresh air.'

Outside it was cool; darkness had fallen but there was still a gentle breeze from the south-east. A few hundred yards away the sea slapped lazily on the beach and over Waterfort the stars of Orion's Belt waited for the Southern Cross to appear.

As Ramage shut the door she walked over to the elaborate tracery of the balcony rail and standing with her back to it faced Ramage as he came towards her. She was silhouetted against the millions of stars that can only be seen from the Tropics, and as Ramage approached she held out her hands. He walked into her arms and as he held her closely he was pleased that she followed the French fashion: the thin cloth of her dress hid her body from the eye but did nothing to conceal it from the touch.

'I am sorry,' she whispered. 'I did not understand. Your officers – they seem so young . . .'

'They are,' Ramage said wryly. 'Aitken is almost my age.'

'But to me – ' she took his right hand. 'This afternoon, only a few hours ago, this hand killed a man.'

'If it had not, that man would have blown me in half – here,' he said roughly, pressing her hand against his stomach. 'That's where the muzzle of his gun was.'

She shuddered and traced the shape of his hand with her fingers. 'All this killing – it never ends.'

'There's been very little of it out here,' Ramage said. His voice was low but harsh; he remembered only too well the guillotine he had seen in every town square during one brief foray into France; he knew only too well what 'The Terror' had done to anyone disagreeing with the Revolution. 'The islands have escaped up to now. You have no idea of the battles being fought in Europe.'

'Jules tells me,' she said.

'Jules?'

'My – last year my father announced my engagement to the first lieutenant of the *Delft* frigate. He is due here. My father hoped his men would dispose of the rebels.'

'Why has he been delayed?'

'I don't know. No explanation has come from the Netherlands.'

Ramage could not see her features clearly in the darkness, but she did not sound like an infatuated young woman grieving over her future husband's absence, and 'my father announced my engagement' was a curious phrase.

She kissed him again and then traced his features with her fingers, as though trying to learn his face by touch. 'Lord Ramage,' she murmured. 'And you are not yet married? So handsome, so brave – and, if you are a lord, no doubt so rich,' she added in a gently bantering voice which asked questions which Ramage had no intention of answering.

'The Navy leaves me no time to do anything but go to sea.'

'Ah – but you are in port now.'

'And you see what happens!'

They moved apart as they heard the door handle rasping, and then the Governor bustled out, followed by the lieutenants. 'How are you now, my dear?' he asked the girl, and when she assured him she was recovered he said: 'I think your mother would like to see you: some trouble with the kitchen staff I think.'

As soon as she left he said to Ramage: 'Perhaps we should discuss plans before dinner; then we can enjoy our food without distraction.'

When Ramage agreed the Governor said: 'Should we talk here? We run no risk of servants hearing too much, and I imagine you want your officers present.'

For the next fifteen minutes van Someren told them all he knew of the rebels' activities, how far they had advanced, and how long – unless something was done quickly – before the rebels reached Amsterdam. At the end of the recital he asked Ramage: 'So what do you propose doing?'

'Thinking about it at dinner, Your Excellency.'

'But you must have some idea, surely?'

Ramage shrugged his shoulders, and then realized that van Someren could not see him in the darkness. 'There are many things we could try to do. But the fact is I have about one hundred and fifty seamen and forty Marines to deal with perhaps five hundred men who know the island well.'

'This I know, but surely . . .'

'I'm sorry, Your Excellency.'

'But – well, I must insist. I am the Governor of the island and I have surrendered it to you. I insist that you defend Amsterdam, and I insist on knowing – knowing now – how you propose to do it.'

Ramage did not feel particularly angry; in fact he more than understood the Governor's concern. But like his daughter earlier, van Someren was talking without considering the facts.

'I think, Your Excellency, that we ought to go down to dinner.'

'Captain Ramage,' van Someren said sharply, 'I insist on knowing.' Clearly he was not going to move from the balcony, and the mosquitoes were beginning to trouble Ramage.

'Your Excellency,' Ramage said quietly, 'yesterday you surrendered this island to me. We signed all the necessary documents. Since then I have continued to address you as "Your Excellency"; you have been treated as though you were the Governor . . .'

Would he need to say more? Van Someren was quick to answer: 'But I *am* the Governor!'

'Forgive me,' Ramage said almost dreamily, 'how can you, a Dutch subject, a citizen of the Batavian Republic, be the Governor of an island which, since yesterday afternoon, belonged to Britain?'

Van Someren was silent for several seconds and Ramage heard two or three of the lieutenants shuffle their feet as they realized the significance of what their captain had said but were far from sure what van Someren was going to do.

'Again, I must apologize,' the Dutchman said. 'You are of course quite correct. You are, I suppose, the new governor – and naval and military commander.'

'More important for the moment,' Ramage said dryly, 'I am your guest for dinner, and I'm sure we all have a good appetite.'

CHAPTER FOURTEEN

Lieutenant Rennick looked at the map yet again. To the trained eye of a Marine officer, the island of Curaçao looked like a femur, or whatever the big thigh bone was called, long and narrow, thinner in the middle. More important than the shape, though, the Governor had sent out a mounted night patrol, at Captain Ramage's request, to find out exactly where the rebels were.

The Governor had been sure they'd be split into three groups, one advancing on Amsterdam by the south coast, another along the road running the length of the island like a spine, and a third skirting the north coast – the island was less than seven miles wide where Amsterdam was built. In fact, though, the patrol had reported back just before the *Calypso*'s officers left Government House at two o'clock in the morning that the rebels were in no sort of formation; they were camped together for the night (and according to local people had spent the previous one there, too) at a place between Willebrordus, on the south coast near Bullen Bay, and the village of Daniel, on the centre road.

This put them ten miles from Amsterdam, which with trained troops would have been dangerously close, but because the rebels were a collection of undisciplined privateersmen, wastrels and troublemakers, the captain had suggested that for the rest of the night a dozen Dutch soldiers with a couple of horses for messengers should be stationed as sentries five miles from Amsterdam along the south coast, another dozen along the centre road level with them, and a third group on the north coast. That ruled out any surprise attack on the port for the rest of the night; a sentry on a horse galloping across this flat country would take very little time to reach Otrabanda.

All this, Rennick reflected, was not the way the Marines had been taught to conduct their business during their brief training at Chatham, but Mr Ramage obviously had some ideas of his own. But Rennick knew that his own father, now a lieutenant-colonel in the 1st Dragoons, would be startled to hear some of Mr Ramage's views. Rennick grinned to himself: his father's ideas about warfare had not changed from the principles drummed into him by his own father, who had also served in the 1st. In fact there had been three generations of Rennicks in the 1st (dating from the day it was first formed in 1683) and his father had expected him to be the fourth. Old Colonel Rennick was appalled (almost apoplectic, in fact) when his son had announced he wanted to go to sea; indeed, he had slammed down his brandy glass so hard that it broke, whereupon his wife had hysterics because it was one of a dozen inherited from her grandfather.

In his ignorance the would-be sailor did not know that eighteen years of age was much too late to begin a naval career, but a chance meeting with another young blood who had made the same mistake put him on to the Marines. His father, finally accepting that his son was lost to the 1st Dragoons (thus saving himself several hundred pounds for a subaltern's commission, with hundreds more for later promotions, since advancement depended on guineas, not glory), mentioned casually that George Villiers, the Member of Parliament for Warwick (the county in which the Rennicks were considerable landowners) was a friend of his.

Father and son had then paid a visit to the Honourable George Villiers at his town house in Portman Square, and there the man who was also Paymaster of the Marines (as well as being the youngest brother of the Earl of Clarendon) seemed glad to see Colonel Rennick and sympathetic towards his son's wish to be a sea soldier. Anyway, a week later a messenger had brought Colonel Rennick an official letter from the Honourable George, and a month later Second Lieutenant Rennick, footsore, shoulders bruised from musketry drill, wrist aching from sword drill, heels blistered from marching, brain weary from (admittedly cursory) lessons in tactics, back weary from drill at the great guns, went to bed at night and if he dreamed it was of commanding his own detachment of Marines in a ship of war.

Now, four years later, it had happened: he commanded his own Marine company of one sergeant, two corporals and forty privates; more important, he commanded them in a frigate which was in turn commanded by the Navy's most brilliant young captain. Others might disagree – if they did you could probably put it down to jealousy – but Captain Ramage had two rare abilities, and you needed to serve with him and to share in the planning and the operations fully to appreciate them.

The two abilities were in many ways contradictory. Rennick had already discovered that the captain was contemptuous of gamblers—both the crazy fellows who wagered small fortunes at the London gambling tables and the captains who just shut their eyes and took their ships into action hoping for the best. Yet Rennick had seen on several occasions that no man was a better gambler than the captain: he would see what ought— or had—to be done, then he would work out the odds, quite cold-bloodedly.

He did not put it into as many words, of course, but in the convoy action off Diamond Rock, for instance, and cutting out the *Jocasta* at Santa Cruz, the odds were (on paper) so much against him that no sane man would accept them. But Captain Ramage did and, Rennick realized later, it was because the captain read figures on paper differently from most people. There were times when he calculated that one of his own men was worth, say, two Frenchmen or three Spaniards. At other times he doubled those figures. In the *Jocasta* business he must have quadrupled them! Yet he knew his men; he never asked for more than they could give (it had taken Rennick a long time to realize that), and he had this ability to lead the men so that they gave it. Rennick still shivered when he thought of how his Marines had captured and blown up the castles at Santa Cruz: it had seemed impossible in prospect, but in retrospect it seemed easy. Which meant, of course, that Mr Ramage had this knack of seeing a problem simultaneously in prospect and, it seemed, in retrospect.

The second ability, of course, was that he took a decision apparently without a moment's doubt, although he was as likely to refuse a particular operation because the odds were wrong as he was to attempt something else. Nor did he give a damn what anyone thought of him; that was what it all meant in the end. He received his orders, did what he thought was right, and damned the consequences. So far the Admiralty and the various admirals had been forced to congratulate him (Rennick gathered much of this from people like Southwick), but if Captain the Lord Ramage ever put a foot wrong then they'd crucify him. They'd put him on the beach on half pay and leave the crabs to chew his uniform and boots (and try to forget the dispatches they'd been only too pleased at the time to print in the *Gazette*).

Indeed, Rennick's own father had written a long letter to this effect quite recently – after the Diamond Rock convoy affair, although before Santa Cruz – warning him that he had reaped enough glory and should at once get transferred to another ship, one commanded by a more conservative captain. The feeling in London, the old Colonel wrote, was that Captain Ramage's luck had held for several years but was bound to change. To be fair, he also mentioned a story from Mr Villiers that the King had been heard to tell the First Lord that had Captain Ramage not had a title in his own right he should have received a knighthood for Diamond Rock and a baronetcy for Santa Cruz, and that the First Lord's reactions had been mixed. So, the Colonel had written: 'Your Captain stands well with the King, but do not forget that Their Lordships are the ones who give the orders and read the reports and pass dispatches for publication in the *London Gazette*.'

For all that, Curaçao looked like a femur, and he could learn nothing more from the map. The Dutch for saint was *sint*, a bay was a *baai*, and a point was *punda*. That much he had learned from the map, but it seemed little more than a chart with roads and villages marked on it. He folded it and left the gunroom to see the captain.

The captain's steward, Silkin, who was blessed with the ability to move without noise or effort, was just clearing away the breakfast table and the captain seemed in a cheerful mood. This, Rennick knew well enough, was lucky; until at least an hour after breakfast the captain often seemed to walk around in the shadow of his own black stormcloud.

'Ah, Rennick; you have the plans for the Battle of Amsterdam?'

The Marine lieutenant grinned and put the map on the desk. 'My only plan, sir – suggestion, rather – is that we take good care not to fight for this side of the city.'

To Rennick's surprise, Ramage nodded in agreement. 'That was my impression, but I'm no soldier. Risk of them turning our flank?'

Rennick nodded. 'We could start off holding the Punda side of the channel, sir – in fact the channel forms a moat in front – but it runs into the lake, Schottegat. We haven't nearly enough men to form a line from the other side of the lake—the far side from here—to the north coast of the island. The rebels could pour through there and come round to attack the eastern side of Amsterdam, Punda, taking us in the rear.'

'Soldiers always design the defences of ports as though they'll only ever be attacked from seaward,' Ramage commented sourly. 'English Harbour, Cartagena, Havana, San Juan in Puerto Rico, Fort Royal in Martinique . . .'

'They should leave it to the Marines, sir.'

'Let them lay bricks, instead of dropping them, eh? Well, what do you suggest?'

'The only way we can't be outflanked or taken in the rear, sir, is to forget the Punda side altogether, simply abandon it, and form a line facing west on the Otrabanda side, with the sea on our left, the channel behind us, and Schottegat, or whatever that lake is called, on our right. If we have to retreat we can get back on board the *Calypso*.'

'We can leave boats ready for us along the Otrabanda quay, you mean. Even shift the privateers alongside.'

Rennick nodded. 'We could evacuate the Governor and his family, and a hundred or so other people.' Even as he spoke he realized that the captain was shaking his head. Rennick was not surprised; the place was indefensible, a fact which, added to their being heavily outnumbered, meant they were better off staying in the *Calypso*. Sailors always got into trouble the moment they set foot on land . . .

'I wasn't thinking of defending Amsterdam, Mr Rennick.' The captain was speaking quietly, and Rennick was relieved to hear the news. It confirmed his own view that it was an impossible task with their force—a hundred Dutchmen, forty Marines and at most a hundred and fifty seamen. Then he realized that there had been a faint emphasis on one of the words which completely changed the meaning of the whole sentence.

'As you quite rightly point out, Mr Rennick, we can't defend Amsterdam, and even if we could—if we had enough men—I'm not sure that would be the right thing to do. I think we should take your Marines and what seamen we can spare, and attack these rebels. Take them by surprise, if possible. And we'll leave the Dutch troops where they are, here in Amsterdam, unless their officers speak English.'

'But sir, there are five hundred rebels and privateersmen . . .'

'And a hundred and fifty or so of us.'

'Exactly, sir, so –'

'You're not suggesting that rebels and privateersmen are better trained than our seamen and Marines?'

'Well, no, sir.' Rennick was wary. All too often the captain's questions-and-answers ended up with some conclusion he could not refute, but for the moment he failed to see the trend of the captain's argument. 'Not better disciplined, anyway.'

'And the odds our men usually reckon against the French?'

'Well, sir, three to one . . .'

'Mr Rennick,' Ramage said in the same quiet voice, 'my mathematics are not particularly good, but if we have one hundred and fifty and they have five hundred, surely the odds are close to three to one?'

Rennick seized the only argument left. 'They're not all French, sir.'

Ramage laughed. 'No, but don't press the point. The French are the privateersmen and will be better trained: they are used to using muskets and pistols. Your Dutchmen, the rebels, will have no training and even less discipline: they'll be the "philosophers", waving their arms in the air and talking loudly of freedom and equality while the privateersmen fire off a dozen rounds each.'

Suddenly Rennick realized that he had given the wrong impression. From the start, for a reason he could no longer fathom, he had thought in terms of defending Amsterdam, although the captain had not made a point of it. He, the Marine officer, was the one who should be arguing that the *Calypso*'s role was to fight out in the open, where they could attack suddenly and retreat, strike again from another direction and vanish, swoop on the enemy when they had bivouacked for the night and then disappear into the darkness. When you had by far the smallest force it was fatal to get trapped in a defensive position.

He glanced up to see the captain watching him and knew those brown eyes had seen and understood his thoughts. The captain's look was friendly. 'Always look all round the horizon first, Rennick; it's very easy to start walking in the wrong direction.'

'I can see that, sir – now!'

'Very well, give me your opinion on these proposals. Don't be afraid to speak out if you disagree. Now, we'll use one hundred and fifty seamen and your forty or so Marines. I think it would be a mistake to mix them: the Marines are the trained soldiers; I see them as the sword, while the seamen are the club. But that being so, aren't forty Marines a little unwieldy?'

Rennick cursed the fact that the *Calypso* did not have the junior Marine lieutenant to which she was entitled, although his sergeant was a reliable man. 'Yes, sir. You remember that at Santa Cruz we put half under the sergeant while I had the other half. That worked out very well.'

'But the seamen,' Ramage said, 'a group of twenty seamen aren't going to be nearly as effective as twenty Marines.'

'Companies of thirty seamen, if you want my opinion. More if you're using fewer officers.'

'There'll be five of us and you and the sergeant. Seven companies, or platoons, or whatever you care to call them. So five companies each of thirty men will take care of the seamen.'

The seamen were light-footed and would be excellent for night work, Rennick realized, providing they did not go blundering into farmyards and set the dogs barking. But none of the deck officers, including Ramage, had the slightest idea about flanking operations or – then he remembered that Captain Ramage was the first to see that Amsterdam could be outflanked from the north and was indefensible. And the first lieutenant, Aitken, came from the Highlands, and there was no telling what tricks he had picked up while hunting (or poaching) deer, when one had to attack silently to windward: deer were too sharp-nosed and sharp-eyed to allow a leeward approach. Wagstaffe came from London, so he wouldn't know the difference between a left wheel and a pink flamingo (of which the island had hundreds, he had heard). The third lieutenant came from Suffolk, so Baker might know a little fieldcraft – it was surprising what one could pick up as a boy while poaching partridges over a neighbour's fields. Kenton was the son of a half-pay captain, so he could not be trusted to walk across an open field at night without bumping into the only bull it contained. That left Captain Ramage, and at that point Rennick stopped speculating: one could never be sure what the captain knew – some of his exploits in Italy with his coxswain, that American fellow Jackson, would be unbelievable if it had not been other people telling the tales.

'Seven groups, then,' Ramage said. 'They can operate as a single force or be divided up. We'll spend today sorting out the seamen, and you can give them instructions in the rudiments of fieldcraft.'

Rennick tried to hide his disappointment but failed. 'We're not moving off today, sir?'

'No,' Ramage said crisply, shaking his head. 'If we move on the rebels in daylight they'll be fully prepared. They seem to camp for the night; get settled in early, no doubt, with a bottle of wine each. Maybe a dozen sentries . . . We want to achieve enough surprise to make up for the odds.'

Rennick knew his captain well enough to make criticisms now, not later. 'Night fighting on land is a very uncertain business, sir.'

'I know,' Ramage said soberly. 'Jackson and I once had some experience of it in Italy against cavalry. And it struck me then that the French cavalrymen could see as little as we could and because there were so many they fell over each other. Darkness puts everyone on the same level. Like death, it's the great leveller!'

'The Marines, sir,' Rennick was quick to point out. 'We lose the advantage of their specialized training.'

'Not their discipline, though, and they're only a quarter of our force. Darkness, Rennick, is like the invention of the gun. Until the gun came along, a skilled swordsman would be sure to kill an unskilled one, but the gun made them both equal. With a pistol, the smallest man can fight and beat a giant. We haven't invented darkness, but we can make use of it. Your Marines should be able to fire three aimed musket shots for everybody else's one.'

Rennick grinned happily as he thought about it. 'We'll be wide awake, too, and the rebels half asleep – except for the sentries.'

'They'll be half asleep and with luck half drunk, too, providing we take them by surprise. Now, we have to arrange with the Governor to keep Dutch patrols out for a few more hours, so we know exactly where the rebels are all day, and where they camp. So we'll make a start issuing and checking pistols and muskets, and get the grindstone up on deck to sharpen cutlasses and pikes. A boarding pike is going to be more useful in the darkness than a pistol. You might emphasize that to the men. Remember a boarding pike is seven and a half feet long – that's the closest the enemy need get to you!'

Lacey brought the schooner *La Créole* into the harbour exactly at noon. Ramage's arrangement with the Governor concerning the seaward lookouts at Waterfort and Riffort had worked perfectly, except that he had forgotten to tell anyone in the *Calypso* about it, so when Aitken heard the sound of ten evenly-spaced musket shots fired at five-second intervals coming up the channel from the entrance he had the Marine drummer beat to quarters while the word was being passed for the captain, who was in his cabin.

As Ramage came up the companionway he guessed what had happened, but the musket shots could also be a warning of an enemy ship. He explained to Aitken the arrangement he had made with the Governor, and the two men watched the British flags which were now flying from the two forts and Government House without the white flags of truce. Then they had seen *La Créole* tacking cautiously across the entrance, at first a good mile out, and then closer as Lacey found the batteries did not open fire.

Ramage did not envy Lacey; the situation was a good test of the young lieutenant. The last time he had seen the *Calypso* she had been off the north-west coast of the island, which was well and truly Dutch-owned. When he returned from escorting *La Perle*, the *Calypso* was at anchor in Amsterdam, apparently undamaged and still under a British flag, while British flags flew from the forts. Yet Lacey had seen what could be done with flags.

It might reassure Lacey if the *Calypso* made some signals, but the lieutenant already knew how *La Perle* had been captured because of a captured French signal book, and he might suspect the Dutch had played the same trick. Paolo Orsini was waiting and Ramage ordered: 'Hoist *La Créole*'s pendant number, and then 243, 63 and 371.'

Ramage knew the first one would puzzle the young midshipman, who had long since shown he knew by heart most of the signals in the book. But as he wrote the numbers on the slate he paused to look up the meanings of all three, then repeated them, obviously worried that Ramage had made mistakes. 'Numbers 243, *Quit prizes or ships under convoy, and join the Admiral;* 63, *Anchor as soon as convenient;* and

371, sir, *The strange ships have been examined.*'

'Correct, Orsini, and then, when she has anchored, the signal for the captain to come on board.'

'Aye aye, sir.'

Aitken wore a broad grin. 'That first one should convince Lacey, sir. No Dutchman, even if he knew about *La Perle* and had the signal book, would think of that. And the harbour must seem full of "strange ships" from his position: he can see the masts of those privateers beyond us!'

Within fifteen minutes of the signal flags being hoisted the schooner was close – reaching through the harbour entrance, guns run out and men with telescopes up the masts: the wary Lacey had obviously not ruled out the chance of a trap and keeping over to the windward side of the channel, was giving himself room to wear round and get out again.

An hour later Lacey was sitting down opposite Ramage as Silkin served the first course of the midday meal.

'I trust that you like callalou soup,' Ramage said.

'I've never tried it, sir,' Lacey admitted.

'Callalou is a sort of local spinach. Silkin is convinced it does me good.'

Lacey, still unused to being treated as a commanding officer, raised his spoon and sipped cautiously, obviously expecting it to be hot. Finding it was being served cold he tackled it boldly and nodded his appreciation.

'Now,' Ramage said, 'tell me the details of the *La Perle* business.'

'There isn't much to tell, sir. She steered a course for the Main, burned lights at night, and pumped. I think the leak was worsening all the time, but her pumps were just about holding. I was watching in case she settled really low in the water, but usually I kept astern of her.'

'Did she keep the same course?'

'Yes, sir. I think they'd decided to make for San Juan de los Cayos. Anyway, that's where we arrived twenty-eight hours after leaving you. I expected her to anchor, but they rounded up, reduced sail, hoisted out boats, made sail again and steered straight for the beach.

'By this time it was getting so shallow that I had a man in the chains with a lead and had the sheets eased, so we were making only a couple of knots, but the French were in a hurry: she hit the shallows making a good five knots.'

'Her draught increased by the leak?'

'By a couple of feet, sir: we were watching the waterline in relation to the height of her gun ports. Anyway, it must have been a soft bottom, although farther out we were finding sand with our lead, and she slowly came to a stop, with courses and topsails still set.'

Ramage nodded. 'It's a strange sight, a ship with canvas set but not moving. A stronger wind, of course, and the masts would have gone by the board.'

'Yes, sir, they didn't wait to let anything run – sheets, tacks, braces, halyards . . . They just tossed booms over the side, hatch covers, anything that would act as rafts. And then they abandoned ship, the boats towing the rest of the men as they clung to anything that floated. Then, when the boats had just about reached the beach – there was quite a heavy surf and two of the boats broached and capsized – we saw smoke coming from the main hatch. Ten minutes later the ship was blazing from stem to stern. The sails burned like sheets of paper in that wind; the rigging was a fantastic sight, with all the tar on it, the rope spluttering like slow match as it burned. Then the masts went by the board, well alight by the time they fell and sending up clouds of steam as they hit the water.'

With his face flushed by the excitement of telling the story, Lacey stopped, embarrassed at his own eloquence, and carried on with his soup. When he had finished and refused more when Silkin offered the tureen, he nodded when Ramage asked if there was anything more to tell.

'When the masts and yards went by the board she lost a lot of weight and this made her float higher – enough for her to move again. The wind caught her and slewed her round parallel to the beach, which runs east to west, and she had her bow to the west. I think the wind then began coming in through the sternlights –' he turned to gesture to the large windows of Ramage's cabin – 'and it was like a pair of bellows starting up. She moved perhaps fifty yards, a little to the westward, and just burned like the fire in a blacksmith's forge. An hour later – we were anchored offshore, just watching her – she had burned almost to the water's edge.'

'And the Spanish?' Ramage asked. 'Any sign of patrols?'

'No, sir. The French ship's company were just scattered along the beach. Some of them were trying to haul the boats higher, so that they wouldn't be smashed by the surf, but three broke up. We saw a group of Spaniards to the east, from the village, but they were keeping away from the French. I have a feeling the French aren't going to get much of a welcome.'

While they finished the meal Ramage told Lacey of Curaçao's problems and the island's surrender, and then described his intended night attack on the rebels. 'I can muster thirty men, sir,' Lacey offered eagerly. 'That would give you eight groups.'

Ramage thought for a moment. *La Créole* was anchored beyond the privateers, almost in the Schottegat. The danger to the ships would come only from a large enemy ship attempting the entrance. The schooner with a much-reduced crew would be safe enough.

'Very well,' he said. 'Rennick has the map of the island. Spend half an hour or so with him, so you'll know what we propose.'

The meal had been finished and Lacey had left when a boat from Punda brought Major Lausser on board with a report from the Governor telling Ramage that the rebels and priva-teersmen had not moved from the camp they had set up the previous night near Daniel; that they had apparently looted the villages of Pannekoek, Willebrordus and Daniel; and in burning down some large estate houses they had collected a large quantity of rum. Patrols had seen men driving cattle into the camp, where presumably they were being slaughtered. And, the Governor commented, tomorrow was the anniversary of the storming of the Bastille. Was it possible, he asked, that the Frenchmen were going to celebrate it? If they were, it seemed highly likely the drinking and feasting would start tonight . . .

CHAPTER FIFTEEN

The Dutch shopkeepers and their families, along with most other people living on the Otrabanda side, had spent most of the day moving over to Punda with as many of their valuables as they could carry or persuade the boatmen to take on board. The rowing boats, laden with furniture on which the owners perched precariously, crossed the channel with the occupants cursing, joking or being reassured in shrill Dutch or Papia-mento, the local language which was a curious mixture of Dutch, Spanish, English and African dialects. Southwick noted to Aitken that it was probably the first time that so many people in Amsterdam had exerted themselves in the blazing midday sun; usually they retired to cool and curtained rooms for a siesta lasting until three o'clock.

Now, half an hour after darkness, the *Calypso*'s boats were landing the last of the eight companies on the Otrabanda quay. Rennick's Marines were formed up as though awaiting the Colonel-Commandant's inspection on the parade ground at Chatham; Lacey was prowling round the thirty men he had brought from *La Créole*. Aitken stood at the head of his group, which he had formed up in three columns each of ten men, and was silent, no doubt congratulating himself that Southwick had lost the argument that the first lieutenant should stay behind in command of the ship, not the master. Ramage had ruled that marching long distances across the Curaçao countryside – and probably running, too – was for youngsters; that masters over sixty with pot-bellies and short of breath could only be rated youngsters if they lived in one of the new charitable homes for old folk. Wagstaffe had his men in four columns of seven men, with a leading seaman ahead and astern. Lacey, Baker and Kenton copied Aitken, who had in turn used the same system as Ramage.

Ramage was thankful that there was still a breeze and knew that with luck it would hold the whole night. As usual it had been cool out in the *Calypso*, but the moment he landed on Otrabanda the heat soaked into him, as though the earth had been storing it all day and would be slowly releasing it through the night. Mosquitoes landed on him like droplets of water in fog and, thwarted at the ankles by his high boots, they made up for it by whining assaults on his wrists and face. The red-hot needle jabs of sandflies showed that Curaçao was not free from the tiny midges which elsewhere the sea-men called 'no-see-'ems'.

Now, as the men scrambled out of the last boat and joined Kenton's company, Ramage checked his own men. Choosing his thirty had been difficult only because it meant refusing at least another thirty. Jackson was the second in command, with Stafford and Rossi. Another dozen or so had been chosen because they had served with him in the *Kathleen* while most of the rest had been in the *Triton*. It had been a case of choosing thirty men out of a hundred or so that, like children expecting a treat, were shouting, 'Me! Me!'

After giving it some thought, Ramage finally had no compunction about risking being accused of favouritism. He had no set plan for the attack (that was impossible until he could see the rebels' position) but he knew that in the darkness it was more likely that he would have to do something special with his own company because of the difficulty of passing orders to one of the others. That being the case, he wanted men around him who would understand his intentions without a lot of explanation. Someone like Jackson, who as a youngster had fought for the rebels in the American War of Independence and probably knew a good deal more than Rennick about this sort of fighting, which was a matter of ambushes, sudden attacks and vanishing again before the victims recovered. Never, in other words, remaining still long enough for an enemy to take aim. Rennick was by training a man of march and countermarch by files, complicated outflanking movements, brave beyond belief but limited by the drill manual, which dealt with routine situations where men fired to order and battalions and armies, friendly and enemy, moved as though in some gigantic quadrille. It was not, Ramage thought wryly, a case of eager seamen scrambling through the night . . .

In the darkness, though, it seemed that he had a small army formed up, but Rennick's suggestion that the first men landed should include one from each company, who would act as a marker – a marker buoy, in fact – and avoid confusion in the dark as the rest of the men landed, had worked perfectly.

Ramage started his inspection at the head of the column, which was led by Rennick's company and followed by the Marine sergeant's. Then came Ramage's company, followed by Kenton and Baker, Lacey and Wagstaffe, with Aitken bringing up the rear. One hundred and eighty seamen and forty Marines – more than two hundred and twenty men, and all silent except for the muted slapping at mosquitoes. The danger in all operations like this was that a man hoarding his tots of rum would get drunk on the march and become rowdy, but each man boarding a boat had to pause at the *Calypso*'s gangway and be inspected by Southwick on one side and the master-at-arms on the other. The master-at-arms had growled as he checked each man: 'Breathe out . . . pistol or musket . . . cutlass or pike . . . yer got any rum hidden on yer?' Only after the test had been passed was the man allowed to go over the side, sober and properly armed.

It was eight o'clock and they had at least ten miles to cover. Ramage finished the inspection, went back to the head of the column and said to Rennick: 'Where are the Dutch guides?'

The Marine indicated the two men standing at the head of the column.

'One had better come with me; there's no point in both being with you.'

'They both speak English, sir,' Rennick said thankfully.

Ramage called one of the guides, gave the order for Rennick to move off and with the guide hurried back to the head of his own company and followed the Marines. His orders to his lieutenants had been simple enough – follow the company in front.

The road out of Amsterdam was cobbled for a few hundred yards past the last house, but after that it was dried earth, so that the marching men made almost no sound. The moon had not risen – nor would it for several hours – but there was very little cloud so the stars were brilliant. And somewhere along the road, close to Amsterdam, Dutch soldiers would be watching them pass – the Governor still had a platoon of soldiers scattered round the west side of Amsterdam to intercept any spies or sympathizers who might try to sneak out of the city to warn the rebels that the British were landing troops and seamen.

Less than a mile up the road Ramage felt the muscles in his shins beginning to tighten up with the unaccustomed marching, and the jarring of his heels was giving him a headache. The road turned inland and then turned west again to form the spine of the island. The figure appearing suddenly in the darkness was Rennick, acting as whipper-in, making sure the companies were keeping closed up.

An hour and a half later, when the guide reckoned that the village of Daniel was only three miles away, Ramage was hot, sticky and tired. His heels were raw, his feet felt swollen to twice their normal size. His jacket was sodden with perspiration, his stock chafing his neck and the band of his hat like an iron strap being tightened with a thumbscrew every half a mile. It was time to call a halt, their second, and a few minutes later the whole column was resting on the side of the road, most of the men lying down with their feet in the air, quietly cursing the blisters but admitting this tip given them by Lieutenant Rennick really worked.

Rennick had just loomed up in the darkness, apparently full of energy and with feet that never swelled or blistered, when the faint popping of muskets stifled every groan. It continued for ten or twelve seconds, by which time Ramage was on his feet and looking in the direction from which the sound came. Then, just as he was refocusing his eyes in the darkness on what seemed to be a faint pink glow low on the horizon, there were several tiny flashes at the base of it, like fireflies, followed by more popping.

Rennick, clicking his heels as if indicating to Ramage that he was speaking officially, gave his verdict: 'Muskets being fired without using ball, in my opinion, sir.'

And Ramage realized that the Marine was right: distant musket fire always sounded unreal, little more than a pop, but the last ones had been fired with the muskets pointing in their direction – that was clear from the brightness of some of the flashes – and the pop was more like the sound of corks leaving bottles. If the muskets had been loaded with shot one would expect a sharper note. That was where Rennick's military training came in useful: he knew instinctively what Ramage might well not have noticed.

Now, Ramage realized, Rennick expected an explanation of the pink glow. Well, it was a fire, obviously, but it was a *steady* glow. The few houses that Ramage had seen burning in darkness at a distance, tended to flare up and die down, then flare again as the flames found fresh wood to consume. This steady glow seemed to indicate a fire that was being fed regularly – a large bonfire, for instance, that had been burning several hours.

'How far away were those shots?'

'Two miles at the most, sir.'

And it was about the fourteenth of July. Then there were more musket shots.

'Round up our other company commanders,' Ramage said. 'I'd better have a word with them.'

It was surprising how the military phrases crept in – company commanders, indeed! But it sounded better, when giving orders to as keen and competent a sea soldier as Rennick, to call the lieutenants and sergeant 'company commanders', even though their companies were no bigger than platoons. However, Ramage thought idly as he waited for them to arrive, it was wiser when you put sailors on shore to divide 'em into companies (after all, they were always known as 'the ship's company'; it was only fishing boats and privateers that had 'crews'). Referring to them as platoons risked a lot of ribaldry.

Finally Aitken, Wagstaffe, Baker and Kenton, Lacey and the sergeant reported themselves and gathered round, blurs in the darkness, waiting to hear what their captain had to say. Ramage, unused to meeting his officers on land, was suddenly reminded of Mr Wesley's preachers conducting services on Cornish roadsides (and having large congregations, too!). He coughed, as much to stifle a laugh as draw their attention.

'All of you heard the musketry and can see the fire. There's no village in that direction and a plantation house would not burn so steadily – or for so long. I think our rebel friends and the privateersmen are beginning a celebration party: we know, from the Dutch patrols, that they have been rounding up cattle. My guess is that they are roasting the carcases on that fire – which is why it is burning so steadily. The musketry is simply firing volleys for fun, celebrating the fall of the Bastille. They're starting early because it's not the fourteenth of July for a few hours yet. So by midnight . . .'

'Aye,' Aitken said, with a wealth of contempt in his voice for men who were not only revolutionaries and drinkers but, until recently at least, avowed Catholics, 'they'll be so besotted by midnight it'll be like picking apples.'

'Bu we're not taking prisoners, are we, sir?' Kenton asked, obviously shocked and clearly thinking Aitken was referring to plucked apples in a basket.

'We'll take them if they come to hand,' Ramage said evenly, remembering the *Tranquil*'s victims. 'Now, your men had better put the bands of cloth round their heads now, so there are no mistakes, and tell 'em once again that anyone without a white headband is an enemy.

'And don't let's forget that whether those rebels are drunk or sober, they outnumber us more than two to one. But we have some advantages, so listen carefully while I explain them.

First, we can't hope to kill them all. Our first objective is to drive them away from Amsterdam, so when we attack we want to make sure that the survivors try to escape to the westward.

'Second, from whichever direction we attack, they are against the light of the bonfire. The wind, such as it is, seems unable to make up its mind whether to be south-east or east, but the point is that the smoke is blowing to the west. If we attack from the windward side – from the east, this side – we can reasonably expect the survivors to run away to the west.'

'But sir,' Baker asked, 'supposing they don't bolt to the west but stand and fight?'

'Then *we'll* bolt to the east,' Ramage said lightly, but added as soon as the others had stopped chuckling: 'Though it is a good question to which there's no answer except that we must make sure they do.

'Now, Rennick, the Marines are the sharpshooters. As the rebels bolt I want your men to pick off as many as possible with muskets and, using your own judgement about numbers, chase the first group. There will be some smoke and a ragged column, I imagine, with our seamen becoming mixed up with the tail of them, which is why we've taken so much of the purser's white duck to make headbands.

'So your Marines will be out on each side of the bonfire while the six companies of seamen attack from this side, driving the rebels past your men, like beaters at the butts. Volleys first from muskets and pistols; then close in with pike and cutlass.'

'Can we be sure the rebels will be gathered this side drinking and eating, sir?' Wagstaffe asked cautiously.

Rennick laughed. 'Spoken like a true Londoner!'

'Well, finish the answer,' Ramage said, laughing with Rennick and Aitken.

'It's a hot night and anyway no one sits on the lee side of a huge bonfire! They'll all be up to windward, clear of the smoke and heat. Even the men tending the roasting carcases will be up to windward.'

'Aye, but they won't be roasting whole carcases on a bonfire like that,' Aitken said. 'The outside flesh would get charred long before the rest was cooked. They'll be roasting nice cuts on long poles, if I know anything about it. A whole carcase means a spit and someone to turn it – and it takes hours. And to feed five hundred or more . . . better to cut up the carcases and issue raw meat and leave it to individuals to do their own cooking.'

'Very well,' Ramage said, 'the main thing is that we don't kill each other accidentally. We all have watches, and the bonfire means we can see the time.' He took out his watch and saw it wanted three-quarters of an hour to midnight.

'We'll allow an hour and a quarter for us to get into position. So at half past midnight, the moment you hear three musket shots one after another at one-second intervals, you all open fire. The three shots should be enough to make the sleepers and the drunks sit up to see what's going on, providing you with more targets, and reveal where the sentries are. One hundred and eighty musket balls, followed by one hundred and eighty pistol balls, should kill a few, because Rennick's Marines have only forty muskets and forty pistols to bring down the rest.'

'That's only four hundred and forty shots, sir, and you said there are five hundred rebels and privateersmen!' Aitken said.

'True enough,' Ramage said with mock seriousness, 'but you speak as a seaman. Rennick's sea soldiers reckon to make one ball go through at least two men at night and three in daylight.

'Now, I want the second company of Marines under the sergeant to go to the rear of our column, then we'll be approaching in the order we attack. Your company will be to the south, Rennick, at the end of the bonfire, then mine, then Baker, Lacey, Kenton and Wagstaffe, who will be roughly in the middle, then Aitken, with the sergeant and the second company of Marines beyond. Any questions or suggestions?'

The earth was baked as hard as pottery by scorching sun, with no rain for many days, and (it seemed to Ramage) liberally covered with small, sharp rocks that dug into hips and elbows and made cutlass hilts clank with the slightest movement.

Ramage pulled out his watch and held it up so that he could read the dial by the light of the great long bonfire burning less than a hundred yards away. Twenty minutes past twelve; ten minutes to wait. His wrists seemed swollen to twice their normal size, the flesh itching in a fiery torture, and mosquitoes were landing boldly on his face.

The bonfire was a good twenty yards long, but low now;

the rebels had obviously started off with a great blaze in the
afternoon and then kept it stoked so that the whole mass
glowed red, just right for roasting. Dozens of shadowy figures
moved about, lit up by flames spurting up from time to time
as more tree branches and brushwood were flung on.

Many rebels were lying on the ground, holding out long
sticks – they might well be boarding pikes – with cuts of meat
cooking on the end, like men fishing from a river bank. There
were few sentries; Ramage could see only one in front of his
position, a man squatting down with a musket clasped in his
arms.

The rebels were drinking – one could see bottles being
passed round, and men were occasionally filling jugs from
some casks propped up clear of the ground, well to windward
of the flames. Occasionally they burst into snatches of revolutionary songs, but the heat, the wine, the mosquitoes and
sheer sleepiness seemed to be draining their martial ardour.
As far as Ramage could make out, only a quarter of the rebels
were actually asleep, dark shadows lying like sheep in a
meadow forty yards or so in front of the bonfire.

He wriggled and carefully moved a sharp stone that was
numbing his left thigh. He looked at his watch again. Only
three minutes had passed. He was sure that if he looked again
he'd find the watch was going backwards. Jackson was lying
to his left, musket in front of him, the butt ready to slide
against his shoulder; Stafford was to his right, with Rossi
beyond. The rest of the men were lying to left and right, so
that Ramage was in the middle of the line, the best place to
shout orders both ways.

Rennick and one company of Marines should be hidden
over there on the left, to one side of the bonfire, while Baker,
Lacey, Wagstaffe and Kenton were on the right, parallel with
the bonfire, with Aitken at the end and the Marine sergeant's
company along the right-hand edge. There had been no
messengers so he presumed they were in position. He had
shocked Rennick by saying he did not want runners bringing
messages that all was well; that they should be reserved for
bad news. Every movement risked them being spotted by the
rebels, so –

'Qui vive?'

The challenge was from over to the right, in front of
Baker's company.

'Qui va là?'

The French sentry, obviously a privateersman, sounded certain that he had spotted someone.

Then Ramage saw the sentry: he was standing bolt upright, staring into the darkness, a darkness which was emphasized by the light of the bonfire behind him. Then suddenly the man raised his musket to his shoulder and fired.

At once scores of rebels began rousing themselves in front of the fire. Now for the signal!

'Jackson, Stafford, Rossi . . . We'll attack now. Ready, Jackson? Fire! . . . Stafford, fire! . . . Rossi, fire!'

To Ramage's right the British muskets fired in a ragged drumroll with the muzzle flashes flickering like summer lightning. Against the bonfire he saw men collapsing like half-filled sacks tossed from a granary steps, while others went down flat in a dive, showing they were unwounded and seeking safety.

Ramage had a pistol in each hand as he scrambled up and began to run towards the fire. 'Forward, men! Pistols when you're within range, then cutlass and pike!'

He was shrieking with excitement, but he knew it; there was no need for self-control now – he wanted his one hundred and eighty men to rout five hundred, and an excited, shouting and howling dash might do it!

Jackson to one side, Stafford the other – and out of the corner of his eye he could see a dark line rising up on his right and sweeping forward. Ahead there were fast-moving shapes against the flames and red glow: startled rebels scrambling up, flashes here and there as flames reflected on sword blades. A few flashes from pistols or muskets, but Ramage knew they must be through the line of sentries.

Cock the left pistol, now the right; cutlass slapping against his left leg. Don't trip and sprain an ankle. Paolo somewhere over to the right, with Aitken, and for Gianna's sake . . . but the boy was excitable and keen and likely to run ahead of the rest.

Some of the rebels crouching now, aiming pistols: several tiny eyes winking in red flashes which only the targets saw. Thirty yards – too far for half-drunk, drowsy and frightened men to aim accurately. And the rebels are half-blinded anyway because they have been in the bright light of the bonfire for hours while the British, the targets, are sweeping in from a dark background.

The smell of roast beef makes the feeling of hunger nudge out fear. They are all running towards rebels with pistols but the British seamen are still obeying orders to hold their fire to be sure of hitting: it takes several moments for an excited man to stop running, aim with any accuracy, and then fire.

A crackling to his right: some of the seamen are firing their pistols. And now movement on the left of the bonfire. Like maggots squirming in rotten meat, dozens of rebels are bolting round the left-hand edge of the bonfire, yelling and tripping, some swaying because they are too drunk to do anything more than follow their friends. In a few moments they will run into a murderous fire from Rennick's Marines. Yes, there go the muskets.

But still there are scores of men in front of the bonfire; men who are not bolting. Far too many for playing around with pistols, he decided, and jamming them back in his waistband as he ran he grabbed his cutlass.

Ten yards to the first men: smells of roast beef, garlic, spilled wine and urine, and the almost aromatic smell of woodsmoke. One man crouching with a pistol, another half cowering with a cutlass, as though trapped by fellow privateersmen each side and the bonfire behind, a dozen more each side ready to fight and Jackson and Stafford shouting wild threats at the top of their voices as they run and Rossi screaming most of the curses developed over the centuries in a country renowned for its blasphemy.

And then – the first man was thick-set, a round head on broad shoulders with no neck, face shiny from the heat, eyes dark holes because the bonfire was behind him. His arm swung out sideways, sword blade flashing in the flames, a great scything movement as he tried to cut Ramage down in a blow which should have decapitated him.

Ramage thrust his sword upwards across his body, deflecting the Frenchman's blade high into the air and bringing the two men face to face, bodies touching. Foul breath, the stench of stale wine, a piggish face unshaven for days, and Ramage chopped his sword down diagonally again and the man grunted as he fell, blood spurting from his neck.

A moment later a metallic flash warned Ramage of a sword

thrust coming from his right. He parried, fighting sideways to avoid standing with his back to more privateersmen between him and the bonfire. This man was big, his face brutish, and he was dressed in the remnants of an officer's uniform. His mouth was moving; Ramage sensed rather than heard in the uproar that the man was cursing him.

A sudden downward slash – a typical sabre blow. The man knew something of swordplay, and Ramage held up his blade horizontally, covering his head and shoulders in the classic parry of quinte. Ramage lunged at the man's chest but his sword jarred against the parry of prime. The Frenchman was a moment late as Ramage switched to the most basic of all positions, called by the fencing masters 'Hit with the point', and a moment later Ramage was dragging at the sword as the Frenchman, the point of the cutlass into his chest just where the ribs divided, collapsed on top of him. The man was too big for Ramage to avoid; together they landed heavily on the ground and a winded Ramage found himself gasping desperately for breath. The pain in his stomach was agonizing, but after a few moments he managed to roll clear of the Frenchman, his cutlass gone and feeling his stomach for the wound. There was none; the only dampness was from perspiration, not blood, and the pain was from the winding.

A moment later Jackson was beside him, helping him to his feet, not asking questions which required breath to answer: Ramage was alive and unwounded.

'My cutlass,' Ramage gasped, and Jackson wrenched one from the dying Frenchman's hands.

Then Ramage was on his feet again, conscious of the scorching heat of the bonfire, but realizing that there were no more rebels between him and the great bed of glowing red embers; instead, muskets were crackling at either end – the two companies of Marines were firing into the Frenchmen as they fled to leeward, to the west, away from Amsterdam.

This was a vital moment, and Ramage was glad to see that his six companies – now scattered men but forming a phalanx – had remembered their orders not to chase helter-skelter after fleeing Frenchmen because this would risk them being shot down by the Marines. In the first rush of fleeing Frenchmen the Marines must have a clear field of fire.

He listened and the shooting was dying down at each end: the Marines had used both muskets and pistols. Now was the time for the chase, using only cutlass or pike.

'Calypsos,' he bawled, and the shout was taken up along the line as the men, hearing the single word that told them the chase had begun, started running round the bonfire, shouting as they went.

As he began to run, leading the way round the left end of the bonfire, Ramage saw for the first time that scores of bodies were lying like stooks of corn scattered by a sudden storm. Then, with his company round him, men still bellowing 'Calypsos! Calypsos!' he passed the end of the bonfire and plunged into the darkness, momentarily blinded and instantly aware that the French now had the advantage, with their pursuers outlined against the bonfire's glow. It was only a glow now, enormous but throwing none of the bright flames made by new branches flaring in the enormous heat.

He ran and caught up with more men wearing white bands round their heads, men in Marine uniforms. Then he heard Rennick's voice bellowing orders. There was no clash of steel; although the Marines were trotting along purposefully, there were no groups of men fighting.

'Rennick! Rennick!'

'Here, sir!'

And there was Rennick facing him, his chubby face even redder in the glow of the fire, eyes sparkling, a great grin showing he was enjoying himself. 'Afraid they can run faster than us, sir!'

Chase them in the darkness while the rebels were disorganized? Or wait for daylight, by which time they would have sorted themselves out? By now the odds were more equal, and there was no chance of the rebels attacking Amsterdam. So he would wait for daylight.

'Have the trumpeter recall our men,' Ramage told Rennick. 'We'll catch up with those rebels in daylight. Now we'll attend to the wounded.'

Back on the windward side of the bonfire Ramage was appalled at what he saw: no mad painter's portrayal of the entrance to hell could be more gory or more terrifying: there were at least a hundred bodies sprawled in a band the length of the bonfire, perhaps fifteen yards, and ten yards wide.

Here and there a wounded man moved; at least one was trying to crawl from under two bodies collapsed across him. Kenton was quietly vomiting, but Aitken stood beside Ramage with Baker, who said bitterly: 'Perhaps I'd feel differently if I hadn't been on board the *Tranquil*. Those women lying there, their clothes torn and their throats cut: I'll never forget that. In fact – ' he was staring at the wounded – 'I could cut some throats myself and never feel an ounce of guilt.'

Kenton had joined them in time to hear Baker's last words. 'I'd help you, even if I've just been sick. This is nothing compared to the *Tranquil*. There the people looked as though they'd been murdered in their own homes. Here – well, it's a battlefield.'

'And, young man,' Aitken said, 'let this be a warning: proper lookouts would have saved most of these men from our attack.'

'True, very true,' Rennick said judicially. 'The sentries should have been at least two hundred yards away. The two I saw with my nightglass were taking a pull from a bottle every five minutes or so. The one who raised the alarm probably noticed a single man and was so drunk he thought he could see twenty!'

By now all the seamen and Marines had returned. 'Form your men up,' Ramage ordered. 'Check that none is missing.' He raised his voice: 'My company fall in here!'

There was Jackson, grimy and bloodstained, and Stafford. And Rossi, looking like the flayer in a slaughterhouse. Paolo raced up and stood to attention in front of Ramage. Even before the boy spoke, Ramage saw the dark stains on the cutlass he held in one hand and the blade of the midshipman's dirk in the other.

'Sir!' he said, and when Ramage nodded he announced: 'I killed two, sir.'

'*Main-gauche?*' Ramage enquired.

'The second one; not the first, sir.'

'Very good; I presume you missed with your pistol, but you must practise. Now rejoin your company.'

'*Mama mia*,' Rossi murmured. 'In Volterra he had the good education.'

'Wot's a "man goes"?' Stafford enquired.

'Is when you have a dagger in the left hand and a sword in the right. The minute you get the other man's sword pointing away from you and him off the balance, you slip in the dagger.'

'Well I never!' Stafford's amazement was quite genuine.

'Wot a good idea. Why don't we use "man goes"?'

Jackson surveyed the pile of bodies. 'Savin' Mr Orsini's presence, we seem to do quite well without 'em.'

Ramage counted the men as they fell in behind Jackson. The Dutch guide, whom Ramage had last seen just before the attack started, arrived mopping his face with a large handkerchief and holding a bloodstained sword in the other.

'Good hunting, good hunting,' he grunted to Ramage. 'I do not think they stop again before West Punt. We kill many here. Some rebels are still alive, though.' There was no mistaking the regret in his voice nor the difference he made between Dutch rebels and French privateersmen.

Ramage resumed his counting. 'Twenty-six . . . are you one of my company? I thought so, fall in, and that's twenty-eight. And you two, you're late. Thirty.'

The heat of the bonfire must be awful for some of those French wounded, and he'd do something about it as soon as he could, but his first concern was his own men, none of whom had forgotten the *Tranquil*. 'Jackson, collect reports from the lieutenants and the sergeant.'

Ten minutes later Ramage was listening to the American, scarcely able to believe his ears. Four Marines wounded (one gunshot and three sword cuts); four seamen known to have been killed and three wounded; and seven more missing. Only eighteen casualties, assuming that the seven missing were dead or wounded. Ramage had reckoned on fifty – although the operation was far from complete.

He turned to his company. 'Working in pairs, I want you to find the enemy wounded. Those that can be moved, bring them here, away from the heat but where there's still some light. Jackson, tell Mr Aitken to send the two surgeon's mates in his company to join us here.'

He turned to the Dutch guide. 'Can you find your way back to Amsterdam?'

'Of course, sir.'

'I'll give you an escort. I want you to report what you've seen to the Governor, but *first* I want you to send out to this place all the horses and carts you can find. Bring straw, mattresses, cloth for bandages – anything that will make the journey easier for the wounded. Some of them,' he added, noting the look in the Dutchman's eyes, 'are our own men. And tell the Governor any surgeons would be welcome – they should ride out at once, bringing bandages and instruments.'

'Yes, sir, but I prefer no escort: I will be faster alone!'

For the next two hours the Calypsos sorted the dead from the living, frequently stoking the bonfire with brushwood to give themselves more light. The moon rose, its light cold and forbidding compared with the yellow flames of the bonfire.

The French casualties round the bonfire would have been horrifying, Ramage thought, but for the *Tranquil*: ninety-eight dead, forty-two badly wounded and eleven wounded but able to walk. A total of one hundred and fifty-one . . . nearly a third of the rebel force, and enough to man a 32-gun frigate. Then he reminded himself that it also meant that two-thirds of the enemy had escaped. Three hundred and fifty of them were at this very moment over there to the west, reorganizing themselves . . .

Three Marines guarded the eleven walking wounded, and Ramage decided to question them. If they had come from the western end of the island, the rest of the rebels might now return to the same place. He saw one man whose wounded leg had been bandaged and who was wearing what seemed to be the remnants of a French Navy officer's uniform. He was a young man, his face hard, narrow and angular, unshaven for several days, his sallow complexion seeming darker in the red glow of the fire.

'Your name and rank?' Ramage enquired in French, kneeling beside the man. He noticed one of the Marine sentries move round a yard or two, so that Ramage did not interfere with his field of fire.

'Brune, Jean Brune.'

For a moment Ramage felt dizzy. 'You command the *Nuestra Señora de Antigua*?'

'No, that is – that was – my brother. I command *L'Actif*.'

'Your brother – where is he?'

'Adolphe? He is over there.' The man gestured to where the bodies had been carried. 'Murdered. And you, *M'sieur*, who are you?'

'Captain Ramage. I commanded the attack.'

'Ah, so you are this Ramage, eh? We heard you were on the coast. We might have guessed.'

'Guessed what?'

'That you would attack treacherously, like an assassin in the dark.'

'I found a British merchant ship after your brother had finished with it in daylight. She was called the *Tranquil*.'

'Yes, he told me of it. A British frigate came in sight.'

'So your brother murdered everyone on board, including several women, who were raped as well, before he fled.'

Jean Brune shrugged his shoulders. 'One woman, but surely not several.'

Ramage looked at the sneering face. No remorse, no surprise, and apparently no regrets. Raping and killing women was unfortunate – because they might have been ransomed.

'Your brother – what does he look like?'

'Very big. Tall and broad, with big moustaches. A man kill him with a cutlass. My brother is – was – a fine swordsman. He must have tripped, for this English sailor to kill him.'

'You saw it happen?'

'Yes, I was lying on the ground, a musket ball in my leg.'

'And your brother fell forward on this British sailor, so they collapsed together?'

'Yes – I tell you, he must have tripped. He was a fine man, my brother.'

Ramage nodded soberly. 'I killed him, and he didn't trip. I am sorry he is dead.'

'You should be,' Jean Brune said bitterly. 'Such a fine man, my brother. My older brother, you understand; he taught me everything of the sea, from when we were boys in Brittany. And he took me privateering, and later he helped me buy my ship.'

'Yes,' Ramage said quietly, 'I am sorry your brother is dead: I had hoped to have him hanged from a gallows in Port Royal. And you – if any of my men find out you are his brother, your life won't be worth a puff of smoke, so guard your tongue.'

Brune sat up on one elbow, his eyes widening in fear. 'But you must give orders to protect me. As an English officer you would not let one of your prisoners be murdered!'

'Wouldn't I? Your brother did. In fact he ordered it.'

CHAPTER SIXTEEN

The first carts arrived an hour after dawn. Two nervous Dutch surgeons had come on horseback, obviously unwilling and acting under orders, and with them was the guide, who told Ramage that he had reported to the Governor.

'Is there any message from His Excellency?'

The guide shook his head. 'More carts come soon and the hospital has been warned to – how do you say? – to stand by.'

'Do you speak French?'

'Some – enough, I think.'

'I'm leaving you a dozen men to help you get the wounded back to Amsterdam. If you have spades and picks you can bury the dead here; otherwise take them back to the city.'

The seven missing British seamen had been found: two were dead, killed in sword fights, and five were wounded, one badly. A total of six dead and twelve wounded. For the moment Ramage did not want to know the names of the dead; there would probably be more before sunset.

'The British dead and wounded – they go in the first carts.'

'Of course,' the Dutchman said. 'The doctors are already attending them with your surgeon's mates.'

The guide was an unimaginative but competent man, and it was clear that he hated Dutch rebels, Frenchmen and anyone else who wilfully interrupted the normal peace and quiet of life in Curaçao. The British were helping to restore that peace and quiet and for that reason (for that reason only, Ramage was certain) they had his loyalty and assistance.

Ramage turned away to look for Rennick but Jackson came up, carrying something carefully.

'Breakfast, sir. Some fine slices o' beef. One of the men has roasted them specially. Just about scorched his eyebrows off, too!'

And suddenly, at the thought of munching juicy slices of beef, Ramage felt faint from hunger. He grinned at Jackson as he took the meat, which was stacked like several thin slices of bread and dripping with juice. 'Have all the men eaten and packed away some for later?'

'Only you and Mr Aitken to eat now, sir. The men have had enough to last a week.'

'And Mr Orsini?'

Jackson began laughing. 'He's been your head chef, sir, standing over the man who was roasting it. Reckon he knows just how you like it, sir, red in the middle and brown at the edges. Most concerned, he was.'

Ramage sat down and began eating. The rising sun was still below the horizon but just beginning to catch the peak of Sint Christoffelberg, which was 1200 feet high, although not yet lighting the top of Tafelberg in front of it, which was only 750 feet.

Where were the rebels making for? There were villages all round Sint Christoffelberg, although it seemed possible they'd make for Sint Kruis Baai, on the coast near the southern slope of the great peak and close to where the *Calypso* had been when she first sighted *La Perle*. Then Ramage dismissed the idea: why make for a bay when you have no boats to rescue you?

This beef is good. It tastes all the better for being eaten with the fingers, juice running down the sleeve and down the chin, tickling, and the chin unshaven and rasping as a sleeve serves as a napkin. All the better, too, knowing that all the men now bustling around have eaten their fill of it. No one at the finest hotel in London could taste such beef – but two hundred Calypsos had just gorged themselves on it. They deserved such a feast, even though there were no vegetables and no tots to wash it down – the Marine sergeant had been ordered to pour away all the wine, otherwise by now several men would be drunk.

It was, of course, a feast in a strangely beautiful cemetery, because the corpses of the Frenchmen were still over there, but the rising sun was casting fantastic long shadows, using rounded hills and mountain peaks and cactus and the small divi-divi trees which always pointed towards the west, leaning in deference to the Trade winds. No clouds yet and the stars have faded, the moon becoming anaemic. In a few minutes the sun will come with its usual rush and the grey country-side will suddenly be dappled with pink as the upper rim – he shook his head and stood up: there had been killing a few hours ago, there was more to come. His cutlass was still stained with the blood of Brune – he refused to think of the grim coincidence which had brought them together, because killing the man gave no satisfaction: he would have preferred a trial. Time, time when Brune was locked alone in a cell and perhaps in the long nights the enormity of what he had done in the *Tranquil* would come to him. Yet it would not; a man who could order the unnecessary massacre of innocent men and women was so beyond the understanding of civilized people that he was almost beyond judicial punishment: one did not try a rabid dog.

'Ah, Rennick!' The Marine officer had seen him get up from his meal, and was ready for orders. 'Well, you still have your guide – I'm leaving mine here to get the casualties back to Amsterdam. So let's ferret out the rest of those rebels. Have your guide question anyone you see on the road: we don't want to march a yard more than necessary.'

'I was just going to report, sir,' Rennick said, 'but I decided to wait until you'd eaten. A Dutch farmer who rode in to see what was happening – the rebels burned down his house two days ago – has just told the guide that he's just seen them beyond a village called Pannekoek, about six or seven miles along the road. It's a couple of miles short of Sint Kruis Baai. They're just gathered there, in no sort of order, and apparently with no leader. He's emphatic they're in no sort of order. They had small campfires lit and went hunting for cattle and goats to cook – there are very few cattle there, he says, so they'll have to be content with goat, which the local people won't normally eat.'

'We can't trap them, I suppose?'

'No, sir, not from what he says and the map shows. When they see us coming they'll just move west. We can only trap them at the far end of the island, West Punt, when they meet the sea.'

'Very well, let's see your Marines stepping out. A steady pace, not too fast: the seamen have some aching muscles after the night's stroll.'

As Ramage watched the French camp through his telescope he cursed the Dutch farmer, although it was not the poor fellow's fault that the French had marched another couple of miles and then spent the busiest morning of their lives since the Dutchman passed. The Frenchmen's backs would be aching, their hands sore, their heads aching from the triple assault of last night's drinking, this morning's effort, and the scorching sun beating down on them as they picked up hundreds – thousands more likely – of the rocks and stones littering the fields and used them to build up three or four dozen little defensive positions, like miniature butts built for a partridge or pheasant drive, along the top of a hill at the eastern side of Sint Kruis Baai.

Obviously this was where the French and the rebels had decided to stand and fight. With the sea at their backs in the protected bay, perhaps they intended to retreat to ships or boats – there might be other privateers around, though Ramage doubted it. Were some privateersmen going to try to seize one or two of those anchored in Amsterdam and sail them round here? That too seemed doubtful, and even if they tried they were unlikely to succeed.

Rennick, who was also lying beside Ramage inspecting the French defences, was impressed by the amount of work but scornful of its effectiveness. 'All that shifting of stone would be admirable if they were building a barracks,' he said. 'The masons could pick and choose. But they've fallen into the trap of fixed defences.'

Ramage smiled to himself; it was a trap from which Rennick had been rescued only yesterday, when he had planned a defence for Amsterdam. 'They've chosen a good place, though,' he said mildly. 'That hill rising gently means they look down on us, and behind there's only a few feet of cliff to jump down if they want to get away in boats.'

'Oh yes,' Rennick said airily, 'they can watch us, but each of our men needs only a dozen rocks and he's safe behind his own musket-proof rampart.'

'But we have to storm them uphill,' Ramage said, curious to see what Rennick had in mind. 'And with all these divi-divi trees and cactus and whatever those other bushes are called, the men will be slowed up. Why, you can't even see the ground for the undergrowth!'

'Attack in the dark, sir,' Rennick said. 'Or, rather, just as darkness falls. Then we can see them against the afterglow of the sunset, but we are coming from the east and attacking out of the dark half.'

'Rennick, is that really a good bet? The odds mean the bookmaker can't lose. Two defenders to one attacker, the attackers slowed up by the slope of the hill and undergrowth, with no surprise possible . . .'

The Marine officer was silent for a minute or two and then admitted: 'Their position does in effect give them another hundred men, I admit; but they'll be fighting with their backs to the sea, so they've cut off their own line of retreat.'

'Then they must be pretty sure they won't have to retreat,' Ramage said, deliberately making his voice sound grim. 'Militarily we don't seem to be in a very good position.'

Rennick wriggled, looked again through his telescope, and then said judicially: 'I have to agree with you, sir.'

'All this military business baffles me,' Ramage suddenly admitted. 'I'd be lost the moment I went through the gateway at the Horse Guards. But as a sailor I can see we have one advantage.'

Rennick waited to hear about it and when Ramage said nothing, finally asked: 'What advantage had you in mind, sir?'

'We have the weather gage; with this south-east wind we are to windward of them.'

'But sir, I don't see how that can help us.'

'Oh, there are many advantages. We can breathe garlic over them. If they look hungry we can roast some beef over a bon-fire and drive them mad with starvation as they smell the aroma. We can call out insults and be sure they hear every word.'

He scrambled back, followed by Rennick, and learned that all the lieutenants had managed to get some sleep after arriving at Sint Kruis, and they reported that except for sentries their companies were also sleeping, the seamen quite cheerfully curling up on the hard ground and in the blazing sun, the only requirement being a small pile of rocks to protect them from French fire. Sentries squatting behind larger piles were also watching for any of their own shipmates who while asleep rolled over beyond the shelter of the rock piles.

The lieutenants soon received their orders, grinning at their simplicity, and Ramage, taking one last look at the French positions, glanced over to his right and saw that the wind was still steady in strength and direction, a breeze from the east, with an extra gust every few minutes that was just strong enough to make the dust rise up in little eddies. Yes, it was east now, but one could never be sure it would not back to the north-east or veer to the south-east. There was very little cloud; a few cotton balls whose whiteness was emphasized by the hard blue of the sky. It was strange to be lying here on earth, smelling all the strange odours that went with life on land. The sharp sweetness of thyme, the spicy smells of plants and shrubs whose names he did not know.

He closed the telescope and slid it into a pocket. The French seemed to be dozing; they had not – so far, anyway – put out sharpshooters to keep up a hail of musket fire every time a Briton moved. Were they short of muskets, powder or shot? Surely not every man had bolted from the bonfire leaving his gun behind? Perhaps, but at least each man would have a cutlass, and this was the sort of situation which must be settled finally with the blade of a sword, the edge of a tomahawk or the point of a pike.

The wind was freshening, there was no doubt about that, and the cotton-ball clouds were swelling up with the warmth of the sun. In half an hour, with the land heating up, the breeze would be brisk as the Trade winds set in for the day. He wanted no more than that, of course. It had taken only five minutes to tell the lieutenants what he wanted done and to make sure they all understood. Some men might be killed or wounded but once again, if they obeyed orders they would have the advantage of surprise, the invisible armour which had so often protected them in the past.

Half an hour gave plenty of time for the preparations. In an hour's time, when the small hand of the watch had moved a twelfth of the way round the dial, the whole thing should be over, one way or the other: either the rebels and Frenchmen would control the island (in which case they'd hang the Governor and most of the Calypsos would be dead) or the bodies of the rebels and Frenchmen would be piled up at the top of the slope, and waggish seamen would refer to the Battle of Sint Kruis Baai. Ramage rubbed his bristly jaw and wished he could shave and clean his teeth.

At first glance it looked as if it would be a repetition of the previous night's attack, except it was broad daylight and instead of being in front of a bonfire the enemy were hiding at the top of a sloping hill. Ramage was lying flat on the hard ground with, from the feel of it, the same sharp stones digging into the same soft parts of his body. Jackson was to his left and Stafford to his right, and the only difference from the previous night's attack was that the companies were grouped evenly on each side, so that his own company was in the middle to form the vanguard, the sharp point of a wedge driving up the hill in – he glanced at his watch yet again – eleven minutes' time.

Now he was holding his watch in front of him, impatiently staring at the dial, unsure whether to regard the slowly-moving hands as friends or enemies. The two pistols pressed against his stomach, the belt hooks held them securely against the waistband of his breeches. His cutlass was beside him, ready to be snatched up. His feet throbbed, the glare made his cheek muscles ache from continually squinting. Insects buzzed or crawled while the air shimmered from the heat, the wind only moving not cooling it. There was no sign of movement up the hill; the French were having a siesta, no doubt, except for their sentries.

Ten minutes to go. They would be hungry and very thirsty, those Frenchmen. Were they waiting for a vessel to come into the bay to take them off? In theory they could, of course, be penned in until thirst forced them to surrender, but in practice many would escape in darkness.

Eight minutes. Some could scramble down the small cliff at night and into the water, and swim for a hundred yards or so, then come ashore beyond the encircling British. Perhaps half of them could swim – that was the usual proportion of swimmers in a British ship.

Seven minutes. Of course, the idea of keeping the French trapped up the hill until they surrendered for lack of water would mean quite a feat of endurance for the British, too, because they had only a quart each. A quart, rather, less what they had already drunk this morning, although they could get more.

Six minutes. This bloody soldiering: how he hated it. Heat, dust, physical weariness, the sheer length of time an action took. If you wanted to move from here to there you walked – marched, rather. If it rained you marched through mud. Then, as night came on, you pitched camp in more mud and at day-break put on your wet clothes and marched again. You could and often did get soaking wet at sea, but once you came off watch you could sleep in the dry and put on dry clothes.

Five minutes. A faint and passing smell of burning. Jackson had noticed it and glanced round him from behind his little cairn of rocks, watching for telltale smoke. Ramage peered round his own cairn and searched the hillside. No movement, and the hillside looked so peaceful one half expected to see a few goats walking delicately among the stones and bushes, standing up on their back legs to wrench at the higher leaves of bushes.

Four minutes. The lack of goats was of course the indication that human beings were hiding up that hill: there were goats over on the flat land to the left and to the right, goats variously quartered in white and black, brown and black, white and brown. The kids born three or four months ago were quite large now, and he realized he had become accustomed to their almost human bleating.

Three minutes. In fact, they sounded like shrill-voiced wives nagging their husbands, or children bleating complaints to their mothers.

Two minutes. They were nimble, though, and often skittish, jumping into the air with all four legs stiff, as though playing a game.

One minute. Jackson was watching him now, poised, tensed and with a white cloth ready in his hand. Ramage said, quietly: 'Three-quarters of a minute . . . half a minute . . . a quarter of a minute . . . now!'

Jackson leapt to his feet, waving the white cloth so that all the men in the eight companies – and the French, if they were looking – could see him; then he dropped flat again. With luck he had given the signal without being spotted by dozing sentries and certainly without noise.

Now three men were running forward from each company, each with a blazing torch in his hand. They ran – like nimble goats, Ramage realized, because each had spent the last quarter of an hour deciding his targets and his route – to bushes and withering shrubs, patches of dried grass, to cacti that had fallen years ago and were now long-dried husks – and held the flaming torches against them. Within seconds the base of the parched hillside had a line of flame sputtering, spurting and then driving up it, fanned by the wind and leaping, flames a few inches high growing to six feet in as many seconds. The smoke as the few green bushes were scorched and then burned by dried shrubs drifted up the hill, like the smoke of a continuous broadside; the crackling of burning twigs and boughs increased until it sounded as though a giant was crashing through a jungle.

Then Ramage realized that he could not see the upper half of the hill: clouds of billowing smoke now covered it and already the flames had swept over several yards, leaving an ever-widening scorched black band which was advancing up the hill as though pulled by the flames.

A wind eddy made a momentary gap in the smoke and Ramage caught sight of several groups of men running about quite aimlessly at the top of the hill. He stood up and shouted to his left and then to his right: 'Stand by, men; they might make a dash for it any moment.'

Immediately the seamen and Marines knelt behind their piles of stones, muskets ready, aiming up the hill into the smoke, so that it would take only a moment's twitch of the muzzle to take precise aim.

Suddenly a section of the hillside seemed to move and he saw figures weaving about in the smoke as they ran down the hill. As some reached thinner patches of smoke Ramage could see they were trying to protect their eyes, and some had rags tied across their faces, probably to try to filter out some of the smoke before it went down into their lungs. But they were clutching muskets and cutlasses; they were men about to fight, not surrender.

With a fearful deliberation Rennick's Marines fired, the muskets delivering what seemed a ragged volley until you realized that no man fired until he had taken proper aim.

Now no one moved up there in the smoke. There were two dozen or more bodies sprawled just this side of the line of flames: Rennick had let them come down clear of the smoke before allowing his men to fire.

Wagstaffe's company would fire at the next target while Rennick's reloaded – and yes, here were another ragged group of the enemy, coughing and spluttering while they ran, firing pistols wildly and yelling as they waved their swords. Two or three, probably blinded by the smoke, sprawled flat on their faces, tripped by rocks or the roots of burned bushes.

There was a crash of musketry as Wagstaffe's men fired, and only two or three of the enemy kept on running – not, Ramage realized, because they intended to attack a couple of hundred British, but because they had no choice: they were escaping the smoke and flame of the hill rather than braving the fire of the British muskets. Ramage was just about to order half a dozen of his own men to pick them off when more muskets fired from Wagstaffe's company. The men were coolly obeying orders, that much was sure!

Lacey's company would take the next group, but if there was a great rush down the hill all the companies would fire. And, Ramage realized, there was probably no one in command of the rebels and privateersmen at the top of the hill; groups were just bolting when they found the smoke and heat became too much.

The line of flames, growing crooked now as stronger eddies of wind drove it on, leaping gaps when sheets of sparks flew into the air, was soon two-thirds of the way up the hill, and the flames themselves were in places six or eight feet high as bushes blazed, their boughs quickly turning to flaming scarecrows.

A few men ran down the hill – too few, Ramage felt; only madmen would come in such small numbers. 'Stand by, men!' he shouted. 'This may be the –'

But before he could finish the flames were momentarily hidden as scores of men came racing down the hill, like a great centipede moving sideways. Lacey's company fired at once – they were already aiming into the flames, waiting for targets to appear, and Ramage could see many of the leading men falling, followed a few moments later by a score shot down by Baker's company. There was too much noise to shout an order and anyway his own thirty men knew it was their turn after the muskets close on their left had fired.

Jackson's musket kicked and then Stafford's, and both men were tugging at their pistols. Ramage grasped his, cocked them, and waited a few moments as the muskets of the next company – that would be Kenton's men – and then the next, Aitken's, fired almost simultaneously.

The effect was ghastly: the enemy appeared to run into an invisible wall and collapse: barely twenty men were still running, the rest had fallen, some among the flames, others in the smouldering debris this side of the flames. Some reached the unburnt shrubs and grass six or seven yards beyond before being cut down.

Ramage realized that neither Jackson nor Stafford had fired their pistols, and his own were still cocked and loaded, but unused. Please, please, let a man come out of the smoke with a white flag or waving a shirt, or just shouting that they have surrendered: there's no point in continuing this aimless slaughter. Except, he realized, that the Dutch rebels knew they'd get no mercy if they fell into the Governor's hands because they were traitors, and French privateersmen by the nature of their bloody trade expected no quarter and rarely gave it. But piles of dead and wounded lying on a scorched hillside . . . this was not the kind of war that Ramage had seen before nor, he realized, queasiness sweeping over him in waves, could he stomach much more of it.

Then, before he could do or say anything, another group of Frenchmen came pouring down the hillside, screaming and coughing, rubbing their eyes and yelling defiance, and, as soon as they broke through the line of flames and made clearer targets, he heard Kenton calmly giving fire orders to his company. Again there was a volley of musketry; then, as some of the enemy still ran on, he heard a crisp voice telling a company to open fire with pistols, and a moment later he realized it was his own, and a crackle of pistol shots brought down the rest of the men.

The Calypsos were now busy reloading their muskets, and he could see, just this side of the flames, what seemed a low parapet and then, as a puff of wind blew the grey coils of smoke clear for a moment, that it was built of bodies. An arm waved here and there, a man staggered upright and collapsed, vague movements which made the barrier seem alive – as indeed parts of it were.

Yet, ghastly as it all was, he was saving his own men; he had dreaded sending them charging up the hill to attack prepared French positions. Those bodies out there, lying dead or, if wounded, coughing in the smoke, were enemy, not Calypsos. Not just regular enemies, either: if they were Dutch they were traitors to their own folk; if French they were privateersmen and little better than pirates, and perhaps a hundred of them came from Brune's ship and had helped murder the *Tranquil* people.

Slowly the scene became less ghastly; his imagination super-imposed the neat staterooms of the *Tranquil*, where the blood of the raped women with their throats cut had stained carpets and settees. He found it a satisfactory thought that by now the Marines and the seamen in all the companies had reloaded their muskets and were kneeling, waiting for the next wave of the enemy to come through the smoke, which was now thinning. The flames were high up the hill, perhaps forty yards away now. Another twenty yards, he guessed, and they would have reached the top.

How many French were left? They must be crowded at the very top of the hill now, unless they were jumping off into the sea, but the Marine 'patrols sent out by Rennick to watch the beaches had not fired, showing that the enemy preferred the devil to the deep blue sea. Or course, from the very first the men on the hill had not known the fate of their comrades once they had run down the hill and plunged through the smoke: they would hear the firing but the clouds of rolling smoke prevented them seeing how the musketry from the Calypsos was cutting them down like corn before a reaper's scythe. When the smoke clears, Ramage guessed, the remaining enemy will surrender. Yet they might all make a dash before the last of the hill burned, preferring a sudden foray through the flames. It would be the flames rather than the smoke that made the men run: they would scorch anyone who stood and waited for them to pass.

And now another group of Frenchmen was running down – and the first of them was waving a white flag: a shirt tied to a cutlass. Ramage shouted to left and right for the companies to hold their fire, but even as he shouted he saw Stafford pause for a moment, and then correct his aim, and Jackson did the same thing, and even as he continued shouting the muskets thudded until the last of the running Frenchmen collapsed, a rag doll thrown on a rubbish heap.

Jackson stood up and turned to him. 'I don't think the men could hear you, sir,' he said quietly, looking Ramage straight in the eye. 'Leastways, not until all the muskets had fired.'

'No, sir,' Stafford confirmed, 'I didn't hear you order nothing; certainly not telling us to hold our fire. Probably deafened by all the shooting. Ain't that right, Rosey?'

The Italian cupped a hand to his ear. 'That's right, Staff; speak up, I can't hear.'

No quarter for the men who murdered the people in the Tranquil: clearly the Calypsos had already decided that, and as a result in that last rush perhaps a few Dutch rebels had been killed, but there had been only ten or fifteen behind the man waving the white flag.

The smoke was thinning out now; in the gusts Ramage could see the top of the hill. No one stood there, although a few men might be crouching behind rocks, seeking shelter from the hail of bullets that could be expected now there were only wisps of smoke to hide them.

He shouted for Rennick, ordering him to search the hilltop with the Marines, and waited for Aitken, whom he could see hurrying towards him. Well, now was the time to get reports from all the lieutenants and see what casualties there were. He took a small silver whistle from a pocket and blew four quick blasts, the signal he had arranged before he left the bonfire.

It was a whistle of a curious pattern; a cylinder with an intricate Moorish design which was unrecognizable unless you looked at it from a particular angle, when it became clear that it was a representation of a woman's breast, the nipple forming the mouthpiece. It had been a present from Gianna, of all people, a present in a tiny velvet-lined case, tucked into his pocket as he left with a mischievous smile and a comment in Italian, spoken with a Neapolitan accent, which he had not understood but was probably lewd. This was the first time he had used it; a silver piece of erotica which signalled the end of the bloodiest and longest action he had ever fought.

The lieutenants came up and reported. No casualties – this was Aitken. One man sprained an ankle when he stumbled over a rock – Kenton. One man with powder burns of the face from a flash in the pan of his musket – Baker. A shoulder wound from a cutlass wielded by an over-enthusiastic shipmate – Wagstaffe. Apart from them, two men had stomach pains – brought on, according to an unsympathetic Aitken, by a surfeit of roast beef – while two of Kenton's men were almost crippled by the hairlike spines of prickly pear cactus which had penetrated the skin of their legs and festered overnight.

The second guide was sent off to Amsterdam, by way of the bonfire site, for more horses and carts to bring in the dead and wounded, and by the time Rennick and his Marines came down the hill to report that it was deserted, the Calypsos were busy carrying the French and Dutch wounded out of the smouldering scrub and making them as comfortable as possible clear of the smoke. The guide was told to bring back doctors if he could, but Ramage had little hope of that: they would still be busy patching up the wounded from the bonfire.

An hour later, leaving behind fifty men to look after the wounded and help load the carts when they arrived, he led his men on the long march back to Amsterdam, twenty miles away. Most of the men still had chunks of roast beef, and the sight of a seaman marching with a musket over one shoulder and a great haunch of beef under the other arm, the meat dusty from having been put down many times, made Ramage feel like Falstaff and wish there was a Hogarth or a Rowland-son to sketch the march. The column stopped from time to time to fill water flasks at the few villages or plantation houses that had wells or enough water in their cisterns, but the sun was well down over the western horizon before Ramage saw the first houses of Amsterdam.

It was then that the fact of the island's surrender really came home to him. The surrender agreement had been signed, the rebels and their privateer allies had been dealt with. Now it would be possible to leave the island with its Dutch garrison and sail for Jamaica, to report to Foxey-Foote about this latest addition to the British flag. He could take three or four privateers with him, and he might decide to burn the rest, just in case some of the Dutch took it into their heads to steal them – after all, Curaçao had surrendered, but Britain was still at war with the Batavian Republic, not to mention France and Spain.

He marched along, cursing his blistered heels, aching shin muscles and dry throat, but the need to talk to the men at the half-hourly halts, making jokes, kept him wide awake. All the men brightened up as they came into the straight stretch of road leading to Amsterdam, now less than a mile away. His eyes seemed full of dust and ached from the glare they had been subjected to all day, but he was glad to see the masts of the *Calypso* above the roofs of the buildings.

Then, as the road turned so that he looked from another angle, he realized there was another set of masts to seaward of her. Another frigate was anchored in the channel almost next to her. He stopped, icy cold with sudden fear, and pulled open his telescope. Yes, a frigate with a Dutch flag. The miss-ing Dutch reinforcements – and Maria's fiancé – had arrived. Had she captured the almost helpless *Calypso*?

CHAPTER SEVENTEEN

Southwick was angry, puzzled and disbelieving. He told Ramage that soon after daylight he had received a letter – or, rather, he had opened a letter – from the Governor addressed to 'Captain Lord Ramage' saying that a Dutch frigate would be arriving in Amsterdam at noon, and that 'normal salutes will be fired'.

' "Normal salutes" indeed!' Southwick said crossly. 'I don't know who the Governor thinks he is, but that letter shows he's forgotten he's no longer the Governor, and how dare he give orders to one of the King's ships. Or, rather, the captain of the King's ship that's taken the island's surrender! As if we'd salute an enemy ship!'

'Not "orders", surely?' Ramage asked mildly.

'Orders, sir: you wait until I show you the letter. I have it locked up at the moment. The *Delft* – that's the frigate – will salute the Governor, then salute us, and we return gun for gun. The British flag will be hauled down half an hour before she comes in through the forts, and the flag of the Batavian Republic hoisted. We will not "commit any hostile act" against her, and so on. And the Dutch flags were still flying at sunset . . .'

'You'd better get me the letter,' Ramage said.

He had come on board weary and apprehensive. The *Delft* was anchored two hundred yards away towards the channel entrance and despite the Governor's letter Southwick had the *Calypso*'s guns loaded, the few men on board had been sent to general quarters, and he had taken in on the spring to the anchor cable to turn the whole ship so that her starboard broadside was aimed at the *Delft*. It was not a noticeable move; the wind was holding the *Calypso* across the channel and she had to be turned only a point for all the guns to bear, and the spring was on the larboard side, away from the *Delft*.

The Dutch flags on the forts: Ramage suspected that could be the most significant part of the whole business. Hoisting them in place of the British flags for an hour or so, so that the *Delft* came in and gave the former Governor a chance to explain the situation – yes, that made sense. Then the British flags should have been hoisted again.

Exactly what was the status of the *Delft*? That was a puzzle. She was a Dutch ship and therefore an enemy, and she had entered the main port of an island which had surrendered to the British, all of which made her a British prize. But the Dutch flags were flying, on the former Governor's orders, so the *Delft*'s captain could claim that he did not know the British now controlled the island, and had the Dutch flags not been hoisted he would not have entered. And so the arguments could go on.

The fact was, Ramage decided, that the Governor (the former Governor, rather) had interfered in something that was not his concern. Unless . . . unless he was going back on the surrender terms, now that the *Delft* had come in – and, Ramage thought ruefully, now that the British had disposed of all the rebels and French privateersmen.

Southwick came up on deck with the letter and Ramage moved closer to the gangway lantern to read it. Shorn of its polite verbiage, it bore out the master's description, except that Southwick had not mentioned that under van Someren's signature was his own description, 'Governor'. In all official communications, especially in circumstances like these, every word was significant.

Ramage folded the letter and put it in his pocket. Aitken and the rest of the ship's officers were below, washing and shaving, while the seamen were washing on deck using head pumps and buckets, tired, but from the singing and joking, cheerful enough.

'I shall be calling on the former Governor. First I'm going to tidy myself. I want two boats rowing guard around us all night, and a third boat watching the *Delft*, from a discreet distance. Any sign of mischief, and it can burn a blue light. Two men at every gun on the starboard side, four lookouts, and plenty of flares ready: we can dazzle any would-be boarders, as well as see them.'

'Aye aye, sir,' Southwick said. 'We won't get caught napping.'

'And I want an officer in the boat watching the *Delft*. They're all short of sleep but that's unfortunate. A senior petty officer in each of the two other boats. Young Orsini can take a turn in one of them.'

With that Ramage went below. An hour later, washed, shaved and in a clean uniform, wearing polished shoes and a ceremonial sword, the former Governor's letter stowed carefully in a pocket, he was being announced at van Someren's residence.

The great drawing room was both hot and crowded: not because of the number of candles burning in the two chandeliers overhead and the candelabra and candlesticks which seemed to be placed at random on every table, but because of the number of people in the room.

Ramage stood at the big double doors, deliberately waiting for van Someren to step forward to greet him, and also to give himself time to see who else was in the room. Van Someren was having an animated talk with two Dutch naval officers, one of whom was probably the *Delft*'s captain: two other Dutch officers, one Army and one Navy, were waiting three or four feet away, as though they were aides expecting to be called.

Major Lausser was over by the big windows, not in uniform and talking to Maria van Someren and her mother. There were half a dozen other men in the room, with their wives. Two were officers from the garrison, the others probably leading citizens. But it was immediately obvious to Ramage that Lausser, Maria and her mother looked thoroughly uncomfortable; embarrassed but, he felt, anxious to talk and pleased (relieved?) to see him.

Why was Lausser not with the former Governor? In the brief moment available to scan the room Ramage had the impression that Lausser was definitely excluded from van Someren's circle. It was hard to explain the impression but it was as tangible as a drop in the temperature.

Finally, deliberately finishing what he had been saying to the *Delft*'s captain, van Someren walked over to Ramage, unsmiling and formal, condescending and giving the impression of a busy man being bothered by a trifle.

'My dear Ramage, I trust you've come to report on the success of your foray.'

Ramage bowed slightly. 'My compliments to your wife and daughter. I trust they are well?'

Van Someren, puzzled, turned and gestured towards them. 'Indeed they are, as you can see. Now, your report – '

'It will be delivered in the normal way,' Ramage interrupted and, lowering his voice so that no one else in the room could hear, added – 'to my admiral. Now, sir, shall we go to your office so that *you* can report to *me*?'

'To you? Why, that is preposterous! Why –'

'I think this is hardly the place to discuss the matter.'

'I am not accustomed to being given orders in my own residence,' van Someren said haughtily.

'That was a habit acquired while you were Governor,' Ramage said, making no attempt to keep the edge out of his voice.

'I am still the Governor, and you will address me as "Your Excellency".'

'You are not the Governor,' Ramage said evenly, and he looked van Someren straight in the eye when he added: 'You surrendered yourself and the island to me as the representative of His Britannic Majesty, and you will therefore obey any orders I find it necessary to give.'

Van Someren looked down, and then glanced round at the groups of Dutch naval officers, as if feeling the need for reinforcements. 'You had better meet the officers from the frigate.'

Ramage nodded briefly but said: 'First I wish to see your wife and daughter.' When van Someren came with him, Ramage added: 'Alone, I think.'

And, he thought as he walked slowly across the room, now van Someren is not quite so sure of himself. The news that I have disposed of the rebels and the privateers must have put the idea into his head that the threat which made him surrender the island and ask for Britain's protection has vanished. And then the *Delft* arrives, giving him the reinforcements he needs and changing the situation radically so that it boils down to this: his strength and safety lies in the *Delft* frigate, while the threat now comes from the *Calypso* frigate. And they are lying almost alongside each other in the harbour. Two gamblers facing each other across a gaming table: on one side Gottlieb van Someren, wagering the island on the *Delft* frigate; on the other Nicholas Ramage, wagering the *Calypso* frigate. The piece of parchment recording the island's surrender was not worth the toss of a worn dice.

Ramage kissed Mrs van Someren's hand, did the same to Maria, and turned to Major Lausser, who was holding out his hand and shook Ramage's firmly. None of them had said a

word, but sides had obviously been taken long before Ramage
arrived back at Otrabanda, let alone landed on Punda.

'You were successful,' Lausser said. 'My congratulations.
I did not think it possible.'

'Much depends on one's enemy making mistakes.'

Lausser glanced up and smiled. 'Indeed, how right you are.
And if one can wait long enough, they usually do.'

Ramage nodded, understanding exactly what Lausser was
telling him. Now to make sure Maria was not just a neutral.
'Your fiancé is still the first lieutenant in the *Delft*, Mademoiselle?'

'My fiancé? Why, My Lord, I am not engaged.' Her hand
moved her fan slowly, and Ramage saw the faint mark on
her finger where until very recently there had been a heavily-
jewelled ring.

'My apologies,' Ramage said quickly. 'I must have heard
idle chatter about someone else. But what a pleasant surprise
for you all, the *Delft* arriving after all this time.'

'Oh yes,' Maria said quietly. 'As you can see, we are all
so delighted that we are giving a ball for all the officers.'

'How kind of you. What evening will it be?'

'Oh, it is now,' Maria said. The edge on her laugh showed
she was not far from tears. 'Can you not see all the gay
couples dancing? Our orchestra here in Amsterdam is like our
honour, invisible and silent.'

'Maria!' her mother protested but without much conviction.
'Your father has his duty to do.'

Ramage wondered why Lausser was not wearing uniform
instead of a soberly-cut grey coat, with matching breeches.
The Dutchman read Ramage's thoughts. 'I resigned my commission at noon,' he said.

'Before the former Governor sent a letter over to the
Calypso?'

'Yes. A few minutes before. Several others resigned at the
same time.'

'I see,' Ramage said. 'But you are in a minority?'

Lausser shrugged his shoulders. 'Yes, because only few
people know what is going on.'

'They can guess, surely?'

'Probably not. The surrender to the British has not yet been
published in the island's official gazette. Only a dozen people

know you in fact lawfully command in Curaçao. The rest believe a rumour, that the British had offered to help. Now the *Delft* has arrived, obviously the British can leave.'

'*Can* they leave?'

Again Lausser shrugged his shoulders. 'At the time I resigned,' he said carefully, 'that decision had not been made.'

Ramage saw that Lausser was watching someone behind him and turned to find van Someren had joined them. He touched Ramage's arm. 'Come now, you must meet the captain of the *Delft*.'

'In your study,' Ramage said firmly. 'This is not a social encounter.'

'But, my dear Lord Ramage, of *course* it is!'

'Mister van Someren,' Ramage said heavily, 'you have no doubt heard of Newmarket Heath, in England?'

'Newmarket? Isn't that where the horses race?'

'Yes, and I must remind you of two things that even the unluckiest gambler on the Heath learned at his father's knee . . .'

'And what are they?'

'The first is that only one horse can win a race.'

Van Someren grunted. 'He did not learn how to choose the winner, though.'

'No, that needs skill. But even the betting man knows the second lesson concerning horses.'

'And I am supposed to ask what that is?' van Someren asked impatiently.

'No, you are supposed to know that it is dangerous to change horses in midstream.'

'Come!' van Someren said crossly. 'We go to my study.' He led the way from the drawing room, snapping fingers at the two naval officers, indicating that they should follow. In the study he began introductions, but Ramage stopped him, even though he was curious about the younger man, who had been engaged to Maria. 'I am forbidden by the laws of the Navy from having any meeting with the enemy. I accepted the surrender of this island from you, which means that you and your people are now under my protection. This gentleman, if he commands the *Delft*, either surrenders his ship to me, or he remains my enemy. Britain is still at war with the Batavian Republic . . .'

'This is ridiculous,' van Someren snapped. 'You don't take that surrender seriously, do you? Why, it was signed under duress.'

'All surrenders are signed under duress,' Ramage said dryly. 'Only I wasn't applying the duress; your own Dutch rebels and the French privateersmen were, if you remember.'

'The duress, or threat, does not exist. You know that.'

'Oh yes, I know that it does not exist now; I removed it for you.'

'So you can see how absurd it is that I should surrender an island like this to a single English frigate! Quite absurd.'

'The instrument of surrender has your signature on it, witnessed by Major Lausser.'

'Lausser no longer holds a commission.'

'Neither do you,' Ramage said quietly. 'You are no longer the Governor of the island, by virtue of the surrender you signed, but that doesn't make the surrender document invalid: nothing –' he paused and then said with more emphasis – 'nothing erases your signature. You surrendered the island of Curaçao.'

Van Someren gave an airy wave of his hand. 'This is just the idle chatter of a young man,' he said in English to the *Delft*'s captain. 'He knows nothing of law, diplomacy or politics.'

And that, Ramage thought, is the end of that: he had given van Someren plenty of time to reconsider: whatever happens to him now is his own fault. Ramage admitted to himself that he was angry because he had taken van Someren for a man of honour, forgetting he was first and foremost a politician and a survivor: he had changed his politics and survived as Governor of Curaçao when the French invaded the Netherlands and his own monarch had fled to England.

'Mister van Someren,' Ramage said, with a slight emphasis on the 'mister', 'I must return to my ship, but before I go I think my admiral would want me to point out two things. First, the instrument of surrender will be published in England, and the moment the French government read it your life won't be worth a worn-out shoe if they can get their hands on you; they'll trot you off to the guillotine. Any question of your going back on it, therefore, is suicide. Second, Curaçao has been surrendered to the British. That a Dutch frigate has since arrived in the port is of no consequence. Now the island is British and we shall keep our word – my signature is on the document by which you place Curaçao under my King's protection. Long before you can send any news to the Netherlands, let alone receive any help, a substantial British force will have arrived here from Jamaica.'

The *Delft*'s captain, a swarthy and stocky man with a plump, white face in which the eyes seemed to be deeply-embedded currants in a suet pudding, tapped Ramage on the shoulder, and grinned, showing yellowed teeth which reminded Ramage of the horse that van Someren was changing in midstream. 'You know the answer, English?'

Ramage shook his head.

'The answer, English, is that this surrender paper must not leave Amsterdam.'

In a fraction of a second Ramage realized that not only was he in a trap and the *Delft* had sprung it, but there was no point in acknowledging defeat. Surprise, that was the secret, helped by a white lie or so. He gave a contemptuous laugh. 'Must not leave Amsterdam? You don't seriously think it is still here, do you?'

The captain looked nervously at van Someren, who had gone white. 'When did you send it away? How? No ship has left Amsterdam!'

'Amsterdam is hardly the only place from which a ship can leave the island. What do you think my admiral would say if I took the surrender of the island and then, without telling him, went off over the hills chasing a horde of pirates and rebels? He would court-martial me!'

He would, too, Ramage thought wryly, if he knew about it. And the contemptuous laugh and the tone of his voice was perfect. The two men believed him at the moment. Later they might have doubts; later they might reassure each other, but that would be – later. Ramage had seen many actors staying on the stage too long after a good performance, remaining until the applause died so that they had to walk off in silence.

'I bid you gentlemen good night,' he said.

'Don't try to escape, English,' the *Delft*'s captain called after him. 'My ship is covering you. You are my prize.'

'That's so,' van Someren repeated. 'You must consider yourselves our prisoners. We shall hoist the Dutch flag over the British in the morning.'

His cabin was cool and the breeze, still strong even though it was ten o'clock at night, made the candles flicker. The lieutenants stood or perched on the settee: Southwick, although only a warrant officer and technically the most junior in rank, sat in the armchair and Ramage was at his desk, the chair pulled round to face the men.

He had just finished telling them about his visit to Government House, and of how the *Delft's* captain had played what he thought was an ace by saying the instrument of surrender would not leave the island.

'Do you think they believed you, sir?' Aitken asked. 'Saying it had already gone sounds likely. A fine trump card, in fact.'

'They believed me at the time because it was such a shock, but by now they may have had second thoughts. Van Someren knows no ship left Amsterdam. The chance of us having a ship waiting in one of the bays – well, it's remote, when you come to think of it.'

Wagstaffe straightened himself up. 'Whether or not they believe it, sir, are we to assume the *Delft* is hostile?'

'Very much so. But her captain and van Someren regard us as her prize. If she needs to sink us, she will.'

Southwick gave one of his contemptuous snorts. 'The *Delft* might be planning to sink us, but what have you in mind for the *Delft*?'

Ramage looked round at the gathered men. 'Any suggestions?'

Lacey said: 'I'd like to start off by bombarding Government House. When I think of all those mosquito and sandfly bites . . . just to kill off some of the former Governor's enemies.'

'It'd be a good idea, if only to teach this damnable former excellency a lesson,' Southwick growled. 'Topple a few tiles round his ears. Teach him that a gentleman keeps his word.'

'He knows that already,' Aitken said sourly. 'That's why a scoundrel can always cheat a man of honour.'

'Oh yes, but there's nothing to stop a man of honour boxing his ears afterwards,' Southwick said.

'I'm waiting for ideas,' Ramage said patiently.

'Just open fire on her, sir. We've springs on our cable and our shooting will be accurate,' Wagstaffe said.

'They can put a spring on their cable – probably have, in fact – and shoot just as well,' Ramage said. 'We end up with a pounding match at a cable's distance. The first ship reduced to splinters is the loser.'

'What had you in mind, sir?' Aitken asked cautiously.

'I'd like to destroy the *Delft* with no damage to the *Calypso* and no casualties to us.'

'Who wouldn't?' Southwick growled impatiently, ruffling his hair. 'No one wants damage or casualties, sir, but short of blowing her out of the water, how can we do that?'

'What's wrong with blowing her out of the water?' Ramage asked innocently.

'It's a waste of our powder,' Southwick chuckled. 'It'd take several tons.'

'Quite,' Ramage said, 'but I had in mind to use hers.'

Six pairs of startled eyes jerked round to stare at him.

'You're teasing us,' Southwick protested.

Ramage shook his head. 'You have to think ahead. After we've destroyed the *Delft* we still have a problem – my original orders.'

'The privateers?' Southwick exclaimed. 'Why, we've dealt with them!'

'I'm sure Admiral Foxe-Foote wouldn't agree. We have ten privateers anchored in Amsterdam, but we can't stay here and guard 'em, and we don't have enough men to sail them all to Jamaica. If we leave any behind, the Dutch might take them – or sell them to the French or Spanish.'

'Let's sink those we can't take with us,' Southwick said gruffly. 'They won't yield much prize money, anyway.'

'That *Nuestra Señora de Antigua*,' Wagstaffe said bitterly. 'I'd like to see her burn. Pity we can't sort out the survivors of her original crew and put them on board. Anyway, her captain's dead, we know that.'

'She would burn well,' Ramage said dreamily, and all movement in the cabin stopped. Suddenly he could hear the water lapping under the *Calypso*'s stern, and the gentle whine of the wind in the rigging, and on deck a sentry coughed and then spat over the side.

'Francis Drake, sir?' Aitken asked.

Ramage nodded. 'Tonight. The wind is holding. About three o'clock, before moonrise. The explosion should take most of the tiles off Government House.'

'Shall I start the preparations, sir?'

'Here, hold hard a moment,' Southwick protested. 'This is all beyond me.'

Wagstaffe laughed happily and said: 'Drake . . . come on, old man, he was a bit before your time, but you must have heard how he launched fireships against the Spanish Armada when it anchored off Gravelines.'

'Ah, yes, but although I wasn't there I did hear tell that he didn't sink any Spanish ships with 'em.'

'No, but they cut their cables and ran for their lives.'

'We don't want the *Delft* cutting and running though; we want her blowing up right where she is,' Southwick declared.

Wagstaffe was enjoying teasing the master. 'Drake would have enjoyed the idea of using a French privateer with a Spanish name to blow up a Dutch frigate.'

'So would I,' Southwick said as he suddenly worked out Ramage's intention. 'And there's a lot of work to be done preparing the *Nuestra Señora*. For a start she hasn't a single sail bent on.'

Silently in the darkness, always keeping the bulk of the *Calypso* between them and the *Delft*, the British frigate's boats had rowed back and forth to the *Nuestra Señora* ferrying across casks, axes and saws, grapnels, lengths of light chain, coils of ropes and several single and double blocks to make up sheets for the sails to save time searching through the schooner for the originals.

While seamen working under the boatswain and Southwick hoisted the sails up on deck and then bent them on to masts and stays, others removed all the hatches, cut big holes in the few permanent bulkheads so that the wind could blow through the ship and up the hatchways, and lifted off skylights to ensure a good draught.

More men climbed up the rigging and secured the grapnels from chains so that they hung down just above the level of the enemy bulwarks, suspended where they would hook into the *Delft*'s rigging. Two axes rested against the anchor cable bitts; all her guns to the starboard side had been loaded with two shots each and a treble charge of powder, although no gunners would fire them because the barrels would probably burst; only heat or sparks falling into the pans would ignite the gunpowder.

Ramage went into the captain's cabin – it was little more than a large cuddy – and was surprised and thankful at the draught blowing through it; a draught that when the time came would fan the flames like a blacksmith's bellows, although for the moment it did its best to remove the stench in which Brune had lived. He walked forward to where the privateersmen normally lived and where their hammocks were still slung. Several seamen were busy breaking up blocks of pitch and wedging them wherever a ledge in the planking would hold a piece. Several of the hammocks swung gently with the sharp outlines of pieces of pitch revealing their contents.

In another corner half a dozen seamen were busy chopping coils of thick rope into ten-foot lengths, while others frayed the ends and jammed them into the piles of pitch. Every few feet were small casks of tar, identifiable only by their smell, because there was always seepage between the staves. They would not be smashed or have their bungs knocked out until the last moment, and many of them rested on piles of spare sails.

Rennick and his sergeant, each with a long coil of slow match slung round his neck, were at work round the main-mast where ten half-casks of powder, each three and a half feet long, were securely lashed in place, each with its bung uppermost. From a point fifteen feet away several lengths of slow match stretched along the deck, like a thin octopus, the ends disappearing in the bungholes, where they went down into the powder and were held lightly in position by wooden bungs.

'Burns at the rate of two feet a minute, sir,' Rennick explained. 'There's fifteen feet from this point to the casks. We don't need a slow match to each cask, of course,' he added hurriedly. 'One would be enough, because when one cask goes up they'll all go, but we have plenty of insurance. When the time comes we light as many as possible, but there's no need to do them all.'

'The guns?' Ramage asked.

'I finally triple-shotted them on the starboard side – those which will point at the *Delft*. Those on the larboard side facing us are triple-charged without shot, and the breechings are cut, so when they go off they'll recoil right across the ship.'

'You still have the port fires to arrange?'

'Yes, sir; I thought I'd set them on deck near the wheel. It'll help us see what we're doing for the last minute or two.'

'And that brandy?'

'Southwick has stowed the casks on deck along the starboard side, forward. I have a Marine sentry guarding it. We were lucky to get it on board without a cask being "accidentally" stove in.'

Ramage nodded. 'The purser's glad to see the back of it. He's been worried ever since he found it.'

On deck Ramage shivered as he considered the *Nuestra Señora de Antigua* as a furnace: pitch and tar with frayed rope, old sails and smashed-up gratings to start a fire, brandy to increase it and finally powder to scatter it – and the schooner – over the *Delft*. The grapnels should catch in the *Delft*'s rigging and hold the *Nuestra Señora* to her long enough for a fatal and fiery embrace.

The men who sailed the schooner, setting fire to her at the last moment as she crashed alongside the *Delft*, would have to take their chance in the water, leaping over the side and swimming, and hoping that the baulks of timber hurled into the air by the explosions did not land on their heads. The *Calypso*'s boats should approach from the side away from the *Delft* and pick them up, providing that flying wreckage and sharks had left anything to save.

Southwick bustled up and said conversationally: 'It's going to take some good timing to shoot up into the wind so that she carries her way and gets alongside the *Delft*, sir.'

'I've been thinking about that.'

'Not above half a mile to get the canvas drawing well and plenty of way on her.'

'A little over half a mile.'

'Doesn't give you much time to get the feel of the ship, and you'll have to start lighting her up below before you're actually alongside, or else there's a chance the Dutchmen will get on board or cut away the grapnels – or if the chain beats 'em, the rigging from which they're hanging.'

'True,' Ramage said patiently.

'And an unlucky shot through that brandy won't help either. They'll be firing at you, of course.'

'I hadn't anticipated them pelting me with flowers, but their broadside guns won't bear until almost the last moment.'

'Musketry, though,' Southwick said gloomily. 'There'll be plenty of that; musket balls falling like rain. You'll need spare men ready to take over at the tiller, because the Dutch will be aiming at them.'

'Look,' Ramage said finally, 'I've made up my mind. I am taking the *Nuestra Señora* alongside, and you are staying on board the *Calypso*. And I don't want to hear that sad story again of how you missed the chase across the island. If you could have run a mile you'd have been welcome. If you can swim a mile you can come with the *Nuestra Señora*.'

'Don't need to swim a mile, begging your pardon.'

'You couldn't swim a hundred yards, so let's have no more arguing.'

'But you are taking Jackson, aren't you, sir?'

'Jackson. Stafford, Rossi, Baker – he'll take over command if anything happens to me – Rennick and fourteen more men. Twenty to handle a fireship – quite apart from those helping to hoist sails who will leave before we get under way. That's quite enough. Half a dozen would be sufficient.'

'I wish you'd tow a boat, sir, so you can be sure of escaping.'

'We've gone over that,' Ramage said impatiently. 'The painter will get foul of the rudder or some such thing: and a boat rowing away would make a fine target for Dutch muskets in the light of the flames. They'll never see swimmers and even if they did they'd never hit them.'

'Well, you know what you're doing, sir,' Southwick said in a voice which implied just the opposite.

'Thank you,' Ramage said stiffly. 'If you'll learn to swim and lose two stone in weight, you can command all the fireships you want.'

By half past two the *Nuestra Señora de Antigua* was ready, Jackson and Stafford stood at the big curved tiller and Ramage waited close by with Baker. Down below Rennick had several lanthorns ready, the new candles inside burning steadily but their light hidden by screens of sacking. When the word came from the quarterdeck the candles would be taken out and used to light the fuses to the powder casks and the piles of combustibles which would start the pitch and tar burning and eventually ignite the brandy in the casks. The powder exploding should in turn send off first the *Nuestra Señora*'s own magazine and then the *Delft*'s.

Ramage could feel the wind steady on his face. It had backed to the east-north-east, so that it was blowing across the channel from the Punda side to Otrabanda not quite at right-angles. The privateers, the *Calypso* and the *Delft* were all lying head to wind, their bows pointing to Punda. The moon had not yet risen – Ramage had planned his attack for an hour earlier – but the stars were bright, the banks of the channel and the quays grey ribbons with the bulky ships black between them.

There had been no sign of Dutch guard boats; they were obviously relying on lookouts on board. What was that captain expecting? Did he anticipate an attack by 'English'? He would expect a battle of broadsides, and perhaps an attempt to board. He knew there was little chance of the *Calypso* weighing and trying to get alongside because the channel was too narrow (particularly without a pilot to warn of shoals) for frigates to manœuvre drawing more than sixteen feet. By now then, the Dutch might have decided the *Calypso* would do nothing until daylight – or even that Ramage might realize he really was trapped and negotiate the surrender of his ship. Or – the thought had only just struck him – perhaps van Someren intended to have the big guns from the two forts hauled round to the town at daylight so that from the quays on each side they could if necessary help the *Delft's* guns pound the *Calypso* to pieces. Each fort had twenty-five or so 24-pounders, which meant that the *Calypso* would be receiving the fire equivalent to a ship of the line, and unable to reply to most of it . . . It was curious how neither he nor any of his lieutenants had thought of the Dutch doing it. Under-estimating the enemy was a bad mistake, but the fireship idea had occupied all their thoughts.

There were groups of men at both the *Nuestra Señora's* masts, ready to haul on halyards to hoist the great mainsail, foresail, forestaysail and jib. There were a couple more head-sails that could be hoisted, but they would take time and meant only more sheets to be trimmed, more ropes to get snagged; trying to free a headsail because of a jammed sheet was a distraction he was anxious to avoid. As it was, the sheets had been led round so that the headsails would be hoisted backed, so that the schooner's bow began to pay off to starboard as the anchor cable was cut, ensuring she was on the right tack and would not have to go about.

Two men waited at the bitts with axes, ready to cut the anchor cable. Rennick and his men were below – Satan and his firemen, Southwick had called them – and Rossi was here on deck with the port fires, sacking, some old sails and blocks of pitch that should cause a fine blaze, helped by the folds of the mainsail as soon as the halyards were let run.

He looked over to starboard and could just make out the black hull of the *Calypso*, but she had the *Delft* beyond and the harbour entrance. The tree frogs sounded sharp and noisy, even this far from the shore, a constant squeaky noise like a block that needed greasing. The four Dutch guards, two on the *Nuestra Señora* and two on the next privateer, now prisoners in the *Calypso*, must wonder what the devil was going on. Very soon, he thought grimly, they would be certain the end of the world had come.

Ramage, calling down to Rennick to stove in the tar barrels so that it began seeping into the wood, began to walk forward. It was a strange sensation. Like all the rest of his party he wore only trousers and a shirt; his bare feet padding over the deck, the soles of his feet detecting the unevenness of the schooner's planking. He had a Sea Service pistol in his waist-belt, just in case, but if he had not fired it when the time came to dive overboard, it would be another weapon for the *Calypso*'s gunner to list as 'lost in action'.

There was no point in waiting any longer to get under way because everything was ready. Everything except the captain's courage, which he knew had vanished: his knees had a curious springiness about them, and his shin and thigh muscles had melted; there seemed to be bile at the back of his throat and his stomach was on the verge of heaving, as though he had eaten bad meat for supper. By now he was at the mainmast, and the men were waiting expectantly. 'Hoist away,' he said, 'and overhaul the mainsheet. And no noise!'

The blocks had been greased within the past hour, but it usually took a few spins of the sheaves to work the grease in. The blocks on the gaff were no exception, but by the time the sail began to creep up the mast he was abreast the foremast, repeating his order for the foresail. The few remaining gaskets were taken off the foresail and its gaff began creeping up the mast, pulling up the sail and having no apparent connection with the men hauling down on the halyards.

The mainsail was up, with a few more swigs on the peak

halyard needed to top up the gaff, but the canvas was only rippling, not flogging, as the wind blew down both sides so that the sail did not draw. Flogging canvas on a night like this would sound like rolling gunfire.

Now the foresail was up and as the men topped up the gaff Ramage gestured to the men at the headsail halyards. At once narrow triangles of canvas rose up the stays, but instead of taking up the bellying curve of sails drawing they became almost flattened, held aback by the sheets so that the wind pushed against them, thrusting the bow over to starboard. But by then Ramage had walked up to the bow, where the two men waited with axes.

Yes, the *Nuestra Señora*'s bow was being pushed round towards the entrance. 'Cut!' he snapped, and the first axe blade thudded into the cable, followed by the second. Five blows and the end of the cable whiplashed out over the bow and at once the schooner, no longer held by her anchor, swung round to starboard so that she headed along the channel, pointing at the *Calypso* and the harbour entrance.

Without further orders men were casting off the headsail sheets and making them up on the starboard side so that the sails began to draw; three men were enough to trim the foresail sheet because for a moment there was no weight on the sail, and four more tailed on to the mainsheet.

And the *Nuestra Señora de Antigua* began to come alive: with all the sails drawing she was already picking up speed and Ramage called: 'Sail hoisters – to your boat!' The boat was towing astern, ready for them, and he walked aft, expecting the dozen or so extra men on board to rush past him to jump into the boat, cast off and row for the *Calypso*. He had reached the quarterdeck, looking up at the set of the sails and glancing forward to see the *Calypso* getting closer, when he realized that not a man had moved. 'Sail handlers! To your boat!' he called.

There seemed many fewer men on deck now. What the devil was going on? Or had he had a momentary lapse and not noticed the men leaving?

'Jackson! Has the sail handling party left?'

'It – er, I haven't been watching them, sir.'

'What the devil is happening? Where are the men?'

'Hiding, sir,' Jackson said bluntly. 'They want to lend a hand setting fire to the ship!'

'But what – '

'They can all swim, sir,' Jackson said, leaning against the great wooden bar of the tiller. 'How close should I pass astern of the *Calypso*, sir? I'm wondering if this side of the channel shoals – there are no quays abreast the *Delft* on the Otrabanda side.'

A fireship with thirty men on board . . . Still, better too many than too few . . . 'Steady as you go,' he said to Jackson. The *Delft* was still out of sight, hidden by the *Calypso*, but the schooner would pass thirty yards astern of the British frigate, which any moment would cease to hide her from lookouts in the *Delft*, even if the Dutchmen had not already spotted the sails. Men tended to see only what they were looking for; with luck no one had told the Dutchmen to do anything but watch the *Calypso*.

Mainsail drawing well – and it was a well-cut sail; he could see that much in the starlight. Foresail rather baggy, probably an older sail, but also drawing well. And the headsails trimmed to perfection, as though the men knew that Southwick had his nightglass trained on them.

And in the calm water the bow wave was a loud hiss as the schooner continued increasing speed, the wind on the larboard beam. Four knots, five and now six, Ramage estimated. Her bottom was clean, that much was certain; the copper sheathing had kept her clear of barnacles and weed. She picked up speed quickly and, he must remember, she would take time to lose way.

The *Calypso* was looming up fast, her three great masts and yards seeming black stripes against the stars. Still no sign of the *Delft*. Jackson and Stafford were quite happy at the tiller, easing the schooner slightly in puffs that were just enough to heel her a few degrees. Everyone would be watching from the *Calypso*, nightglasses jammed to straining eyes; lookouts on the seaward side would be hard put not to glance over their shoulders at the sight of a schooner racing up the channel in the starlight under all plain sail. There was phosphorescence in here too, so her bow wave would be a pale green flame, seeming alive.

There! A vague dark blob beyond the *Calypso*'s stern; a blurring of stars low on the horizon, hidden by the Dutch frigate's masts and rigging. Two hundred yards to go!

'Rennick, ahoy down there! Start lighting up!'

Almost at once he could see black hatchways becoming pale yellow squares as lanthorns came out from behind screens and the candles were snatched up to light fuses and combustibles. The reek of tar, and also the sooty smell of guttering candles – no, that was from Rossi's lanthorns, which he had, very sensibly, put in the schooner's binnacle box.

'Rossi, stand by to light those port fires!'

One hundred and fifty yards to go, six ship's lengths or more. Flickering at the hatchways – Rennick's men were making a good start and the tar was probably flaring. The *Delft* must see the lights now – the flames, still small, were reflecting on the underside of the fore and main booms, lighting the rigging as delicate tracery and just catching the weave of the canvas. And the phosphorescence must make the bow wave and wash very obvious. Were the Dutch waiting with a broadside? He gave a quick order to Jackson which brought the schooner a point to larboard but the Dutch still could not train round their broadside guns far enough.

No point in trimming sails; the *Nuestra Señora* would carry more than enough way to shoot her up into the wind and alongside the frigate. For a moment he thought the crackling was musket and pistol fire from the *Delft*; then he realized it was the sound of flames inside the schooner. The pitch must have caught – yes, and here was the beginning of the smoke, sharp in the throat.

The only thing (apart from his bad seamanship) that could save the Dutch now would be for the fire down below to get out of hand, so that it reached those half-casks of powder before the *Nuestra Señora* could get alongside . . . A hundred yards to go, perhaps less. The schooner was seventy feet long, twenty-five yards.

'Stand by at all the halyards!'

He could see men, the extra men, materializing from their hiding places behind masts, behind guns, behind coils of rope. He needed them now; it saved him calling up Rennick's men, as he'd planned. And – yes, he could improve the plan.

'A man to every grapnel,' he bellowed. 'Up the ratlines with you and haul 'em on board, ready to toss into the Dutchman's rigging as we come alongside – I'll give the word!'

There was Rossi, waiting calmly. 'Get your lanterns out but keep them down so you don't blind us!'

Rennick was shouting up through the skylight (now a gaping

hole) of the captain's cuddy that all was well below. The smoke was swirling up through the hatches; he could hear men coughing and cursing.

'Get your men on deck, then!' he ordered Rennick.

The *Delft* was huge now, fine on the larboard bow. Left on this course, the *Nuestra Señora* would pass across her stern and race out through the harbour entrance. No – don't look at those flashes along the *Delft*'s upper decks: the Dutchmen are blazing away with muskets. Wounded Calypsos – that was his great fear: any man wounded had to be left behind: he had given strict orders about that.

Seventy-five yards. Jackson was watching him, the luffs of the sails and the *Delft*. The schooner's hatchways were yellow and red rectangles of light and flames: the draught below was more than he expected, roaring, a blacksmith's bellows. And here was Rennick, breathless.

'Everything going fine, sir!'

'Not burning too quickly?'

'No – it just looks like it from up here!'

'Rossi,' Ramage called. 'Start those port fires!'

And there was the stern of the *Delft* on the larboard bow, the flashes of muskets making her seem like a house surrounded by fireflies. This was the moment.

'Hard over, Jackson!' It was not a regular helm order but far more effective. Smoothly the *Delft* herself seemed to move quite slowly from the larboard side, across the schooner's bow – just missing the bowsprit – to place herself on the starboard bow, forty yards or so ahead and now heading the same way.

The schooner's sails began flogging, the masts shaking the ship.

'Make up topping lifts . . . Let go all halyards! Stand from under! Mind the booms and gaffs!'

Rossi's port fires burst into flame and Ramage saw Jackson, face calm, eyes sparkling in the reflection, looking up and over to the *Delft*. There was no need to give him any more helm orders; the American could lay the schooner alongside the *Delft* using the last of her way.

The Dutch musketry was now nearly deafening; the sound of balls ricocheting off metal fittings and guns varied from a sharp ping to clangs like pealing church bells. Now the *Delft*'s taffrail was abreast the foremast and the *Nuestra Señora* was making perhaps two knots. Now abreast the mainmast.

'Throw those grapnels, men – high and true!'

There was a great thud as the schooner's hull caught the *Delft*'s side, but everyone was expecting it. Then Ramage realized that all the sails, with their great booms and gaffs, had dropped several moments before and he had not noticed the crashing and flapping as he concentrated on the *Delft*. And there was Rossi, calmly stuffing spluttering port fires into the folds of the mainsail.

Ramage took the silver whistle which was slung round his neck on a piece of line. One last glance round. The grapnels were holding the two ships together and the men were out of the rigging. There was no sign of wounded men lying on deck – a miracle in view of the rattling musketry, but until a few moments ago the Dutchmen were trying to hit men running around on a moving vessel.

'Abandon ship!' he bellowed, and put the whistle to his lips and blew a piercing note, and suddenly the whistle seemed to explode and everything went black.

CHAPTER EIGHTEEN

•

Seas were breaking over him and the side of his head was crushed in. His left arm felt as if it was seized in a vice. A loud voice was cursing in fluent Italian; then a Cockney began swearing violently. His whole body was suddenly lifted up, rolled sideways and dropped with a thud, and then he was violently sick, bringing up salt water which tore at the back of his throat.

The spasm was over quickly, but the violent red flickering stayed, the wound in his head numb except for the sharp etching by salt water. Then he realized the red flickering was not in his head; it came from two ships that were less than fifty yards away, and he was now sprawled in a boat whose seamen were rowing away from the flames as though the Devil was chasing them.

'You all right nar, sir?'

He glanced up and recognized the shadowy face of Stafford, whose hair had come loose from the queue and was plastered over his face so that he seemed to be a witch after a ducking.

'I think so. Left arm feels strange. My head, too.'

'*Accidente!* You is alive then, *commandante*,' gasped an excited Rossi. 'Any minute those *stronzi* blow up!'

'Where . . . where is Jackson?'

'Here, sir, at the tiller. And Mr Rennick, too.'

Slowly everything stopped spinning and Ramage looked round. The *Nuestra Señora* was ablaze forward and aft, her masts like trees in a forest fire, but as they had planned, nothing was burning near the mainmast, where the burning fuses should be sputtering their way towards the powder casks. But the blaze started by Rossi's port fires on the schooner's quarterdeck had spread to the *Delft*, perhaps by sparks. But no – her mizenmast and yards had collapsed across the *Nuestra Señora*'s quarterdeck, probably because the shrouds had burned through, and now the great spar formed a column of flames joining the two ships.

There was the *Calypso* ahead, all her masts, yards and rigging looking like yellowish-red lacework in the light of the flames, but the hull was solid black and menacing. And beyond her dancing reflection of the flames just caught the masts of the rest of the privateers and beyond, in the distance, *La Créole*.

And the buildings. The flames lit up every building in Otrabanda. And Punda – there was Government House, the white walls this side showing stark, but the northern side was in harsh shadow with the harbour entrance a gaping black mouth with a fort on each side.

Suddenly there was a blinding double flash, followed immediately by a great rolling and reverberating boom that seemed solid noise. The night was black again as the shock of the explosion caught them, and then men, stunned by what they had seen but realizing that now they were safe, stopped rowing. The boom continued echoing down the channel towards the Schottegat, seeming to leave a terrified silence in its wake.

Then it began to rain: a pattering on the water grew heavier and suddenly Ramage realized what it was: the wreckage of two blown-up ships was beginning to land.

'Duck!' he shouted. 'Crouch down – under the thwarts!' But his voice came out as a croak and Stafford repeated it, adding his own oaths.

Great splashes told of heavy pieces of timber crashing into

the water, and amid the noise Ramage heard Stafford say conversationally: 'That flash left it all bloody dark, didn't it? You're orf course for the *Calypso*, Jacko.'

'All right, all right, it isn't every night we see a frigate blow up.'

'Nar, but I'm soakin' wet and cold, and the capting is shivering like a sick dog.'

'Give way, men!' Jackson called, and the men began rowing again.

'The Dutch survivors,' Ramage croaked. 'Our boats . . . search for them . . .'

'*Mama mia*, all is blown to Heaven, sir,' Rossi said, 'or is sitting on the clouds wondering how to make the down.'

'We'll send boats as soon as we get to the *Calypso*, sir,' Jackson called, 'but they'll probably send 'em anyway. We want to get you and Mr Rennick and the rest back on board quickly.'

'What's happened to Mr Rennick?'

'Don't rightly know, sir. It's his shoulder, and he's lost a lot of blood.'

'Where's Mr Baker?'

'He – well, sir, a musket ball caught him.'

'Badly wounded?'

'Dead, sir. Him and several men. You and Mr Rennick and a few wounded men were all we could get over the side in time.'

But the effort of concentrating was too much; Ramage tried to fight off the faintness draining him but he had no strength, and the next time he opened his eyes he was lying on the *Calypso*'s deck, Southwick shining a lantern on him as Bowen, the surgeon, ripped the seams of his shirt and trousers and said quietly to the master: 'Nasty cut on the skull but the cranium not damaged: musket or pistol ball still lodged in his left forearm. Get him to his cabin and clean him up: for the moment I've more urgent cases to attend –'

'But it's the captain!' Southwick protested.

'Yes,' Bowen said crisply, 'and that's what he'd want.'

Ramage seemed to be floating in a dream. Someone was scrubbing him with a harsh towel and he felt warmer; it was dark again and then someone was trying to persuade him to drink some brandy and then gradually – it seemed to take hours, but he found out afterwards it was only thirty minutes – he was wide awake, warm, sitting up in his cot and calling for clothes.

Silkin disappeared and came back with Southwick, who announced in the pompous tones that most people adopt when talking to a sick person: 'The surgeon says you must stay in bed, sir.'

'Get me some clothes, Silkin!' Ramage snapped. 'I've got to get on shore!'

'Sir!' Southwick protested.

'Don't argue! What time is it?'

'Half past four, sir. It'll soon be dawn.'

Ramage swung out of the cot and had to grab at the armchair to steady himself against the dizziness. 'Silkin, get a damp cloth and clean up this mess on my head.'

'It is clean, sir,' Silkin said, 'and that's a dry bandage. Your arm, too, sir: Mr Bowen says it will soon get very painful.'

'Soon!' Ramage exclaimed. 'It hurts like the devil already. Now, help me to get dressed and tell Mr Aitken to have a boat ready and I want him to accompany me on shore. The sergeant and a dozen Marines, too.'

And that reminded him. 'Rennick,' he said to Southwick, 'how is Rennick?'

'Bowen thinks he'll be all right. Musket ball in the right shoulder. He lost a lot of blood. So did you, sir.'

Silkin was putting out clothes, and Southwick hustled off to warn Aitken.

'A hot drink before you go, sir?' Silkin said coaxingly.

'It would make me sick. All that salt water I swallowed.'

'A bite to eat, then, sir?'

'Nothing – now, don't jerk my breeches like that, blast you; my head feels as though it's going to fall off.'

It took ten minutes for Ramage to dress, but at the end of it his stock was tied neatly, his sword hung properly, and apart from the broad bandage round his head which forced him to carry his hat under his right arm, and his left arm in a sling and throbbing as though it was going to burst, he felt better than he guessed he looked.

Aitken met him at the gangway. 'The Marines are in the boat, sir. And Bowen –'

At that moment the surgeon came bustling up. 'Sir, I must

forbid this madness. You should be in bed and—'

'How are your other patients, Bowen?'

'As well as can be expected, sir.'

'Then you'd better be with them.'

'Yes, sir,' Bowen said contritely. 'I understand.'

Did he? Did Southwick? Aitken certainly did; he was a shrewd fellow. But he was probably the only other man in the ship who realized that blowing up the *Delft* was not the end of it: there was still van Someren and the potential of the guns of his forts to deal with. Now, with it still dark and the sight of the exploding ship fresh in the Dutchman's mind, was the time to deal with Gottlieb van Someren.

The walk up to the residence with Aitken seemed ten times as long as before, but the marching Marines gave the impression of a whole battalion striding along the cobbled street. Aitken directed the sergeant to the big gateway and with a bellow and stamping the Marines halted.

'Wait here,' Ramage told the sergeant.

The sentry box outside the gate was empty but there were lights in several of the windows of the residence. When the main door opened to Aitken's banging a startled major domo immediately retreated up the stairs when he saw Ramage.

'Come on,' Ramage said, following him, 'he's going to report to van Someren.'

The former Governor was in his study, sitting at his desk and facing several men who were probably town councillors. Two Army officers sat slightly apart.

As Ramage walked into the room, followed by Aitken, the major domo was bent over van Someren, obviously trying to whisper to him that the English captain had arrived. The moment he saw Ramage the former Governor leapt up so violently his chair fell over backwards.

'You murderer!' he exclaimed.

'Every one of those men would still be alive had you kept your word,' Ramage said bitterly. 'You wave white flags and surrender when the rebels frighten you, and then you tear up the surrender document the moment you think you are safe. And with the captain of the *Delft* you planned to imprison the very people who took great risks to save you. You surrendered; then you committed treachery.'

'You—you . . .' van Someren fought to control his temper.

'This is a matter of honour: you must choose, swords or pistols. My – '

'You are such a scoundrel,' Ramage said contemptuously, 'that no gentleman would meet you on a field of honour. Anyway, you are under arrest. Your escort is waiting at the gate.'

'But – where are you taking me?'

'To Jamaica. This gentleman – ' he indicated Aitken – 'sails at noon in the schooner *Créole*. You will go with him.'

'And you?'

'I remain with my ship until I receive orders from my admiral. You will go at once. Call the sergeant,' he told Aitken as he felt the dizziness pulling him down.

Van Someren came over to him. 'Are you badly wounded?'

Ramage shook his head and felt as though he had been clubbed. 'No, just a cut or two.'

Aitken was standing beside him. 'Are you all right, sir? I'll get this fellow on board and come back when you've had a bit of a rest.'

'Yes, do that,' Ramage said, and managed to stay on his feet until van Someren and Aitken had gone through the door, and then quite slowly the floor came up at a steep angle and hit him in the face.

He woke to find himself in a cool bedroom lying in a large four-poster bed with a portly Dutchman peering at him through enormously thick spectacle lenses and examining his head, while Maria van Someren held his left arm as though any moment it might crumble into a dozen pieces.

The Dutchman caught his eye. 'Ah, you wake. You ask the usual question, "Where am I?" and I answer, "In Government House." I am a doctor.'

Ramage was conscious of a gentle pressure on the palm of his left hand and he looked at Maria. 'You have been unconscious a long time – you see, the sun has risen,' she said. 'Mr Aitken has been up to see you with – Mr Sousewick, is it? He leaves at noon. And one of your lieutenants is waiting, Mr Wagstaffe, and three seamen. He asked if when you recover consciousness they could see you – I have their names written – '

'Don't worry,' Ramage said, 'I know who they'll be.'

The Dutch doctor interrupted. 'I must insist you rest now. No more of the talking. I have bandaged the head and this afternoon we remove the musket ball from the arm. You will need all the strength for that.'

'Quite,' Ramage said, 'and I am grateful for your treatment, but I have a lot to do.'

'My dear sir, your ship is safely at anchor, and Miss van Someren has told you that the schooner leaves at noon – with her father. There is nothing else to bother you.'

'The island all round my ship happens to be my responsibility too, Doctor. If the French arrive and murder you all in your beds, I don't want your ghosts haunting me.'

'But surely there is no risk of that, my dear sir. Why, the island has been surrendered to you. We are now under British protection.'

'Look at me, Doctor,' Ramage said sarcastically. 'I am your British protection. Now, if you have finished, would you send in my men as you go out.'

Maria continued holding his hand to her breast and he was just becoming conscious that she wore no stays when there was a knock at the door and she answered. Wagstaffe looked in, saw Ramage was awake and grinned. 'Good morning, sir. We had no time to get you a posy of flowers, but I bring greetings from the Calypsos. Did you get a message about Jackson and –'

'Bring them in!'

The three seamen trooped in, startled to see Maria, and lined up at the foot of the bed. 'Glad to see you looking a bit better, sir,' Jackson said. 'More colour in your face.'

'I have my own doctor and my own nurse. These men,' he said to Maria, 'disobeyed orders and deserve to be punished.'

Maria looked startled and said, wide-eyed: 'I am sure they meant no harm.'

'Oh no,' Ramage said mildly, 'it was disobedience that saved me from being blown up. Now, Jackson, tell me what happened.'

The American looked embarrassed. 'Well, sir, there's not much to tell. While we had way on we were moving targets and those Dutchmen's muskets did no harm, but the minute we stopped alongside of 'em we were sitting ducks. But funny how it is, I don't think they actually hit anybody until after you gave the order to abandon ship.'

'Is right,' Rossi confirmed. 'Is a miracle but no one was hit.'

'Then as you blew the whistle, I saw Mr Baker hit. One shot took off the side of his face, and then he was hit again.'

'How do you know?' Ramage asked out of curiosity.

'Staff was holding him – just making sure there was no hope. Then we saw Mr Rennick was hit. He ordered us – Staff and me, that is, 'cos Rosey had already seen you were hit but we hadn't – to leave him be.'

'What happened then?'

'Staff and the Marine sergeant picked him up and dropped him over the side, and the sergeant swam with him towards the boat.'

'And then . . . ?'

'Well, sir, Rosey let out a yell and we saw you lying down, sort of hidden by the binnacle, and you was lying on your left side, so all the blood from the wound on the right was running down all over your face.

'I thought you was gone, sir, but –' he looked embarrassed – 'well, Rosey and Staff and me picked you up anyway and tossed you over the side and went in after you. We thought the schooner would blow up any minute, and – well, somehow it didn't seem right to leave you dead on a half-breed ship like that.'

'A half-breed ship?' Maria murmured, both horrified by the story and puzzled by the expression.

'Well, ma'am, she had a Spanish name and a French owner, and they were all murderers. At least the sea made a better resting place for the captain – not that he needed it,' he added hastily.

Maria looked at Ramage. 'When he says "murderers" does he really mean –'

'Yes,' Ramage said abruptly. 'Now, Jackson, the other wounded seamen?'

'They were tossed over the same way. You see, sir, I'm afraid no one took too much notice about your order about leaving the wounded.'

'But I made it quite clear when I called for volunteers. I said that anyone wounded and unable to fend for himself would have to be left behind.'

'Oh yes, sir, and bless you for it, but you didn't expect that to stop anyone.'

'No – the whole ship's company volunteered.'

'And you only picked sixteen, not counting the officers and the sergeant. That's why the sail handlers stowed away.'

Ramage sighed. He realized that he had watched the last strands of the *Nuestra Señora*'s anchor cable part under the axe blows, and as the ship gathered way he thought he was in command . . . and the men, he had to admit, were kind enough to leave him with that illusion.

He looked over at Wagstaffe. 'How is Rennick now?'

'He'll be all right, sir. Bowen has removed the ball in one piece and nothing vital is damaged. He's sleeping now.'

'And the rest of the butcher's bill?'

'Apart from Baker, we know six seamen were killed, and two more are missing. We can find no trace of them. Five were wounded – that includes you and Mr Rennick, sir.'

'And Dutch survivors?'

Wagstaffe glanced at Maria, but Ramage nodded.

'None, sir.'

Maria said quietly, 'It was better that way. That dreadful man, the captain, he threatened my father with the guillotine, and he was going to seize you today when you came on shore. He was certain you would try to negotiate. And then tonight, after you had been . . . after you had been shot, they were going to board the *Calypso* . . .'

'And that was why you gave back the ring and Lausser resigned his commission?'

She nodded, weeping quietly. 'I could not ever marry a man who agreed with his captain doing that, and Major Lausser could not persuade my father . . .'

Ramage looked up at the three seamen and grinned. 'You will tell the ship's company that any further disobedience will be punished.'

'Oh, natcherly, sir,' Stafford said. 'Fact o' the matter is,' he added soberly, 'I 'spect that before next Michaelmas some of 'em will be regretting their disobedience!'

With that the three men left the room and Maria asked: 'What is a mickle mouse?'

'I'll tell you in a moment,' Ramage said. 'Now, Wagstaffe, as the second lieutenant you are in temporary command of the *Calypso*. I want a dozen Marines in each of the forts until we establish discipline on shore. I am making Major Lausser the acting governor, but all his orders will be countersigned by me. And have a guard boat rowing across the harbour entrance from sunset until sunrise. Can you think of anything else?'

'Bowen was worrying about your medical treatment, sir. That ball still in your arm . . .'

'You can report the evidence of your own eyes,' Ramage said. 'He can inspect the ball tomorrow – the doctor removes it this afternoon. In the meantime it hurts, I can tell you that much.'

Two weeks later to the day Ramage climbed down into a boat, wearing a hat for the first time over the large scar on his scalp, and sat back as Jackson gave the orders which sent the boat surging towards the ship of the line which had just anchored a hundred yards to seaward of where the *Delft* had blown up.

Fifteen minutes after that he was on board the *Queen*, reporting to Admiral Foxe-Foote, whose first words were a complaint, not a greeting: 'I expected to receive a written report, Ramage, and all I get is a verbal report from your first lieutenant.'

'I trust you received the instrument of surrender for this island, sir, and the former Governor.'

'Yes, yes,' Foxe-Foote said impatiently. 'Now, what about those privateers. Young Aitken tells me there are only nine left. And I hope the wreckage of this damned Dutch frigate hasn't blocked the harbour. The channel's narrow enough as it is.'

'The area has been buoyed, sir.'

'I should think so. An enemy frigate and a schooner lost. Not a penn'orth of prize money; thousands of guineas just sunk. Bad business, Ramage; no forethought, that's your trouble. Oh yes, a convoy came in two days before I sailed, and some young woman was asking about you. She had a foreign name.'

Ramage looked blankly at Aitken, who was standing behind the Admiral. The Scotsman winked.

'A name like Volterra, sir?' Ramage asked.

'Yes, that was it. Miss Volterra. You know her?'

'I know a Marchesa di Volterra, sir.'

'*Marchesa?* Why, is she related to the lady that rules Volterra?'

'Yes, sir. In fact she is the lady.'

'Good heavens! Why – well, had I known, my wife would . . .'

'I am sure the Marchesa is quite comfortable, sir,' Ramage said politely, watching the Admiral's face as he realized that this 'Miss Volterra' not only had her own kingdom, but probably had enough influence in London to make or break admirals on distant stations. 'Now, sir, about those nine privateers . . .'

AUTHOR'S POSTSCRIPT

The fourth edition of *Steele's Naval Chronologist of the Late War* was published in London in 1806, and on page 100, under the heading 'Colonies, Settlements &c, captured from the enemy', is the following brief reference:

> The island of Curaçao, in the West Indies, D[utch]: surrendered after having claimed the protection of his Britannic Majesty, to the *Néréide*, 36, Capt. F. Watkins, September 12, 1800.

William James, in his *Naval History of Great Britain*, Volume III, gives more details:

> On the 11th of September, while the British 12-pounder 36-gun frigate *Néréide* . . . was cruising off the port of Amsterdam, in the island of Curaçao, the Dutch inhabitants of the latter, tired out with the enormities of the band of 1500 republican ruffians that were in possession of the west end of the island, sent off a deputation to claim the protection of England. On the 13th the capitulation surrendering the island . . . was signed . . . The vessels, large and small, lying in the harbour of Amsterdam, numbering 44; but no ships of war were among them.

The rest of the story is told by the redoubtable James, who recorded the whole war in great detail. The island was subsequently returned to the Dutch, and Amsterdam's name was later changed to Willemstad.

D. P.
Yacht Ramage
English Harbour
Antigua
West Indies